Halsey's Bluff

[signature]

LARRY SCHWEIKART

To Ryan Brown
a big "what-if"
for you to enjoy !

D1563768

Zmok Books

THE KNOX
PRESS

Halsey's Bluff
By Larry Schweikart
Cover by Barney Geary

Zmok Books an imprint of Winged Hussar Publishing, LLC, 1525 Hulse Road, Unit 1, Point Pleasant, NJ 08742

In conjunction with Knox Press

This edition published in 2016 Copyright ©Winged Hussar Publishing, LLC

ISBN 978-0-9963657-3-4
Library of Congress No 2016931697
Bibliographical references and index
1.   Alternative History 2. Military History 3. Action & Adventure

Winged Hussar Publishing, LLC All rights reserved

For more information on Winged Hussar Publishing, LLC, visit us at:
https://www.WingedHussarPublishing.com
Twitter: WingHusPubLLC
Facebook: Winged Hussar Publishing LLC

Proudly produced in the United States of America

INTRODUCTION

A few years ago, I opened a gaming magazine to find an ad for a war game featuring a picture of the flag-raising at Iwo Jima . . . except that the flag being raised was a Japanese flag, and the caption read, "History is in your hands . . . Don't screw it up!" While in fact history shows that it would have been extremely difficult for Japan to have defeated the United States in the Pacific in World War II, it was not at all unlikely that, had a few events gone differently, the war could have gone on much longer.

One of those turning points came in June 1942 at the Battle of Midway, where American carrier forces under Rear Adm. Ray Spruance (who had replaced Bill Halsey, hospitalized with a severe skin rash) defeated a superior Japanese force, in the process sinking four of Japan's fleet carriers and killing more than 340 pilots, as well as thousands of Japanese sailors. But Midway could easily have gone differently. The unlikely and amazing arrival of the carrier Yorktown put American dive bombers over the Japanese carriers at precisely the moment they were loaded with their own recovered aircraft, as well as aviation fuel and bombs. They were sitting ducks for the Americans. Yorktown's arrival on scene had itself been a miracle, the badly damaged ship having returned to Pearl Harbor and been repaired in 48 hours, despite initial assessments that it would take months to get her back in action.

While any number of battles in World War II could, conceivably, have gone differently, virtually no other fight hinged so delicately on a handful of key decisions and mistakes, from Yamamoto splitting his carrier force to invade the Aleutians to the failure of a Japanese scout plane, which apparently flew right over Spruance's carriers, to see the Americans immediately below him. The successful attack by the Yorktown's aircraft itself constituted the last in a series of previous 'what ifs': what if Japanese planes had knocked out Midway's airstrip on their first strike? What if Japanese Admiral Nagumo, in charge of the carrier force, had waited before ordering his planes to re-arm for ground attack, only to learn, in the midst of that re-arming, that his scouts had found the American carriers? What if Fletcher's scattered and largely blind dive bomber and torpedo squadrons, which somehow managed to arrive nearly simultaneously over the Japanese fleet, had not drawn off the fighter planes that provided the combat air patrol, and thus used up its fuel, forcing them to return to the carrier decks . . . just as the York-town's attackers arrived?

In Halsey's Bluff, I have offered a much different 'what if.' What if Halsey commanded the American forces as Yamamoto expected? What if Yamamoto did not divide his carrier forces? What if Halsey was lured into a trap that Fletcher, by sheer luck, avoided? Could Halsey, fighting against his nature, run rather than attack? In this speculative history, the fate of the Pacific rested on the answers to those questions.

The idea of a counter-factual Battle of Midway came to me as I was reading the Civil War trilogy by Newt Gingrich and Bill Forstchen. Few individual battles lend themselves to the kind of plausible alternatives as Gettysburg, except perhaps Waterloo and Midway. As an American historian, Midway was the logical choice for me to pursue. Over the year or so that it took to write this, I had extended discussions or e-mails with members of the Battle of Midway Roundtable, many read parts, or even all, of the manuscript, correcting my deeply inadequate knowledge of historical details when it came to carrier operations in World War II. These men lived those operations, and their brothers-in-arms often died in the process. It was an exchange that reminded me of the deadly reality they faced some 60 years ago. Regardless, however, any mistakes are my own and any flaws are solely the result of me not listening to their excellent advice. Ronald Russell, of the Battle of Midway Roundtable, is especially due a debt of gratitude, as are Sam Laser, Frank DeLorenzo, Otis Kight, Alvin Kernan, and my cousin, Marine Col. (Ret.) Michael Jackson.

So, at the risk of repeating myself, what follows is not what really happened in 1942. But it very well could have.

Larry Schweikart Centerville, OH 2009

FOREWARD

by Ronald Russell

Halsey's Bluff didn't happen—readers will recognize that basic fact at the outset. Author Larry Schweikart has written a tale not about World War II in the Pacific, but about the war that very nearly came to be, the one that the Japanese intended themselves. And while most of the occurrences in the book are remarkable for their deviation from true history, the fact is that all of them very easily could have happened, perhaps should have happened.

Many of the war's actual battles turned out as they did because of strange twists of fate that were contrary to expectations, often surprising to both sides. That was especially true of the Battle of Midway in 1942. What if the unlikely American victory at Midway had been a Japanese triumph instead? That certainly could have happened if the enemy commander had simply concentrated his forces in classic fashion. His subsequent victory would have profoundly impacted the rest of the war in a manner seldom envisioned.

Schweikart has that vision in a sweeping spectacle of bloody, desperate naval and air combat around Hawaii and even off the American west coast. It is a chilling story of what easily could have befallen U.S. forces in the war's first year if only a few events, some very minor, had gone the other way. Readers will find Halsey's Bluff hard to put down, and finishing it should send most of them to their reference books to find out how and why it is a work of fiction and not history.

Ronald W. Russell, author of No Right to Win: a Continuing Dialogue with Veterans of the Battle of Midway and moderator, The Battle of Midway Roundtable.

PROLOGUE

Chuichi Nagumo (Wikipedia)

Pacific Ocean, North of the Hawaiian Islands
7 Dec 41 0937

He puffed hard as he ran up the tiny, narrow, curved metal stairway, up from the radio room of the Imperial Japanese Navy aircraft carrier Akagi. The smell of the cold Pacific air filled his lungs, tinged with the odor of aviation fuel and grease. At the third level, he had smacked his head hard on an overhang, then slipped on the salt brine scum on the deck outside the bridge. Supporting himself with his right hand, he was careful to keep the paper he held in his left hand off the wet deck. Regaining his balance, he darted through a door and took another ladder to the command center and observation deck. The officers had been watching the planes come in from the east and touch down on the carrier deck, when their concentration was interrupted by the young officer. He blurted out, "Admiral- san! Victory! It is an overwhelming victory!" Only then, after sprinting from the communications center two decks below with the first official report of the Pearl Harbor strike force did the ensign realize that he had badly violated protocol. He instantly straightened up, and saluted.
"Sir."
Holding his salute and panting, he watched as the figure in a dark blue uniform stood in front of the others at the command center. The man did not to turn at his unseemly interruption, and only after several moments did Vice Admiral Chuichi Nagumo slowly lower his binoculars, glare at the ensign, and raise his white-gloved hand to return the salute motioning Ensign Yuri Ito to read the message.
"And?" the admiral asked. His voice was flat, without emotion.
Ito smiled slightly. "We have the first official reports of the Pearl Harbor strike force under Commander Fuchida, and they

add up to a marvelous victory."

"I appreciate your enthusiasm, Ensign," he stated coldly. "Perhaps you should let us be the judge of what qualifies as a victory?"

The chastised ensign bowed deeply, hoping he had not lost face and quietly responded, "Hai!"

Nagumo then gestured for him to continue. "Specifics, please."

"Yes, Sir. Commander Fuchida reports the surprise was complete. The Americans got no fighter planes up until twenty minutes into the attack. At least six, and possibly all seven, battleships are sunk or capsized. One, it seems, got underway, but ran aground. There are reports, however, that dive bombers hit her. In the smoke, damage assessment was getting difficult." He reported with complete assurance that the *Arizona* was utterly destroyed. One of Commander Fuchida's pilots reported it went down in less than ten minutes, broken in half. "Two other battleships were capsized as a result of torpedo hits. All other capital ships in the harbor took major damage, including all cruisers. In addition, a dozen support ships — oilers, tankers, repair vessels — were sunk. Commander Fuchida estimated the American casualties in the thousands; not counting civilians."

Several officers, crowded inside the small bridge, exchanged cautiously satisfied glances, but Nagumo remained impassive, then jerked his head upward, indicating that Ensign Ito continue.

"The pilots charged with destroying the airfields reported virtually all of the American fighters, bombers, and scout planes were annihilated. A handful got off the ground, but landing will be difficult because of the effective bombing of the runways. Commander Fuchida also reported that an entire flight of B-17s arrived in the middle of the battle, unarmed and apparently out of fuel from their trip from the mainland. They were all shot down. I checked with the submarine communications unit, and the two midget subs in Pearl Harbor also claimed major hits on three battleships."

"Virtually all of their aircraft," Nagumo repeated, looking with some skepticism at the other officers. With sarcasm dripping from his voice, he added, "In wartime, it's truly miraculous how 'virtually all' of enemy aircraft and ships that pilots claim are destroyed mysteriously seem to find new life." He saw that Ensign Ito was not following his monologue, so he waved his hand for him to continue. "And our losses?"

Nagumo had not smiled throughout the entire report of successes. It was as if Ito had told him the entire attack failed, but he continued nonetheless. "Commander Fuchida counts fewer than thirty planes missing, although some are badly damaged and may be irreparable. If no other aircraft return, and if we can repair those which did, the total loss will be under thirty ... Sir." The ensign's eyes swept the room, taking in the now-broad smiles and nods of approval. Rear Admiral Hiro Konichi, like Nagumo, was a known critic of the Pearl Harbor attack, predicting it would cost Japan several aircraft carriers and hundreds of planes. Now, he stared incredulously at Ito, then at Nagumo, and realized both he and his superior would bear some shame for their inaccurate prophecies. Konichi's smile disappeared as he realized what the successful attack did to his reputation.

"You say, fewer than thirty? And we got *all* the American ships?" Konichi shook his head and approached Nagumo. He hoped to buffer the obvious conclusion all would draw. "It seems, Admiral, that you and I were wrong, and Admiral Yamamoto was right. Nevertheless, it is you who has led this force, and therefore you are due great honor for this victory. All the American ships ..." he said, shaking his head and turning away to the other officers, who as yet to appreciate the internal politics, still beamed. "And to think Admiral Yamamoto had to convince the general staff of this attack when he said we should decide the fate of the war on the very first day, and it appears we have done so ... "

Nagumo held up his hand to Konichi and cut him off, then looked at Ito. "Ensign, is that all they sent? Are those all the dispatches?" he asked.

Ito was still at attention and remembering his breach of protocol, nodded and answered, "*Hai*." He was puzzled thinking, *Isn't that enough, Admiral?*

"So Commander Fuchida makes no mention of aircraft carriers?" Nagumo looked at Ito, who re-read the dispatches.

That's what is bothering you? "No, Sir. Commander Fuchida had nothing to say about aircraft carriers, one way or another." Again, his eyes surveyed the command center, the light from the windows almost obscured by the shoulder-to-shoulder officers standing inside. He noticed that some of the smiles started to vanish, turning to looks of concern. Several officers began to shift nervously.

Konichi realized that the only thing worse than his and Nagumo's earlier warnings of failure would be failure itself. "Admiral," he offered, "perhaps Commander Fuchida's report was just incomplete. Or perhaps the ensign, in his excitement, failed to take down all the information. Perhaps we only need to send down for a follow-up, even before Commander Fuchida himself comes in with his official report."

Nagumo glumly shook his head while staring at the deck, then folded his hands behind his back. "I know Commander Fuchida well. He is nothing if not thorough. For him to deliberately exclude the American carriers from his report speaks volumes. We must conclude that they were not in Pearl Harbor today. And if that is the case, we must also assume that they are preparing to swoop down on us at this moment as we recover aircraft and are completely vulnerable. Cancel the pending third strike."

"Sir?" Captain Iture Tanaka, one of the strongest proponents of the strike, added, "We have them defeated. One more attack will utterly destroy the Americans."

"Then what, Captain? Invade San Francisco?"

Nagumo shook his head. "No, the strategic objective of this mission was to so cripple the Americans that they could not pursue war with us for at least a year. If we have failed to destroy the carriers, then we have not completely succeeded. Further, Captain Tanaka," Nagumo coldly continued, "it would take us another two hours to prepare another strike. You are, I trust, aware of the time it takes our elevators to bring the aircraft up, to spot them, to fuel them, to re-arm them? And we must recover all of Commander Fuchida's strike force first. At the end of two hours, do you think the Americans might be prepared? Do you think they would have all their anti-aircraft guns manned, what few aircraft they have left on alert? Meanwhile, our fleet is running low on fuel, and we have no idea where the American carrier force is. If they strike us at the moment we send a third wave against Pearl Harbor, we would lose in a few minutes all that we have gained."

Sufficiently rebuked, Tanaka nodded and instructed a staff officer to carry the abort message to the commander of the third strike group.

"Admiral," Konichi interjected, "given your concern, shouldn't Kido Butai move at full speed away, putting more ocean between us and the Americans?"

"We cannot do that either, Admiral. Not yet. First, we still have not recovered all our aircraft. I will not sacrifice our brave fliers to run from an enemy. Nor do we know where that enemy is. He might well be southwest of us, laying an ambush. No, we will have our full complement of air power, and if we must fight, our strike force, our Kido Butai will destroy the carriers in a sea battle, despite the greater cost than striking them in Pearl Harbor. Nevertheless, I agree with Captain Tanaka. It is not a complete victory without those carriers." Other officers, having now established the correct political position, soberly nodded.

Radio silence, no longer needed, had been lifted since the attack started. "I must report to Admiral Yamamoto, unless any of you have further comments." He scanned the room. No one moved. "Very well. Dismissed."

CHAPTER ONE

Tokyo, Ministry of the Imperial Japanese Navy
8 Dec 41 0950 (Tokyo time)

Shigeru Fokodome (Wikipedia)

Admiral Isoroku Yamamoto returned the communications officer's salute and watched as the young lieutenant dashed from the room with his latest dispatch. The Combined Fleet commander had just sent a message to Admiral Nagumo: "Concur with your assessment. After recovery of aircraft, redeploy to rendezvous point 'Leopard.' Await further orders. Well done, Admiral Nagumo." Yamamoto then addressed the other members of the Naval General Staff, who listened intently. "We have struck an important blow. It waits to be seen whether this is the mortal strike that we hoped when we designed it." Aside from Yamamoto's *bete noir*, Rear Admiral Shigeru Fukodome, who simply glowered, his comments were greeted with approving nods around the table, which featured a detailed papier Mache model of Pearl Harbor. Fukodome, who favored a less aggressive stance toward the fleet at Hawaii, thought Yamamoto out of control. He was seething at his inability to control his egotistical admiral.

Yamamoto continued. "When Nagumo arrives at his rendezvous point, we will confer and assess our overall position. By then we will have more information on the Singapore and Philippine operations. Until then, I will return to the *Nagato*." The officers, as one, silently filed out of the room. Temporarily disarmed, even Fukodome departed, saying only, "Congratulations, Admiral Yamamoto."

One of his admirals, who had never supported the Pearl Harbor attack, commented something to the effect that Japan had stirred a sleeping giant. The diminutive Yamamoto said nothing, although he certainly agreed with that sentiment. He was all too familiar with American industrial capabilities, and he well knew that one way or the other, nothing had been resolved this day. He attended Harvard as a young man, and lived in the United States' capital, Washington, D.C., for a year while serving as a naval attaché.

Washington! The cherry tree blossoms! They so reminded me of Japan when I was there. Americans. So full of energy, yet so lazy. Which characteristic will they display now? So free, yet so willing to sacrifice their freedom temporarily for a cause. A half million died in their Civil War to free Africans? He shook his head, baffled. *So improper. So impolite. They do not understand order. Yet is that a strength?* He remembered how average Americans freely spoke their minds about anything and everything, even to superiors, and without fear of any retaliation or even censure. *Coarse. They are an unrefined people. Brash.* Yet from his analysis of their aviation industry and air pioneers, he knew it was precisely the coarse, unafraid individualists who had designed and produced new, often astounding aircraft. *And what they do in the air, they can do on land or sea. America's freedom, quite unappealing to a Japanese, strangely is their source of strength. It allows everyone to participate in the debate of ideas, in business, in technology, even in their military. Strange. They don't work out of obligation but often for fulfillment. What Japanese does that? They lack a code of honor. Or do they? Is their commitment to individualism and freedom itself a code?*

As Yamamoto circled the table, looking at the small red X placed on each American ship in Pearl Harbor that was considered sunk or damaged beyond repair, he recalled his trip to Dayton, Ohio. *Even that, a small city in the middle of America, was a site of explosive growth and invention.* He sighed. If it had just been Dayton, he knew Japan could match it, and Pittsburgh, and, perhaps, Detroit. But having flown across the United States, and taken trains to various cities, Yamamoto knew that there were a thousand Daytons spread across the United States. *How many more will suddenly spring to life now that we have given them cause? We import all of our oil – they, if necessary, can pump all they need from their single state of Texas alone! We must acquire entire regions of China for iron ore and coal – they ship iron from Minnesota and dig coal from West Virginia, and have still more untapped. And if they had to make all-wooden aircraft, they have enough forests to fill the skies. Before Admiral Nagumo even reaches his rendezvous point, American men will be joining their army and navy in numbers that even the Chinese would envy – and they are far more capable than the Russians or Chinese we have fought in the past. Ah, why do I wrestle with myself? The die is cast. I have lost my argument. Now I can only serve. Serve, and seek to win.*

"Sir?" Yamamoto had not noticed his aide, Captain Ure Sagata, standing in the corner next to a steward with a tray of tea. "You seemed lost in thought."

Yamamoto grimaced that he had become so transparent. "Indeed, Captain, indeed." He took a cup of tea from the steward and dismissed him. Then, seeing his chief of staff, Captain Yasuji Watanabe, also standing nearby, announced, "Captain Watanabe, you are dismissed." Watanabe displayed a pained look, but saluted and left. Despite his official position as chief of staff and his intense loyalty to Yamamoto, Watanabe seemed to lack the imagination displayed by his younger counterpart, Sagata. Yamamoto looked at the lone remaining officer, Captain Sagata, and set the tea down. Absent-mindedly rubbing his left hand, where two fingers were missing due to an explosion near him during the Russo-Japanese War, Yamamoto surveyed his eager young aide, whom he had treated for months as an unofficial chief of staff. "From Kobe, are you not?" The Admiral gestured to Sagata to join him.

"Thank you, Admiral," replied Sagata, as he poured himself a cup. "Yes, Sir. My parents are in the silk trade."

"Merchants." Then he smiled. *Didn't the Prime Minister make some disparaging comment about the American president — a "merchant" he called him? How silly.* He surveyed Sagata, perhaps the first time he ever really looked at the man. *Something of a giant*, Yamamoto thought. Sagata stood close to six feet tall. He also looked unusually young, completely devoid of facial hair, with smooth, golden skin, and fire in his eyes. *Ah, to be that young again.* Sagata was careful never to imply criticism or questioning of orders. *Must never give offense. Only the gods know how the most innocuous comment from a Japanese can be interpreted as an offense. Westerners think our incessant politeness, our compulsion for courtesy, is derived from inherent goodness. It's just the opposite: it comes from our insecurity, and the concern that the tiniest slight could cost you your entrails.*

"Merchants," Yamamoto repeated. "Good for you, Sagata. Merchants are level-headed, common-sense people, who understand resources and tradeoffs, gains and losses. Tell me, Captain, what you think of our operations today."

Sagata seemed surprised by the Admiral's candor, especially given his reputation of disregarding advice that conflicted with his own. Many admirals had reaped Yamamoto's wrath by challenging his conclusions, and legend had it that the Admiral had fixed several war-game scenarios to favor his own strategies by intimidating referees to miraculously "revive" sunken carriers, or minimize "damage" done to other vessels. Sagata knew he should tread carefully, and attempted to humbly deflect the question. "I am only a captain, Sir. What do I know of grand strategy?"

Yamamoto smiled. *A wise response for one wishing to avoid assassination by the ultra-militarists in Tokyo.* "I will tell you something few have ever heard me say. Sailors often know more than captains, and captains more than admirals. We are not the Imperial Army, Sagata, and we do not treat our junior officers like so much rice to be tossed to the winds. My admirals often have ulterior motives—a desire to advance in rank, or, more likely take my job. I cannot always give their comments an unbiased hearing; some are simply fools. But you? You already could have had your own command. Now put your humility aside. What do you think? You officers talk among yourselves. What is the view among the junior officers here at Imperial Headquarters? Remember, most of the time anymore I have been banished to my flagship, the *Nagato*, in Hashirajima harbor."

Choosing his words carefully, Sagata complied. "I will answer, Admiral, but first, if I may beg your indulgence, I wished to thank you on behalf of all the junior officers for your generosity in the wardroom."

"How did you ...?" Yamamoto began, but Sagata interrupted. "Admiral, permit me, but even here at the Ministry they speak of your kindness. Although honor prevents the men from saying so personally, I know they greatly appreciate the fact that you have subsidized their meals. They refer to you as Yamamoto the Beneficent."

Yamamoto shook his head in disbelief. "You surely exaggerate, honorable Captain. It is nothing."

"No, Admiral. It is an impressive act. The men are grateful beyond measure. They know that the tradition in the Imperial Navy has been for officers to pay their own meal and wardroom expenses. What may seem insignificant sums for senior officers is an extreme financial burden on younger men. We learned that it was your doing—that prior to your assignment to sea duty, you instructed that all junior officers' food bills be applied to your own." Sagata remembered more than one officer slapping him for minor performance flaws, and knew others who had suffered brutal discipline at the hands of vicious superiors in the Imperial Navy. Yamamoto was nothing like those men, at least, not while Sagata had been around him.

"I am honored by their compliment, Captain," Yamamoto replied. "Between us, it is a silly tradition, and one that I intend to change. Unfortunately, I can battle only one navy at a time, and at present it is the Americans', not my own, that I must engage. From the top down," he paused, not wishing to name Fukodome, "we suffer from the light of dimmed stars."

Sagata smiled broadly — *that's a shot at Fukodome, and probably Nagumo!* He paused — and bowed. "I understand Admiral-san, and we shall speak no more of it. Now, Sir, do you still wish my opinion of our officers' attitudes as we enter our current conflict?" The captain waited to ensure that Yamamoto was serious. *No need to end my career so early, or without honor.* Yamamoto gave him a sharp nod, then gestured for Sagata to sit in one of the Ministry's fine leather chairs, arranged next to a large globe. Sagata sat, placed his tea cup and saucer on the table at to the other side of the leather chair, then straightened himself as befitting an officer of the Imperial Japanese Navy.

"Obviously, Sir," Sagata began, "the men are excited. Most, of course, have never seen combat before, and many anticipate great opportunities for honor and glory."

"Honor and glory?" Yamamoto grunted. "Is that truly what killing is about?"

Puzzled, Sagata shrugged. "Of course not. One does not engage in war lightly. But to die for the Emperor ..."

Yamamoto's sigh interrupted him, but even Sagata seemed to lack a certain conviction, which Yamamoto noted. "Of course. Dying for the Emperor. How glorious."

Sagata was not sure if he detected sarcasm in the Admiral's voice, yet knew that Isoroku Yamamoto was a complex man, and certainly no mindless *banzai* warrior who ran headlong into gunfire. On occasion, he had caught glimpses of another Yamamoto. The 57-year-old Admiral stood 5' 3" and weighed no more than 130 pounds, although he was now putting on somewhat of a paunch — a result of his decreased physical regimen and affinity for fine dining. Sagata had never seen him in anything but a perfectly pressed blue or white Imperial Japanese Navy uniform. Because he was his aid he had seen the other side of Yamamoto when on leave and gambling. Equally, Sagata rarely saw Yamamoto's dazzling smile with perfectly white teeth. A study in formality, known for his paucity of words, the man could at times be blunt and course, once describing another officer as an "asshole," and frankly admitting about another, "I hate his guts." He had heard about the Admiral's gambling, playing *shogi* endlessly, and wagering about almost anything. Some even thought his Pearl Harbor plan was little more than a reckless bet of some sort, perhaps with one of his critics, such as Admiral Nagumo. During his gambling binges, Yamamoto puffed cigars relentlessly, although strangely he refused to smoke cigarettes, and even in staff meetings, would glower at anyone who lit up a cigarette, even if other, more senior officers permitted smoking. The cigarettes quickly disappeared when he was in the room.

Most of all, Sagata was privy to the Admiral's shore exploits, where he disappeared to unknown places for many hours at a time to enjoy geishas, despite his marriage of twenty-two years to Reiko. Sagata had not witnessed it personally, but some reported Yamamoto, Mohammedesque, would hit two or three geisha houses a night. The next morning it always fell to Sagata to cover for him with the swarm of irritating reporters who followed his every move. Sataga never exactly made excuses for the admiral, but was coming ever closer to doing so, and privately looked forward to getting his boss out to sea, far from women.

Ah, the press. Despite their probing, the admiral was their master. Many reporters fawned over him, referring to him as Isoroku, a presumptuous informality. What would they say if they knew of his obsession with gambling or women? Or did they, and they just didn't care?

Sagata had seen a political side of Yamamoto as well, a man capable of cultivating civilian supporters who referred to him as sensei ("respected teacher"), an unusual designation for a military man. He carefully orchestrated every meeting, whether with the press or the politicians, often arriving late to ensure that he remained in control. When it came to his subordinate admirals, however, Yamamoto took advice and listened to opposing views, but never forgot who stood by him and who abandoned him.

The man hates ceremony. What will he do if he is the conquering hero when we win this war? Will he respond to the desires of the public to be the object of national affection? He could easily rival the loyalty afforded the Emperor. Will he take advantage of it? Will he make speeches and public appearances? No, not Yamamoto. Sagata recalled that when the admiral received his appointment as Commander in Chief of the Combined Fleet, he merely issued a terse statement referring only obliquely to the "task facing the Imperial Navy," which he predicted would "be graver than ever." *Yet neither does he shrink away from power. While he might abhor the trappings of office, Yamamoto would not hesitate to rule, and with a firm hand.*

Sagata, for all his insight, had not known how politically vulnerable Yamamoto was prior to Pearl Harbor, and how much the admiral had opposed the current policy of Imperial aggression, especially the earlier invasion of China. In Japan, such opposition did not come cheaply, and several paid with their lives for challenging the Army. Many wondered how Yamamoto had managed to avoid assassination, which increasingly seemed to befall any critic of expansionism. Before accepting the current assignment, Sagata had researched what he could on the admiral and his family.

Born in Nagaoka, Yamamoto's grandfather had been on the losing side of a civil war in the 1800s, and the family had been forced to live down its opposition to the government. Perhaps that had been one of the motivating factors in the admiral's remarkable ascent through the ranks — the desire to prove loyalty — but it was nevertheless ironic that 50 years later, another son of Nagaoka again found himself opposing the administration. Although Yamamoto certainly had his share of political friends, even they could not protect him forever, and many inside the Japanese government suspected this appointment to sea command was little more than an attempt to get another war opponent out of Tokyo and out of the bull's- eye of the Army expansionists - literally and figuratively.

A year ago, Sagata had been offered his choice: command of a light cruiser, the *Jintsu*, or the opportunity to serve as Yamamoto's aide. As much as he wanted his own command, he could not turn down the opportunity to learn from the most brilliant man in the Navy, and one of the visionaries of naval air operations. And learn he did, though surprisingly Sagata found that Yamamoto's command of the Pacific forces brought with it a great deal of empty time. The admiral designed maneuvers, then did very little for several days, aside from eating exquisitely prepared meals and listening to martial music — and, of course, gambling. Sagata looked forward to the times when the admiral would entertain officers of his flagship in his wardroom, a fashionable dining facility replete with white tablecloths and teak inlays. Delicacies such as *urume-iwashi* — dried sardines from Tosa—were in abundance, plus sliced fish, various stews, rice, then the traditional soup. Egg custard was brought out for dessert. Yamamoto insisted on full meals at all mess calls. Eating was, perhaps, the one vice that surpassed Yamamoto's obsession with gambling and geishas, and Sagata watched him down remarkable portions of food for someone so small.

*These are understandable weaknesses for one in his position, Saga*ta rationalized, *and he has few of them. They are not fatal. Certainly they are nothing compared to his strategic vision and tactical understanding.*

Sagata had heard rumors that Yamamoto received one of the rare "First Grades" to be awarded a fleet admiral by the Imperial Navy, a singular acknowledgment of his talent. Although he admired the Americans—he had a biography of American President Abraham Lincoln, by Carl Sandberg, by his bedside—Yamamoto was one hundred percent Japanese, and scorned the Army only because he saw it as hopelessly clumsy and incapable of winning the strategic fight. *Many mistake him for an "American lover." Nonsense. He knows who our main enemy is, and he alone has the skill to defeat him. He is an unusual man. Above all, he has a sense of duty and loyalty – not the blind "bushido" loyalty of so many of my fellow officers, but a sense of traditional duty to Japan, and to the Navy. But bull-headed? Absolutely. Often unwilling to hear criticism? Definitely. He's often right – but what happens when he's wrong?*

"Sagata!" The captain had apparently entertained his thoughts quietly for an uncomfortable length of time, and Yamamoto snapped him out of it. "You were saying about our current war? What did you think of the Army's incursions into China? Of the ..." and suddenly Yamamoto searched for a word, "... the incidents in Nanking?"

The mention of Nanking, which Japanese newspapers had virtually blacked out, made Sagata blanch. This was too much, and Sagata deferred. "It is not good for one's health to express negative opinions of the Imperial Army." The stories of the mass beheadings, the twenty thousand young Chinese men slaughtered by machine-gun outside the city walls, and the endless raping, followed by the shipping of all females to so-called "comfort stations" to service the Army had turned Sagata's stomach.

"Diplomatically stated, Captain. Very well. So, your view of our Pearl Harbor operation?"

"Permission to speak freely, Sir?" Sagata proceeded with

caution.

"Absolutely, Captain. There are just the two of us here. I need to know what the attitudes of my junior officers are—after all, the admirals who surround me are capable military men, and as you know, many opposed the operation because they thought we would fail. We have not. It unfolded exactly as I anticipated, except, perhaps, for the absence of the American carriers."

Clearing his throat, the younger man nodded. "Admiral, forgive me. There is no doubt you have designed and carried out an exceptional operation—and from what I hear about our operations elsewhere, it is only the beginning of unprecedented victories, victories such as the world has never seen ..." His voice trailed off.

"But ..." Yamamoto coaxed him on.

"But anyone who thinks that we have knocked America out of the war, or dealt some death blow to the United States, is living in a fantasy." Sagata suddenly realized he had overstepped his bounds and insulted the Admiral. "I'm sorry, Admiral. I should be silent. I meant no offense."

Yamamoto smiled. "Not at all, Captain. We need fantasies, at times, as something to aim for. Continue your analysis. It seems contrary to the line of thinking of my other admirals, who oppose my plans for other reasons. Why do you think the United States will not be seriously hurt by this attack?"

"I didn't say that Sir. You—ah, we—have indeed stung the Americans, badly. However, I fear that it is akin to whipping a elephant: the blows only make him angry— then what can you do with him?"

Yamamoto pondered the example. "Why do you say that? Do you not have confidence in the military prowess of the Empire of Japan?"

"Do you mean *bushido*? The "*yamato damashii*" —our warrior spirit that no one else possesses?" Sagata asked, gazing now at the globe, and the region of China where his brother had disappeared over a year earlier. With a whiff of sarcasm in his voice, he shouted, "Banzai!" mockingly raising his arm. Again, he realized he had gone too far, offered an unintended insult to the admiral, who had lost two fingers on his left hand at Tsushima. Before he could apologize, Yamamoto gestured with his bad hand, then impatiently circled it in a signal to continue.

"Very well, Admiral." *Fish or cut bait, as the Americans say.*

"Here is what I see. When we have naval reviews and our ships mass, when our air force darkens the skies, or when the Army marches through downtown Tokyo, it looks like an impressive ... no, an unbeatable force. Perhaps to many Asian nations, it is." He chuckled, "Perhaps even to some Europeans, who thought Germany was a paper tiger. You, sir, have studied in America, and I have not. You have lived there, and I have not. But I read everything I can about the United States. I have had friends from American businesses and we talked. Admiral, I mean no disrespect to you, or to our glorious Empire, when I say that previously in China we were an annoyance to the United States, like the flu, striking our neighbor's house, but a disease contained in Asia. The Americans were smugly insulated from us. It was, after all, yellow people oppressing yellow people. But this attack! Our propa ... er, our newspapers portray the Americans as violent and warlike, but I believe they are essentially peaceful, even lazy to a point. It was their apathy we should have fed, not created a lust for revenge. In ten years they would have stood by as we marched into Brisbane or Canberra. Now, however, we have galvanized and motivated the Americans, and they are fearsome." Concerned he was treading perilously close to treason, Sagata paused, "But I have already said too much." Yamamoto slowly looked up, almost with disgust at having to coax him yet again, and rolled his hand once more, urging him to continue.

What did the English say? In for a penny, in for a pound? Sagata stood up and paced, as if delivering a lecture at a military school. "Sir, I studied the physical resources of the United States, which you have seen first-hand. The Americans have the potential to out produce us in steel twenty-to-one; in coal, fifty-to-one; in aircraft — just going by existing plants — three-to-one. Admiral, I conducted a study for the Imperial Navy of American shipyard construction facilities three years ago, and even then, they had the capacity to build ten warships to our one ... and that was before they were aroused and angered... who knows how many new facilities, how many shipyards, they will build now out of a desire for vengeance? And food? We are nothing compared to their vast food resources. If we have a single bad harvest, our armies in the field could starve. And oil? Even if we are so skilled or fortunate to gain the Dutch East Indies oil fields ..." Yamamoto looked up, surprised that a captain knew of the planned operation, but said nothing, "... all it would take is a single, well-executed naval strike by the British, Australians, Indians, or Americans to sever our oil lifeline, and our massive navy would be little more than a fleet of coastal barges."

"Which is why," Yamamoto sighed, looking away, "I urged the invasion of Siberia. For the only time in my career, I sided with the Army, and for one of the few times in my experience, the Army lost the argument. Now the Russians are at war with the Germans, having sucked all their reserves out of Siberia, leaving it an empty shell that we easily could overrun. Instead we are gambling all on the most massive conquest in human history, engaging not one, but three formidable foes in England, Australia, and America. Forgive me for interrupting your analysis, Captain. Oh, and I did see your study of the raw materials. In fact, Commander Genda and I used many of your numbers in our presentation to the General Staff when we argued for the *Kido Butai* operation against Pearl Harbor."

"You used it to argue *in favor* of an attack on the United States, Sir? I ... I don't understand."

"I'll explain in a moment, but I want you to finish. So far, your dissertation has been thorough and impressive."

Thrown off stride, Sagata hesitated a moment, then, buoyed by the Admiral's encouragement, returned to his argument with boldness. "My conclusion, Sir, is that I think we have engaged an enemy whose manpower reserves and raw materials are so staggeringly superior to our own that even our best planners have not really appreciated the danger to which this attack exposes us." He thought about continuing, but concluded he had said more than enough for a junior officer, and any more statements might well result in time spent alone with his Mayonaka, or *seppaku* knife, that night.

Yamamoto gestured to the captain to sit. "Captain Sagata, it may surprise you to learn that I think you are correct in most of your assessments, and certainly in those regarding the relative strengths of the Americans and our own military." Sagata's brow furrowed, and Yamamoto continued. "The one element of your analysis that is missing, however, is character. Spirit. Forget *yamato-damashii* for a moment. I do not refer to anything special to Japan—I mean the warrior spirit that has been with all great armies since the dawn of time, the Mongols, the Romans, the Hun, the English. What is the true nature of the American character? You mentioned several aspects of Americans: sloth, anger, violence, isolationism, arrogance, resolve, confidence, resourcefulness. Ancient Greeks believed that for every good form of government there was a bad form, and that it was not the design of government that was important so much as the character: monarchy vs. tyranny, aristocracy vs. oligarchy, *polis* vs. democracy. Is this not true of character as well? When does a determined man become stubborn? When does a loyal man become foolish? Some of the very things you identified as American weaknesses may be strengths. That is bad for us. But, on the other hand, some of their perceived strengths may be exploited as weaknesses. Will they be angry, and vengeful? No doubt. As would we. But how will that thirst for revenge manifest itself? Will they be impetuous? Careless? Can we manipulate their desire for retribution, leverage it?

"There is no question that the productive capacity of the United States utterly dwarfs our own, even should we be successful in many of our military operations in the next few months. I dare say—and I cannot give you details— that if every one of our goals set for the end of 1942 were to be achieved, the outcome of a war will still be, as the Americans say, 'touch and go.' Given that I presented all of your objections to the government more than six months ago, and was overridden, my task—as is yours—is to find a way to win. So, how do we overcome these significant— and contrary to what some in the Army say---very real advantages?"

Sagata stared at him and shook his head. "You presented the arguments I just made?" Yamamoto stared back at him. "Admiral, I do not know. Can we? Is it possible?"

"Likely? No. But it is possible if the Americans do exactly as we hope, and if we make virtually no mistakes. Then, somewhere along the line, I believe we will still need some stroke of fortune as well, some favor of the gods. I'm not speaking of a 'kamikaze'-type typhoon that utterly destroys the enemy, but rather a key piece of information at the right time, or the wrong move by one of our enemy's generals or admirals."

Frowning, Sagata said, "Yes, anything is possible. Is it reasonable to expect one's enemy to behave precisely as one hopes? Exactly as we need him to behave?" He shook his head. "This does not happen much in war."

"But, honorable Captain, it did happen in the Russo- Japanese War," Yamamoto offered.

"At Tsushima." Sagata slowly agreed. "But the Americans ..." He pursed his lips as if to say something else.

Yamamoto finished his thought for him. "... are not the Russians. Indeed, Captain Sagata, the Americans, I venture to say, are like no foe we have ever fought. And I'm not referring to their material wealth and productive capacity."

Puzzled, Sagata replied, "What, then?"

Yamamoto now stood, his turn to deliver a lecture to a class of midshipmen. "I refer to their mental capacity, their confidence, their almost reckless sense of providence, as though their God rescues them even when they err."

Sagata raised an eyebrow; then, holding up his hand as a student would, he offered, "You mean the saying in the west that 'God watches out for drunks and Americans?'"

Yamamoto smiled. *They are often the same.* "Yes, that saying. There is, however, something to it. Look at their Revolutionary War with England—have you studied it?" Sagata nodded. "Well, then, you know that their armies under their General Washington lost repeatedly, yet turned the entire war with a single courageous raid at Trenton."

By now, Sagata rose and paced with him. "And providence! The French navy showed up to lure off the British fleet and defeat them—the only time in history the French navy ..." the term came out as an epithet, " ... ever defeated the Royal Navy!" Yamamoto glowed with pride at his aide, who had the enthusiasm of a prize student.

"Very good. You have learned your enemy's history well." Then Yamamoto's broad smile disappeared and his face grew serious. "We could go on and on, but unfortunately the point of all this is that all too often, the Americans believe that their God is protecting them, giving them victory." His voice tailed off with those words.

"Surely, Admiral, you do not believe this—that they are blessed by some god? They are barbarians. *Gaijin.* We may admire some of their military prowess, but they are nothing compared to us. Only Nipponese are the true descendants of the gods. The rest? Sub-humans."

Yamamoto put his hand on Sagata's shoulder. "Certainly. You are absolutely right, Captain, and no, I do not believe that they have supernatural favor, but—this is the key—I believe they believe it. It can, therefore, be either a disadvantage for us, or an opportunity."

"Opportunity, Admiral? How?"

"Patience, Captain. In all due time the plans to defeat the Americans will be revealed."

"I don't understand. I thought Pearl Harbor ..."

Yamamoto shook his head like a wise father. "Pearl Harbor was a goad, the spur. We need the Americans angry, looking for retaliation. Have you ever watched a bullfight, Sagata?"

First American history lessons. Now Spanish bullfights? "Yes, Admiral, to my shame I've seen the torture of one of these animals in what was called a fight."

Yamamoto nodded. "Yes, they are barbaric, but the structure of the fight illustrates a great deal about our current situation. America, the bull, is wounded, and angry. We are smaller, weaker perhaps in resources and manpower — but smarter. The trick is to make sure the bull stays angry, lure him in, keep his focus on what he will do to you, not what you are about to do to him. Until that time, however, one blow, or even several, will not kill such a large animal until he is bled out. Captain, do you know when the bull dies?"

Sagata started to tire of the game, and he felt a headache coming on. It was all too much grand strategy. "No, Admiral."

"He dies when he lowers his head in fatigue. That is when the brain, the nervous system is vulnerable. When he is tired, and when his will has been sapped, he gets careless. At that point the matador can easily kill him."

Sensing the lesson was over, Sagata leaned outside and gestured to the steward to remove the cups and saucers. "So what is the next move?"

Yamamoto patted him gently on the shoulder as he escorted the captain to the door. "We show him the red cape, honorable Captain. We show him the red cape."

CHAPTER TWO

Naval Station Pearl Harbor
25 Dec 41 1400

Chester W. Nimitz (Wikipedia)

"Attention on deck!" The shout brought two dozen Navy, Army, and Marine Corps officers to their feet as the new commander-in-chief of the Pacific Fleet, Admiral Chester W. Nimitz, entered the auditorium. Looking tired from his seventeen-hour flight from San Diego, Nimitz strode down the aisle between the two rows. Arriving at the lectern, he announced "Be seated," and waited for the brief rustle of men finding chairs to subside. Nimitz wore service dress khakis, with the long-sleeved shirt required by winter months, even in Hawaii. Four sparkling stars adorned each collar. His black tie, too, was at regulation length, meaning it looked too short, ending abruptly about a half inch above his belt and giving him the appearance—as it did with all officers—of having more of a paunch than he really possessed. Nimitz's Chief of Staff, the jovial Captain Arthur Lamar, who in fact did run to the portly side, trailed the "CINC," pronounced "sink" for commander-in-chief. Standing near the stage, Lamar assumed the "at ease" position and momentarily brushed back the shock of thick brown hair that contrasted him instantly with his white- haired boss.

The CINC surveyed the room, noting several empty seats. The missing were most likely victims of the attack eighteen days earlier. He shook his head, dropped down in thought then looked out to those left in the room. Among the missing was his close friend, Admiral Husband Kimmel, the commanding officer at Pearl Harbor, who fell early in the battle on Sunday from a stray American anti-aircraft round outside his headquarters building. *Just as well,* thought Nimitz. *Now he can be buried a hero rather than investigated endlessly and scapegoated. We will omit any mention that it was an American bullet that killed him. Ironic. Kimmel's last words were, "It was merciful that the Japs got me," unaware a round from his own guns had accidentally taken his life. My old friend, you are already missed.*

Nimitz, looking like a thinner Spencer Tracy, leaned over the lectern to study the audience, which sat in total silence. The 56-year-old Texan probably seemed ancient to them because of his white hair, and was unusually gaunt, thanks to the marathon plane ride from San Diego by a PB2Y-3 Coronado, a big, four-engine seaplane. Despite the fact that the Coronado was a reasonably comfortable and plane, Nimitz found he still couldn't sleep much on the trip.

Upon arriving at Pearl Harbor at mid-morning of Christmas day, 1941, the pilot had asked Nimitz if he wanted to observe the damage from the air, and the Admiral accepted the offer, sliding into the left hand seat as the Coronado flew wide circles around the harbor and Hickam Field. Clucking his tongue and shaking his head, Nimitz said nothing as he stared down at the hulks of the American battleships, some of them half-submerged. A thick oil covered most of Pearl Harbor, streaking the aqua water, while at Hickam the flight lines were littered with shattered aircraft, parts, and rubble. As he departed the Coronado at 0900, he shook the hands of every member of the exhausted crew per his usual routine and apologized to them for infringing on their Christmas Eve.

Nimitz immediately instructed his staff to take him to inspect the battle damage at Pearl Harbor Naval Base from ground level. What he saw when he arrived there shocked him even more. Sailors in dungarees, paddling small boats, still searched for bodies pinned under wreckage. Oil slicks, which looked bad enough from the air, now seemed so thick Nimitz thought he could walk on them. In Dry Dock #1, the *Oklahoma* was being repaired, having been righted from its capsized position several days after the attack. He'd heard stories of work crews at the *Oklahoma* covering their faces with bandanas to block the putrid smell of death from the battleship's lower decks, caused by scores of unrecovered bodies.

Despite the gruesome tour, Nimitz knew it was important that he eat breakfast for appearances' sake. He could not allow his officers to see any signs of weakness. Putting aside the images from the harbor, he downed some orange juice, toast, and a local favorite, fried Spam. Nimitz needn't have worried about maintaining his tough-as-nails reputation, which had preceded him and was well-earned. Although unafraid of making hard decisions, he willingly delegated authority to more talented subordinates when necessary. But, would that matter now? In front of these men?

As he continued to assess the officers in front of him, his eyes rested on several men in U.S. Army uniforms over on the right side of the room. *This is a new kind of war, he thought. This will involve amphibious warfare and island fighting as we've never seen it, and it will take cooperation of an unprecedented kind between the Army and Navy. That means I'm going to have to get along with MacArthur.* The thought sent a shudder down Nimitz's spine. He knew of MacArthur's reputation as an excellent tactician whose ego and insatiable thirst for publicity often clouded his military instincts. *All problems in due time, Chet. Now's not the time to worry about Mac. Reassure the men, and jump start the Navy here in Hawaii. That's what you're here for today.*

When the bombs had started falling at Pearl, Nimitz had been working in Washington as Chief of the Navy's Bureau of Navigation; although he was hardly a desk jockey, having commanded the USS *Augusta*, then Battle Division One. Nimitz had seen plenty of duty aboard fighting ships, and, more important, three years earlier he had sounded very much like Col. Billy Mitchell when he warned that war with Japan was coming, and would likely be started by a surprise attack. Despite his credentials and foresight, some hard-chargers and aviators still regarded him as a "battleship admiral," insufficiently attuned to the new power of aircraft carriers and aviation. They couldn't be more wrong, but Nimitz brushed off the criticisms. He had a healthy appreciation of his own strengths and weaknesses, and knew that he didn't understand carrier operations as intimately as some. But he knew plenty of commanders who did, most notably Vice Admiral Bill Halsey. And there were others who showed great potential for task force leadership, such as Rear Admiral Ray Spruance.

Nimitz suddenly realized he had been standing in front of the men for several seconds, lost in thought, and they looked at him quizzically. He examined the fleet officers who stared back at him, searching for indications of fear, apprehension, or timidity. *None. They're mad. They want revenge. Good. They'll need that anger to get them through the next several months. The tough times have only begun. The Japs did us a cruel and perverse favor by sinking the battleships, because now, more than ever, we'll have to become a carrier navy.*

He cleared his throat, and began with the obvious. "Gentlemen. Three weeks ago the United States Navy sustained the worst defeat in its history."

Nimitz could sense the officers bristle at the word "defeat," but he wanted them angry. "We allowed ourselves to be surprised, and then, once the attack started, responded poorly. Slow response to man anti-aircraft guns, inexcusable delays in getting our aircraft off the fields ..." at which point he cast a glance at the officers from the Army Air Force, who glared at him, "... inept gunfire, and ineffective fire containment and rescue operations all combined to give the Japanese an even more comprehensive victory than probably even they imagined. I'll be blunt and coarse so that no man here misses my meaning: with or without the element of surprise, they kicked our asses." There was some uncomfortable shifting among the officers, who likely had thought they were coming for a pep talk. *Pep talk, hell! We don't have time for self-pity, and I'm sure not going to play cheerleader.*

Nimitz continued. "When we meet the Japanese again, we will have to improve in every aspect if we hope to defeat them. Nothing less than the safety of Hawaii and even the west coast of the United States may depend on it." Officers flashed glances at each other. "President Roosevelt has stated to me in no uncertain terms that he does not question anyone's courage at Pearl Harbor; nor do I. He thinks you are the bravest soldiers, sailors, and Marines on earth; so do I. But, he also made it clear that he will not tolerate—the nation cannot tolerate—another disaster of the type we had three weeks ago - *Nor will I.*"

"On the other hand, I want to make something else clear. I do not blame any of the officers in this room, and certainly not Admiral Kimmel or General Short, for this despicable attack. Had Admiral Kimmel received proper warning, he likely would have done exactly what I would have done—what the 'book' would have called for: he would have sailed out, rendezvoused with Admiral Halsey's *Enterprise,* and attacked. Well, gentlemen, sometimes the 'book' is wrong. In deep water, outnumbered six carriers to three, we likely would have lost that fight, no matter how bravely our men fought or how well they were led. And then where would we be? All ships would have been lost in deep water. All three carriers gone, our veteran pilots, killed. No, gentlemen, the Japanese don't know it, but by attacking us here, with the carriers out to sea, they made a strategic mistake of the most profound kind. And because I do not think anyone here should suffer blame for this attack, I am personally requesting as many of Admiral Kimmel's existing staff as can be arranged to remain with me."

Puzzled, yet relieved, looks were exchanged as the officers realized none of them were to be made scapegoats.

"Here's the reality, gentlemen. Both President Roosevelt and I realize that we will likely suffer several more setbacks until we can go on offense. You are aware that immediately after the attack, orders went out for Wake Island to be reinforced, then that mission was scrapped, and just two days ago, Wake fell."

Even though they'd lived with the reality of the scrapped rescue mission for weeks, Nimitz still heard some muffled comments of "That ain't right!" and "What crap." The brotherly feelings he'd received only moments earlier now turned to resentment over the thought of abandoning their comrades on Wake, even though Nimitz had no part in the decision—and supported it as sound judgment. *Couldn't be helped. It was a lost cause, and Admiral Pye was right not to pour out more good blood in a symbolic gesture.* Nimitz slowly scanned the room with a steely look that immediately restored order. He continued.

"It was Wake's sad, but necessary and ultimately heroic fate to fall." A few resigned nods were seen in audience. Nimitz gestured to Lamar, who strode to the podium and raised the canvas revealing the large map behind the admiral. "Now," he continued, with a gleam in his eye, "I bet you'd like to know how we can hit those sons of bitches." Instantly the mood changed and a cheer went up.

Nimitz picked up his pointer and turned to the map. "At this moment, we are tracking two Japanese strike forces." Pointing to the Indochina/Malaya area, Nimitz continued, "One is almost certainly heading for the British stronghold of Singapore. The British think they can hold, but I'm skeptical. Fixed fortifications, whether in Europe or here in the Pacific, belong to the medieval period of war, and are no match for modern bombers or long-range naval gunnery. If the Japanese gain control of Singapore, all of the Dutch East Indies are open and virtually defenseless. At best, there are a dozen heavy and light cruisers of the Dutch, British, Royal Indian, and Australian navies in the region, and the British have battleships *Repulse* and *Prince of Wales* still in Singapore, although they are close to evacuating them. There is one British carrier, the *Hermes*, in the Indian Ocean, probably too far away to help. Without air power, those cruisers will be helpless. The Dutch have no troops to speak of left in the East Indies, having already pulled those out to resist Hitler a year ago."

Nimitz next trained his pointer on the Philippines. "We know where the other task force was: in the Philippines. Our forces there fell and only a few are hanging on. We are guessing that task force will substantially remain in the area to lend support and raid near Australia. As an aside, the Philippines reiterated the lessons we learned in China, and now in our own skies over Hawaii, namely that our P-40 Warhawk is sadly inferior to the Japanese Zero." Sharp nods, along with some well-placed curses from the Navy and Army aviators, responded to Nimitz's assessment of the Warhawk. "We pray for the success of our forces and their Filipino allies there, but the reality is they likely cannot hold out for more than a few weeks. Ultimately, their fate will be the same as that of our men on Wake Island." Officers exchanged concerned looks, often seeking confirmation or scuttlebutt from their peers. No one disputed Nimitz's assessment.

"Then," Nimitz continued, "there are at least two other major Japanese strike forces out there that we cannot find. One, we think, but cannot verify, is heading for the islands northwest of Australia, to carve out a string of bases that will act as forward buffers. The other group — the one that struck us, plus large numbers of additional ships attached to it that we did not even encounter — is lurking in the north Pacific. It is our belief, gentlemen, that the other three forces, while they will gain territory and raw materials, are largely sideshows in Admiral Yamamoto's plan, and that this force of multiple carriers in the north with its supporting vessels is his real sword. Make no mistake, Yamamoto is frustrated that he did not sink our three aircraft carriers, and he will try again, though I doubt he would attempt another strike here at Pearl Harbor. The Japanese want us to fight — it's in their tradition of Tsushima, the great single decisive battle of the Russo-Japanese War, by which they think they can make us beg for peace."

"Never!" "The rat bastards!" "We'll show 'em, Admiral!" came the cries from officers who could no longer contain themselves.

For a second, Nimitz smiled slightly, then reverted to his granite look as he held up his hand. "I know, gentlemen. Just because I'm an admiral, don't think I don't know how you feel. There are times I wish I didn't wear these stars; times that I could just take the helm of the nearest cruiser and sail out there and start lobbing shells, or grab a fifty caliber and blast away at the nearest Jap ship. We all want to get into action. There are more than two thousand dead Americans, friends, shipmates, and family from the December 7 attack. Many of you lost buddies, some with horrific wounds or burns. Others ... well, I heard about the horror of those sailors trapped in air pockets inside the *Oklahoma*. Admirals are not insulated to loss — my good friend, Admiral Kimmel, is just one example. Perhaps President Roosevelt would not approve of me saying so, but on top of everything else, on top of the obvious human and material losses, our national ego has been badly bloodied in this despicable attack. The destruction of the *Maine* was nothing compared to this treachery. However, just as I will never rest until the Japs pay, and pay dearly, for this infamy, neither will I recklessly waste our last capital ships between Japan and the west coast. Our time will come, gentlemen. Your time will come; and when it does, there will not be the slightest doubt in your minds that your training, your weapons, and your skills will be vastly superior to that of our enemies."

"I'm telling you much more than normally you would be allowed to hear, because I think — and the President agreed — you deserve to know that we're not just sitting on our hands. I'm also telling you this because we will need more out of you in the coming struggle than you even thought you had in you. In the coming months, we will need repair crews to work at an inhuman pace. We will need training to be ratcheted up to unprecedented levels. We must compress several years' worth of preparation into a few months. We need officers to make every move without mistake or hesitation, in full confidence that what you're doing is right. This is a tall order. At the same time, we'll be counting on our civilian brothers to do their part, and to supply us with new and better ships." Nimitz raised his voice. "Mark my words, though, gentlemen," Nimitz said, his voice quivering with emotion for the first time. "When the moment arrives, we will rise up like a mighty wave and avenge our comrades! We will teach the Japs a lesson they and history will never forget!"

As one, the officers leaped to their feet and let out a primal yell, with all of their rage, pain, and sorrow of the last few days exploding in cheers and applause and adrenaline. Nimitz paused for a moment, then gestured to Lamar, who lowered the map canvas, allowed the frustration to vent for a few moments, then turned to shout loudly over the cheers, "Atten-shion." Immediately the sound of dozens of pairs of shoes and boots slamming together was followed by silence as fifty Naval and Army officers watched Admiral Chester Nimitz walk out of the room, every one of them now confident that they would finish what the Japanese started on December 7.

Lamar swelled with pride in the performance of his boss. He'd never heard the old man talk like that. He watched Nimitz leave, then announced, "Dis-missed," he smiled as he ran to catch up with the admiral. Shorter than Nimitz, Lamar had to almost double-time to keep up with the admiral's quick pace. Lamar found himself sweating, even though it was December, the mild Hawaiian air and gently swaying palm trees made the air soft. Nimitz seemed lost in thought, and finally, out of boredom, Lamar broke the silence. "Looks like you hit the nerves you wanted to hit, Admiral." He was careful to speak loudly, due to Nimitz's slight deafness, then knew he connected when he saw the twinkle in Nimitz's eye.

They kept walking, and, after a moment, Nimitz replied, "They'll be motivated, that's for sure. We're going to need that, because I wasn't lying when I said the task before us is nothing less than daunting. Japan has ten fleet carriers, the two largest battleships ever made, and enough ships to carry out four separate invasions simultaneously. They have the best naval fighter aircraft in the world, and more than five hundred well-trained pilots, each of whom has a warrior spirit that, frankly, we've never encountered before. We, on the other hand, at present have only three carriers, with the Enterprise on its way, no escorts to speak of, and a badly damaged naval base."

"And," added Lamar, "Japan really isn't at war on the other side of the world with an equally dangerous enemy."

"You had to bring that up," noted Nimitz in a tinge of graveyard humor. "What I could not tell the boys was that the President decided that the overwhelming amount of men, ships, and resources will be going to the European theater. Privately, I'm told we may not get more than twenty percent of the resources."

Lamar shook his head and let out a low whistle. "Twenty percent? Admiral, that barely puts us on a par with Japan. We'll have no significant advantage anywhere then. How are we supposed to whip them?"

Nimitz looked at him reassuringly. "Did you think I was kidding when I said we were going to have to be better trained than the Japs? Guess I needed to add 'lucky,' too. The fact is, we have three aircraft carriers, and now maybe a fourth, between Japan and an invasion of San Francisco. I don't think they'd actually try that—they aren't that crazy —but we would be hard pressed to stop them if they did."

Nimitz did not find it necessary to mention his own qualities that would help tip the scales in America's favor: he was a born administrator; could organize a herd of cats through a fence gate at a moment's notice, and he seemed able to squeeze blood out of a turnip when it came to extracting the maximum from available resources. Both traits would be desperately needed at Pearl Harbor in the coming months. Nor did he share with anyone, including Lamar, his view that whatever happened in the short run, in the long run the United States would simply overwhelm Japan with men and weapons—but he hoped it didn't come to that, with its accompanying casualty lists.

"When does the *Yorktown* head out this way, Admiral?"

"I've been informed that *Yorktown* will be ordered out next week. By February we'll have four CVs: the *Enterprise*, *Lexington*, *Saratoga*, and *Yorktown*. The *Hornet* just finished her shakedown, and could be here in a month." "So, at best, we have four, maybe five, to Japan's six, and perhaps ten?" Lamar asked.

"There are some ways to overcome superior numbers, but for now, we have to be cautious and make sure that we don't take disproportionate losses anywhere. At any rate, we'll have to do the best we can until the cavalry arrives." The two officers ascended the stairs of the Pacific Fleet Headquarters building past the Marine guards, who presented arms. Inside, Nimitz and Lamar turned down a row of desks into a hallway, before coming to the office of "Commander-in-Chief". This office was divided into a chart room filled with officers performing routine duties and beyond that Nimitz's private office.

"Art, we're fighting a holding action. I can't risk much with only three or four carriers, and I have the whole damned Pacific to patrol. At the same time, we can't let them get away with uncontested invasions. I want Halsey and Spruance over here as soon as Ray gets back from Midway. I want to speak to them together." Nimitz took off his hat and flipped it onto his desk, over his clock.

Lamar produced a small notepad and copied the orders. "Aye aye, Sir. Halsey's *Enterprise* came in three days ago. Spruance should be back here tomorrow."

Nimitz studied the map of the Pacific that hung on his wall. He had two favorite subordinate commanders, the aggressive Halsey, with his exceptional instincts for battle, and the more cautious Raymond Spruance, who tended to see the big strategic picture more than the tactical situation. Where Nimitz knew he would have to keep a tight rein on Halsey at times, he would probably have to kick Spruance in the butt. But together, they offset each other's weaknesses and were a near perfect tag-team.

"It was damned stupid of King to order Halsey after the Japs like that. He could have gotten caught out there and we'd be in a hell of a mess." Nimitz had little love for his imperious superior, Admiral Ernest King, a superb organizer but frequent poor judge of commanders in the field. King had ordered Halsey to pursue the Japanese fleet. Even Halsey, who never ducked a fight, disagreed with the order, but went out anyway—and had nothing but trouble. A jinx on the mission, some said: a destroyer had a man fall overboard and drown; a sailor was crushed when a turret malfunctioned aboard the *Salt Lake City*; a scout plane aboard the Enterprise crashed onto the deck, decapitating a machinist's mate; a Wildcat from the Enterprise plummeted into the sea, killing the pilot; another torpedo plane simply disappeared; and two destroyers collided and had to return to Pearl Harbor for repairs. *With that kind of record, it's a good thing Halsey didn't find the Japanese.*

"Sir," Lamar offered, "Admiral Halsey might well have found the Jap carriers and gotten in some licks." Nimitz glanced skeptically at him, then turned to the map. "At any rate, Sir, we'll have the carriers re-fitted and ready within a week."

"Provided there are no new surprises, that is. Very well. That's all for now. Thank you, Captain. Make sure we have constant B-17 and PBY patrols at maximum range in a 180-degree arc, and I don't want any crap from General Emmons, although I doubt he'll be in any mood to buck me on this. And request, in the strongest possible terms, to keep that damned radar unit on at all times."

"Yes, Sir. Are you hosting the officers for dinner tonight, Sir?" Lamar knew the admiral held the best dinners in the Navy, and he hoped to use both the carrot and the stick when it came to the officers under his command. Knowing he'd be giving a hard-hitting speech earlier in the day, Nimitz planned a get-together for the base's top brass as a carrot. Nimitz's dinner parties featured the finest filets, fresh vegetables, and many flavors of ice cream. Lamar also knew of the admiral's habit of drinking two old fashions before dinner, and never any more. And it was Lamar's job to have everything in order.

"I am. You know the drill, so expect twelve, plus the two of us."

"Aye aye, Admiral."

"And one more thing, Art: tell Captain Layton that I want any intel that Commander Rochefort gets about Jap fleet movements and anything mentioning Yamamoto by name, no matter how trivial it may seem, the minute it gets processed over at Hypo. And I want it *before* Rochefort sends it to Washington."

"That's not protocol, Sir. Do you think he'll comply?"

"The hell with protocol. Rochefort doesn't exactly go by the book, anyway. From what I heard of Rochefort, he was begging Kimmel to take his information. Hell, I even heard ..." Nimitz realized Lamar had no need to know, and clipped his thought. "Well, let's just say Rochefort did everything he could to bring that information to the attention of those who should see it."

Lamar knew he'd been slotted in the Intel pecking order, and said, "Aye aye, Admiral." Then, in the doorway, he paused again. "Sir, one more question ...?"

Nimitz nodded impatiently. "I've heard that Commander Rochefort walks around in a bathrobe, and that he doesn't, well, bathe a lot."

Nimitz chuckled. "Son, that's two comments, not a question. In fact, I had heard some things too, but people here tell me it's all part of an image the Commander cultivates. The one, brief time I met him, he was squared away. But, for the record, Commander Rochefort can wear a brassiere on his head and smell like French cheese if his bunch of codebreakers can tell me where those Jap ships are."

"Aye aye, Admiral." Lamar laughed, then gently closed the door behind him.

Nimitz sat down and rocked back in his chair. When he was certain no one was watching, he put his feet up on his desk and closed his eyes. *Lord, I'm not a praying man — as You well know — but I ask this one thing: give me three months. Hold the Japs off just three months.* He took out a cigarette, looked at it, and put it in the ashtray, unlit. Then Admiral Chester Nimitz did something else he hadn't done in more than twenty-four hours. He fell asleep.

CHAPTER THREE

Henry Kaiser (Wikipedia)

Northern California
3 Feb 42

"Mr. Kaiser, it's the White House on the phone." Henry Kaiser's secretary, Eunice, pointed to the receiver from her outside office.

Kaiser, his desk full of designs and plans from his latest dam construction project, squinted. *Franklin Roosevelt? What the heck could he want we me? We aren't exactly best pals.* He nodded and picked up in his office, gesturing to Eunice to close the door. Then he pointed to his wife, Bess, to come in. She had just stopped by to bring her husband some homemade rolls, and entered with a puzzled look. As she shut the door behind her, Kaiser swung his arm to the empty chair, urging her to sit.

"Henry Kaiser," he announced into the telephone. "Please hold for the President of the United States," said an unidentified female voice at the other end. Kaiser slowly lowered himself into his chair.

"Henry!" came the bubbly voice of Franklin Roosevelt just a moment later. "How are you?" Without waiting for an answer, Roosevelt added, "Henry, I need your help."

Roosevelt's New Deal administration has systematically harassed and hounded me for a decade — me! One of the few businessmen in this country actually trying to employ people! "My help, Mr. President," Kaiser responded coldly. "It doesn't seem like you've needed my help for the last ten years."

Roosevelt brushed off the sarcasm. "Henry, I want you to handle the bulk of merchant shipbuilding for the war effort. We need you, Henry. America needs you."

Kaiser certainly didn't trust the man, and at any rate had no intention of letting him off that easily. "I appreciate that, Mr. President," Kaiser replied. "Indeed I do. Yes, very kind. But over the last ten years, your Brains Trusters have been taxing the hell out of my businesses and sending your labor thugs to my plants. Why should I help you now? Why should I believe you now?"

Roosevelt played coy. "Why, Henry ..." always familiar — a clever trick the politician had cultivated, "... I have no idea what you're talking about."

Kaiser smiled. "Very well, Mr. President. You don't know what I'm talking about, and therefore I must decline your invitation ... unless your memory suddenly improves." He really didn't think he could bluff the President of the United States, and actually didn't care if he worked with FDR or not, but was surprised me when Roosevelt conceded.

"All right, Henry. We both know the dance. I need you more than you need me. What do you want?"

Kaiser's round face broke into a massive smile, and he turned to Bess. He covered the mouthpiece and whispered, "I've got the son of a bitch, Bess!" She had grinned, and shook her head.

"That's better, Mr. President. Don't want to be accused of hampering the war effort. Okay, first, I need all your New Deal, union-loving, socialist regulations temporarily suspended in all my yards. All of them. Get your votes somewhere else."

Roosevelt bristled — Kaiser could feel it over the phone line — but the President had no choice. Roosevelt had his own staff nearby and was dictating the conditions to them as Kaiser listed them. "You don't mince adjectives, do you, Henry? Very well, agreed. What else?"

"Second, Mr. President, I need you to keep the boys in the War Department off my back. None of this 'excess profits' crap. No 'Merchants of Death' hearings. I'll make ships so fast it will make your head spin. It will make those sons-a-bitches at the Philadelphia shipyard look like first- year pipefitters, but I can't do it with your admirals down here every week and those damned bureaucrats crawling through my books. The Navy gives us the plans, leaves us alone, and we'll give Uncle Sam back a damn fine ship in ninety days. Your boys can come in here twice a year to snoop around, do audits, whatever. All the rest of the time, I need to be building ships, not shuffling paperwork."

"All right. I think I can get Secretary Knox to sign off on that," Roosevelt sighed loud enough for Kaiser to hear over the phone, and Kaiser chuckled at Roosevelt's theatrics, knowing that the President hadn't given him much at all yet. "Anything else, Henry?"

"Yes. One more thing. California doesn't have the work force I need—nowhere near it. I'm going to have to bring in thousands of shipwrights, pipefitters, electricians, welders and other skilled people from all over the country, and, well, Mr. President, a lot of them will be Negroes. I plan to run ads in every major eastern and mid-western city offering top wages, and I'm going to hire whoever shows up, colored or white, pink or purple, makes no difference to me if they can weld. Hell, I'll hire Japanese midgets if I can trust 'em."

Roosevelt laughed at that one. "So why should that be a problem for me—aside from Japanese, of course. Haven't you read the newspapers? Eleanor is a champion of the Negro, or so they say."

"I'm serious, Franklin." Kaiser changed tactics, using Roosevelt's first name deliberately. "There's going to be a lot of people out in California who don't particularly want to see a river of darkies coming here, even if it's to work. I want your Justice boys to keep an eye on this. I'm not going to brook any lynchings, burnings, Klan, or any of that stuff here. And unlike Eleanor, I'm no champion of the Negro. I just want the best, most motivated work force I can get, and I don't give a damn what color they are. I'll take one-armed Irishman or an un-circumcised rabbi if he can build a ship."

Roosevelt emitted a hearty laugh at the image. "Rest assured, Henry, there will be no racial distractions for your work. If nothing else, Pearl Harbor taught us—well, most of us---that we're all Americans and that we have more to deal with right now than skin color." Then he paused for a moment, and, with a twinkle in his eye, added, "But, if you also want me to send Eleanor ..."

It was then Kaiser's turn to laugh. "That won't be necessary, Mr. President. Franklin, thank you. I won't let you down. In return, you are going to see shipbuilding on a scale you've never thought possible. And we will win this damned war."

"I have no doubt about that. No doubt at all. Tell me, Henry, do you already have your shipyard sites selected?"

"I do, sir." Kaiser changed to more formal references, again, deliberately. "I've found suitable places in San Diego and Santa Monica, but my main shipyards will be in Richmond, California and in Washington State. Within two months, I can have over fifty thousand workers at five main sites. Using some of the new modular construction techniques my plants have perfected already, we think we can build ships in large sections, cutting hundreds of hours off the construction of each vessel. We can drop interior sections — navigation, mess, and so on — into the partially completed hull while we continue building the bow portion of the ship, then just weld the large, already-completed sections together. When I said we'd turn out a new ship every ninety days, you need to understand that's a starting estimate." Kaiser jabbed his finger in the air, even though Roosevelt couldn't see him. "Between us, I expect that this time next year we ought to be able to turn out a completed Liberty Ship in a month or less."

"A month? Henry, isn't that a tad optimistic?" FDR had heard more than his share of bluster from generals and politicians, but Henry Kaiser exuded genuine confidence. The man believed he could do it, and, based on his track record of building the nation's largest dams, on time and under budget, Roosevelt believed he could do it, too. A pregnant silence hung on the line for a moment, then Roosevelt added, "Henry, I think you can. I'm betting the lives of thousands of Americans that you can. By the end of this war, we may have you building aircraft carriers, too. And I'll uphold my end of the bargain. You won't get any interference from the federal government when it comes to construction."

"I appreciate that very much, Mr. President. One last thing, though: you haven't said anything about cost. I assume we will be on a strict War Department austere budget?"

"Now, Henry. You really do underestimate me. You build ships and send me the bills. If you can indeed turn out a ship in ninety days, I can guarantee you no one in Washington will question for a moment your invoices. They'll just chalk it up to the cost of freedom, and happily pay it."

Kaiser snorted, "That's not unusual. Most politicians don't mind paying bills with the taxpayer's money." Then he realized he'd gone too far. "I'm sorry, Franklin. It's a good deal, Mr. President." *Back to "Mr. President now."* Henry laughed, noting his own manipulation. "I'll update you regularly. You won't be disappointed in our efforts."

"Of that, I'm certain, Henry. Good bye, and God bless your efforts."

A moment of silence had hung in the office as Bess raised both hands as if to ask, "What did he say?" Henry quietly folded his hands in front of him, mentally noting the innumerable tasks to take care of—ordering steel, building small, modular homes to accommodate the influx of workers, and, above all, setting up a system for his managers to teach the welders the "Kaiser method" of welding. *Relax, Henry. It can't be any tougher than building a dam.* When he finally reviewed the phone call with Bess, and munched down a roll with no butter, his wife had said only, "Henry, if Franklin Roosevelt was willing to swallow his pride and ask for your help, you owe it to him, and the country, to do your best."

Kaiser nodded. "And that's exactly what I intend to give."

Shortly after Bess left, Kaiser began contacting some of his peers in the business community—titans who made steel, autos, electrical facilities, dams, concrete, aluminum, and ships. Their reaction to Pearl Harbor was almost identical: what the hell were the Japs thinking? To a man, they had assured Kaiser that in their own area of production, they'd bury both Japan and Germany within a year after ramping up. One automaker swore his plants could turn out a tank in five hours from scratch; the head of Oldsmobile had completely re-tooled for torpedo production; and Donald Douglas, the aircraft manufacturer, said that six months after Pearl Harbor, his factories could be producing 200 planes a month. When multiplied by the facilities at Boeing, Convair, Fairchild, Grumman, Hughes, and others ... Well, Henry did the math. By the end of 1942 American aircraft companies would be turning out 50,000 airplanes a year. And one parts manufacturer promised "a billion bullets" a year, by himself. *My business pals were right. What the hell were they thinking?*

CHAPTER FOUR

Naval Air Station, Alameda, California
1 Apr 42 0943

James Doolittle (Wikipedia)

Captain Marc Mitscher stared at the dock from the starboard bridge wing of the *USS Hornet*, having been ordered two days earlier to prepare the ship for departure, but had still had not been told what his mission was. Below, pulling alongside the 19,800-ton aircraft carrier, was a long convoy of trucks, each with its cargo covered, crawling up to the dock where a massive crane and crew stood ready. *Any fool can tell those are airplanes,* thought Mitscher observing the equipment concealed by the tarps. *So what the hell's the big mystery?* Chomping down on his unlit cigar, Mitscher hustled down the Hornet's ladders to the hangar deck, where an Army Air Force colonel strode up to him.

"Lieutenant Colonel James Doolittle, Sir, reporting for duty." Jimmy Doolittle saluted, then smiled at the confusion that registered on the captain's face.

Returning Doolittle's salute, Mitscher gazed at the green uniform and said with suspicion, "Army Air Force?"

Doolittle replied, "Affirmative, Sir. Mitscher surveyed the aircraft concealed beneath the tarps. "Colonel, I'm afraid I don't understand. I have not been briefed on this mission. What are we doing with the Army?"

"I know you have not been briefed, Sir. I have sealed orders for you. Classified, to the top. Perhaps if we could retire to your wardroom?"

"That would be a good idea, Colonel Doolittle." Mitscher, looking over Doolittle's shoulder, noticed that the first aircraft, still concealed, was being fitted with a harness to hoist it aboard the Hornet. "But in the meantime, Colonel, do you want to tell me what those aircraft are?"

"Yes, Sir. They are specially adapted B-25 Mitchell medium

bombers. 'Billys' we call 'em." Doolittle smiled.

"Land-based bombers?" Mitscher asked, peering even more intently over Doolittle's shoulder. "You mean like the two that staged practice takeoffs here in February?" Doolittle grinned and nodded again. "Don't tell me. You're going to bomb Tokyo from an aircraft carrier." Mitscher was joking. Doolittle wasn't. His toothy smile now stretched from ear to ear.

Mitscher's eyes widened. "Holy Christ! Come on, Colonel," Mitscher turned on his heel and headed toward the wardroom. "I can already tell, this is going to be good." "Yes, Sir, it is," Doolittle said, almost running to keep up with the captain.

500 nautical miles west of Hawaii
3 Apr 42 1149

Doolittle and Mitscher watched in anticipation as the lead B-25, "*Mama's Boy*," raced its engines. Although in just over two weeks Doolittle would fly the lead plane off himself, his co-pilot, Lt. Richard Cole, was conducting this routine test. Each day, every one of the 16 Mitchells fired up its engines and pushed it to take-off speed, with the aircraft tied down and restrained by wheel chocks. And, each day, a full system maintenance was performed on every plane. Today Cole had kicked out the maintenance man and warmed up "*Mama's Boy*" himself, anxious for the mission ahead. After satisfying himself that the B-25's engines were working fine, he looked up to the carrier's bridge and gave a thumbs up to Doolittle and Mitscher and shut the engines down.

Doolittle's 133 officers and men had practiced relentlessly since Navy Captain Francis Low first conceived of the plan not long after Pearl Harbor. The idea was passed from the Navy to the Army Air Force and Gen. "Hap" Arnold, who turned it over to his special project officer, Doolittle. Over the next several months, Doolittle recruited volunteers from the 17th Bombardment Group. They mastered taking off their planes within the confines of a carrier's flight deck, no small feat for the 14-ton, 50-foot- long planes with 67-foot wingspans. Doolittle's lead plane, with the least takeoff space, would only have 467 feet to clear the flight deck, even as the tail section of the last B-25s hung off the aft of the *Hornet's* deck. The basic problem, of course, was that large Army bombers had never launched on a combat mission from an aircraft carrier before, and they were going to have only one chance to get it right.

"A raid on Japan," Mitscher said. "Just four months after Pearl Harbor! I have to admit, I thought it might be a year before we could even strike at the outer fringes of the Empire."

"You're probably right, Captain. If this were a normal mission ... well, it wouldn't be happening. Between you and me, this is all about image and propaganda. We have to show the Japanese they are in a war. Let them know that they picked the wrong damned fight, with the wrong damned enemy." Doolittle leaned over the map of the Pacific spread across a wardroom table. "This is just pure psychology, Captain, nothing more. We can't do much damage to Japan with a handful of bombers and five hundred pound bombs. But what we can do is tell everyone out there who is still fighting — all the Aussies and Kiwis and Malays and Indians and Chinese — they aren't alone, and they aren't forgotten. Uncle Sam is coming for them, sooner rather than later."

"Well," added Mitscher, "don't tell my crew that they are risking their lives to haul your asses over almost two thousand miles of the Pacific Ocean for a propaganda victory. As far as they're concerned, we're going to sting that son of a bitch Tojo badly."

"Fine. I have no problem making them think we're blowing Tokyo to hell."

"Look, Colonel Doolittle, I want you to know that I fully appreciate the impact of what you're doing. Remember over a year ago the Brits were on the ropes against Hitler's air force when Churchill ordered that gutsy raid on Berlin. Threw Hitler into a frenzy, caused him to change all of his targeting of the Royal Air Force landing fields just as that strategy had been paying off."

"Remember it? Hell, that was what Captain Low said gave him the idea we could do the same thing to the Japs. Who knows what this raid might provoke them to do? Anyway, we have to do something. Americans don't like playing defense."

"One more thing, Colonel. You haven't had a live drill with these things since we went to sea, since we can't land one back on a carrier. Are you sure you can take off on this length of deck?"

"Captain, we were hitting the four hundred-fifty foot markers in practice." Mitscher started to protest, but Doolittle held up his hand. "I know, I know. Practice isn't real conditions. But it's all we have — and remember in our practice takeoffs, we were on dry land, and didn't have a headwind, so I'm counting on you to give us a little extra boost."

Mitscher shrugged and replied, "Well, not much we can do about it now anyway. And since you're the lead aircraft, we'll be fishing you out first if this doesn't work. I'll give you every edge I can."

"I know you will, Sir. We'll get these babies off your deck, don't worry." Doolittle saluted and bounded down the outer island ladder to the *Hornet's* deck, then abruptly turned and yelled back, "Captain, please don't forget, we need to have a little ceremony before we lift off." Mitscher nodded, but he continued looking at the flight deck. God, I hope that lunatic can take off a B-25 from a carrier, or it will be the Japs who get the last laugh.

USS Hornet
17 Apr 42 1300

Sixteen B-25 bombers, tied down, faced each other at an angle, like a deck of cards about to be shuffled. Far too large to be stored below, and the planes had endured the salt spray and elements for several days. Crews in khakis and leather bombardier jackets had all gathered on the flight deck, some sitting, some standing. As many of the *Hornet's* personnel as were not needed for the ship to function were excused to attend the ceremony. The barrel- chested Halsey, whose *USS Enterprise* had joined the Hornet four days earlier to provide air cover for the small task force, had also been piped aboard. Yet neither he, nor Mitscher, nor Doolittle himself was the center of attention. Rather, the "guest of honor" — a 500-pound bomb to be loaded in one of the B-25s — sat in its cradle in the center of the men.

"Gentlemen," announced Doolittle, "we are here to send personal greetings to the Emperor of Japan." A robust laugh and hoots went up from the crews. "Lieutenant," Doolittle said, holding out his hand, "may I please have our gift for the Emperor." Another chuckle accompanied a lieutenant as he marched up to the colonel, saluted, and handed him a Japanese medal from a pilot shot down at Pearl Harbor. Doolittle took a piece of wire and attached the medal to the tail fin of the bomb. "I hereby mark this medal for 'Return to Sender': the Empire of Japan!" A cheer went up as he pointed to the "greeting."

For the next half hour, crewmen attached medals or painted slogans—"Remember Pearl Harbor!" or "Compliments of the

USS *Arizona*" — on several other bombs before the serious business of loading the B-25s with their deadly cargo began in earnest. Preparing the planes for an afternoon takeoff the following day took almost all night, but was finished by five in the morning. No sooner had the exhausted crews finished their last cross-check of the aircraft than spotters noticed Japanese picket boats on the horizon, and "Battle Stations" was sounded. Halsey's *Enterprise* planes, combined with 3-inch gunfire, sank most of the picket boats, but they likely had gotten off radio warnings. Doolittle's men ran to their aircraft, a full 150 miles farther away from their targets than anticipated. Already, all extra weight including some of the guns had been removed to allow for extra fuel, and now there was nothing else left to strip. The planes would have to fly as they were. A small gale had battered the ships all night, but now it was welcome, and Mitscher turned his carrier into the wind. Doolittle revved his twin Wright R260013 Double Cyclone fourteen-cylinder air-cooled radial engines to half-throttle. They belched grayish smoke, then hummed to life.

When the launch officer received the signal from the bridge that the *Hornet* was fully into the wind, he directed the deck crew to remove the restraining blocks from the wheels of "*Mama's Boy.*" Then Doolittle cranked the massive twin Wrights up to their maximum takeoff power of 1700 horsepower and gave the deck officer the thumbs up. The flight deck crews carefully timed the swells of the ocean to allow the bombers to take off when the ship was at its highest. At the proper moment the launch officer returned a thumbs up, saluted, pointed toward the end of the deck. He knelt down so as not to be beheaded by the bomber's wing. Doolittle released the brakes and the bomber bolted down the deck, amazingly fast, and yet, it seemed to Mitscher watching from the bridge above, all too slow. Seemingly against all logic, the B-25 lifted off seconds before reaching the end of the flight deck, and a cheer erupted from the *Hornet*'s crew. Already, the next B-25 had positioned itself and was racing its engines. In less than 30 minutes, all 16 bombers had lifted off, and were winging their way toward Tokyo with a message that they hoped would change the course of the war. Sure of that fact, Mitscher recorded the operation in his diary that night, with a map. "*I don't know how, but those bombers are going to do a helluva lot of damage,*" he wrote.

CHAPTER FIVE

Pacific Ocean, Chart/Map Room of the Imperial Japanese Battleship
Yamato
21 Apr 42 0850

The Kongo (Wikipedia)

Admiral Isoroku Yamamoto circled the map table of his new flagship, the goliath battleship Yamato, peering at the several small ship models, one group near Port Morseby in New Guinea, and a second near the island of Tulagi. Other admirals and generals stood back near the bulkheads as Yamamoto walked by them, careful to give him room to study. He had transferred his flag in February from the Nagato, although all the battleships—except those of Battle Division 3 that had accompanied Nagumo on his Pearl Harbor attack, the Kongo and Hiei—remained in the protected Hiroshima Bay in their fleet anchorage off Hashirajima Island. Aside from gunnery practice, they never left the protection of the land-based aircraft and anti- aircraft guns, and had been christened the "Hashirajima Fleet" by sailors in the Imperial Navy. Even the Yamato, with its 18-inch guns, giving it a range greater than any battleship in the world, needed air power to operate effectively. It had therefore ceded its role as the shining star of the fleet to the carrier *Akagi* and her sister ships, drenched in the glory of Pearl Harbor and other victorious operations. Now, the powerful battleships sat some 20 twenty miles from the bustling port cities of Hiroshima and Ture, where still more hardware and vessels for the Imperial Navy were being produced.

Yamamoto, an aviation advocate and pioneer, had still not grasped the irony of transferring his flag to a dinosaur whose construction he had vehemently opposed, then, after Yamato became a reality, whose presence he used as a recurring joke. Yet today, Yamamoto was in the Yamato's chart room planning new operations, which themselves were required because of an attack by an American aircraft carrier on the homeland. In a war that had been fought, so far, almost exclusively by carriers, Japan's premier admiral found himself commanding a battleship he knew was all but obsolete.

"What will the Americans do?" he asked quietly, mostly to himself. "What will the Americans do?"

His mind drifted back to a visit with the newly-installed Prime Minister, Fumimaro Konoe, in September 1940, shortly after Japan had signed the Tripartite Pact. He had met Konoe at the minister's private residence, the Kantei, in Nagatacho, across the street from the Diet Building—no easy place to hold private meetings, as the press hovered outside the gate. Konoe had grilled the admiral about the Navy's view of the Pact, as well as the prospect for war with America. Konoe well knew that Yamamoto personally opposed the Pact, yet now he demanded to know why the Navy officially had supported something that he found dangerous.

"What would the Americans do?" was Konoe's question then. "What would they do if war came? More important," the Prime Minister had asked, "what can we do? What will you ..." and Konoe had insultingly jabbed his finger at Yamamoto "... do?" It was telling that he had posed the question to Yamamoto, and not Fukodome, who had accompanied him to the meeting.

Yamamoto had bristled at the lack of respect, and wanted to grab the slimy politician by the throat and strangle him. Yet he knew then that the Navy could not rely on these politicians, and the course to war was already set. How dare he imply that the Navy's response would change Japanese policy! Instead, Yamamoto stiffly answered, "If we are ordered to war, I can guarantee we will give the Americans a tough fight for six months, but if matters drag on for two or three years, I can make absolutely no guarantees. I suggest you. . ," and then Yamamoto had uncharacteristically pointed his own finger at Konoe, "and the rest of the politicians avoid war with the United States. That is my recommendation." And he was summarily dismissed from the presence of the Prime Minister. And war came.

Not long after that, Fukodome appointed Yamamoto head of all naval operations in the Pacific—a promotion, to be sure, but perhaps also a convenient means to remove his dissenting voice from headquarters. Yet it was also a sign of Fukodome's discomfort with the Admiral. He had gotten too influential to ignore, and too powerful to control.

And now, here Yamamoto was asking himself, *"What will the Americans do?"* Earlier that month, American aircraft had appeared out of nowhere and bombed Tokyo in broad daylight. The Japanese homeland! He had received the itemized damage list: 50 dead, 250 wounded, and 90 buildings destroyed, including a steel factory and the Mitsubishi Heavy Industrial Corporation factory. It took courage. Their president, Roosevelt, saying the attacks came from "Shangri-La." Clever. And some want to think that only we have Yamato damashii—"warrior spirit." We are engaged with a fearsome enemy who has unlimited resources. We are counting only on him lacking the will to win. This is our first test. If they take the bait and contest our invasions, then we'll know.

He looked at his officers, and asked for comments.

Vice Admiral Nagumo, his Pearl Harbor fleet strike leader, spoke first. "Honorable Admiral, my best guess is that the Americans will attempt to engage our strike forces one at a time." Gesturing at the table, seeking permission, Nagumo saw Yamamoto nod. The 55-year old veteran torpedo expert, known for his utter lack of humor, was nevertheless a favorite of junior officers, whom he carefully trained and endowed with considerable (some said too much) responsibility. He had served in virtually all positions, and at one time was the Imperial Navy's rising star, whose brilliance had now been eclipsed by Yamamoto. Prematurely aged and arthritic, Nagumo was once a fencing master. Whatever had diminished his reputation, Nagumo, while he was hardly friendly with his superior Yamamoto, was not averse to acting as a subordinate. Indeed, one of the complaints about him was that he was better as a carrier commander under the authority of a more strategic thinker, and that too often, he expected detailed instructions rather than acting on his own initiative.

Watching Nagumo begin, Yamamoto, without noticing the irony attached to his own suppression of dissenting opinions, noted Nagumo perfectly represented Japan's great strengths and her great weaknesses. He lacks the nerve to act autonomously. His need for consensus from his other officers—and superiors—limits his abilities as a commander. Nagumo will do exactly as told, but I cannot count on him to make the critical decision in battle on his own. Yamamoto sighed quietly. It is a trait that stains our entire service. We slap it into our sailors physically, and emotionally drill it into our junior and senior officers. Obey. Don't question. Don't think for yourself. That's wonderful for building discipline—and fatal for the battlefield, where conditions require men to act on their own.

Given the floor, Nagumo walked to the map and picked up the pointer. "If I were the Americans—and let me remind everyone that we do not know at this point which commander we may be facing, only that this man, Nimitz, is the Pacific Commander in Chief ..." which was met with indications of affirmation around the table, "I would move all four carriers to intercept our forces individually." He swept the pointer toward the Tulagi strike force. "It seems logical that they would strike the nearest enemy fleet, and I believe they cannot afford another defeat like Pearl Harbor. Aside from their theatrics of bombing our homeland,   they have only suffered losses. They are unsure of our abilities, and, for their own morale, must fight us and win somewhere. Therefore, I believe they not only will fight, but that they will commit a sufficient force to ensure victory."

Yamamoto folded his arms. "Which means, Admiral?"

Encouraged, Nagumo continued. "Which means, Admiral, that I believe the Americans will commit at least two of their carriers to this battle. They must win, and they do not want to risk being outnumbered."

Yamamoto was impressed by Nagumo's analysis. The man is not known as an original thinker or innovator. Perhaps I have been too quick to judge him. Still staring at the map, Yamamoto asked, "Your recommendation, then?"

Gaining confidence, Nagumo pointed to the Japanese carrier icons on the map. "We have committed the *Shokaku* and *Zuikaku* to this engagement, plus the light carrier *Shoho*, as cover for the invasion forces. That gives us roughly one hundred and ninety aircraft. If the Americans send the *Yorktown* to join the *Lexington*, which our intelligence says is already in the area, it would give them approximately two hundred aircraft, because their Yorktown-class carriers carry one hundred aircraft each, providing them with a very slight advantage in the air. For an attack to succeed, I believe we need a much greater margin for error. There is a chance, however, to hurt them badly. If we commit the *Akagi* to this battle, that will give us an additional sixty aircraft and, when combined with the Army's land-based air forces, should give us an advantage over the Americans' force."

Yamamoto studied the map. *Akagi* was the best the Imperial

Japanese Navy had to offer. At 41,000 tons, the carrier was the result of a hasty adaptation to the Washington Treaty of 1922—a cruiser hull converted into an aircraft carrier, little different than the American carriers *Lexington* or *Saratoga*. Her design, while extremely effective, reflected the ad hoc way she was constructed, with large, slanting supports for the walkways, a tiny command island, and catacombs of walkways and ladders, leading more than five levels up to her flight deck. But she had plenty of space for aircraft and could make 31 knots. That's one of the problems, Yamamoto noted. Carriers such as the *Akagi* are too fast for most of our battleships. To escort carriers with our battleships merely slows them down, depriving them of their speed. Hence, the "Hashirajima Fleet."

Akagi had not come cheap: the conversion cost 53 million yen, making her the most expensive warship in the fleet, even more so than the *Yamato* and *Mushashi*. If Japan was committing the *Akagi*, it was a serious operation indeed, with high expectations of success. Calculating the distances, Yamamoto observed, *Akagi* would have to turn southeast from her present location and make a good twenty knots to join the task force in time." It is possible, but only if fortune is on our side. The slightest delay would leave *Akagi* and her escorts alone in the ocean and the existing invasion force at present strength, which Nagumo thinks is insufficient. "Admiral, you are aware that even if *Akagi* makes good speed, this will likely delay your attack on Port Morseby by perhaps a day, perhaps two?"

Before Nagumo could respond, there was a knock.

A guard opened the door and announced that a courier had an urgent message for Admiral Nagumo. Yamamoto gestured first to Nagumo to take the message and then to a steward to pour a cup of tea while watching Nagumo read it and break into a wide grin.

"I have some information, Admiral. Two hours ago, I received a radio message from a collaborator on one of the islands east of Tulagi. He had been sailing far to the south, when he saw what appeared to be warships—many warships."

Yamamoto's brow furrowed. He hated surprises, especially from subordinates, and such independent action was highly unlike the passive Nagumo. "And you just now are informing me of this?"

"Honorable Admiral, he has been reliable in the past, but this report was too important to rest on the words of a gaijin alone. I wanted to obtain confirmation before mentioning it. I dispatched a seaplane, which has just radioed back that an American force with two aircraft carriers is steaming toward Port Morseby. That force should reach there by tomorrow night. Admiral, this is our chance. If we order the *Akagi* to move immediately, it could arrive in time to be the deciding factor in the battle. We have the advantage over the Americans—we know where they will be, and when they will arrive. We can be prepared to spring a decisive trap."

It is true. We have been favored with the element of surprise yet again. Destroy two more American carriers, eliminate the base at Midway, and then occupy Hawaii. The Americans could not defend their territory with their two remaining aircraft carriers. "Very well, Admiral Nagumo. Well done. You were wise, both to cultivate your source and to confirm his report." Nagumo bowed with deep satisfaction at his superior's compliment. "And I concur with your recommendation.

"Immediately Order the *Akagi* to immediately come about and make all deliberate speed for your task force north of Tulagi. But when you locate the American ships, do not wait on Akagi's arrival. Strike immediately. Be bold. We have the advantage, and for perhaps the only time in the war, we can trade the Americans plane for plane. Even if Shokaku and Zuikaku cannot complete the victory, or if they suffer damage, it is only important that they weaken and occupy the American force sufficiently that Akagi can finish it off. I do not expect them to be mere decoys, but neither do I expect them to launch the critical strike."

"Yes, Admiral. I understand." Nagumo saluted and left the room to radio his instructions. The other admirals looked on, and a few still seemed apprehensive.

"Admiral Tagawa, does something concern you?" Yamamoto asked.

Yushii Tagawa had just received his command two months earlier, and it was surprising that someone so new to the inner circle of Japanese naval leadership would express an opinion, but Tagawa spoke with confidence. "Sir, my only concern is that if we do not wait for *Akagi* to arrive, and the Americans somehow locate our carriers while our strike forces are out searching for them, we could be the ones outnumbered and outgunned. If somehow they damage one of our carriers before Akagi arrives, they might even have a genuine aerial advantage. Does the famous Mahan doctrine not teach consolidation of forces and critical mass?"

It seems several of my commanders suddenly think themselves tactical geniuses. Yamamoto sighed. *At least he's not a sheep like some in this room.* "You may well be right, Admiral. There is a chance we could be destroyed piecemeal under the wrong circumstances. On the other hand, by waiting for *Akagi,* we would give the Americans more opportunity to find us, and to possibly strike first. Again, because of *Shoho* and the ground-based aircraft, we have numbers on our side. We can afford to sustain some losses if we inflict as many — and it will not always be so. For if this war goes beyond this year, I fear that American resources will build two, three, or even five carriers for every one we can construct. You are correct to be cautious, Admiral, but there are times one must trust in the gods to enhance an already good situation. I believe this may be one of those times. Most important, our intelligence does not suggest the Americans are that close yet."

Tagawa bowed, and no one else offered a comment, for Yamamoto's reputation as respecting the opinions of those whose views were similar to his own were well known. "Very well, report to your ships. We are embarking on one of the most important battles of the war, one which, if it goes as I hope, will possibly force the Americans to negotiate a peace treaty and end our involvement with them."

CHAPTER SIX

Naval Station Pearl Harbor, Commander in Chief, Pacific Fleet (CINCPAC)
22 Apr 42 0900

William Halsey (Wikipedia)

"Bill, Ray, I asked you here because there's going to be a battle in the South Pacific, and we need to decide what to do after that engagement." Nimitz shook the hands of his trusted commanders, Bill Halsey and Ray Spruance, as they came into his office. Two men could not be more different, yet they were close friends. Nimitz gestured at the two empty chairs, and the admirals sat. Halsey half-pulled his pack of Lucky Strikes out of his pocket and raised his eyebrow at Nimitz, who responded, "Go ahead." When Halsey offered Nimitz the pack, he shook his head. Nimitz smoked, but rarely in meetings. "Bull," as the press called him, took out a Lucky Strike and lit it up.

Nimitz gestured to the pot in the corner. "Oh, I'm sorry. Coffee?" Spruance shook his head but Halsey was already out of his chair, pouring before the words were out of Nimitz's mouth before returning to his seat.

"As of last report," Nimitz began, "it looks like the Japs are sending a pair of invasion forces, one to take Tulagi and one to take Port Moresby, and they are covering those forces with at least two fleet carriers. We think there may be a smaller carrier with them. I sent Fletcher and Fitch down there with the Lex and the *Yorktown* to poke around. That ought to be sufficient to interrupt the landings and, perhaps, engage the Japanese carriers or even drive them off. But I don't think that's their main thrust."

Halsey jumped to his feet and grabbed the pointer,

"Hell, you're right Chet. There's no question in my mind they want Midway," slapping the map board with the pointer for emphasis. Pacing as he talked, Halsey's barrel chest caused him to resemble a rooster when he walked; his thick eyebrows and deep set eyes gave his face a perpetual scowl until he laughed. Taking the cigarette out of his mouth, Halsey continued, "They can't afford to leave this outpost in their lines of communication and supply. It's a sub and air base that could threaten them twenty-four hours a day. If we fly more B-17s in there, we could raise hell with their sea lanes for seven hundred miles in any direction. Couple that with the damage some subs can do, and the little yellow bastards have a real problem." Nimitz winced at Halsey's racial slurs, which were common, although he shared Halsey's views of the enemy's morality.

"Bill," Nimitz said, "sit down please. Your analysis is right as far as it goes, but I think some other information may be pertinent here."

"What else could be pertinent except where the Japs are and how many of them are there?" Halsey routinely had little tolerance for psychological studies or sophisticated operations, but now he appeared to Nimitz particularly agitated, and continually scratched his arms and back.

"Something wrong, Bill?"

"Ah, hell, Chet, I seemed to have picked up a skin condition. Doc's treating it, but he isn't entirely sure what it is. Between you and me, I haven't been able to sleep. It's getting bad."

Nimitz looked at him soberly. "Bill ..."

"Don't bother, Chet. I know. If it gets to the point that I can't perform my duty, I'll relieve myself and go to the hospital. Trust me. I'm not so foolish as to jeopardize a command with some damned fungus. I'm not there yet, though."

"Ok, Admiral, I'll take you at your word. Now, back to our opponent. It helps to know who you are dealing with, and in this case, we will be dealing with Isoroku Yamamoto," Nimitz replied, swinging his arm back to a picture of Yamamoto on his desk. "No matter who else is commanding the actual attacks, make no mistake, it is Yamamoto we are fighting. If we can think like him, if we can get inside his head, we can anticipate his next move and beat him to the spot. Then we'll know where he will   be ... because we, in essence, will put him there."

Halsey grunted, said nothing, and continued to scratch his left arm. I know, Bill, too sophisticated for you. You and Custer. Brilliant and aggressive, but too damned reckless. Spruance, Nimitz noticed, had characteristically remained silent, staring intently at the photo of Yamamoto on Nimitz's desk. "Something you want to add, Ray?"

"Not at this time, Sir. I'd prefer to know more about this Yamamoto." Spruance reclined in his chair and folded his hands.

Halsey and Nimitz looked at each other, and Nimitz squinted at him. "Ray, still waters run deep. Really, is something on your mind?"

Spruance briefly grinned, a rare occurrence for him. "Admiral, some people believe that when I'm quiet, I'm thinking some profound and important thoughts. The fact is, I'm thinking nothing at all."

Nimitz peered at him for a moment, thinking of the comments of other officers about Spruance—that he was so cautious that by the time he decided to laugh, a joke was already by him—then shook his head good-naturedly. "Ray, Ray. You can't sandbag me. All right, here's the scoop on Yamamoto. He's quite a character. Born in Nagaoka. His family was on the wrong side of a civil war in the Meiji period. He spent time in the U.S., both at Harvard and as a naval attaché in Washington. A pioneer in post-World War I aviation in Japan, Yamamoto visited Wright Field in Dayton, Ohio and has seen the extent of our country."

"Then he should know we have the capability to take his little island apart," Halsey snorted.

"Which," Nimitz continued, ignoring the interruption, "is likely why Yamamoto opposed war with the United States. Our spies tell us, in fact, that he did everything except stage a coup, and that is one of the main reasons he was hustled off to sea command. They wanted get him out of harm's way in Tokyo. Bill, he *fully* understands our capabilities, and it is precisely because of that understanding that he has worked so diligently to bring about the Tsushima-type battle that would give Japan a couple of years' worth of breathing space."

Halsey was still not convinced. "Even then—and I'm only agreeing with you for the sake of discussion—say that he could achieve a Tsushima-type victory in the Pacific, does he really think we wouldn't transfer every ship possible over here from the Atlantic? Or build new ones? Or keep building them until we absolutely crush Japan?"

"We can only get inside his head so much. It's sufficient to say—and obvious—that all the Japanese vastly underestimated us. So what now? We need to focus on who he is, and what he would be most likely to do, not whether he is rational in doing it."

Halsey reluctantly agreed. "So what do we know that can help us? That can help me and Ray and our carriers?"

Typically, the quiet warrior Spruance said nothing, but was pleased that the boisterous Halsey continually put him on equal footing.

"We've learned a great deal about the man. For example, he eats an inordinate amount for someone his size, and apparently has developed a taste for fine cuisine. I doubt that's a factor any time soon, but it's worth keeping in mind. Then there is the gambling and the geishas." Both admirals suddenly cast sideways glances at each other and leaned forward. "Yamamoto is one of the best poker players in Japan and wagers relentlessly on Japanese chess, called *shogi*. He's one of these guys who would place a bet on when his own mother would die. This may be something we can take advantage of. It makes him prone to going for the jugular, but at the cost of dropping his guard. If we can catch him in an attempt to deliver a roundhouse, we might do some serious damage to the Japanese naval forces, even before we have overwhelming ship superiority."

"And the geishas?" asked Spruance, whose own inability to hold his liquor had caused him to swear off drinking except at public toasts, making him particularly sensitive to personal character weaknesses. "Does he have a wife?"

"He does, and the geishas are definitely a flaw. At some point, it might reveal his location to us or otherwise present some opportunity. For now, I'm basing my reading of the man on two factors: first, his familiarity with America and his view that the only way to beat us is to defeat us in a single decisive naval engagement, and second, his affinity for gambling, for taking risks."

Both Spruance and Halsey understood Nimitz's point, but typically Halsey spoke first. "You think we can use that over-aggressiveness against him, feign weakness and draw him into an ambush somewhere?" He had directed his comments at the map, and, remembering Nimitz's deafness, said more loudly a second time, "Can we lure him into an ambush?"

"It's possible. We have to keep in mind that he will have operational objectives, whether it's taking Tulagi, or, down the line, Midway, but within the scope of those operations, I believe he will bite if we can throw him the bait. Word is that once he makes up his mind, he latches on, and isn't easily talked out of a position." The latter part drifted by as both admirals shifted nervously at the term "bait." Sensing their unease, Nimitz said, "Of course, you two are wondering who will be the bait, and who gets to be the hook. Well, gentlemen, that's going to depend entirely on where Yamamoto shows up, and where we need him to be. I can't give you a better answer than that."

Nimitz then gestured to Halsey, who was still holding the pointer, to relinquish control. Nimitz pointed to the Coral Sea: "Much of what we do, gentlemen, will be decided here. If Fletcher and Fitch can repulse those invasions or engage the Japanese fleets without suffering serious loss, it might actually persuade Yamamoto to be more cautious. It might signal to him that he must have overwhelming force to beat us. And that might curb his reckless nature — the trait we are counting on."

Halsey's face flushed. "Sounds like you're almost pulling for a Jap victory?" and immediately knew he'd overstepped his bounds, both professionally and personally. "I'm sorry, Chet ... Admiral. Hell, you know I didn't mean ..."

Nimitz, though hurt, knew it was just Halsey being "Bull." He gave a dismissive wave. "I'm not saying that at all, Bill. I'm saying, if Fletcher and Fitch are extremely successful, it might make it harder to provoke Yamamoto into a big mistake. It would mean we'd have to fight this war the way the Army and MacArthur want to, island by island. Well, by God ..." a phrase that got both admirals' attention, given Nimitz's reputation as less than a "holy Joe" ". . . I'm not going to slog it out through every jungle hell-hole in the South Pacific. No, I think we can end this war quicker if we can cut off their supply lines and starve 'em out."

"Look, you both know tactics, but the Army, especially in the Civil War, used to do something we in the Navy rarely do, and that was to 'demonstrate' — put on a sideshow to distract the enemy while the real deal was building up to hit him somewhere else. I think that's what we're going to have to do with Yamamoto: put on a dog and pony show in one spot, and hit him somewhere else." Both admirals now moved to the edge of their chairs. Halsey was intermittently smoking, shifting the coffee into the hand with his cigarette, and scratching. Spruance alternately stared at the ceiling in thought, then studying the picture on Nimitz's desk.

"So," asked Spruance, "do you have an idea of how and when

you want this 'show' to begin?"

"Not yet, Ray, but something in my gut tells me that before this is over, we're gonna have a helluva fight around Midway."

Halsey and Spruance glanced at each other, and bobbed their heads in agreement.

"That is all, gentlemen. Layton is watching Rochefort's de-crypts carefully. We'll know more after Jack reports from down south. Meanwhile, Bill, you get that skin condition addressed. That's an order."

Halsey snuffed out his cigarette in Nimitz's ashtray, saluted, and replied, "Aye aye, Admiral."

As the two admirals exited, Nimitz pondered the picture once again, then turned to watch his two commanders walking down the hall. Fire and ice. Aggressiveness and caution. Maybe that's the key. *Yamamoto will know those men, too. He'll be expecting them to act in character. But what if he's wrong? What if, instead of Spruance, he gets Halsey? And instead of Halsey, he gets Spruance?*

Honolulu, Hawaii Territory
25 Apr 42 1312

The residence of Sam Tomita looked like any other small Honolulu home—well trimmed yard, plenty of palm trees, fading paint, and, as usual, Ensign Elliot Gibbons' 1938 Ford parked out front. Elliot had come to take Sam's daughter, Miko, for a picnic. Prior to December 7, no one thought there was anything unusual about an American sailor dating a typical Japanese-American girl living in Hawaii. However, none of the Tomita's were typical. Sam, a local photographer, had a small studio outside Honolulu, where he had carved out a good living from shots of graduating seniors and smiling babies to more professional work that involved making official photos for local contractors, surveyors, and even, on occa-sion, the Army or Navy. Once, when the Honolulu police photog-rapher was ill, they had summoned Sam to photograph a murder victim's body—a task he never wanted to repeat.

Miko's mother had died two years earlier, killed by a drunk driver while walking home from her waitress job, and the family was still having trouble coping with the loss. A despondent Jerry Tomita, Miko's brother, was draft age and already serving in the Hawaiian Territorial National Guard. He'd put in for a transfer to the 100th Battalion, which the War Department was already considering reorganizing as an all-Japanese-American regiment. If his paperwork went through, he'd be transferred to Camp McCoy in Wisconsin. For now, he stood duty guarding supplies.

Miko herself was a stunning beauty, part Japanese, part Hawaiian, and part English, with a touch of Cherokee Indian thrown in. Her high cheekbones, jet black, waist- length hair, perfect smile, and trim figure made her the object of attention for years at the shipping company where she worked, until Elliot came along. They made the perfect couple, the young American officer and his Hawaiian fiancée. It had been six months since they announced their engagement, and no locals found anything unusual about the beautiful secretary and the ensign. Perhaps, if they had had they lived on the west coast of the U.S. mainland, Miko's entire family might have been in an internment camp. In Hawaii, though, they were just another of the many interracial couples who populated the islands.

Sam joked with them as they loaded the car, teasing Elliot about still being an ensign. He saw them off, waving goodbye as the yellow Ford pulled away from the house and disappeared over the hill. Waiting until he was certain they hadn't forgotten something and would return, he casually walked inside, went into his room, pushed his desk aside, and pulled back a trap door that led to a basement that neither Miko nor Elliot knew anything about. He turned on a light, revealing several photographs he had taken yesterday of the American ships in the harbor, to which he had affixed name labels. Then he powered up his radio transmitter and receiver, used for sending messages to the Japanese submarine *I-23*, located just 100 miles off shore, and proceeded to report the number, and type, of ships in Pearl Harbor the previous day. The decade he had spent establishing his cover as an ordinary Japanese- Hawaiian photographer was now paying off for Ishii Tomita, and for the Empire of Japan, for whom he worked.

CHAPTER SEVEN

Task Force 17, Coral Sea 3 May 42 2015

USS Yorktown (Wikipedia)

"Makin' good speed, Admiral." Captain Elliot Buckmaster checked the grid coordinates on the chart, and pointed to Rabaul. "We'll be just south of where we figure the Japs are sometime tomorrow morning, maybe even tonight."

Rear Admiral Frank Jack Fletcher had just come up from the flag bridge of the USS *Yorktown*, his flagship for Task Force 17, to join Buckmaster on the navigation bridge. An admiral was always welcome, at least in theory, on the captain's bridge, but a captain could only enter the flag bridge by invitation. Buckmaster gestured to the empty captain's chair, but Fletcher shook his head, and paced in the narrow space around the helmsmen, more anxious than usual.

"Captain, I know you know this, but just a reminder, our charts on this region are really old, so keep your screens well out. I don't want to end up on a beach."

"Aye aye, Sir. We've got 'em out. Care to go outside, Admiral? Might be easier to walk."

Fletcher took the hint. *God, I'm getting in the way of his crew.* "Very well, Captain, let's smell the salt air for a few minutes."

No sooner did they walk outside than the two officers felt sand blowing in their faces, a sign that land may be imminent.

"Good God!" Fletcher said, looking at Buckmaster. The captain seemed just as astounded. "Can't be, Admiral. Our destroyers are miles away. They aren't reporting land. OOD, are our lookouts reporting land?" Suddenly Fletcher started to laugh.

"What are you laughing about?" asked the panicked Buckmaster.

"Captain, it's not sand. Taste it." Fletcher had wiped his finger down his cheek on a whim and had licked it. Buckmaster did the same.

What the hell? Looking at Fletcher like he needed a rubber room, Buckmaster ran his finger down his cheek to pick up some of the grit and reluctantly touched it to the tip of his tongue. *Sugar?* The two looked at the lookout/radar decks above them, where they saw two sailors on watch. One had a cup of coffee. "Sugar." Fletcher pointed upwards. "Seems one of our lookouts tried to pour sugar into a coffee cup."

Fletcher shook his head. *Are we this spooked?* Eight days earlier he had put out from Tongatabu, and two days ago Task Force 11, with the USS *Lexington* under Rear Admiral Aubrey Fitch, had joined Task Force 17 southwest of the New Hebrides Islands. Both forces had been raiding Japanese shipping and landings in the Rabaul area, generally harassing the enemy and, more important, building fighting experience for the flyers. The missions had been remarkably free of losses, with only two of 104 aircraft shot down by enemy fire.

He gestured to Buckmaster to return to the bridge. "Signal Admiral Fitch to commence fueling operations with the *Neosho*. I want our tanks topped if we get into a fight." Buckmaster, in turn, ordered a subordinate to immediately send the order.

"Sir, is Admiral Fitch still about a hundred miles south of us?" asked Buckmaster, signing the order.

"That was their last communication, Captain. As soon as we are refueled, I want the oiler and her escort, the Sims, to get the hell out of here. And I'll order Fitch to close up. I don't like being this far apart. It's too easy to get picked off, one group at a time."

"Aye aye, Admiral. Then head for Tulagi?"

"That's what we're here for, Captain. Knock out the Japanese landing force on Tulagi ..." Fletcher paused.

"But you think there's more to this mission, don't you, Admiral?"

"Elliott, I think we're going to run head long into a fight. Probably some Jap carriers. They wouldn't send a landing force down here uncovered, and they wouldn't send two carriers if they didn't think we were going to see significant action."

Buckmaster did some quick calculations. "If Lexington finishes fueling within the hour, and brings her speed up to twenty-seven knots, and we reduce speed to twenty, Task Force Eleven should be pretty close by tomorrow morning, and we can be coordinating our attacks on Tulagi. That way, we can keep a reserve strike spotted on one carrier in case the Japs suddenly appear out of nowhere."

Fletcher slapped him on the shoulder. "You're reading my mind, Captain. My orders left lots of operational discretion, and the subtle message was to find those enemy carriers. Sending carriers to raid land bases is a waste of good Navy ships! They rarely achieve any success."

"Sir?" Buckmaster stared at him incredulously. When Fletcher did not realize what he had said, the Captain prodded him again. "Pearl Harbor? Taranto?"

"Of course, Captain, if you can surprise your enemy in a port, hell, yeah, you should be able to do some damage. But I'm talking about raiding land targets that have some idea you're coming."

"Well, Sir, it's my understanding that those orders specifically reflected Admiral Nimitz's wishes to contest the Japanese everywhere, and not allow them to figure out where we're going to hit them next. Ever since Pearl Harbor, we've been stinging them all over the Pacific."

"And with what to show for it? Captain, there's a time to jab and weave, and a time for the uppercut. If we can find the enemy carriers that I'm sure have accompanied the landing force, we can do some real damage to the banzai boys."

"Aye aye, Admiral. Well, we're on course and on schedule to do just that."

Fletcher thought for a moment, then added, "Send a message to Admiral Crace. I'm detaching him to a likely course to block the invasion fleet. Tell him I'm giving him the cruisers *Australia*, *Chicago*, and *Hobart*, and destroyers *Perkins*, *Walke*, and *Farragut*. I know he'll be in range of Jap land-based air, but I think he can handle it. If we don't get the landing force from the air, he should rip it apart from the sea." *Crace is a go-getter Aussie, and nobody's going to have to kick him in the ass to get him to attack,* Fletcher thought. *Just watch your back from those land- based planes, John.*

Vice Admiral Nagumo lay in his bunk, his joints aching, trying to sleep before the battle that appeared imminent tomorrow. He
would rather be on the Akagi, which he would have commanded
under normal circumstances. But, it was still 200 miles behind the
Zuikaku, Shokaku, and *Shoho,* and more important, for Nagumo to
maintain the subterfuge that there were only two fleet carriers and
the smaller *Shoho,* he had to keep *Zuikaku* as his flagship. Japanese
radiomen were deliberate in their "laxity" of concealing this during
supposedly "coded" messages. American codebreakers, delight-
ed with their good fortune, passed the information back to Pearl,
where Nimitz, in turn, had relayed it to Fletcher.

*If we have acted our parts well, the Americans will think they are
facing two fleet and one small carrier, instead of three fleet and a small
carrier, plus land-based aircraft. We must continue our ruse throughout
the first attack.* Nagumo had transferred a half-dozen planes from the
slow *Shoho* to the *Akagi,* allowing the former to appear fully operational, while giving the bigger, faster carrier even more aircraft. *That
was not easy. Our operational doctrine restricts aircraft to a single carrier,
unlike the Americans. Airmen are trained and spend their entire careers
aboard one ship. The Americans are far more flexible, moving aircraft units
around as needed. Such re- organizations raise hell with our men, but in
this case it cannot be helped.* Akagi *will just have to adjust her hangar and
deck space.*

Nagumo knew such "adjustments" for Imperial Japanese
Navy carriers were neither simple nor easy. Each aircraft on any
one of the fleet carriers was stowed below in a specific position, with
only a few feet separating them. They fit together like a jigsaw puz-
zle, and it affected not only how they were transported, but how
they were "spotted" — prepared on the decks to launch — when it
came to battle. Adding even six more planes required exceptional
aircraft handling, making sure that fighters were always up in combat air patrol and then having the decks cleared to recover aircraft.
Nagumo guessed that the Akagi, the largest of Japan's new carriers,
alone could handle the overload. Her 857-foot length and 817-foot-
long flight deck were the fleet's largest, giving her far more space
than the *Hiryu* or *Soryu,* and slightly more than the *Kaga.* It would
just be up to the *Akagi's* captain, Taijiro Aoki, to manage.

Nagumo had not told Captain Tagichi of the *Shoho* that he fully expected to lose that carrier at least, and possibly one of his other big carriers. *Such is the sacrifice I must make to accompany the strike forces with larger numbers of fighter escorts. Either way, the plan is mine. I alone shall receive the honor, or the shame for what transpires.*

He had almost drifted off, still in his uniform, when a rap at his cabin door jerked him awake. "Yes?"

"Sir, we have a report from a land-based scout plane one hundred miles south of Tulagi. It has sighted an American carrier, which we think is the *Yorktown*."

So, the Americans are behaving exactly as expected.

"Any sign of other carriers?"

"Not at present, Sir. Only a screen of four cruisers and half a dozen destroyers.

Another raiding party of a single carrier? Or just the first of two, three, or even four?

"Radio Akagi to increase speed to twenty eight knots, but she is to remain behind *Shokaku* and *Zuikaku* by at least fifty miles. Inform Captain Urema that he is to dispatch two scout planes out at dawn in the direction of the American carrier, and they are *not* to stop until they have searched at least one hundred miles to the south of this American carrier."

"Yes, Admiral-san."

Nagumo wanted his intention understood. "One hundred miles south, is that clear?"

"*Hai!*" came the response.

The lieutenant turned to leave, when Nagumo added, "One more thing. Radio to the captain of *Shoho*: she is to move to the lead of our force."

"Sir?" The lieutenant was surprised by the command. It was highly unusual to place a small, slow carrier with less than half a compliment of planes in the lead of an attack force.

"Do as you are told, Lieutenant!" Nagumo snapped. "Yes, Admiral." The officer rapidly departed.

Shoho may soon have the honor of being the most important ship in the Imperial Navy, Nomura concluded, and without knowing why, Captain Tagichi may become one of the most honored commanders in history. Too bad he'll have to die before he learns of his honor.

Nagumo picked up the telephone to the flight officers' wardroom. "Inform Commander Genda I want a search grid prepared immediately." Minoru Genda, despite being assigned to the *Akagi*, was Nagumo's head of aviation, and was required to stay with the admiral, so he had joined him on the *Zuikaku*. Appearances were critical if the ruse was to be pulled off, and if the Americans learned that either Nagumo or his chief air officer were not with the main carrier body, their suspicious would have been aroused. Genda, more than anyone else, had conceptualized the Pearl Harbor operation, and, in general, he had thrived under Nagumo, who delegated extensive responsibility to him. He had full operational authority over the planning of the air attacks for the Tulagi operation.

Genda appeared in less than 10 minutes, and Nagumo directed him to the map room.

"We have found the American carrier *Yorktown*," Nagumo began. I want you to prepare a search to her south to see who else is with her. Then, depending on what we find, it is up to you to design and coordinate the attack on the American carrier or carriers if there's more than one." He pointed to the spot where the scout had seen *Yorktown*.

Genda surveyed the chart, looking at the disposition of the *Shoho* in particular, and raised an eyebrow, but said nothing. *Obviously Admiral Nagumo expects the Americans to use up their attack on the* Shoho, *saving our larger carriers for counterattacks.* Developing a search pattern was no small task for such a force. The Imperial Japanese Navy expected the scout planes from the cruisers to handle the burden of scouting, augmented only by carrier aircraft if absolutely necessary. Each airplane had to fly a disciplined route out, make a left turn, fly a specified distance at a 90-degree angle from its original course, then make another left turn for home. If all aircraft were perfectly coordinated and flew at the same speed, the design would resemble that of the spokes of a wheel, with each aircraft reaching the turning point of the aircraft to its left before going home. That would have been difficult enough using aircraft from a single carrier, which might be better coordinated. But using the cruisers to do the dirty work?

Genda sighed. *In Japanese naval doctrine, all carrier planes are reserved for striking the enemy, not boring patrols, yet it is the boring patrols that locates our foe.*

Coordinating such a search grid from many different ships took talent, of which Commander Genda possessed a great deal. Once he had settled on a search strategy, Genda considered the various options for a follow- up attack. He knew better than to waste the details on Nagumo. *It is a great responsibility being the resident genius for air operations – and a great curse, for I cannot foresee everything, yet there is no one to check my work.* Genda came to attention, saluted, and said, "I shall plan the scouting mission and have it for you in an hour, Admiral, and within three hours have a plan for any strike that we may need to conduct."

Nagumo returned his salute, having received precisely the response he wanted.

CHAPTER EIGHT

South of the Solomon Islands, USS **Yorktown**
4 May 42 0700

SBD Dauntless dive bombers (Wikipedia)

Officers could barely talk to each other over the din of aircraft engines, cupping their hands and yelling into the ear of the man next to them in order to be heard. Frank Jack Fletcher stood outside the bridge above the cacophony, looking down at a flight of 18 F4F-3 "Wildcat" fighters, 12 TBD "Devastator" torpedo bombers, and 28 SBD "Dauntless" dive bombers—which the Japanese had appropriately named "hell divers." The Americans liked that name.

Since 0300, the nearly 400 mechanics aboard the *Yorktown* had been carefully re-checking the aircraft, and as each one cleared inspection it was pushed onto the elevators and raised to the flight deck. In the hangar area, the odors of grease, oil, aviation fuel, paint, and other chemicals hung in the air as massive ventilators labored to pump the aroma out. While the mechanics examined their assigned aircraft, armorers attached bombs and torpedoes to the Dauntlesses and Devastators. If space permitted, American aircraft were armed and fueled on the flight deck, speeding up the process, as carts with ordnance and the aircraft would go up together. In either case, hauling small carts loaded with 500-lb. bombs was no easy labor, and the thirteen-foot- long torpedoes were even more cumbersome. Crews with the long, tin fish would wind their way through the forest of wings and landing gear to the appropriate aircraft. While some worked to attach bombs and torpedoes, other crewmen manipulated python-like belts of ammunition for the machine guns in the fighters and for the rear gunners, feeding them into wing mountings and rear cockpit canisters.

Only a few feet separated one plane from another, meaning that many crewman had smacked their heads at one time or another on a wing. Worse, it meant that any aircraft whose wheel chocks had not been fastened could pose a danger should the *Yorktown* suddenly pitch the wrong way, and the carrier sickbays in all fleets experienced a steady stream of men with smashed hands, feet, or broken ribs from a runaway. If the ship pitched suddenly, fuel lines could come loose, then the more serious problem of a rogue spark could make for an interesting day. Care had to be taken at all times, and nothing happened without extreme caution inside a carrier or on its flight deck. In particular, a hangar deck fire could shut down a carrier. American crews took damage control very seriously and continually trained to handle fires. Once the aircraft engines were running, matters got even dicier. At those times, live propellers in limited space posed a constant hazard to the inattentive or lazy.

Merely lining the aircraft up properly—in Navy parlance, "spotting" them—was of critical importance. For a carrier to maintain a combat air patrol, decks had to be kept clear unless being readied for an attack. It was possible to take off a scout plane or two while re-arming on deck, but obviously impossible to recover any aircraft. Once an attack was ordered, crews had to bring aircraft to the flight deck by elevator in the correct launch sequence.

While Americans were far more flexible about this than their enemies, it generally required fighters to be brought up first and spotted in the rear, with the torpedo planes next, and the Dauntless dive bombers forward. Merely pushing a Wildcat or TBD to the elevator, which might be several hundred feet away if the aircraft was in the wrong spot, required a team of ten men. After Coral Sea, when the planes were outfitted with folding wings, the wings were unfolded on the way up. Then on deck, more pushers would position the aircraft. While pilots were still in their briefing rooms, the flight deck crews would climb inside the cockpits to start the aircraft while several others stood by with fire extinguishers in case of a problem. Deck hands, their uniforms blasted against their skin by the prop-wash, stood ready to remove the wheel chocks. Other flight personnel retreated to the carrier's catwalks, ready to observe and cheer the takeoffs.

Fletcher watched these preparations, regretting as all commanders do that his men did not have more training time. He also mulled the fact that somewhere, 40 or 50 miles to his south and moving toward the *Yorktown*, Admiral Fitch was preparing a similar force for takeoff from the *Lexington*'s flight deck. *If he hasn't hit a snag*, Fletcher thought.

Yorktown's planes would target the invasion force around Tulagi, while *Lexington*'s aircraft were to arrive just in time to attack the Japanese after they had dispatched their own attack force against Fletcher. *It's a juggling act, that's for sure. But we first have to lure him out. He won't just show himself. With luck, just as his planes are coming for the* Yorktown, *Fitch's forces will be hitting his relatively unprotected carriers.*

With the carrier already into the wind, the pilots performed their final checks—stabilizers, flaps, rudder. When their checklist was complete, they gave the launch officer the thumbs up. In the distance, a destroyer had taken up a position in case any aircraft had a problem on takeoff and had to ditch. Satisfied from his perspective that an aircraft was ready, the launch officer signaled the bridge, and the chief air officer, empowered to order the launch, gave the command. Overhead, the wind sock also signified sufficient wind speed for takeoff. The lead pilot, his canopy open until after launch in case of emergency, saluted to the flight officer as the crewmen removed the wheel blocks. One by one the Dauntlesses, then the Devastators, then the F4Fs lumbered down the deck and climbed into the south Pacific sky, where they head for their target and rendezvous with the other aircraft en route—a practice called the "running rendezvous," originated with the *Yorktown*. No sooner had the last strike aircraft departed than the *Yorktown* began launching its combat air patrol aircraft, which would take up positions at different altitudes around the carrier.

Before the last of his aircraft left the *Yorktown*, Fletcher's radar picked up a Japanese scout plane. High above, hidden from eyesight in the clouds, the scout watched this impressive display and reported his position. The scout then continued on south. Less than a half-hour later, it transmitted a second report, of another American carrier rapidly steaming northward.

Coral Sea, over the Japanese invasion fleet
4 May 42 0742

Randy "Tex" Ryan, leader of VB-1, the first squadron of Dauntlesses, conducted a quick assessment of the island that came up on the horizon. Within minutes, he concluded that the primary target would be the landing ships and the transports. "Boys, looks like we're too late to hit the first wave—they're already on the beach—but we can sure raise hell with the reinforcements." At 12,000 feet, Ryan rolled his plane over and put it into a 70-degree dive right over one of the large landing ships, teeming with troops. With its red tail stripes, at that angle the Dauntless looked almost like a red bolt of lightning coming out of the Pacific sky to rain judgment on America's enemies.

"Roger, skip," confirmed Ed Osowski in the squadron's second Dauntless. "Tally ho, boys." He followed Ryan into the dive. Immediately behind were the other six bombers. The 3-inch anti-aircraft guns on the transports and destroyers were already blazing. Their flak was ineffective, but Ryan soon found himself in "the funnel," as they called the hail of fire ahead. Osowski engaged his SBD's dive brakes, to reduce the load on the aircraft's wings when he pulled out of his dive. He ignored the occasional antiaircraft round that found its mark, one glancing off his windscreen without penetrating. He resisted the natural temptation to dodge the enemy's tracers, focusing totally on the bridge of his target, a Japanese landing craft packed with troops.

Now he saw Ryan's plane release its bomb, then a second later the Dauntless burst into flames and careened wildly away from the ship. Osowski stayed on target, watching Ryan's bomb explode harmlessly 20 feet to the port of the lumbering vessel. "And ... away," he announced to his gunner, Lou Deluca, just as his wing recorded a half- dozen taps of enemy lead penetrating the metal skin. Osowski pulled back on the stick firmly but steadily. The Dauntless lifted up as a massive explosion below provided an additional burst of wind and heat, nearly seizing control from the pilot. As he banked away, he heard the third pilot in the squadron, Rick Goings also claim a hit. "Got 'em. Dead on near the stack." Osowski continued to bank away, accelerating to full speed. Climbing back to 15,000 feet, he searched for other targets on which to unload his 100-lb. bombs and to confirm damage—no fewer than five ships were on fire and one appeared to be listing—when he heard a Wildcat from their escort announce, "Blue Boy, you got a Zero comin' in." DeLuca, in the gunner's open cockpit, blasted away with his .30 caliber, but the distance was such he wasn't registering many hits, and the Zero was homing in on him. "Keep present course, I'm comin'," announced the Wildcat, then, suddenly,   he heard, "Oh my God!

They're on me! Jack, Billy, get these guys. Jack ..." Then nothing except Lou's continued bursts behind him and the unending plink-plink of Japanese bullets raking his Dauntless.

As the Dauntlesses were savaging the landing ships and their covering force from high above, *Yorktown*'s Devastator squadron was coming in low with their torpedoes. Cliff Mazzolo, leader of the second Devastator torpedo squadron, watched the lead squadron go in against heavy fire from the ships, but saw no Zeros. "Come on, boys, we got 'em. They haven't got fighters on us yet. They must be busy with the dive bombers." Mazzolo brought his plane down to 100 feet above the waves, opened his throttle to the 120-mph attack speed, and checked once more with his gunner, Robbie Zans. "Anyone on our back?"

"No one yet, skip. Can we be this lucky?" Zans, a stocky Chicagoan—whose family had likely changed their name from something Polish—scoured the skies for enemy planes. The Devastators were far slower than the Zeros, which could reach 310 mph, even with a full load of fuel and ammo, making it little contest between the two if fighters appeared on the TBD's tail. Mazzolo lined up his plane on a destroyer, the *Kikuzuki*.

"Almost there," said Mazzolo. "Three, two, one, torpedo away!" The 1900-lb Mark 13 fell away from the aircraft, splashing into the water and flattening out, accelerating to an expected 33 knots. *Thirty-three knots? God! That's this fish's top speed, thought Mazzolo. If that commander has any sense, he'll turn away, and at their speeds, he can probably put enough distance between himself and our torpedo that it fizzles out before it hits.*

When Mazzolo felt the 13-foot-long fish drop, he banked the TBD right, straight into a hail of gunfire from the *Kikuzuki* that ripped through the cockpit. He felt something wet on his arm, and looked down to see his flight jacket punctured and blood oozing out, but he didn't feel anything. After a brief inventory he concluded this body was intact and he'd only been scratched. "Imagine that, Robbie! They missed my heart by about six inches!"

Mazzolo heard no response. "Robbie?" Now flying away from the sinking destroyer, he craned his head to where he could barely see down the long greenhouse canopy. The entire rear was perforated with bullet holes and Zans slumped over. "DAMMIT," Mazzolo screamed, then almost instantly noticed his oil gauge dropping and noticed a black streak pouring from his cowling. To top it off, his arm was now hurting like hell. The TBD's engine had taken several rounds, and Cliff knew he wasn't getting back to the *Yorktown*. "This is Blue Fourteen. I'm going down. I'm ditching on a bearing straight for the Briar Patch," which was the *Yorktown*'s code name. "We got a destroyer. Their ships were all lit up and smokin'." Then he felt the big Pratt & Whitney "Double Wasp" air-cooled radial engine sputter and give one final cough. The Devastator dropped like a rock and smashed into a wall of water. *Thank God for safety harnesses.* Punching the release, Mazzolo half-crawled, half swam out of the sinking TBD, inflating his Mae West. Salt water raced into his wound and he screamed. He choked as he took a big mouthful of the Pacific.

As he bobbed on the surface, he scoured the skies. In the distance he could occasionally see planes coming or going—many of those coming his direction were smoking or nearly out of control. Smoke from the burning ships was visible on the horizon.

Catalinas and the subs are already out looking for pilots who had to ditch and could reach designated zones. Hope I'm in their search pattern. Then a bleaker thought came to mind. *Hope I'm not in some shark's search pattern,* and he looked at the blood seeping out of his arm and coloring the ocean red, causing him to swivel his head in all directions for any sign of a black fin cutting the surface.

Bridge of the Yorktown
4 May 42 0815

Yorktown was recovering planes, each one coming in and snagging the wire, then waiting for the crash barrier to be lowered so it could taxi past. It was then pushed to the elevator, to await rearmament, refueling, and repairs on the hangar deck. Reports were coming in now—at least six landing ships destroyed, a destroyer sunk, and a dozen other ships damaged. Fletcher knew better than to accept at face value the assessments of his pilots, not that they were given to exaggeration, but it was simply a fact that pilots always thought they did more damage than they really had. Still, the multiple confirmations of a destroyer and at least two other ships sunk gave him some measure of satisfaction. That's the good news. The bad news is we have at least twelve Dauntlesses and half a dozen TBDs down, and others shot up pretty bad.

"Admiral, here are the preliminary numbers." Buckmaster handed him the list, but repeated the information anyway. "Looks like we may have gotten two or three troop ships and a destroyer, and lost twenty-one planes — twelve dive bombers, six torpedo planes, and three fighters. There are a few still out, and some might not make it, so those number may go up."

"What about search and rescue?"

"We've got Catalina's up from Australia — had 'em up before the battle began — and there will be some subs in the area, but it's going to be hours before we find out if we've rescued anyone."

"Fine. Any sign of their carriers yet?"

"No, Sir. *Lexington's* force ought to be getting there about now, so we'll see if they took the bait."

Fletcher looked at Captain Buckmaster. "The worst part, Captain, is that I hate being on the receiving end." Then he gave a grim shrug and again raised his binoculars to search the skies. No sooner had he done so than the search radars lit up and radio reports from the escort screen farther out came in.

"Incoming enemy aircraft, bearing three three zero."

Fletcher saw the 3-inch guns of the escort ships opening up, yet it seemed like only seconds later the *Yorktown's* own full complement of anti-aircraft guns were being elevated as in a single motion. *God, they got here fast.* "Elliott," Fletcher asked, binoculars still trained on the enemy planes, "how much fighter cover do you have up?"

"Only eight Wildcats, Admiral. We sent the rest with the attack squadrons, and we have just recovered them."

"Very well." Fletcher knew the answer before he asked, yet hoped somehow it would be a different number. "Let's hope those eight are your best fliers."

"Lieutenant Kunkle's up there, sir. He's my top guy, but ..." Buckmaster's voice trailed off as he brought his own glasses up and discovered that at least four squadrons were approaching, somewhere around 80-100 planes including the fighter escorts. "Holy God, Admiral," he said quietly. "Looks like they threw the kitchen sink at us."

Fletcher lowered the glasses. "Captain Buckmaster, it's going to take a miracle for us to get out of this. All we can do is hope Lex's planes catch them with their pants down, because sure to God this day we're going to take a beating."

Above the **Yorktown**
4 May 42 0817

Jumpin' Jesus! It's the whole Jap air force. Lieutenant Earl Kunkle and his wingman, Ernie Stampp, carefully dodged in and out of the clouds above what appeared to be several squadrons of Japanese dive bombers and torpedo planes. *But no fighters. What the hell?* "Stampp, you see any Zeros?"

"Not a one, boss man. I don't like this."

"Neither do I, but we've got no choice. In ten minutes, the Yorktown's gonna be a Roman candle. Come on."

Kunkle, with Stampp right behind him, banked directly for the eight Aichi D3A "Val" dive bombers nearest to him, and it took only a few moments for the Japanese machine gunner in the rear of the cockpit to train his weapon on the Wildcats. His first bursts went wild high— common for excited gunners—and Kunkle wasn't going to give him a second try. He felt his stick hand sweating as he lined up the Val in his sights, pressed down on the firing button, and ripped out three consecutive bursts. The dive bomber's cockpit disintegrated and the Val wheeled over to the left and started its death spiral, its pilot obviously dead.

"Good shootin', Earl. Pick up the next one. Holy crap, Earl, we got Nips on our tails!"

Stampp heard 7.7 millimeter rounds perforating his rear fuselage before he could roll out, leaving Kunkle alone. "Clear out, Earl!" Stampp warned.

"I see him." Kunkle counted two Zeros coming in from 2 o'clock, and watched the tracers whiz by his wing, but felt no damage. "You okay, Ernie?"

"Yeah, but they're after you. I'm coming around." Earl knew the physics as well as anyone. Stampp couldn't swing the Wildcat back in time to help him unless he flew toward his wingman.

"I'm comin' to you, Ernie." He banked the F4F steeply to the right, then rolled down where he could see Ernie coming in behind him in the distance, but the Zeros had copied his movements. Another burst of tracers, and the sound of shattering glass filled the cockpit. Two rounds whistled past his head, lodging in the instrument panel and sending out a burst of sparks. The oil gauge immediately fell to zero, although he doubted that his oil pressure was gone, or the engine would seize up. Miraculously, the photo of Betty Grable in a bathing suit clipped to his instrument panel was untouched. "Damn," he muttered.

More tracers followed, and a line of bullet holes marched its way up Earl's wing, stopping just short of the cockpit. "Come on, Ernie! This is getting serious," Kunkle bellowed. He pushed the stick down and put the Wildcat into a dive, then rolled it over to the left, but the Zeros seemed stuck to him.

"Got him!" Ernie screamed. He had blasted the trailing Zero out of the sky, but the lead plane remained glued to Earl Kunkle.

"He's too fast for me, Ernie. I'm gonna hit the brakes, and make him stop dead in his tracks for you!'

"Earl, what the hell ...? No, Earl, I'll get him, don't ..." But Kunkle had already pulled up the stick, putting the Wildcat into a near stall, and making it a sitting duck. Still, the faster Zero had to match his slower speed, a maneuver that obviously surprised even the veteran Japanese pilot. He de-throttled and hit his flaps, giving the American one brief chance to line him up. Ernie depressed the firing button and loosed a long burst that seemed to last minutes. The Zero hung motionless, then exploded.

"Wha-hooo," shouted Stampp into the radio, but Kunkle was gone, too. Stampp traced a long trail of smoke, down to the Pacific, where a Wildcat was already slipping beneath the waves. Before he could even grieve, Stampp noticed something else right above the waves: a squadron of Nakajima B5N "Kate" torpedo planes, moving in for the kill. Listening to the chatter from the Wildcats, he now knew that most of the Vals were splashed, but the *Yorktown* now had a towering cloud of smoke in the distance. Now the Kates were lining her up for the *coup de grace*. Stampp dove at the nearest one, closing in seconds, and firing relentlessly. He set it on fire, then he immediately targeted the next, ignoring what he knew to be a Zero on his tail. He managed to cause a second Kate to explode, but six others released their torpedoes in a spread covering some 300 yards, and the last thing Ernie Stampp thought before he felt the stabbing pain in his chest was that he had failed to protect the Yorktown.

Off the **Yorktown's** *port side*
4 May 42 0833

"Captain. Six torpedo bombers, starboard quarter."

Buckmaster and Fletcher both trained their glasses in the direction of the Kates, and Captain Buckmaster stated calmly, "Hard starboard rudder, engines ahead flank!" The helmsman spun the wheel to the right, and even though the carrier's 25,000 tons barely seemed to respond, the nine enormous boilers in fact were pushing the behemoth into a right turn at nearly 30 knots. Buckmaster grabbed the handset to damage control. "Report damage from those bombs."

"We've got the one put out, Captain. Still working on the other, but I think they can contain it in front of the number one elevator." Machinist Oscar W. Myers, the Air Department's fuel officer, had installed a new fire-control apparatus in which the fuel system of the carrier was drained immediately after usage and filled with inert CO_2 gas. Captain Buckmaster had approved Myers' innovation and quickly adopted it, in stark contrast to the Japanese carriers, whose 30 fueling points each could become high- explosive valves in the event of a fire. Fletcher greatly appreciated the changes in U.S. Navy doctrine that made almost every member of a carrier crew a member of a damage control party, and which directed damage control personnel to flatten out on the deck during surface actions to avoid unnecessary casualties from shrapnel. At least we've got the edge in a few things, ruminated Fletcher.

"Prepare for impact, gentlemen," Buckmaster stated calmly as he watched the streaks heading toward the carrier at over 40 knots. *They didn't bunch their spread close enough. We're gonna take one, maybe two, but not all of 'em. They're too far out, too, outside those torps' 2000-yard range. The fish will die before they hit.* "Well, Admiral," he noted to Fletcher, "you damn sure called this one."

Fletcher shot him a disgusted look, then braced himself against the bulkhead. Amazingly, *Yorktown*, despite seeming to move in slow motion, had turned significantly since Buckmaster's order. The first torpedo, then a second, then a third sailed wide. Men on the forward part of the ship manning the .50 caliber antiaircraft guns saw a fourth suddenly begin to swirl crazily 100 feet from the carrier without exploding. The vessel would not be so fortunate with the next two, each of which hit just in front of the first elevator where the fire crews were already battling the blaze from the bomb. It sent a monstrous explosion through the ship. Smoke poured out, and fires licked out onto the flight deck as fuel and ammunition in the storage areas succumbed to the blast, causing residual explosions. Gunners continued to blast away with their .50 calibers the quads, and the five-inchers, but they were nearly blinded by the smoke. They still somehow managed to bring down four Kates, but the port gunners suddenly found the ship listing so badly their fully elevated guns were looking almost entirely blue ocean. Buckmaster was again on the intercom to damage control.

All *Yorktown* pilots still in the air were ordered to the *Lexington,* and for a couple who were already short on fuel, the extra flight southward proved fatal. Two Devastator's dropped out of the sky, along with a Dauntless and a Wildcat.

"Admiral, may I recommend you transfer your flag to the *Minneapolis*, Sir?" Fletcher looked out over the flaming deck, and replied, "Very well. Buckmaster, do you think you can save this ship?"

"Yes Sir, I believe we can get her back to Pearl if we don't take any further hits. But you might need a more effective command platform, just in case."

"Very well, Captain. Contact the *Minneapolis*. I'm transferring the flag. And, Captain Buckmaster ... well done."

Over the **Zuikaku**
4 May 42 0851

Warning bugles sounded as Ichibei Yokokawa, the captain of the Japanese carrier *Zuikaku*, commenced evasive maneuvers to avoid the incoming American aircraft. Lacking the search radars of the American ships, the Japanese still relied on often-unreliable visual spotting. The screening destroyers, further out, usually saw the enemy aircraft first, and began laying down smoke to signal the carrier that attackers were incoming. Yokokawa could see his sister ship, *Shokaku*, making similar zig-zags. Their escorts, including the cruisers *Myoko* and *Haguro,* along with five destroyers, poured fire into the sky as the waves of American dive bombers and torpedo planes honed in. Together the carriers had only a dozen Zeros for combat air patrol, as Vice Admiral Takeo Takagi, who commanded the strike force, had sent the rest with the Vals and Kates attacking the Yorktown.

"Is this what Admiral Nagumo expected?" asked Yokokawa, now swinging the carrier back to port.

"So far, Captain, it is exactly as he expected," replied Takagi. "It was impossible to hide the invasion force, and it is still under attack. But Admiral Nagumo guessed that the Americans would only strike with part of their aircraft there, and send the rest to look for us in our vulnerable state."

They watched, mesmerized, as two Devastators appeared to come straight at the island, banking off only at the last minute as they released their "fish." Both men knew there was no evasion for two torpedoes dropped at that range.

"Well, Admiral, let us hope that our destruction here plays the role Admiral Nagumo expects of it."

Then *Zuikaku* was rocked by two ear-shattering explosions, as both torpedoes dug into the side and, simultaneously, a Dauntless that neither man had seen planted a 500-lb bomb right near the bridge. Glass shattered, sending sharp fragments riddling Takagi and Yokokawa, who fell where they had stood. Fire then swept the bridge, and explosions of fuel and bombs rocked the *Zuikaku*. Japanese fire and damage control teams, were helpless in the face of the blaze were added to by the confusion and shouting. Ammunition, bombs and fuel lines were exposed to the flame, triggering multiple massive bursts below decks that roasted the crews in entire sub-sections of the carrier. Two more hits rocked *Zuikaku*. Leaks became gushers, and *Zuikaku* began to sink.

Less than a mile away, Captain Matsubara Hiroshi on *Shokaku* stared in remorse as his sister ship slipped below the waves. Reports were already coming in that the *Shoho*, a light carrier assisting the invasion forces, had been spotted by American aircraft and also sunk. *We will be next*, thought Hiroshi. His sixteen 5-inch guns and nearly 100 25 mm. guns blackened the sky with antiaircraft bursts, putting out nearly 2,500 rounds per minute. But Hiroshi understood the dynamics of shipboard anti-aircraft fire, in which the 5- inch guns did not so much target an individual airplane as they aimed at a pre-set box in the sky and covered that box in a net of metal through which an attacker had to fly. If the gunners had sufficient warning and got their grid coordinates up to the guns in time, an attacker—in this case, Dauntlesses, coming in at 225 knots—might be exposed to the barrage. But if gunners had to wait longer for their solutions (the fire-control calculations of where to aim), they might only actually have guns on an enemy for 30 to 40 seconds. In short, Hiroshi knew that pinning his hopes on 30 to 40 seconds' worth of gunnery was a losing proposition, and like all carrier commanders, he understood that the only reliable protection against dive bombers and torpedo planes was his fighter umbrella. Only now, they were spread out, chasing individual planes. His vessel sat wide open to attack if the Americans could just coordinate their efforts.

CHAPTER NINE

Lexington *Strike Force, two miles north of* **Zuikaku**
4 May 42 0900

"There they are, Skip," exclaimed Toby Emmert, the radioman-gunner for Lexington's 2-T-12. He pointed down and to the left, where a small force of destroyers and cruisers screened a carrier. "It has to be the *Shokaku* — that's the only one

TBD Devestator Bomber (Wikipedia)

left." Lieutenant Roger Merton merely nodded and announced to the squadron, "Red Squadron, enemy carrier sighted seven o'clock. Commence attack. Repeat, all aircraft, attack."

"Look behind us, Tob, and see if you can find the torpedo squadron." He gestured with his thumb over his shoulder, and Emmert scanned the ocean behind him, finally picking up several small shapes perhaps a few miles back.

"I got 'em, Skip. They should be hitting the carrier just about the same time we come in from the top. Whoa!" A 25 mm. exploded right outside the canopy, sending hot shrapnel through the glass. "Dammit! I'm hit, Skip." Emmert checked the blood coming from his face — glass from the cockpit, nothing serious. "I'm okay, Skip, just get us into the funnel quick."

Despite the flak, Merton was suspicious. *Too damned easy,* he thought. *Where's their fighter cover? Chatter says we already got two Jap carriers. It can't be this easy.* Cautiously, he said, "Commencing dive approach," and he flayed the dive brakes open and pushed the stick forward as the Dauntless nosed down into its 70-degree angle. *Shokaku's* fat deck was dead in his sights, the huge rising sun goose egg painted in the middle. *Do the Nips have any clue what kind of target they give us?* Behind him were six other Dauntlesses, bearing down, and a second squadron behind them, then, in the distance, the Devastators lined up the carrier amidst a hail of fire.

"They've got no fighter cover, guys. Tally ho!" He felt the plane lighten as he released the 500-lb. armor piercing bomb, and jerked the stick back, turning the bomber away from the carrier and its murderous fire. "Damn!" screamed Emmert in exultation. "Direct hit! Do you believe it? Right in the center of the deck! Hot damn! I mean, dead center!" No sooner had he admired his handiwork than three other Dauntlesses planted bombs on the Shokaku's deck.

Coming around, Merton could see the low-flying Devastators, some exploding, some crashing into the water, but still others relentlessly coming on, parallel to the waves, releasing their metal fish which streaked toward the smoking *Shokaku*. "My God," said Merton softly, "we caught 'em with their pants down. Scratch one flattop! Yeeee-hoooo! Come on, boys, we've still got some 100-pounders left." The smaller bombs did minor damage, but collectively they sent the Japanese scurrying in all directions to put out fires and move ordinance. In general, the smaller explosives added to the chaos on decks, and, if nothing else, gave the American crews great satisfaction. Once empty of bombs, the squadron's survivors accelerated to full speed. Minus the seven planes destroyed by Japanese fire, the Dauntlesses headed back to the *Lexington*.

Merton did not see in the distance behind him the air armada of Japanese Zeros, Kates, and Vals from the *Akagi*, which now followed him back to the "Lady Lex."

Bridge of the Lexington
4 May 42 1006

"Our strike force is inbound, two zero zero. Captain, it sounds like we really did some damage." Lieutenant John Billings, Officer of the Deck, had listened intently to the radio chatter from the attack squadrons. Standing on the bridge next to Captain Fred Sherman, he pointed in the distance to the black silhouettes that already had been picked up on the Lex's radar.

Sherman nodded, but added, "We better have scored some hits. Looks like *Yorktown* is hurt bad. And I don't trust initial pilot reports of three carriers hit. I've been shot at by too many ships that were 'sunk.' Still, if even half of what we're hearing is true, we might have taken out at least a couple of Jap carriers today. 'Course, we've already paid a high price. Besides *Yorktown*, the cruiser *Asto-*

ria was hit. Don't know if she'll make it home. All right, Mr. Billings, prepare to recover aircraft."

"Aye aye, Captain." Billings gave the order and deck crews scurried to extend the arresting gear, while damage control personnel prepared for the inevitable problems associated with shot-up aircraft. Billings counted the black silhouettes.

"Sir, so far I've got what appear to be six Dauntlesses, and a couple more I can't make out, which are probably the slower Devastators. No sign yet of the Wildcats."

Damned odd, thought Sherman. One or two of the Wildcats should have gotten back here already.

"Contact the lead Dauntlesses and ask if they've seen the Wildcats."

A few moments later, Billings returned. "Strange, Sir. None of them have seen the Wildcats since the battle. But they have a flight of planes a couple of miles behind them. Radar says it's a big group."

Strange as hell. "I want full preparation for air attack. We'll recover the incoming planes, but something doesn't feel right." The lead Dauntless was already on approach, gear down, arresting hook deployed, and the pilot watching the landing signal officer with his two big paddles. Unlike the Japanese, who had an effective system of red and green lights that the pilot could line up like the sights of a rifle, American fliers relied on their LSOs to get them down safely. Behind the leader, two more Dauntlesses were circling to get in the landing cue. Then he saw the escort vessels open up. "They're shooting at our boys! Radio them to stop ... They're not shooting at our guys— they're shooting at the planes behind our guys!" Billings saw the black puffs of smoke from the outer ring of destroyers and cruisers, opening up on the enemy aircraft at the same time he heard the claxons as the Lex's spotters pointed at the inbound Japanese swarm, easily 40-50, bearing straight for the carrier.

Two Dauntlesses had come in and a third was on final approach, but the horde in the background was closing much faster. "Wave 'em off! We aren't landing anyone!" Billings knew it was nearly useless—the enemy planes would be on them in seconds. The *Lexington*'s combat air patrol of 15 Wildcats had already pounced, but the Japanese attackers were escorted by several Zeros that now bore in on the American fighters.

"Evasive action, now," Sherman shouted. "Helmsman, full right rudder!" The helmsman spun the wheel to the right, and the carrier began a slow turn as the rising sun insignia on the incoming aircraft became clearer. *Lexington's* anti-aircraft guns opened up, but were hindered by the presence of so many American planes now diverting and trying to clear the battle space overhead. Everyone knew they had no hope of landing aboard the *Lex* and with *Yorktown* on fire, they would have to ditch. Destroyers and cruisers around the carrier blackened the sky with antiaircraft fire, but some Japanese planes made it through.

"Bandits on our tail, *Lexington*, repeat, bandits." Numerous calls started to come in from the carriers' embattled planes, which had started to peel away from their landing formations to evade the attackers. Another group of Japanese attackers ignored the American dive and torpedo bombers and honed in on the carriers. Billings could only watch as the torpedo planes dropped low into their attack levels. He also knew the Vals were above them already. Soon the spotters for the guns would direct the eight 5-inch guns, the 1.1-inch batteries and many of the .50 caliber machine guns upward. Crews set the 5-inch fuses for three seconds, hoping to blanket the box through which the Vals would fly. Much more effective were the four 1.1-inch .75 caliber quad mounts, augmented by more than thirty .50 caliber machine guns manned on the catwalks and on the island by sailors and Marines.

For the *Lexington* alone, that meant that at least a dozen machine guns on any one side of the ship at the moment would bring fire to bear on torpedo planes, and four or five more on the dive bombers, while crews could direct fire at the dive bombers when the angle permitted. When combined with the average destroyer's compliment of five .50 caliber guns and four 5-inch guns, and the average cruiser's armament of nine to twelve 5-inch guns and another eight .50 caliber machine guns, the Lexington's screen could throw up an absolute blizzard of metal. Sherman's carrier was surrounded by the *Morris, Anderson, Hammann,* and *Russell* close by. In addition, Admiral Thomas Kinkaid's Task Group 17.2, which included the cruisers *Minneapolis, New Orleans, Chester, Portland,* and the damaged *Astoria*, plus Kinkaid's destroyers *Phelps, Dewey, Farragut, Aylwin,* and *Monaghan,* also provided covering fire. In total, Sherman's protective force could hurl 100 5-inch shells and some 40,000 .50

caliber or 40 millimeter rounds, plus thousands of 1.1-inch rounds into the air every minute.

And still, the Japanese leaked through. Two Vals plummeted through the 5-inch flak and streaked straight for the *Lexington's* deck. Fire control teams were already pulling out hoses and abatement gear when the first bomb exploded on the deck, blasting a four-foot gap in the wood. A second punctured the forward elevator, and exploded below decks, sending pieces of aircraft shooting out the open side of the hangar bay into the Pacific. No sooner had the damage control crews started to contain the first two fires than a Kate, whose torpedo missed badly, headed straight for the island. It missed a direct hit, clipping its wing and careening wildly into the sea, but another fire now engulfed the aft part of the island. And still they came. Three Kates targeted the Lex. It could not turn quickly enough to avoid two hits, and horrific explosions ripped through the hull. Watertight compartments kept her from sinking immediately, but she listed badly and became a wounded duck, inviting more attacks from the Vals and Kates.

Meanwhile, seven miles away aboard *Yorktown*, gun crews blasted away at another Kate with a Wildcat close on his tail, braving the U.S. anti-aircraft fire. The American pilot riddled the torpedo plane, but it did not explode until seconds after it released its fish. Streaking toward the center of the *Yorktown*, the torpedo miraculously passed under the carrier, then proceeded to spin in slow circles. But the Wildcat pilot was not so fortunate: when the Kate exploded, the Wildcat attempted to pull out, but the shipboard gunners could not adjust their firing quickly enough, and his plane was ripped to pieces, spinning off near the circling torpedo.

Finally, after what seemed an eternity, the last of the Kates and Vals either disappeared into the distance or crashed into the sea. *Yorktown*, smoke billowing, could not divert its planes to the *Lexington*, which now was rapidly sinking. Instead, they had to ditch near the screen of American destroyers and cruisers and hope that someone could pick them up as the battle subsided. Damage control crews on the *Yorktown* worked furiously, containing the blaze on the forward deck but still struggling to seal the inferno engulfing the elevator. In normal times, simply moving on board a ship is trying — the passageways are tiny, wiring and plumbing exposed and uncovered to save weight, and stairs only half the size of normal metal steps to save space—but in combat, with a ship smoking, sometimes listing, it was damned near impossible.

Before transferring Fletcher to the *Minneapolis*, Buckmaster had brought the *Yorktown* around to a bearing of due east, weighing the relative proximity to subsequent attacks against the greater problems posed by sailing the carrier even farther from Pearl Harbor. If we can just get her to Pearl, we can patch her up.

"Captain, it's Lex," announced a lieutenant, pointing to the handset. "She's sinking. Admiral Fitch has transferred his command to the *New Orleans*."

"God help us," Buckmaster replied quietly. "All right, OOD, as soon as we can, I need every bit of speed *Yorktown*'s got."

CHAPTER TEN

Naval Station Pearl Harbor, Headquarters, Commander in Chief, Pacific Fleet
9 May 42 1013

Pearl Harbor (Wikipedia)

Admiral Nimitz was smoking, a development that greatly concerned Capt. Arthur Lamar, who watched through the glass from the chart room. *That can't be good. I've never seen him smoke indoors before.* Lamar watched through the office glass as Nimitz, Halsey — smoking and drinking coffee by the cupful — and Spruance talked quietly. Every few moments an officer from communications entering with another message from the Coral Sea battle.

Nimitz waved Lamar into the office. "Art, I want you in on this. We may have to cut some orders here. Pull the shades, please, Captain."

My God. This is big if we're blacking out the room. Lamar replied "Aye aye, Admiral." He pulled down the darkened shades and closed the blinds to the outer offices as a further precaution. Then, after Nimitz indicated, he took a seat and pulled out his note pad.

"All right, gentlemen, here's what we know. *Lexington* is gone." Lamar blanched. Rumors had been flying, but this was the first official word. Halsey nervously pulled out a Lucky and lit up as Nimitz continued. "Fitch transferred to the *New Orleans*, and he is repositioning southeast, hoping to get close to Australia. Fletcher is on the *Minneapolis*, heading back with the *Yorktown*, but it's slow going. Three boilers are completely out. At best, they are on half power, and won't even get back here for more than a week — if we can keep her from getting hit again. *Astoria* is shot up, too. The British are hustling another carrier and two cruisers from the Indian Ocean. We've recalled Crace with his cruisers, to rendezvous with the Brits near New Caledonia to keep the Aussies and New Zealanders happy."

Halsey, now furiously puffing his third Lucky since arriving, cursed under his breath. "What kind of damage did we do to the Japs?"

"Not inconsiderable: we sank a small carrier, the *Shoho*, and left two others, which we think are the *Shokaku* and *Zuikaku*, seriously damaged, perhaps even sank the *Shokaku*. Both were reported smoking badly and on fire, with conflicting reports about the *Shokaku*."

"Two and a half for two," muttered Halsey, "if we are lucky and that carrier goes under. Normally, that would be a good tradeoff, but today ..." His voice trailed off. Everyone knew what he meant. "Well, maybe *Yorktown* can make it back. In that case, it would be one for one and a half or two and a half." Then he asked the question they all were thinking. "How did Jack Fletcher let this happen? Hell, he's a good commander."

"I don't think Fletch is to blame on this one, Bill. From all the reports I have, our guys were tearing up the Jap fleet and were on their way home, when they were followed by a very large enemy formation."

Spruance lifted his head. "Another full strike, Sir?

But you said we sank one carrier for sure and damaged two others badly. Where did the planes come from?"

"We don't know if they did. Rochefort's mind- readers think Yamamoto assigned a third fleet carrier to the attack. They have some evidence that the planes that sank Lex were from the *Akagi*."

"I'll be a horse's ass," exclaimed Halsey. "That son of a bitch guessed right."

Spruance, seemingly oblivious to the losses, stepped to the map. "Admiral, they think they've got us. By God, Yamamoto thinks he has us now. And he's going to come straight for us, here ....", slapping the pointer against Midway. "If I were him, I'd get *Akagi* back and push straight for Midway, now. He has to think that we'll be gun-shy—and perhaps if he hits quickly, we would be overly cautious with our last two carriers."

"How many more carriers can he muster that quickly?" Halsey asked, studying the map and considering Spruance's reasoning.

Nimitz tapped his pencil against his hand. "We know — that is, Rochefort tells us — that the *Kaga*, *Soryu*, and *Hiryu* are unaccounted for. Even if our reports about *Shokaku* are wrong, and it gets back to a port where it can be repaired, Yamamoto won't have it for months. But if he can rendezvous the *Akagi* with the *Kaga*, *Hiryu*, and *Soryu*, he'll have four full-sized carriers to our two."

Halsey grimly looked at the map. "Are you still thinking of taking them on at Midway?"

Spruance put down the pointer. "It's a good opportunity, Admiral. Midway has an airfield itself, so that would even the odds somewhat. Who knows? Maybe *Yorktown* can be patched up by the time we need her."

Both men looked at Nimitz, who felt a headache coming on. *The blessings of command.* "What do you think, Bill?"

Halsey first looked at Spruance, then nodded. "Ray's right. They'll come after us, all right. We still have Rochefort's boys. If we can find out where they are and when they're coming, maybe we can get the jump on them. If we manage to take out a carrier, then it's close to even with the land-based aircraft, although I'm not too high on B-17s in anti-ship work. They've yet to prove they can hit a barn door with a baseball bat. At any rate, the Japs are sucking oil, that's for sure, and they can't stay out long, so if we give 'em a bloody nose, Yamamoto will have to regroup. It would give us time to get the Essex-class carriers out and bring on our new, fast battleships."

Spruance agreed. "From what you've told us about Yamamoto, Admiral, he won't quit while he thinks he has the advantage. Have you run any of this by King?"

King, thought Nimitz. *Of course I have to "run this by King." The name fits. King Ernest. Ernest King. Runs the Navy like it's his personal yacht club. Nearly destroyed his career through the bottle until he got it under control. And they think I'm harsh, arrogant, and impatient?* "Not yet. I will, of course."

Halsey temporarily forgot himself and uttered a curse. "Damned King."

Spruance chuckled. "Not your favorite commander- in-chief?" Spruance knew better. Halsey had served under King in the late 1930s with a pair of carriers and gotten chewed out after a slight delay during a launch. King held Halsey in high regard, but never told him so, contributing to Halsey's insecurity around the boss. Spruance intoned, regally, "A greater perfectionist cannot be found in any navy! You can't have too much affection for him, either, Admiral, knowing how he disparaged 'detailers' and all," a reference to Nimitz's position in the Bureau of Navigation.

Spruance continued. "I've got to give him credit, though. He stood up to Roosevelt. You were there, Bill."

Before Halsey could reply, Nimitz intervened. "That's enough, gentlemen. We're not discussing the Commander in Chief of the U.S. Navy." *God, I hate coming to King's rescue, the ambitious SOB. But the man knows carriers. His solution to Fleet Problem XIX in the late 1930s, well ... He and Billy Mitchell had the same idea. But King saw Billy's attack and raised him, coming from the northwest in a thunderstorm that concealed the Saratoga attack force. He achieved complete surprise. Yet he was about to be kicked into retirement, and even then refused to play the game. Have to give him that. He never was chummy with FDR, even when it apparently meant his career. Ironic. Yamamoto may have saved King's career, putting him in the one position where his grating personality would not interfere with his genius.* "Let's get back to Midway." Nimitz again studied the map. "Bill, do you have that skin condition under control?"

Halsey, suddenly reminded of the dermatitis, began to subconsciously scratch. "I do." Nimitz looked skeptical, but Halsey added, "I'm fine, Admiral. What do you want me to do?"

Studying both Halsey and Spruance, Nimitz continued. "All right. Bill, I want you to take *Enterprise* and *Hornet* out the moment they are ready. If *Yorktown* gets here anytime soon, I'll send her along, too, but for now, I want our remaining carriers at Midway." Halsey grinned. It was just the assignment he wanted. "Ray, I want you here at Pearl." Spruance started to protest but Nimitz cut him off. "If *Yorktown* comes in, I'll want you to head up her task force. If she doesn't, I need someone here with experience in case ... well, in case Jack Fletcher doesn't make it back. I can't risk having my two remaining combat commanders in the same place. Sorry, but that's the reality we all face now. We're it, gentlemen. We are all that stands between the Japanese and the west coast. We need to be aggressive, but not foolhardy." Spruance nodded, knowing Nimitz was right.

"Bill, your orders are to take up a position northeast of Midway. I want you close enough to support and strike, but not so close as to be discovered by Japanese scout planes who aren't specifically looking for you. Am I clear?"

"Aye aye, Admiral," Halsey responded.

"Your mission is to first, assist in repelling any attempted invasion of Midway. However, if in the course of performing said mission you find an opportunity to strike the enemy carrier fleet, do so. The best defense is a good offense. Am I clear on that?"

Again, Halsey bobbed his head. "Yes, Sir." Spruance quietly looked on, expressing full agreement and support of his friend.

Nimitz continued. "Finally, Admiral, since we do not know the disposition of the *Yorktown*, and since you have the only remaining fleet carriers in the Pacific for at least a few weeks, I want you to exercise due caution in any engagement with the enemy. In other words, I want you to strike, if possible. But if, in your judgment, you would get into a tit-for-tat exchange that would cost you both carriers, you are to withdraw. Midway is not worth both our remaining carriers. Bill, I know you made your reputation by being aggressive, but here you must be cautious. If *Yorktown* doesn't get back, that will be two disasters in a row for the U.S. Navy. We can't afford three."

Halsey still nodded. "Chet, I swear I won't let you down." Then, looking at Spruance, he added, "And Ray, if you get *Yorktown*, you get your ass up to me as fast as possible and we'll really show Yamamoto and the purple-pissing Japs who they're messing with!"

Spruance, no racist, nevertheless had to grin at Halseys's colorful description of the enemy. "You have my word, I'll make every effort, Bill." He extended his hand, and the beetle-browed Halsey shook it furiously.

Nimitz concluded the meeting. "Very well, gentlemen. Bill, make ready for sea, and we'll stay on top of Rochefort to keep you up to speed with the latest intelligence." Both men stood, and Nimitz shook their hands. *God go with you, Bill*, he thought as they exited. *You're going to need all the help you can get on this one.*

Although it was Tuesday, a good business day, Sam Tomita scrawled a cardboard sign that he hung in the window of his photography shop: "Closed due to illness." He locked the door, climbed into his 1938 Buick and drove down to an observation spot overlooking Pearl Harbor. Shutting off the car, he gave the bay a cursory glance, opened his trunk, pulled out his camera tripod, and hiked up Aiea Heights. The cool winds came off the Pacific there, and it was a perfect scenic view.

But Sam was there for other reasons that day. He setup his camera so that it faced back toward Honolulu. *It won't take long for the Marine patrol to come by.* The Navy was building a new hospital on this hill, which provided a panoramic view of Honolulu — or, if one came about in the other direction, Pearl Harbor. Sam squinted in the sunlight and peered through the lens as he began snapping pictures of the city, outlined against the puffy green mountains capped in their wispy fog. He interspersed these with pictures of the hospital site. He'd been at it perhaps fifteen minutes when two Marine guards spotted him while making their rounds to prevent the theft of building materials. Sam shaded his eyes so he could see their faces. He had met many of the guards who routinely patrolled the Heights, but not these two. *No matter. My credentials have never failed.*

A red-haired sergeant — and a large fellow at that — advanced, all business.

"Who are you, and what are you doing up here?" he asked. "Let me see some identification."

Sam nodded. "My name is Sam Tomita. I'm a professional photographer. Occasionally I work for the Honolulu police, and even for the Navy." He pulled out his wallet, and also flashed his temporary duty identification from the Honolulu Police Department. *Except they don't know that it was temporary, and that it's long expired.* The Marines whispered something among themselves.

"What are you doing up here?" The red-head repeated, holding Sam's driver's license and looking suspiciously at the camera.

"I told you. I'm a professional photographer. Right now, I'm taking pictures of the mountains. The Navy wanted to see what the view of the city was like for the hospital, I guess to know where to put the convalescent wards, and they hired me to do the job."

Red looked skeptical. "The Navy has its own surveyors and photographers."

Sam laughed. "I know. I'm one of them, although the only picture I have is one we took with the Army guys." He pulled out a photo he'd taken for the Army Air Force's 13th Reconnaissance Squadron, which had held a party before heading to Australia to become part of the 43rd Bomber Group. A big banner, "Willing, Ready, and Able" stood behind the men, who were clustered in front in Hawaiian leis and a couple comically dressed as hula "girls." Sam handed the photo to Red. "I do some freelance work for the Army, too." In the corner was his logo and signature, "Sam Tomita Photography."

The Army reference certainly didn't impress either of the Marines, but the Navy's use of a photographer seemed reasonable. Looking at the picture, he quipped, "I'm surprised they let you see them in this condition." He held it over his shoulder, whereupon the other Marine leaned forward, shook his head disapprovingly. "Flyboys," he snorted.

"Okay," said Red. "We just have to be careful about Japs ... er, I mean, about anyone up here photographing the harbor. You know, enemies." Red handed back Sam's identification and the photo.

Sam gave an understanding smile and stuffed his identification back in his wallet and pocketed the picture. "Of course, Sergeant. Actually, I think photos like this ..." he smiled as he patted his pocket, "are almost as dangerous to the war effort." Both Marines grinned at that.

"Very well." Red jerked his head to the other Marine, and the pair headed away from Sam, down a small ridge where they lost sight of him. Waiting an extra minute after they left, Sam methodically turned his camera around on the tripod and began snapping pictures of Pearl Harbor, where an aircraft carrier was coming into port. After an hour, Sam packed up his gear. Although it would be risky, he needed to come back again this afternoon before making an important radio transmission later tonight. Of course, he would verify the two carriers he saw in Pearl Harbor, but he'd seen one before, the *Enterprise*, and used his telescopic lens to see the name of the other on the fantail— the *Hornet*. Neither of the carriers he saw leave in April had come back—the *Lexington* nor the *Yorktown*. Sam would pay close attention in the next days to see if either returned. Meanwhile, at 1:00 in the morning, Sam would go to his basement, turn on his transmitter, and send a cryptic message: "Two pineapples are on the tree." Then he would shut off his equipment, and Sam Tomita, photographer, would return to his innocent business of photographing graduations, babies, and an occasional military reunion or party.

CHAPTER ELEVEN

The **Yamato,** *Hashirajima Bay*
27 May 42 0815

The Yamato (Wikipedia)

"Our task is clear." Admiral Yamamoto addressed the admirals of the Combined Fleets as they prepared to put to sea. "Our information confirms that the Americans only have two aircraft carriers sailing from Pearl Harbor. We have no reports, however, of the *Yorktown*, but I believe its damage could not possibly be repaired soon enough to join them. The *Saratoga* is thought to be on the west coast, and unavailable for Nimitz. I have decided against the Imperial General Headquarters and Naval General Staff's recommendation to send a task force to occupy the islands of Attu and Kiska. While this would extend our circle of control, and would indeed protect our northern flank, I have made other plans." Several admirals, including Nagumo, were hardly surprised that Yamamoto defied his superiors, as he had done so often. In this case, however, Nagumo agreed that the Alaskan adventure merely diluted their effective force.

Yamamoto continued. "Admiral Nagumo, you will command the advance carrier force consisting of *Hiryu, Soryu, Kaga*, and *Akagi*. I have assigned to you the heavy cruisers *Tone* and *Chikuma* of the Eighth Cruiser Division, along with battleships *Kongo* and *Hiei* of the Third Battleship Division." Nagumo's face brightened. "As at Pearl Harbor, you shall be my sword."

"That force," he continued, looking at the other officers, "will be followed by the carriers of the Fourth Carrier Division, *Ryujo* and *Junyo*, and cruisers *Takeo* and *Maya*, under the command of Admiral Kakuji Kakuda." These were smaller carriers—light carriers, mainly useful for providing a small combat air patrol above a strike force, but incapable of launching many dive bombers or torpedo planes.

Kakuda bowed, then shot Yamamoto a look. Yamamoto indulged him. "You have something to say, Admiral?"

Again, Kakuda bowed. "I would like to again express my concern that without the General Staff's recommended simultaneous invasions of the Aleutians, the Americans will surely know where our main thrust is going. We have always used multiple operations as a form of deception, and because we have the ability to do so. Why do we now abandon this approach now?"

"Your objection is noted, Admiral," answered Yamamoto. "I alone am responsible for this decision, but for once I decided to try to think like an American." Eyebrows went up around the room. Yamamoto smiled. "Our enemy knows by now we use multiple offensives, and has adapted. He will not be fooled the same way again. Moreover, he knows we cannot do much to threaten him from Attu and Kiska, even if they fall. Nor can we launch operation AL in time to act as a lure for the enemy carriers. No, Admiral Kakuda, the key to the Pacific is controlling Midway and Hawaii. They know that as well. We will not have to look hard for their forces, and I do not want our forces dispersed. Admiral Mahan taught mass. Mass, it is."

Kakuda could do little else but bow and step back. "All our forces will mass at Midway. We will have twelve transports with landing forces, which have already left Saipan and will rendezvous with us, and they will also bring five cruisers and eleven destroyers under the command of Admiral Kurita. We will fight, therefore, with a force of six carriers, two battleships, and more than enough cruisers and destroyers to overwhelm the enemy. Following our force will be Admiral Hosogaya's occupation force, consisting of the heavy cruisers *Atago*, *Chokai*, *Myoko*, and *Haguro*, the battleships *Haruna* and *Kirishima*, light carrier *Zuiho*, a light cruiser, and eight destroyers. I will cover and support the entire operation with battleships *Nagato*, *Yamato*, *Ise*, *Hyuga*, *Fuso*, *Mutsu*, and *Yamashira*, three light cruisers, and the light carrier *Hosho*. This fleet represents most of our vessels, but it is far superior to the entire U.S. Pacific Fleet, let alone what they are likely to have at Midway. In short, there is no excuse for anything but an overwhelming victory."

All around the room the admirals nodded as Yamamoto continued. "Your orders are simple: destroy the airfield on Midway, lure out the enemy ships and eliminate them, then take the island. From there, we will sail for Hawaii." Several of the admirals broke out in smiles, followed by spontaneous shouts of "Banzai!"

Yamamoto raised his hand. "There is more. The American carriers will counterattack. I'm sure of this." He displayed a tight, small grin. "In fact, I'm counting on it. The moment we are confident that we have engaged the main attacks of the enemy carrier planes, I will split my strike force in two. I will take the *Nagato, Yamato, Ise,* the *Hosho,* and half the destroyers and cruisers to the south of Midway, while Admiral Kurita will temporarily assume command of a force designated Task Force Niitaka — in honor of our Pearl Harbor strike command ..." Kurita smiled and bowed deeply. "... and he will take that force, including battleships *Hyuga, Fuso, Mutsu,* and *Yamashira* to the north of Midway. We will sail at top speed to set up a blocking position behind the Americans. If any of their ships escapes from the initial battle, we will eradicate them before they can break out of the trap."

Eyes widened around the room. They were stunned. Smiles started to appear on some faces. "Truly this is an opportunity greater than even Tsushima. It is as complete a knockout blow as Japan could hope for. There can be no excuse for anything other than complete, total victory." Yamamoto surveyed the room. The excitement was electric. "Any questions?" Of course there would be none. The officers were stunned at the opportunity to utterly destroy the American Navy. "Dismissed."

The officers filed out of the room, but Sagata remained. He watched Yamamoto fold his personal map and his order of battle chart for the coming operation. Sagata was puzzled. For someone who had just outlined plans for what should be a crowning jewel of a great military career, the Admiral seems unusually pensive. The captain's expression must have given away his thoughts.

"A question, Captain?" Yamamoto asked, slowly sinking into a large leather chair.

"Showing the bull the red flag again, Admiral-san?" Sagata inquired.

Yamamoto nodded. "Perhaps. The loss of the *Zuikaku* and *Shoho,* and the inability of our work force to repair *Shokaku* in time for this operation, was a more severe blow than the admirals here appreciated. *Shokaku* may be in dry dock for a month."

"But the Americans? Didn't they lose two carriers - of their four or five? Isn't that proportionally a greater loss?"

"In strict numbers, yes. In terms of who we are fighting, no. While their production has not yet begun to come on line, the Americans will nevertheless quickly turn out two, three, or four aircraft carriers per year. Regardless, with or without those ships, the only way we can buy time is to eliminate the entire U.S. carrier force and the Hawaiian Islands as their base. That would greatly change the balance of power, and perhaps, if China can be brought to heel and if operations in Burma and elsewhere are successful, the Americans may yet decide that Germany is such a threat that we are an annoyance. Perhaps ..." his voice trailed off.

"Do you believe that, Admiral?"

Yamamoto gazed at Sagata with a profound sadness. "No, Sagata. The sad truth is the Americans will never negotiate, never forget, and never stop. I fear that even a great victory in the coming days, no matter how impressive, will merely feed the overconfidence of our government, and steel the resolve of the Americans even more."

"What about showing the bull the red flag? I'm puzzled Admiral. Just a month ago, I thought ... well, that is, it seemed you thought we could win."

Yamamoto laughed loudly, slapping his leg. "Win? Sagata! Is that what you thought I meant? I never thought we had a hope of winning. Think of what victory entails. We have not even 'won' in China or Burma. While we have large population centers under our control, there are two immense armies still out there, either of which is capable of defeating us. Have we 'won' in the south Pacific? With or without the Americans, do you seriously think the Empire of Japan can conquer the Australian mainland? Then there is the matter of the Americans: how do you propose to invade a nation with fifty million more people than we have and many times our industrial superior? And without invasion, how can you 'win?' We could not even invade Hawaii now, and certainly could not resupply it unless we moved the majority of its population somewhere else. It would take sixty ships a month to bring in enough food and supplies for the current population of Hawaii.

"No, Sagata, I thought all along that possibly if we hurt the Americans badly enough, we could buy enough time for other factors to intervene—perhaps the war in Europe would go badly, perhaps her allies would press for peace, especially if we could threaten Australia." He stopped, and sighed. "I don't know what I thought. The truth is, I was thinking like an Imperial Navy officer, and not as a logical person. We had our orders. We always had our orders. I could do nothing else."

A grim reality descended on Sagata. "So, Admiral, if we win this battle, what do you plan?"

"We can only keep all options open. Certainly, I want Hawaii, eventually. Perhaps we would turn our attention to Australia. Right now, the central threat is the presence of the U.S. carrier force, and, secondarily, Midway."

"It appears, Admiral, that we have the tiger by the tail. We cannot eat him, but surely we cannot let go."

Yamamoto looked up with a sadness that Sagata had never seen before, but only momentarily. His visage lightened, and he said. "Well, Sagata, we must hope there is a third option."

"What might that be, Admiral?"

"That the tiger gets tired of trying to shake us off and decides to live with the annoyance."

"But you said they would never relent, never forget."

"I did. Let us hope I am wrong in this instance. Aside from their Revolution, the Americans have never fought a war that lasted longer than four years."

In that flicker of time, Sagata understood that any chance for option number three rested entirely on what happened the next few days.

Kaiser Shipyards, Richmond, California
28 May 42 0840

"No, dammit, no." Henry Kaiser puffed as he jogged his portly body over to the construction site of the *Meriwether Lewis.* "Lay the plates down. Don't try to weld anything vertically if you can help it." Kaiser gestured for the welder to yield his helmet and gloves, which Kaiser put on quickly. With his mask up, he delivered a terse lecture as he aligned the steel plates on the ground. "Make your work easy. Use gravity. Don't lift anything until you have to, and when you lift something, weld the biggest sections you can so as to minimize the number of welds you perform." He snapped the visor down and fired up the welder. In moments he completed a perfect weld. The ship workers were astonished at the speed and precision with which the "old man" melded the two sheets of steel together. He clicked off the welder and took off the helmet and gloves. "See? Easy as pie. Now, save yourself some energy, and let's get efficient around here."

Men bolted into action in every direction as Kaiser smiled. Johnnie Eugland, his assistant and right hand man, shook his head. "Boss, you got 'em hoppin', that's for sure."

Kaiser headed toward his office and ticked off the numbers both of them knew by heart. "John, we've knocked almost ninety days off the build time of one hundred fifty days. I know that's impressive, but we have two problems. Number one, word has come back that four of the first twenty vessels split apart in heavy seas in the Atlantic. Our design has a flaw. I want you to come up with a fix. We don't have time to reconfigure the whole she- bang—just find a simple, effective way to strengthen what we have and make it safe for those boys."

Eugland took notes and stabbed the pad with his pencil as he put his period down. "Right, Boss. And number two?"

"We gotta shave more time."

"Boss?" Eugland surveyed the vast panorama of construction within his eyesight—at least thirty ships in some stage of construction. "The men are cranking out ships like they were pancakes at the Rotary breakfast. And you want 'em faster?"

Kaiser pulled out a cigar and chomped the end off, lighting it as he spoke. "Faster, dammit. We can do better. The Nazis are sending fifty thousand tons a month to the bottom. That means for every five Liberty Ships we turn out, two of them won't reach England at all, and those that do won't have enough supplies to sustain what forces we have over there now, much less be able to supply an invasion of Europe. No, we have to get more out of 'em."

Eugland shook his head. "How ya gonna do it, Boss? I mean, we've restructured the whole construction process twice; we've streamlined the management; we've cut out all extraneous movements on the lines. We can't bring in any more workers—they'll just get in each other's way. Heck, as it is, we have all these Negroes workin' here ...."

Kaiser shot the foreman a glance. "I thought we understood each other when we started this. When I told FDR I would make him ships in record time, I didn't say they'd be ships built by white hands, black hands, or even men's hands. I ran ads in every newspaper I could find, and if Negroes replied to the want ads, then God bless 'em. You've seen them work — if they have the same training, they are every bit as good as a white. Now, I don't have time for this kind of distraction, so do you have any problem with coloreds working in the yards?"
Eugland gulped. "No, Mr. Kaiser."

"Good. Now, Johnnie, I'm not sure how we're going to squeeze out any more production, but I have a meeting tomorrow with two fellas that might help us: Andrew Jackson Higgins and Preston Tucker of the Higgins Boat Works down in Louisiana. They've been building wooden landing craft at a God-unbelievable rate. I wouldn't think it was possible if I hadn't seen the numbers.

…and, like us, they've been making adjustments to the process on the fly. Word is Higgins and Tucker don't get along too well — kinda the same personality — but they both think big, build big, and dream big, so it can't hurt to talk to them."

"Oh, that reminds me, Boss, you had a call earlier today from a Mr. Howard Hughes. He wouldn't say what it was about. Damn strange fella, that's for sure. All he said was that he'd be willing to talk. That's it. 'I'd be willing to talk to Henry. Have him call me.' Here's the number, Boss. Isn't he the guy building wooden airplanes? Hey, wooden ships in Louisiana, wooden airplanes? This isn't some sort of attempt to get us to start makin' our Liberty Ships out of wood is it?"

Kaiser laughed. "You don't have to worry about that, Johnnie. These guys are all misfits of one sort or another. I read about this guy Tucker in the 1930s while I was building dams in Arizona and Washington. Seems he had an 'armored car' that would go forty-five miles per hour and ran rings around everything the Army had at the time. Embarrassed them damn bad. That's one thing you can't do, Johnnie: embarrass the generals. You give them the credit, give them the glory, and they'll let you make your weapons your way. Higgins figured that out — he let a Marine help design his landing craft, and the Marines loved it. Buyin' 'em by the thousands. But Tucker? He's a hot dog. Really knows his stuff, design-wise, but is a showboater who lifted up the Army's skirt, if you know what I mean. Needless to say, they didn't buy any of his armored cars."

"Even though they were faster than anything the Japs or Krauts had?"

"Nope. But they weren't stupid. The car had a Plexiglas rotating turret on it, and they liked that, so they gave him a contract to make ball turrets for the B-17s and B-24s when the war broke out. Still, Tucker is a car man— he used to win a lot of races, if I recall. Lousy with money. I never loaned him anything, but he's asked two or three times. Between you and me, I'm surprised Higgins ever got tied up with him. Higgins seems pragmatic, and profit- minded." Kaiser looked at his cigar, which by now was almost half smoked. "Maybe you need both. Maybe you need the dreamer and the builder, the visionary and the carpenter, to actually get stuff done. I've always been more the latter. Build it. Fix it on the fly if something is wrong, but keep building. Hell, I don't want to give our boys inferior crap, but inferior is better than nothing. How many of 'em will die waiting on the perfect tank or the perfect ship? Not from my yards! I'm gonna give them everything I can, as fast as I can, and as good as I can make it at the time and work on 'perfect' as we go."

Eugland nodded. "Sounds about right to me, Boss.

So, what do you want me to tell this Mr. Hughes?" "Nothing. You're right. He's a strange bird. Makes Tucker look damn well sane. I'll call Hughes myself. Meanwhile, I want you to go back through and interview every one of our supervisors for ideas to cut build time. Every one, you got it? I don't want any suggestion ignored, no matter how trivial it seems. Let's see if we can't cut our production time in half by this time next month."

Eugland stopped taking notes. "By half?"

Kaiser smiled and walked off, waving his cigar. "I don't care if you have to hire women and midgets. Add more workers."

"More workers, right, boss."

"Just get it done, Johnnie. FDR trusted me, and I trust you." Eugland looked at his notepad and suddenly felt 80 years old.

CHAPTER TWELVE

Coronados and Catalinas (Wikipedia)

Midway Island
3 Jun 42 0930

"Fer Chris' sakes, Commander, willya put that camera down? It's hard enough getting these lunkheads to work without you pointin' that thing in their faces all day—Sir." Marine Lieutenant Able Cozner positioned himself directly in front of Commander John Ford's lens, displaying prominently his nose hairs. "No disrespect, Sir, but we're we're tryin' to keep from getting killed out here ... you too, Sir. We don't want you killed either ... Sir."

Ford doubted the last part of the lieutenant's sentence, and lowered the camera. "I know I'm no fighting man. But the Navy Department says you have to be nice to me. 'Render full cooperation,' or words to that effect? What's the matter, Lieutenant, don't you leathernecks appreciate the value of propaganda?"

Cozner smiled. "My idea of propaganda is what Doolittle did a couple of months ago—drop bombs on those sumbiches."

"Look, Lieutenant. I know I'm a pest when it comes to your work. But let me put it this way. You're a Marine, right?"

"Damn straight, Commander ... Sir."

"Marines—I know you're really tough—but Marines need guns, and grenades, and even a ship now and then to get them to the beaches, isn't that right?"

"Yes sir, we do need those things."

"That stuff costs money. We're not talking the- biggest-poker-game-you've-ever-won money. We're not even talking Hollywood-makes-a-blockbuster movie money. I mean *real money,* so much money it'd make you think about joinin' the *Army* just to get your hands on it."

Cozner laughed at that image, and Ford, now knowing he had gotten through, continued. "Lieutenant, what I'm doing is getting you and your men that money— getting you those rifles, machine guns, airplanes. These documentaries that I'm shooting are going straight back to the states and will open every movie in every theater, telling the folks back home what brave soldiers you guys are and how you need their help. And you know what comes after the newsreel?"

Clearly, Cozner hadn't been to a movie in years, and certainly didn't know. He shook his head.

"Bond sales. Victory bonds, war bonds. There will be ushers in the aisles selling bonds like they were popcorn, like so many candy bars. And those movie audiences, having just seen what heroes you guys are . . . well. They'll be falling all over themselves to buy those bonds — bonds, Lieutenant Cozner, that send money to the Treasury, which turns right around and gives it to Congress to write checks for General Motors to make tanks, Convair to make bombers, and old Henry Kaiser to make Liberty Ships. Heck, somewhere in there I bet they have a special fund for Purple Hearts for eager-beaver young louies like yourself."

Cozner spat on the ground. "I bet they've already got two or three of those with my name on 'em already. Commander Ford, you sound a lot like Santa Claus."

"Next to your rifle, Lieutenant, I'm your best friend on this God-forsaken island. I know how to make movies. I can yank a tear out of your eye, or have you standing in the aisles. I'm every bit as good at my job as you are at yours, Lieutenant. Now, what's say you let me do my job, and I'll try to stay out of your way when it's really necessary."

Cozner thought for a moment, and then said. "Deal, Commander Ford, as long as you make sure you take cover when the shooting starts."

Ford rejected the offer. "Come on, now, Lieutenant. It is precisely my job to film you boys shooting down Jap planes. I can't do that from inside a pillbox, can I?"

Before Cozner could answer, a sergeant came running down the beach. "We got contact," he yelled. "About twenty minutes ago, a PBY reported some Jap minesweepers headed straight this way. You know what that means. And a PBY also sighted another whole fleet to the west. We're sending up some B-17s now. Ford flipped on his camera again as Cozner shouted to the men digging trenches and foxholes. "Listen up! We got company. We'll probably be seeing some Japs in the next few hours, so we keep working, but every man keep your weapon and helmet close at all times. And put your shirts on. I know it's hot, but it'll be a lot hotter if you get stuck out in this sun under a bombing attack without any covering. Sergeant, post a lookout on our sector of the beach. And keep your eyes open!"

Ford captured it all on film, but he knew this was filler, and the real thing would be here soon enough. "Lieutenant," he shouted. Cozner gave him a disgusted look, like *"What now?"*

"I'd prefer it if you didn't call me 'Commander.' I might not answer when called. How about just 'Ford?'

Cozner beamed and said, "Whatever you want, Fordie."

John Ford just sighed, and checked his film.

U.S. Task Force 16, Northeast of Midway Island
4 Jun 42 0104

"Another confirmation, Admiral. This time a PBY hit a Jap transport ship. Damaged it. They're heading straight for Midway, that's for sure." Lieutenant Charles LeBoutiller, Halsey's aide, saluted as he handed the radio message to the admiral. At 26, the dark-haired, tall, smooth-cheeked, LeBoutiller seemed an unexpected fit for the Admiral's right-hand man. He had finished Harvard just as the war in Europe heated up, prompting him to put his career on hold. LeBoutiller joined the Navy, which immediately put him into Officer Candidate School. He had planned to go into the rough and tumble world of advertising, already putting feelers out to J. Walter Thompson and Batton, Barton, Durstine, & Osborne before joining up. Several superiors had appreciated his clarity of language, which provided a natural skill for an aide. Halsey had spotted him at a lower level of King's staff and stolen him. Once in Halsey's employ, though, LeBoutiller became an appendage, a mind- reader who knew Halsey's needs almost when the admiral did.

"Admiral Nimitz was right. They're right out there to the southeast, right where he figured. Not like Yamamoto to come in without a diversion. He's like those vaudeville magicians. 'Watch my hand,' while he pulls the rabbit out of the hat with the other hand."

"Sir," said LeBoutiller, "Midway will put up PBYs at first light to find the carriers, and when they do, they'll launch their B-17s."

"Useless waste of time. Damn land-based bombers couldn't hit a barn door with a blowtorch. The Army ought to save them for use against the landings, or, if things get really bad, for bombing coconut forests to get us something to eat. That's about all they're good for. But if our forward positions fall, those bombers could pulverize the Japs on the beaches." He signed deeply.

"All true, sir, but if the Army at least finds the carriers, we'll know where they are."

"That we will, ensign. Lieutenant, I want every squadron ready to launch the moment we get a fix on the Japanese. Let them rest until about 0500, then they need to get ready to kick ass. And pass this information on to Hornet. We will not lose a battle because of poor communication."

"Aye aye, Admiral." "Oh, and Charlie?" "Yes, Admiral?"

"What was the last known disposition of our subs?" "They are fanned out in an arc to our east."

"Who do we have to the south?" Halsey walked over to the chart and began calculating speeds and distances from the point of the PBY's dispatch.

"Right now, just the destroyer Balch, plus the Hammann, which should get on station tomorrow. Why, Admiral, what are you thinking?"

Halsey pulled off his cap and ran his hands back over his hair. "Something isn't right. Yamamoto doesn't work like this. He wouldn't put everything he had into one attack. He always has a couple of balls in the air at once. I want the *Balch,* and later, the *Hammann* to take up a patrol position south of Midway. We have the north covered: between us and the submarine screen, they can't get around us here. But we're naked as a jaybird on the south. Yamamoto's got something up that sleeve of his, and we need to know what it is."

As LeBoutiller saluted and left, Halsey walked outside the flag bridge deck and leaned over the railing. "Tomorrow's going to be a helluva day," he said, and lit a cigarette.

Carrier **Akagi,** *200 miles northwest of Midway*
4 Jun42 0530

"No doubt, he saw us." Several Japanese officers scanned the skies with their binoculars, and two of them had seen the PBY simultaneously. "And where is our fighter cover?" In fact, they could see and hear their fighters racing above them, but the PBY had dipped in and out of a cloud formation just long enough to spot the strike force and escape.

"So!" Nagumo said. "The element of surprise is at last gone. No matter. We have gotten well within range. Prepare for high-level bombing attack. The Americans will use the B-17s they have on Midway. As soon as that attack has passed, launch the Midway strike force. Is Commander Genda ready?"

"Yes, Admiral," reported a lieutenant. "He has fully recovered from the flu he had a week ago."

"And Commander Fuchida is sure he can go?" Misuo Fuchida had been the leader of the Pearl Harbor attack, and his infamous radio message, "Tora! Tora! Tora!" — "Tiger! Tiger! Tiger!" officially started World War II for the Americans. Only a month ago, Fuchida had come down with acute appendicitis and it was questionable whether he would recover, but he reported for duty the previous day with a doctor's clearance. Now, Japan would have two of its best aviators when the Navy sent its planes into action.

Again, the lieutenant responded affirmatively.

"And the American carriers? Still no word of their location?"

"No, Admiral. We sent out scout planes in the search pattern ordered by Commander Genda," pointing to a chart showing a massive fan shape. "Every one of them should be at maximum range in the next ten minutes. If there are any carriers there, the scout aircraft will find them."

Nagumo seemed satisfied. "Perhaps, then, the gods will favor us today. We have taken every precaution."

Carrier **Akagi**
4 Jun 42 0602

"As you expected, Admiral. The American bombers, right on schedule."   They could not see the B-17s except for a few moments between the clouds — which was good news for the Japanese fleet, as the bombers also couldn't easily see them.

Nagumo lowered his binoculars as the geysers shot up 50 yards away from the *Akagi*. "Once again, they have proven their high-level bombers are completely ineffective against ships at sea. Good. They will likely send their PBYs out on torpedo runs next, unless they have learned how ineffective those are as well. If we do not see any Catalinas in the next ten minutes, Genda is to prepare for the assault on Midway."

"As you wish, Admiral."

A thin smile crossed Nagumo's face. *All developing as we planned. The key will be the American counterstrike. If we survive that, we have them.*

Midway Atoll
4 Jun 42 0615

"Ensign, stand down." Commander Van Brogan stood on the airstrip next to the PBY-5As that sat with their engines running and a load of torpedoes. Brogan gave the "cut" sign with his hand across his throat. "We have new orders. Scrap the torpedo run, unload those fish, and prepare for some scouting."

Ensign Everett Mason was clearly upset. "No torpedo attacks, Sir? We just gonna let 'em walk onto the island?"

"That's enough, Ensign! Our mission now is to find the Japanese strike force. We will worry about the landing craft later, but everything depends on finding those carriers, and you will get yourself up there as soon as possible."

"Yes, Sir," replied Mason, saluting. *Does he understand that unloading a torpedo takes at least ten minutes?*

"All right, you heard the Commander. Get these fish off and top off the tanks."

Over the carrier **Soryu**
4 Jun 42 0845

"Jeee-zus, skip, must be the whole Jap navy down there." Mason's bombardier/observer, Earl Dobson, counted and consulted his Navy silhouette charts. "That's the *Kaga* down there," he observed, confusing it with *Soryu*. "That one looks like the *Hiryu*, and I can't see those two in the distance, but there's two more."

Mason began transmitting immediately. "Midway, this is Alfalfa Six, repeat, Alfalfa Six. We have multiple enemy carriers — Main Body! Repeat, Main Body! - bearing three two zero, distance one seven five, speed two five. At least twenty ships. More in the distance, four carriers sighted. Repeat, four carriers sighted. Course one three five, speed two five." As he ended transmission, he rolled the Catalina over into the clouds. "Now, let's get out of here before the Zeros put us in the Pacific."

Ensign Mason had not seen the massive flight of Vals, Kates, and Zeros that had passed him to the north just 45 minutes earlier, headed straight for Midway. His radio message came as the first wave of Japanese attackers were pummeling the airstrip and harbor facilities on the atoll.

Carrier **Enterprise**
4 Jun 42 0853

"Admiral, reports from Midway are that the Japs failed to knock out the air strip." LeBoutiller stood with Halsey on the flag bridge, copying notes as he took messages from the radio room phone. "They did take out the PBY hangar, but those ducks can tie up almost anywhere. And we've got the location of the Jap fleet," he added, waving a sheet of paper.

Halsey slapped his thigh. "Gotcha," he exclaimed. He picked up the intercom to the captain's bridge. "Captain, launch all attack aircraft on the following coordinates. Do not wait to mass formations. Repeat, don't wait or we'll miss the chance. If they get their running rendezvous in, fine. Even if not, the Jap planes are hitting Midway now, and they won't have a lot of air cover and they'll have a bunch of out-of-gas Vals dropping into the sea." Halsey knew that the captain had listened to the same information, but relayed the coordinates of the enemy's last known position again as LeBoutiller rattled off them off.

On deck, Lieutenant Richard Best and Lieutenant Commander Eugene Lindsey already had their squadrons - 19 Dauntlesses and 14 Devastators—ready to lift off. Lieutenant James Gray's 27 Wildcats would follow. Aboard the Hornet, another 12 dive bombers under Lieutenant Commander Robert Johnson and 10 torpedo bombers under Lieutenant. Commander John Waldron simultaneously prepared to take off. Only a handful of planes, including all of the *Hornet*'s 27 fighters, five Devastators and six Dauntlesses, would remain. The *Hornet*'s Wildcats would provide combat air patrol over both carriers, while the remaining attack aircraft would remain below decks as the reserve in case follow-on attacks were needed.

Halsey already knew they would be needed, but didn't dare

send in everything. *I could sure use Spruance and the Yorktown now,* thought Halsey as he calculated the substantial disadvantage in aircraft that he faced. *Would have been better if the Army had waited to send in the Flying Forts and coordinated with us, but that's too much to ask.* "LeBoutiller, we are going to need Lieutenant Gallaher's 19 scout Dauntlesses, too."

"What's the status on Midway?" Halsey leaned over the bridge, looking in the direction of the atoll, which was well outside visual range.

"The airstrip has survived the first attack, Admiral. They only shot down a few Jap planes. Word from the Army is that the B-17s think they scored one hit on a Japanese cruiser, which probably means they didn't hit anything. Admiral, if I may be so bold, I don't think we're going to get much help from the air units on Midway. About all it's good for is to serve as a magnet for the Jap attacks. And their fighter planes—the Brewster Buffaloes?" He just shook his head and Halsey confirmed his thoughts with a disgusted look.

Suddenly a sailor interrupted. "Admiral, they said you'd want to see this immediately." He handed Halsey a note, saluted, and left. Halsey read the first few words, noticeably blanched, and leaned backward against the bulkhead, as though the strength just left his legs.

"Admiral?" said LeBoutiller, but Halsey only handed him the note.

SECRET
FM: CINCPAC TO: CTF 16
SUBJ: MATERIAL CONDITION USS YORKTOWN
EXPECT USS YORKTOWN TO BE UNAVAILABLE UNTIL 31 JULY 1942 DUE TO ENGINEERING CASUALTY. ABLE TO MAKE 9 KTS. ALL HANDS AND PHNSY WORKING TO MAKE READY FOR SEA.

"God." The word came out of LeBoutiller's mouth more as a plea than an exclamation. "We're outnumbered at least four to two." Halsey hung his head, took off his cap, and ran his hand through his hair again.

"This changes everything, Charlie. Dammit, I have no room for error now. None. If our first attack wave doesn't get them, we can't risk our reserves. Dammit!" Halsey smacked his fist against the bulkhead, causing the steersman to flinch. He thought for a moment. "All right. Charlie, send this message to Spruance: 'Continue repairs all deliberate speed at PH.' Then I want you to get a message to Nimitz. I'm sure he's informed of the situation, but remind him that we will need more carrier power here, in this theater, and I mean soon. He'll know what that means."

"You mean arm-twisting to get some ships from the Atlantic?"

"That's exactly what I mean, Charlie, but even if he can convince the brass tomorrow, it will be weeks before we can have more carriers in the Pacific besides *Saratoga*." He let out a loud sigh. "All right, it all rests with Best, Lindsey, Waldron, and Johnson. If those boys can do their job, the rest of it is irrelevant."

CHAPTER THIRTEEN

Over the **Soryu**
4 Jun 42 0916

Zero (Wikipedia)

Dick Best, still thinking the *Soryu* was the *Kaga*, was stunned at his good fortune. The carrier was recovering planes from the Midway attack and had not yet seen the Americans. "This is our chance! Let's hit 'em." He rolled the Dauntless over into its 70-degree dive, followed by 17 other bombers. One had already ditched due to an engine malfunction. *Still no Zeros, though. Damned odd.* Five- inchers from the Japanese cruisers and destroyers laced the sky with flak. But as Best started his dive he heard the last man in his formation shout over the radio, "Zeroes on our tails. Zeroes on our tails."

Now the *Soryu*'s machine guns and her own 5-inch guns opened up, every tenth 25 mm. shot a tracer that zipped by Best's canopy. How can they not hit me? "Chief, you watchin' the back door?" he said into the radio microphone as the tracers seemed now to be a steady ribbon zoning in on his aircraft.

Aviation Chief Radioman James Murray, Best's radioman/ gunner, called back, "Skip, they've already splashed three of our guys—they're just working their way down the list. They'll be on us in no time."

"We don't need much time." Best lined up the sight on the big red sun painted in the middle of the *Soryu*'s deck. "See how you like this, Tojo!" He pulled the release and his bomb sailed away just as a flak explosion rocked the aircraft sharply to the left. Best pulled out of the dive, only to hear Murray say, "Dammit. Wide left. Musta missed by twenty yards." Then, *"Behind us, Skip."* Two Zeros had banked in, coming straight at Best's tail. Murray blasted away, but one was near dead center to the rear and he couldn't line up a shot without clipping off his own tail. So Murray took the Zeke's wingman, higher but to the left. "I got him, Skip. I got him!" Smoke billowed out of the Zero, but the attacker to Best's immediate rear was riddling the Douglas with bullet holes, and it was starting to lose both fuel and hydraulics.

"We're gonna have to ditch, Chief. Keep him occupied for a few seconds. I don't care if you have to shoot the damn tail off!"

"Aye aye, Skip." Murray blasted away, and despite taking care not to shoot off his own tail, he watched fabric and metal chipping off nonetheless.

"Brace for impact." Best tried to level the Dauntless at the last minute but he'd lost too much speed, and it slammed into the Pacific like a hammer on an anvil. Murray felt a sharp pain in his lower back, then nothing, as water flooded in.

"Get out! Get out," screamed Best, already out of his harness and crawling over the side of the rapidly sinking plane. But Murray looked at him helplessly.

"Skip," the gunner cried, "I think my back is broke." Water filled up to his chest as Best swam to him, unhooking the harness. "Skip. Can't move anything below my waist."

"Come on, Chief, push yourself out. I'll pull you away from the plane, but I can't lift you out by myself. You gotta help!" But Murray was in shock, looking at his limp legs. The Dauntless was slipping beneath the waterline, and water swirled up to his neck. Then, as he gazed at Best with a look of horror and helplessness, the aircraft suddenly dropped below the waves with Murray inside.

Best's Mae West kept him above water, but the waves splashed enough into his lungs to keep him coughing. He stared upward, where the battle raged, and saw smoking trails marking the sky. In the distance, a single carrier appeared to be burning. At least we got one, you bastards.

Over the **Hiryu**
4 Jun 42 0927

As the Dauntlesses plunged into the sea, beset by Zeros from behind and anti-aircraft fire from below, the torpedo squadrons angled in for the low-level attack. John Waldron tried to maintain his composure, but the sight of so many American planes going down so quickly hit him like a fist in his gut. A single Dauntless had placed a bomb perfectly on the deck of the *Soryu*, which penetrated to her hangar deck, where her ordnance and fuel went up like a Roman candle; but it had cost the Americans an entire squadron. Now, Waldron's Devastators lined up for the *Hiryu*; and unlike the lead element of dive bombers, they knew the Zeros were above them.

"Almost got him," Waldron said to no one in particular, even though his radioman/gunner, Horace Dobbs kept focused on enemy planes to their rear. Waldron talked his way through his own runs. "Release in three, two, one ... Away!" Relieved of its weight, the Devastator lurched upward as Waldron banked out of the way, noting two other Devastators releasing at the same time. But the *Hiryu* had already taken evasive action, and he could tell that by the time the torpedoes reached her, the target would be much smaller. In fact, *Hiryu* was now sailing away from the fish at nearly 30 knots, meaning that if it got enough distance, the American Mark 13 would run out of steam before it reached its target.

"Get out of here," Waldron ordered his squadron, now down to four. "Dobbs, can you see if we got a hit?" Dobbs, who had no action moments earlier, now was fully occupied with the Zero bearing down.

"Don't think so, Mr. Waldron, but we've got problems. The Nips are everywhere." He cranked out five straight short bursts, to no effect. Taking one last look in the direction of the carrier, he saw no smoke and no explosions. "I think that's a negative, Commander." Then the Zero required his attention again.

"Keep him occupied, Dobbsie. I think I can climb us into that cloud cover there." But the climb slowed the fat Devastator even more, and Dobbs' twin .30 caliber guns were clattering non-stop now.

"He's getting too close, Commander. We ain't gonna make it." A burst ripped into the fuselage.

"Just a few more seconds. Hold 'em off, Dobbs." Waldron had to choose between a maneuver that might catch the Zero pilot by surprise and buy them time, or take the direct, shorter route straight to the clouds.

"We've only got one chance," shouted Waldron, as he banked the Devastator hard left. The Zero, still certain his prey was headed straight for the clouds, took a few critical seconds to adjust, and was by Waldron before he knew it. Waldron smiled, then grimly banked the Devastator toward the next nearest cloud accumulation. Although the Zero had re-acquired him, it was too far back, and his shots were going wide. As Waldron and Dobbs burst into the puffy cotton, Lieutenant Commander John Waldron, USN, let out an un-officer-like "Yeeee-haaaa!" He didn't know that only one other

Devastator from his squadron had escaped, and none had achieved hits.

Near the Imperial Japanese Carrier Kaga
4 Jun 42 0944

Lieutenant Commander Eugene Lindsey had already watched six of the 14 aircraft in his squadron go down, and Zeros were fast targeting the rest. Normally he would have coordinated his attack with Dick Best, but in the hopes of catching the Japanese with their fighters away and in the process of recovering planes, each unit had gone in on its own. Now, they were paying the price. Invisible rounds streamed at him and two penetrated the canopy, but he wasn't hurt and neither was Aviation Chief Radioman Charles Grenat, a short, squat Coloradan who worked on the railroads back home.

"Chief, I've got a stabilizer problem. The ailerons aren't responding. She's fighting me."

"Need to be a little closer, Sir. It's still too far — and at this angle and we'll miss by a mile. Hey, we've got company," announced Grenat. The gunner began firing at an attacking Zero. They both heard the thwack, thwack, thwack, thwack of lead ripping into the wing, and Lindsey seemed to lose whatever control he had left as the Devastator pitched upward sharply, right into a torrent of fire from the *Kaga* and her escorts.

"No good. We're too low to bail out, and I can't control her if we get any higher. We're ditching." Lindsey fought the joystick until the lumbering plane, slammed into the water still taking hits from the Zero. The Zero made one strafing pass, but it was not needed. Both Americans were dead on impact. Of Lindsey's remaining seven planes, two got close enough to release torpedoes; one actually was a direct hit, but the warhead did not explode. Lindsey's 14 planes, just like Waldron's 15, had failed to score a single hit.

The only hope now lay with Lt. Commander Bob "Ruff" Johnson's 12 Dauntlesses, as they screamed down toward the *Kaga*. They had come closer than anyone in launching a coordinated attack with Lindsey, although their squadrons were from two different carriers. Johnson benefited from exceptional protection by the *Hornet*'s Wildcats, who kept their tails clear of Zeros.

"Come on, Clay," Johnson said to his wingman, Ensign Clay Fisher. "The fighter boys are doing their bit. Let's put a couple down the funnel!"

Johnson activated his dive brakes, which splayed out with their more than 300 perforations that allowed a slipstream of 240 knots to pass through. It was a brilliant concept, envied by the Japanese, which permitted the bomber to maintain exceptional stability in its 70-degree dive. The Dauntless seemingly shook off flak and small anti-aircraft hits and within seconds, Johnson had the rising sun lined up. He had no sooner released than the *Kaga* seemed to pitch portside, and instead of hitting dead-on in the middle of the flight deck, and the bomb struck the aft end of the ship, setting off a large but non-fatal explosion. Fisher released his bomb immediately after Johnson, but it glanced off the ship's starboard side. The near-miss buckled some of the *Kaga*'s plates, but the damage was minor. "Those are negatives, Commander," reported Fisher to Johnson. "We hit her, but not enough to slow the Japs down. I think they can still even recover aircraft," and indeed, moments later, fire control crews had the aft fire under control and within minutes would be recovering fuel- starved airplanes. Another Dauntless from Johnson's squadron had been damaged, and, unable to reach the Kaga, put a bomb on the forecastle of the battleship Haruna, which also billowed black smoke. No other American planes scored hits that day. The surviving aircraft returned to the Enterprise and Hornet.

Aboard the **Akagi**
4 Jun 42 1017

"Admiral, the Americans have severely damaged the *Soryu* and the *Haruna,* and done light damage to the *Kaga*. However, flight operations on the *Kaga* have already been restored."

Nagumo nodded. "And the *Soryu*? Is she unsalvageable?"

"As of fifteen minutes ago, the fire control crews had not been able to contain the blaze, which is nearing the elevators. It's only a matter of time, Admiral, before the bomb storage areas go up."

Again, Nagumo solemnly nodded. "Very well, authorize Captain Ryusaku to abandon ship. Instruct him he is ordered to leave the vessel. We are about to achieve a great, great victory, and I will not minimize it by allowing my captains to go down with their ships."

Somewhat surprised, the ensign nevertheless repeated the order, and concluded, "Yes, Sir."

Even though he had officially transferred his flag back to the *Akagi* for operations with the *Kido Butai* (First Carrier Striking Force), Nagumo always requested permission of the captain of the *Akagi* to enter his bridge. "It is my honor, Admiral, please." Nagumo stood in the front of the cramped space, with a half-dozen other officers, and knew that in the next hour much of the war in the Pacific might be decided. Fifteen minutes earlier he had received vectors from the scout planes sent out early that day. They had spotted the American carriers northwest of Midway. In fact, they were so far northwest that Admiral Kurita would run right into them, rather than envelop them ... if Nagumo's strike force didn't destroy them first.

"Captain Aoki, have you recovered all your aircraft yet?"

The diminutive Aoki, a veteran of several campaigns and one of Nagumo's best carrier commanders, replied, "Yes, Sir. In fact, we will have the last of the fighters refueled in the next twenty minutes." Anticipating Nagumo's next move, Aoki asked, "Should I send for Commander Genda?"

Nagumo smiled. "You read me like a book, Captain. Yes, and get Commander Fuchida up here as well. He seems to have special insight into American tactics."

Aoki immediately tasked a sailor to locate the airmen, who reported to the bridge within a few minutes, still in their flight suits. Nagumo motioned to the chart table and gave them the last-known vectors of the American carriers. "The Americans have utterly failed in their attack. Now is the time to destroy them. Commander Genda, you will take all remaining aircraft to this spot," he slapped the chart northwest of Midway, "and finish off the American fleet. You have prepared for this, have you not?"

"*Hai!*" Genda exclaimed, and a smile crossed his face.

"Commander Fuchida, do you have anything to add? Have the Americans adapted to your tactics in any way?"

"No, Admiral-san. If I may ...?"

Genda raised an eyebrow and started to reprimand Fuchida, but Nagumo waved him off.

"Continue, Commander. You have a question?"

"Sir, it is not my place, but is it wise to leave an air base in our rear? We know their bombers and torpedo planes are not a threat to your ships, but if they know when my aircraft are returning, we could fly into an ambush at the very time we are low on fuel."

Nagumo rubbed his chin and nodded. "Good point, Commander. I shall suppress any activity from that air base with naval gunfire from Hosogaya's invasion force. He has enough guns to keep them pinned down. Does that reassure you?"

Fuchida nodded. "*Hai!*"

Then it was Genda's turn. "Sir?" "You, too, Commander? What is it?"

"Sir, my concern was less for my flyers than for your fleet left without air cover. Suppose for a moment our intelligence was wrong, and the other American carrier appears. Are you not committing all of your air cover to escort our strike force?"

"I am. As soon as your force departs, I will have the reserve fighters brought up. At the same time, I am ordering forward aircraft from the carriers *Ryujo* and *Junyo*, as well as Hosogaya's air patrol carrier, the *Zuiho*, for a combat air patrol around Midway." Fuchida and Genda exchanged concern looks. On paper, it provided the necessary airplanes, but in reality, it entrusted the protection of the fleet to the air crews from two other carriers almost 50 miles away. Their time-on-station would be cut as they guzzled gas getting there and returning, and they could not land on any of the fleet carriers without completely disrupting the flow of rearming and refueling those carriers' own aircraft. Still, Nagumo's mind was made up, and they said nothing. "Now, commanders, if you are finished reviewing my strategic plan, I suggest you go to your airplanes and win this war."

The two aviators snapped to attention and saluted, then ran off. Aoki chuckled. "Aviators! Such know-it-alls."

Nagumo smiled. "They asked intelligent questions.

They are two of our best. We are wasting them by having them drop bombs on the Americans."

Aoki gave only an affirmative "Uuummmmm," and nodded. *Now, if Admiral Halsey behaves as is his character, he will move forward rather than pull back, and we will have him.*

Midway Island
4 Jun 42 1035

"Commander Ford, get down!" Lieutenant Cozner jerked

Ford down into a slit trench just an instant before an incoming shell covered them with sand. Undeterred, Ford popped up, scraped the dirt off his lens and trained his camera on the devastation. "Yer some piece of work, Sir. You're going to get us both killed."

Ford ignored the comment. "Looks like they're laying down fire on the airstrip." Midway's airfield, some 300 yards away, was an inferno, as explosion after explosion swept the length of the two runways. Ford looked at Cozner. "Seems the Japs don't want you guys taking off or landing anything."

Cozner snorted. "That's the least of our worries. See those ships there?" He pointed to the bobbing silhouettes a few thousand yards off shore. "They're landing ships, and they will be coming closer, and when they do, we're gonna have our hands full with a whole invasion force. Between you and me, I don't know if we can stop 'em. By the way, Commander, you did a good job in that movie 'Drums Along the Mohawk.'"

Ford looked at him in astonishment. "I thought you said you hadn't seen any movies."

The lieutenant shrugged. "So I lied. Some of 'em. 'Young Mr. Lincoln' was a helluva movie. Same thing with 'Stagecoach.' That Wayne fella is a man's man, that's for sure. But I didn't care for 'Grapes of Wrath' too much. I don't particularly like that actor, Fonder? Fonda? Did hear that he enlisted in the Navy, though, so guess that makes him okay."

"Where'd you get the time to see movies, Lieutenant?"

Cozner smiled coyly. "Well, I did have a girl before this mess. We were kinda serious. Anyway, she liked Marines, and she liked movies, and I was determined to give her what she wanted." He now sported a wide grin. Another shell burst nearby, causing both men to duck and cover their heads as dirt and sand rained down on them.

"I can't imagine any girl would take to you, Lieutenant. Must be your taste in movies." Ford then smiled at him and the Marine grinned back through the dirt.

Ford reached into his bag and took out a telephoto lens, then scanned the horizon. "Seems there are some big boys out there blasting away at us. I take it that means our air attacks weren't successful."

Another shell exploded just feet from them, and Cozner let

out a groan. His arm was perforated with shrapnel, and hung limp at his side.

"Crap!" Ford put his camera away. "Come on, Lieutenant, you need to get to a corpsman."

Cozner, in shock and his arm shattered, mumbled only, "tell Sergeant Perkins he's in charge ... Tell Perkins."

"I'll tell him, the minute I get you to the hospital."

Ford put his arm around the burley lieutenant and they moved 30 feet when another explosion overhead covered them in debris. The two staggered out of the tree line and Ford realized that to reach the hospital they had to cross the airstrip, which was under heavy fire. "Come on, Marine, we're going to have to jog it." Half-pushing, half-carrying the lieutenant, Ford managed to get Cozner across the field of fire to the hospital, which was already jammed with two dozen wounded men, some of them badly mauled. A medic gestured him to a vacant cot, and Cozner sat down. Ford said only, "His arm ..." and the corpsman nodded, held up a finger to Cozner as if to say, "one minute," and disappeared. Cozner, still groggy, looked at Ford.

"Go take yer pictures, Ford. Show America what this war's all about." Cozner gave him a thumbs up, then yelled, "Wait a minnit, Commander." The filmmaker stopped and Cozner added, "Make it as good as 'Stagecoach.' Make it good." Ford felt a tear welling up, and he obediently bobbed his head, and jogged out of the hospital, back across the inferno that was now the southern part of the airfield, and toward the beach to find Sergeant Perkins, and the war.

CHAPTER FOURTEEN

South of Midway, aboard the destroyer USS **Balch**
4 Jun42 1053

Akagi "Val" (Wikipedia)

The bridge lookout had his binoculars trained to the north, toward Midway. "What the hell do you think you're doing?" roared the *Balch's* XO, Commander Harold Tiemroth. "Train your eyes to the east, right now! We aren't sent out here to be spectators. Admiral Halsey is concerned that the Japs may try an end run, and we are it until the *Hammann* gets here tomorrow. I damn well don't want to be called into Halsey's office because we let his fleet get blindsided. Now stay sharp!" The seaman simultaneously replied "Aye aye, Sir," and focused his attention to the east, where, sure enough, he thought he saw something.

"Captain, objects on the horizon, port beam. They may be ships." He pointed to the northeast, where first a pair of destroyers, then a pair of cruisers, then finally a battleship came into view.

"Shottlemeir, radio Admiral Halsey immediately. Inform him we have sighted large enemy force south- southeast of Midway, speed twenty-five knots, heading due east. And tell him the Balch will retire at the same speed, remaining exactly at this distance so as to keep him informed of the force's location. Is that clear?"

"Aye aye, Captain, clear." Lt. Commander Bill Shottlemeir, Tiemroth's communications officer, reached for the handset. "Helmsman, come about one eight zero. All engines ahead full." *We've got the whole Jap navy coming, and we're right in front of it. Help me, Jesus!*

Over the **Enterprise**
4 Jun 42 1057

Wave after wave of Vals and Kates swooped in, defying Halsey's screen to shoot them down, bearing straight for the *Hornet* and *Enterprise*. American Wildcats, alerted to the incoming force by radar and by their own scouts, riddled the Japanese, but there were too many Zeros for them to handle. One by one, the American fighters were overwhelmed or pulled away. Already the cruiser *Vincennes* and the destroyer *Gwin* were dead in the water, having intercepted torpedoes meant for the carriers.

A fresh radio message in hand, LeBoutiller entered the navigation bridge where Admiral Halsey was watching the battle with Captain Murray. "Admiral, this just came from the *Balch*," he said. It seems we have a force coming in from the south. Do you suppose the Japs are trying to slip in on us from behind?" He was interrupted by a flag radio messenger with another message.

"Sir, we just got this. I was told to bring it to you without writeup." The messenger handed LeBoutiller a carbon "flimsy," taken directly from a radio operator's typewriter in flag radio. LeBoutiller returned the messenger's salute and quickly scanned the rough copy.

"Admiral," announced LeBoutiller, "this dispatch is from the USS *Trout*. It's kind of garbled, sir. Seems they were on the surface sending this when a Jap patrol plane hit him, but it says there's a force coming through the sector where the subs are. Apparently a helluva battle sir." He looked outside as a Val screamed in at an odd angle. He's not on a dive-bombing run! "Admiral, get down!" LeBoutiller dove at Halsey, who was standing by the captain's chair, knocking both him and the captain down. The Val barely missed the island, its wing cracking off against the edge as the plane cartwheeled into the ocean.

Halsey stood up, brushed himself off, took off his cap and ran his hand over his hair. He cast a glance at Murray. "You okay, George?" Murray looked angry, and nodded. "Damn close one."

Halsey looked at LeBoutiller. "Now, you were saying about this dispatch?"

"Sir, the garbled message we got from the submarine *Trout* was that it was under attack, but that a Japanese force of heavy ships, including battleships, was coming through the sector patrolled by our subs. Its time reads ..." the ensign looked at the clock, "eight minutes ago."

"Well, Admiral," observed Murray, whose attention had remained focused on the battle, "our boys are giving them hell, that's for sure. But it's only a matter of time before one of them gets through. If we don't get hit, though, I can have all the reserves and the re-armed scout squadrons ready for a counter attack in thirty minutes."

"Good job, George. What do you gentlemen think?"

Murray, still directing the carrier in battle, ordered the helms-men to turn 30 degrees to port, then he answered Halsey. "It's clear they're trying to flank us, Admiral, and not just on one side, but completely envelop us. They must have thrown the whole Jap navy into this attack, because we just had a dispatch a few minutes ago saying they were laying down fire on Midway and that landing craft were in the water. Now, you don't launch an amphibious invasion without some air cover, no matter what you hope the outcome of the battle at sea is, so I'm guessing ..."

" ... that the Japs have more than the four carriers we already confirmed out there? That's what I'm thinking too. Several more."

"Admiral," Murray, was pointing. "Over there. The *Hornet*!" Despite the risk, all three officers moved outside the pilot house to look at the savage explosions on the *Hornet*. "My God! She must have taken three or four hits!" Shaking their heads, they returned to the interior of the bridge, as Murray continued to direct the *En-terprise*. Halsey was watching the battle when LeBoutiller shouted and pointing, "Over there!" Halsey trained his glasses on a pair of Kates, leveling off on a bearing straight for the *Enterprise*. "Captain, you've got torpedo planes to port, three o'clock and getting ready to release." A burst of fire tore the leader apart but the wingman stayed on course and released.

"You've got a fish in the water, George!" just as the warning claxons went off.

Murray immediately ordered "Hard starboard rudder! En-gines full ahead!" The helmsman spun the wheel, causing the ship to turn directly into the torpedo's path. Halsey froze as he watched the torpedo head   straight for the massive carrier, then went out of his sight, disappearing under the side of the vessel. A massive "CLUNG" rang out as the torpedo bounced off the hull. It failed to explode, malfunctioned as it spun twice in a circle, then petered out.

"Jesus, that was close, George!" Halsey redirected his atten-tion to the *Hornet*, which now was listing badly. The intercom from radio central rang and LeBoutiller picked up the handset.

"Admiral, Hornet is sinking. Captain Mitscher is transferring to the *Portland*, and he can't get any of his aircraft off." He had to yell into Halsey's ear due to the incessant drum of anti-aircraft fire outside.

Halsey swept his cap off. "Dammit. It's bad enough we lose

a carrier, but we need *Hornet*'s planes." LeBoutiller had already calculated the numbers.

"Sir," the lieutenant yelled again, "assuming none of his
planes got off, that reduces our force by a two dozen Dauntlesses
and five Devastators."

"Twenty-nine aircraft. In a battle like this, that's the difference between victory and defeat," Halsey added, in a voice so low
neither LeBoutiller nor Murray heard him.

The same sailor who had delivered the earlier dispatch from
the radio room now reappeared. Again, he saluted LeBoutiller and
delivered his message. LeBoutiller looked at the sailor. "Why don't
they just call these up?" Seaman Pellagrano replied, "Sir, the IC is
out from radio central. So they sent me to deliver these in person."
Then he smiled a gap-toothed smile. "Between you and me sir," he
yelled, "it's wearing me out!" LeBoutiller grinned, and jerked his
head as to dismiss the seaman, who saluted and left.

"Admiral, another message from one of the subs up north.
Seems they nailed two more Jap heavy ships. They think one is the
battleship *Fuso*. They got it good, sir. It's sinking."

It was good news, but not good enough to offset the peril-
ous position Halsey's task force was now in. "George, what do you
think? These bastards are trying to envelop us?" Murray only started to answer when the scream of a smoking Val started to drown
them out. Through the pilot house window they saw the plane
heading straight for them. "Down!" Halsey screamed, and they hit
the deck as a massive explosion rocked the *Enterprise*. Murray was
immediately up, on the intercom to damage control central himself,
his bridge crew back at their stations. Within minutes they learned
that a suicidal Val pilot, out of bombs, had plunged his plane deliberately into the carrier. A gaping hole was torn out of the island and
some 200 sailors were dead. Firefighting crews were already containing the blaze, and fortunately there was no damage done to the
flight deck. Halsey looked out, through the plumes of smoke, to see
sailors dashing everywhere, pulling hoses, pushing airplanes out of
the way, and often ducking when a Zero or Val would swoop by to
strafe. "Now, as I was saying, George, what do you think?"

Murray frowned, first looking toward the burning, listing
Hornet, then to the aerial battles going on above. "Admiral, you
know me. I'm not one to run from a fight. We do have enough planes
here to launch one more counterattack. We might get lucky and get

ourselves another carrier. We might not."

"Go on, George." Halsey, for the first time all day, really wanted a cigarette.

"We might think about saving what is left, Admiral. If it's true that the Japs are coming in like pincers, we stand to lose not only the *Enterprise* and her planes, but the entire task force. And Midway is likely already gone. We can't protect it anymore."

Halsey slumped, then looked at LeBoutiller. "Charlie, do you concur?"

LeBoutiller glumly nodded, and spoke loudly, over the din of gunfire outside. "I do, Admiral. It looks like Yamamoto may have outguessed us on this. He rolled the dice, sent everything he had, and now simply has us by attrition. Without *Yorktown*, we just don't have enough planes. And if we direct another strike at Nagumo's carriers, and get hit from the south by a force of battleships, well, we won't have enough air cover. *Enterprise* might as well be a big, fat oiler in that case. Especially if they have even one carrier in that group."

Every fighting urge inside Halsey said "attack," but his common sense and the tactical situation screamed retreat. "Very well, gentlemen. Charlie, get this sent to all ships: Task Force Sixteen will withdraw immediately, due east, maximum speed. As soon as this attack is over, I want all our strike aircraft ready, but nothing other than scouts are to leave our deck until we're sure what we're facing. Maintain steady contact with the *Balch*. Charlie, communicate my regrets to Midway. We did our best, but if they bitch, they can tell it to the crew of the *Hornet* and the *Vincennes*. That's it, gentlemen. Break off as soon as possible."

"Aye aye, Admiral," echoed Murray. LeBoutiller turned into the chart room to draft the orders, only to be interrupted by the Seaman Pellagrano again. Handing the dispatch to LeBoutiller, he saluted and smiled, bracing himself in the doorway as the carrier pitched.

LeBoutiller shouted to Halsey and Murray, "The sub boys are doing a helluva job. They got another battleship, dead in the water." He dismissed the seaman, who again flashed his gap-toothed smile.

"Why is that man always so damned happy?" groused Halsey. He and LeBoutiller walked into the chart room. "Anyway, if these reports are accurate, whatever was coming our way from the north has been somewhat compromised. Maybe the Japs will slow down there some. Maybe they'll be spooked. It's that force in the south that concerns me now," jabbing his finger in the rough area where the Balch was patrolling. "They've got the angle on us, and I'd bet my bottom dollar Yamamoto himself is in charge of that group."

Before LeBoutiller could act, Halsey held up his hand. "Wait up, Charlie." The Admiral closed his eyes and thought a moment, despite the cacophony outside. He opened his eyes as a near-miss threw up a massive geyser whose peak came up nearly five decks to the flag bridge.

"All right, Charlie, here's what we're going to do. Message to Tom Kinkaid," and Halsey dictated the following orders:

SECRET FM: CTF 16
TO: COM CRUISER GRP
4Jun42

DETACH ATLANTA AND NEW ORLEANS TO TF16 CRUDIV 6 TO MAINTAIN CURRENT POSITION NORTHWEST OF TF 16
ENGAGE IF ENEMY ENCOUNTERED. PREVENT ENEMY MOVEMENT NORTH OF TF 16
REPEAT AS NECESSARY BUT MAINTAIN, REPEAT, MAINTAIN POSITION NORTHWEST OF TF 16

That's it, Charlie. Send it."

LeBoutiller dispatched a sailor to the com room. "Now, Charlie, I want you to find out where the *Hammann* is. When you do, send this," and the admiral dictated a second set of orders:

SECRET FM: CTF 16
TO: USS HAMMANN
4Jun42

USS BALCH RETREATING YOUR BEARING AHEAD OF ENEMY TF RENDEZVOUS WITH BALCH AND DESRON 6 AT ..."

Halsey moved around the map and swept off some of the glass from the chart room window that had shattered when the Val hit.

".. POINT SPADES ALL SHIPS THEN ASSUME BEARING 240 DEGREES TRUE AT MAXIMUM SPEED DO NOT, REPEAT, DO NOT AVOID OBSERVATION

BY ENEMY FIGHT IF ENGAGED"

"Sir." LeBoutiller scribbled off more orders and sent them, then looked up in disbelief. "You want the destroyers to form a battle line against cruisers and battleships if they are engaged? Yamamoto probably has the *Yamato* out there."

"Not exactly, Lieutenant. I'm hoping it won't come to that, but they may have to buy us some time. Okay, now, I need an immediate estimate of where our four oilers stand with fuel." LeBoutiller quickly stepped through the chart room into flag radio. He returned in minutes.

"Sir, Dewey is still near capacity. The *Monssen* and *Platte* are at half, and *Cimarron*, which just topped off Kinkaid's cruisers, is damn near empty."

"Very well. Send this to the Cimarron, Platte, and Monssen," and Halsey provided yet another set of orders:

SECRET FM: CTF 16
TO: USS CIMARRON PLATTE AND MONSSEN
4 Jun 42
RENDEZVOUS WITH DESRON 6 AT POINT SPADES AND REPORT TO COMDESRON 6
PROCEED WITH ALL DELIBERATE SPEED

And as soon as you send that, send this to the rest of the Task Force:

SECRET FM: CTF 16
TO: TF 16 AND 17.2(CRUISER DIV6, COMDESRON 1,DESRON 6, CI-MARRON, PLATTE, MONSSEN EXEMPTED)
4 Jun 42
PROCEED ALL DELIBERATE SPEED TO POINT ACES.
AVOID ENGAGEMENT IF POSSIBLE
STRICT RADIO SILENCE IN EFFECT

Halsey folded his hands and tapped one finger nervously. "Let's see if that slows down Yamamoto." "What are you thinking, Admiral?" LeBoutiller asked. "Do you plan to engage one of these prongs?"

"Not unless I have to, Charlie. I doubt if Nagumo personally is in charge of that northern prong. I figure he's still on the west side of Midway with his carriers. Either way, the carriers will have to go around the atoll. That will take some time. Kinkaid might be able to slow down that force in the north, and it's already taken some damage from the subs. That leaves the southern pincer. I'm betting, by the way, that Yamamoto is heading up that one. He might have a carrier, but probably not a fleet carrier. Most of the Japs' air is wrapped around Midway. This isn't a battle we can win right now. But if we have to engage, I might need to buy some time in our retreat. Either way, the destroyers are going to have an important mission. I promised Nimitz I wouldn't leave Pearl Harbor defenseless, and by damn, I intend to keep that promise. We were badly outnumbered today. It's tragic, but true; we traded Yamamoto carrier for carrier again. In the short run, that won't cut it. But both he and I know in the long run, he loses every time we do that. No, Charlie, we don't have any options right now. If they are coming in from both the north and south, the worst thing we can do is let them encircle us and fight them both at once. So if we have to take on one pincer, it might as well be the one closest to Pearl, but I don't even want to risk that if I can avoid it. There are too many unknowns with three separate groups out there. Let's get closer to home. Who knows? Maybe the repair crews can work a miracle on the *Yorktown*, or maybe we can get within range of Hawaii's air cover."

They both knew neither of those options were likely. The Japanese had the angle. Unless he could offset the angle that the southern force had on him, Halsey might have to engage one fleet. And if the Japanese could block their way, the second pincer would fall on his rear.

"Admiral, if the reports from the *Balch* are correct about the speed of that force, though, they'll be able to get between us and Hawaii. They have too much of a head start."

"Charlie, that's why the destroyers and the oilers are going on a little mission."

LeBoutiller took that as a statement of confidence, saluted and left. Halsey wasn't smiling. He lit another cigarette. *We're still going to need a miracle.*

CHAPTER FIFTEEN

Ray Spruance (Wikipedia)

The Battleship **Yamato,** *100 miles south of Midway*
4 Jun 42 1120

Yamamoto had ordered Kurita's northern task force and his own southern force to maintain radio silence during their pincer movement, but their radiomen maintained a tight listening watch for any sign of enemy activity to the north. Yamamoto knew about the loss of the *Soryu,* the *Fuso,* and the damage to the *Haruna,* as well as of the Americans' loss of the *Hornet* and *Vincennes.* He also knew, unfortunately, that he had been spotted. That damnable American destroyer remained too far ahead for his guns, or to waste precious air assets on. It was like a herald with a lantern, running through the villages, screaming "The barbarians are upon us!" Worse, the loss of the *Fuso* indicated that the American submarine patrols have detected our northern pincer. We have no element of surprise, either north or south, now. Can we count on Halsey to be aggressive? Does it matter? We already have the angle on him. He cannot reach Pearl Harbor.

Sagata was handed several dispatches and reports of the combat at Midway, confirming what Yamamoto had already known. They had exchanged carriers, and the Americans had lost a cruiser and the Japanese, the *Fuso.* On the surface, an even exchange. By dawn tomorrow, Hosogaya will have completed his assault on Midway Atoll and possibly have its airstrip functioning.

"Is the American destroyer still pacing us?" Yamamoto asked Sagata, even though he knew the answer.

"As of last report, it was still out of range of even our longest-range guns, and maintaining a speed and bearing as to stay directly in front of us, but we have lost contact."

Lost contact? It has clearly alerted Halsey. Does he know he's being enveloped? Does he care? Does he think with a single carrier he can defeat three? Or does he think Midway's airfield is still operational? Is there another factor I have not considered? "Sagata, I want you to order every patrol plane we have into the air. I want them to sweep in an arc to our east-southeast. If Halsey has any surprises, I want to know about them."

"Immediately, Admiral." Sagata hustled off. Each cruiser and battleship had several seaplane scouts, and the light carrier accompanying Yamamoto's fleet had five aircraft capable of long-range reconnaissance. They would all be airborne within the hour.

I do not think you can escape this trap, Admiral Halsey. We are too far in your rear.

Midway Atoll
5 Jun 42 1500

"God in heaven! There must be a hundred ships out there." John Ford scanned the horizon with his camera, despite the shells bursting behind him. At least 25 initial invasion craft were inbound, and Midway's heavy guns were already blasting away, spewing massive geysers among the vessels. One boat went up in a fireball. Through his telephoto lens, Ford could see the barges and discerned body parts flying from the explosion. Two Marine privates peeked over the edge of their foxholes, and one double-checked the loading mechanism of his .30 caliber air-cooled machine gun while he sighted in the landing craft. Japanese landing barges could carry up to 100 soldiers, but only as far as the reef, where they had to unload under fire from Midway's defenders, then wade ashore. The Americans would get several minutes' worth of free shots at the attackers—when they could dodge Admiral Kurita's cruisers that provided fire support. One of the Marine privates suddenly noticed Ford. Jerking his head backwards, he shouted, "You might want to take your camera a little farther back, Sir," he yelled. "It's gonna get mighty hot here in a minute."

Ford acknowledged the suggestion, but shook his head. "I'm staying right here, Private. Someone's got to film this stuff." The private just shrugged. On came the landing craft, now stopping at the reef and disgorging their troops, when Ford felt someone slide in beside him in the narrow foxhole. Lt. Able Cozner, his arm bandaged and taped to his side, wielded his .45. He still appeared to be slightly in shock.

"What? Thought you'd seen the last of me, Commander? Well, whatcha lookin' at, Sir? Film the war!" Cozner waved his pistol toward the enemy.

Ford smiled and resumed filming. "Lieutenant, did anyone tell you that you are wounded?"

"Nope," replied Cozner. "Nobody."

"Did anyone tell you that you are crazy?" "Yep. Everybody."

A burst of machine-gun fire raked the dirt right in front of the foxhole, and the landing forces closed rapidly, despite the chest-deep lagoon water. Farther to the north, Ford could see hundreds of Japanese marines pouring out of the boats—and dozens falling. Their numbers, however, were overwhelming, blowing right through the mine fields on the beaches, through the barbed wire, and seemingly brushing off the defensive fire. Already, Americans in the foxholes were being overrun, battling backwards across the sand, using the craters dug out by Japanese gunfire as pre-formed foxholes. Naval gunfire had pockmarked the airfield by now, and most of the remaining Midway-based aircraft, even those in protective shelters, were in pieces or on fire.

Ford absorbed this scene in a matter of seconds, before he felt Cozner tapping him on the shoulder with his .45. "Time to pull out, Commander Ford." He pointed to the wave of Japanese infantry slogging ashore, and the Marine casualties that were mounting all around him. "Pull back!" he ordered, and a dozen Marines jumped out of their defensive positions and ran to the small trench, where they had prepared more positions. And all the while, more Japanese craft kept arriving, discharging more troops. Hopeless, thought Ford. Too many. We can't hold. We'll be overrun within an hour. No sooner had Ford again started to train his camera on the beach area than Cozner yelled at the team repositioning the .30 caliber machine gun.

"What are you waiting for? Get that sucker firing!" he bellowed, when suddenly his chest exploded in a gush of blood, and five Japanese soldiers, who had flanked the machine-gun team, shot the Marines. Four more were immediately on top of Ford, who raised his hands with his camera. One soldier cocked his head, gave a quizzical look at the camera, then knocked it out of Ford's hand with the butt of his rifle and rammed his bayonet in John Ford's stomach. The four moved on to the next trench, firing at the Marines who returned fire from their positions, ignoring Ford as he stared at his wound in shock at the life pouring out of his body.

Naval Station Pearl Harbor, Headquarters CINCPAC
5 Jun 42 1645

Nimitz rested his head in his hands, as Spruance re-read the dispatch from Midway. Obviously sent in haste, it lacked even the minimum normal coding and routing classifications:

**MIDWAY BEING OVERRUN; AIRFIELD OUT; RESISTANCE BEING ELIM-
INATED; DETONATING DYNAMITE
(SHANNON)**

Colonel Harold Shannon, USMC, had taken over command of the ground forces on Midway in October 1941. Under his orders, the garrison had booby-trapped so much of the atoll with dynamite that American forces were concerned they'd blow themselves up accidentally. If the colonel was actually blowing up large portions of the two islands, the situation was indeed hopeless. Shannon's message came on the heels of Halsey's earlier radio transmission relating the Hornet's loss. Halsey was withdrawing to the east, but gave few details.

Nimitz wasn't melodramatic, but his voice cracked with emotion. "Nearly a total disaster, Ray. It's my fault. I sent them out there without the *Yorktown.* I thought we could ambush the Japs. Now they may be on our doorstep, and they may still trap Halsey."

Admiral Sprucance and Captain Edwin Layton, Nimitz's Fleet Intelligence Officer, read the dispatches. "Chet," replied Spruance firmly, "you did exactly the right thing, and for all we know, Bill has done exactly the right thing. We had to engage them at Midway, and we simply couldn't wait on *Yorktown.* There just wasn't any choice. God love Halsey! I thought he'd stay on offense despite your order, but he surprised me — he fought against his own tendencies and may well save the fleet. We still don't know what's happening out there, but if the subs were actually intercepting a sweeping pincer movement to the north, Halsey did the right thing. Now we need to know what's happening with that fleet that our destroyer is watching."

He looked up. "I suppose you're right, Ray. We've still got *Yorktown,* which might be ready the day after tomorrow. I cabled Washington, and King met with FDR personally and got *Wasp* transferred over. She'll be here in two weeks, maybe sooner. But if they get Halsey and *Enterprise* ... well, that would be demoralizing as all hell. I don't know how we can hold Hawaii with just one carrier."

"You think Yamamoto's trying to encircle Halsey? If the destroyer's position plots are any indication, they have the angle on him. He can't get out of their net. Then Yamamoto will head straight for Hawaii—he'll have the men, the ships, and perhaps for the only time in this war, he's going to have the oil."

"No question, Ray. He'll push on to see what we've got here. But if he doesn't get Halsey's force? What then?" Nimitz stood up and paced back and forth.

A staff yeoman entered and handed Layton several more messages from Halsey. Layton's brow furrowed. "Something wrong, Captain?" Nimitz asked, "Or I guess I should say, after the way this day has gone something else wrong?"

Layton gave Nimitz the messages. "Admiral, if Halsey is doing what I think he's doing, he knows the Japs have the angle on him and he's going to give them something to think about." Nimitz read the messages, then re-read them, then a quizzical look crossed his face.

"Ed," Nimitz said, "is there any way we can give Bill a little help?"

"Those destroyers will be under radio silence, Admiral."

"I know that. But they don't need to send, only receive. And they really don't even have to actually receive, do they?"

Layton started to understand. "We could have our nearest PBYs start transmitting to the destroyers, Admiral. They could send the last known position of the southern pincer."

"Do it," ordered Nimitz. "I want as much radio traffic going in to that zone as you can manage."

CHAPTER SIXTEEN

Destroyer **Balch**, *300 miles southeast of Midway*
5 Jun 42 1700

Akagi flight deck (Wikipedia)

"Captain, we're starting to get all sorts of PBY radio traffic reporting the position of the Japanese fleet, which we already know. It's like they're shining a big spotlight on us, almost like they're trying to give our position away." The ship's second in command, Lt. Commander Shottlemeir, scanned a number of radio messages just brought to the bridge. He obviously wasn't happy with the situation.

"That's exactly what it is, Mr. Shottlemeir," said Tiemroth.

The lieutenant commander couldn't contain himself. "Well, that's goddam brilliant!"

Tiemroth disregarded his second-in-command's outburst. "How long until we rendezvous with DESRON 6?"

"Approximately two hours and twenty minutes, Captain. Oh, and a minute ago this came in—why is Admiral Halsey giving us all the oilers?"

Tiemroth had initially been baffled when Halsey detached the task force's oilers to him. Now, he was starting to understand. *Over four hours ago, Halsey instructs me to come about and head due north, right behind the Jap fleet and barely outside their gunnery range. It's a miracle we weren't spotted. Now, he's going to have all his destroyers and most of the oilers in one spot. It'll be a stroke of genius if it works, but if the Japs figure it out early, every ship here will be at the bottom of the Pacific by tonight, and God only knows how Halsey will get home without fuel.*

Headquarters, 6th Marine Defense Battalion, Midway Atoll
5 Jun 42 1900

Private Yaguro Ichi had fought his way ashore and hadn't stopped for several hours. His pants were still soaked, and he still had sand in his shoes. None of the troops had eaten since last night—or if they had eaten some fish in the landing craft, they promptly puked it up in the choppy water. His canteen was empty and his mouth was parched. Four hours earlier, his best friend, Ichii—soldiers called them "the twins" because their names were similar—had been blown apart by an American grenade, and sometime during the day he'd encountered the oddest sight—an American with a camera instead of a rifle. *On this beach? Today? What was that man thinking?* Ichi's sergeant had bayoneted the American, and they moved on. An hour ago, he had fought through several defensive positions, finally breaking into the atoll's communications center.

It was virtually empty. The Japanese found an abandoned facility. *Or maybe they just underestimated the ferocity and speed of our attack,* thought Ichi. No matter. As Ichi and six other men burst in, the radios were unattended. They appear to have destroyed the codebooks, but he nevertheless thought the materials important, and he turned them over to his commanders, who, to cover their own backsides, decided to turn them over to their commanders. Before long, the materials—which contained several un-sent messages from Midway---were handed over to Admiral Yamamoto's intelligence chief, who decided to inform the Admiral.

The **Yamato,** *320 miles southeast of Midway*
5 Jun 42 2010

"It is not clear how we came by this message, Admiral. Apparently our infantry captured the American radio bunker intact, and this message was being transmitted at the time. Perhaps the Americans did not know Midway had fallen." Sagata had given Yamamoto the translation of the captured radio message just minutes earlier.

Yamamoto studied the message and shook his head. "PBYs transmitting our coordinates. But why? The destroyers already knew where we were ..."

" ... unless the destroyer has broken contact. Admiral," Sagata suggested, "We should reestablish contact with that destroyer. Something tells me it is no longer heading for Pearl Harbor. What if the destroyer was not there to pace us as much as to lure us away from the real position of the American fleet?"

"You mean slip in behind us and escape, Captain? Unlikely." *Unlikely, yet exactly what the aggressive Halsey might do — come in behind us.* Yamamoto thought for a moment, and reconsidered. "We cannot take a chance, however. Unfortunately, we won't be able to see anything until morning. If you have two pilots who are experts at night flying, start them immediately searching a grid one hundred miles to our north and northwest."

"*Hai!* Should we maintain present speed and course?"

Yamamoto nodded. "We have no choice. Until we know otherwise, I will still assume Halsey is trying to extract his fleet directly toward Pearl Harbor."

"Point Spades," 200 miles southeast of Midway
5 Jun 42 2213

"Oilers *Platte, Cimarron*, and *Monssen* will rendezvous with us in less than an hour, Captain. *Balch* is already here, and *Hammann* will arrive by twenty-four hundred hours." Commander Edward Sauer looked through the darkness at his little fleet of five destroyers, soon to be joined by a sixth and three oilers. "Sir, what the hell is it with the radio traffic from these PBYs from French Frigate Shoals and the subs? They've absolutely been bombarding us with radio traffic. If our location ever was a secret, the Japs sure know where we are now. Why don't they just get on a loudspeaker and broadcast where we are? Frankly, Sir, it's weird. Some of the messages don't make a lick of sense, almost as though they were sent specifically to tell the Japs our location."

Sauer leaned back in his chair and locked his hands behind his head. "That's just now dawning on you, Ensign? I'll tell you where we are. We're one hundred-fifty miles behind the whole Jap navy with a handful of destroyers and some oilers? And up until now this made sense to you? Son, I worry about you."

Ensign Milos Riccardi — everyone called him by the Americanized "Miles Ricky" — spread his hands. "What do I know, Sir? I'm just an ensign. But it seems to me like we're being set up."

Letting out a long breath, Sauer stood up and put his hand on Riccardi's shoulder. "That's exactly what it is, Ensign Riccardi."

"You mean they want the Japs to know we're here?"

Sauer shrugged. "So it would seem."

*Aboard the **Yamato** 335 miles southeast of Midway*
5 Jun 42 2240

"All resistance on Midway has been eliminated." Captain Sagata reviewed the latest reports from Midway, then presented the stack to Yamamoto, who ignored it. "The airfield?" he asked.

"It seems the American commander had rigged large parts of the landing strip to blow up if they were in danger of losing the island. It will need major repairs before we can land planes there. Our chief engineer, Major Mifume, who conducted a preliminary inspection, thinks it will be out of action for perhaps a week."

"A week ..." Yamamoto's voice trailed off. "We should be flying long-range reconnaissance missions out of that base tomorrow."

"Sir, we did capture all port facilities intact. Oh, and Admiral, we translated a message that was about to be sent from Midway to an oiler, the *Platte*. What's interesting about this, Sir, is that just about thirty minutes ago, submarine I-723, which was out of torpedoes and en route home to re-arm, came into contact with the *Platte*."

"So?" Yamamoto's mind was blurry from exhaustion. He hadn't slept in 24 hours and was still focused on intercepting Halsey.

"Admiral, the submarine's position was here," pointing to a map point some 150 miles behind Yamamoto's force.

Yamamoto stood up and stared at the map. "They are absolutely certain it was an oiler?"

"No doubt, Sir. The submarine crew was despondent—it would have been so easy to sink, and they almost surfaced to use their deck gun, but the captain said something didn't feel right and he decided to send us this information and await orders. He wasn't sure we wanted the Americans to know that we knew where they were. Moreover, Admiral, we were picking up a great deal of radio traffic directed to that zone just before nightfall, although nothing coming out of that area."

As you would expect if Halsey's force was observing radio silence. Have we been steaming away from Halsey for eight hours chasing a single destroyer? If so, he has put enough distance between us that our strike aircraft would be at their most extreme range. And he continues to gain separation tonight. Yet, what if he is exactly where I thought he was—just a few hundred miles to the north, running like a rabbit for Hawaii? Or what if there is a third alternative I haven't yet considered? What if Halsey intends to fight, slip in behind me, and attack the invasion fleet? He could occupy Nagumo's planes with his own, while the American cruisers and destroyers annihilate the landing ships, which are only in the first stages of reinforcing Midway. At this point, Nagumo is already swinging his carriers around to the north, making it difficult to come back and support the invasion fleet. Hosogaya has the Zuiho, and Kakuda has light carriers, but did Nagumo strip them of their aircraft during the battle to reinforce his own air cover?

"The submarine commander was wise. Compliment him on his restraint." An ensign wrote the message for the admiral's approval, then quickly departed.

Sagata handed Yamamoto the dispatches. The admiral is lost in thought. He bowed and went outside the bridge. Yamamoto joined him a few moments later. "Beautiful night, Admiral," he said. "The morning might be even more wondrous."

"Don't tell me you're a romantic, Sagata." Yamamoto rubbed his eyes.

"Not really, but you must admit, it is one of those nights that we sailors live for."

"Perhaps, Sagata, I would be more enthusiastic about the current condition of the heavens if I felt better about the disposition of my forces."

"Still troubled about the activity behind us, Admiral?"

Yamamoto gave a nearly unnoticeable shrug. The *Yamato* crashed effortlessly through the foam. The salt breeze slapped them in the face, reminding Yamamoto of his youth on destroyers. "I miss the counsel of my other admirals," he confided. "True, they are a contentious and often disagreeable lot, especially that ass Kondo ..." he noticed Sagata smiling, and added, "but you did not hear me say that. After each one speaks—the aggressors, the timid commanders, the glory hounds, the plodding bureaucrats—I always feel as though I have heard the best advice from the man best suited to make an argument for his case. But alone, out here, I cannot be sure how Nagumo, or even Hosogaya, will react. Nagumo is a good man, but we are not in harmony. He and Hosogaya each sees the war from his own perspective, and worse, cannot envision it from the perspective of another. I do not say this with resentment or hostility. It is not a criticism of them personally, but I must tell you that I cannot trust implicitly any of my admirals. And in turn, that makes me weak. My own strategy has now placed me at the head of only one of three great prongs, but success now partly relies on the other commanders making the right decisions. I fear I have allowed myself to become too personally involved in this battle, on the one hand, and yet, removed on the other." He let out a deep sigh.

Sagata stood quietly, wiped the brine from his cheek, and replied, "Permission to speak freely, Admiral?" Yamamoto gave a sharp nod. But Sagata rephrased the question.

"Permission to speak as you asked me earlier, Admiral?"

Yamamoto turned to him, anger flashed in his eyes, and said, "*Hai!*"

"Very well, Admiral. So far, we have achieved an impressive, but not overwhelming, victory. In two battles, we have sunk two American carriers and damaged a third ..."

" ... which, may I remind you, is still unaccounted for at this moment," Yamamoto inserted.

"Indeed, Admiral. For our success, we have lost two fleet carriers and one light carrier. In the short run, acceptable losses, but in the long run, as we discussed, completely unacceptable. I might be short-sighted, Admiral ... I'm only a captain ... but without a more significant victory than we've had so far, it is difficult to see how you can achieve your objective of seeping the Americans of their patience—of ensuring that the war is drawn out long enough that they reconsider."

"Agreed, Sagata, but you are telling me nothing I don't know. Do you think Halsey is trying to escape behind us? Or even slip back to attack Hosogaya's invasion force?"

"We don't know, Admiral. We will know early tomorrow morning. I don't think ..." Sagata stopped, wary of offering Japan's finest naval thinker advice.

But Yamamoto was growing impatient with this tactic: "Sagata, I have told you to speak freely. Do not make me prompt you again."

"Yes, Admiral. Apologies. We are much better off with Halsey, whatever his force strength, in front of us than behind us. Admiral Hosogaya is an experienced amphibious commander, but he knows little of carriers. If he is attacked, and hesitates or has a single misstep, we could lose another carrier, or worse, and the

American heavy gunships would slaughter our invasion force. We have committed such a large component of our amphibious forces to this, if they were substantially lost, we might not be able to evacuate the troops that are there. Certainly we would not be able to mount major invasions in the future ..."

"... such as Hawaii, if the opportunity arose," Yamamoto interrupted, and Sagata nodded in agreement.

Yamamoto absent-mindedly rubbed his missing fingers. "Halsey is aggressive and impetuous, no doubt. He certainly would not like to run, and slipping behind us to strike at our blind side would be a masterful recovery." Sagata agreed. "And Nagumo is already proceeding eastward, you think, in an attempt to close a net that may already have a hole in it? Possibly leaving Hosogaya defenseless against air attacks?"

Sagata nodded again. Yamamoto thought for a moment, then replied. "If there is the slightest sign tomorrow morning that Halsey's fleet is indeed behind us, we will come about and chase him down. This *will* be the decisive battle. I will not allow him to fight again."

CHAPTER SEVENTEEN

The **Yamato**
5 Jun42 0530

Nakajima E8N "Dave" (Wikipedia)

In the distance, Yama-moto could see the battleships and cruisers launching scout planes to the north and north-west, each firing off their two-man seaplanes from catapults.

They would be over their reconnaissance areas just as the full light of daybreak struck. If Halsey's fleet was indeed behind him, he would know within the next hour. The uneven nature of the scout force concerned Yamamoto—it was not as though all of the planes were from a unified command. His own carrier, *Hosho,* was techni-cally the first aircraft carrier Japan ever built. It carried only 21 air-craft, giving it only about one-third the striking power of a fleet car-rier. But Yamamoto was aware of that limitation when he decided to envelop Halsey. None of the *Hosho*'s planes could be spared for scouting, and none were primarily scouts, anyway—he had insisted that the *Hosho*'s entire compliment be fighters, in case his fleet was attacked. No, the scout planes would come from his battleships and heavy cruisers, each of which had dual seaplane catapults, and the battleships had a third replacement seaplane stowed below. That meant he had 16 scout planes flying in an arc back to the north and to Midway—if the pilots, from different ship and not used to sweep-ing vast areas as a team, could coordinate their search.

Like anything in war, Yamamoto noted, scouting is a discipline, and unit scouting requires practicing together, which these men had not done. We are so far ahead of the Americans in air doctrine, yet so lacking in many respects. After a battle in which our combat air power was superior, something as simple as scouting may be our undoing.

The Nakajima E8N was a biplane with two crew members that cruised along at a leisurely 100 miles per hour. What it lacked in speed, it made up for in its 485 nautical-mile range. Ironically thought, Nagumo—who didn't need them because of his carri-er-based scout planes—had the only cruisers bearing the newer Ai-chi E13A scout planes, which were a good 40 miles per hour faster than the E8N and had almost triple the range. *Should I have foreseen that when I assigned cruisers to escort Nagumo's carriers? Perhaps. An error on my part.* It would mean the difference of a report coming in perhaps 15 minutes sooner, or if Halsey's ships were further away, an additional 250 miles of operating room. Yamamoto shook his head at his misjudgment. *How could I not have envisioned this?*

As light crept up on the horizon, Yamamoto could now barely see the specks in the distance, a handful of pilots in whose hands rested the fate of the Empire.

DESRON 6, 280 miles southwest of Midway
5 Jun 42 0714

"Commander Sauer, we have radar picking up an aircraft. Looks like a loner."

Sauer strained through the binoculars, but could see nothing. "How long until he's over us?"

"Probably another three minutes, Sir."

"Fine. They don't know we have radar. Pretend we don't see him. Come on, Tojo, take the bait."

Above DESRON 6, Imperial Japanese Scout #18
5 Jun 42 0718

"Most puzzling, Tamanika," shouted the observer into his pilot's ear, pointing down at the destroyers. "It's at least a half dozen destroyers. And look there — in the distance — oilers. But I don't see battleships or the carrier. They have to be around here somewhere."

"Send a message to Admiral Yamamoto. Destroyer screen sighted. Three, repeat, three oilers. No sign of carrier or battleships." He swung the "Dave" in a giant U-turn. "It has to be nearby, but we're actually a little past our turnaround point. Even now we'll be fortunate to get back to the *Mutsu* intact. Surely one of the other scouts will confirm the main body. It's inevitable if they are this spread out."

"*Hai!* How does it feel to be the hero of the Empire —the crew that delivered the critical coordinates to the Imperial Japanese Navy for its most significant victory?" Tamanika just grinned and nodded as he turned his plane on its return leg toward his cruiser.

On the ships below, the Americans watched with a perverse,

grim satisfaction. They'd been spotted.

"POINT ACES," 532 miles southeast of Midway
5 Jun 42 0730

"We'll know in the next hour or so if Yamamoto bought it." Halsey stood in his chart room, surrounded by other officers on the Enterprise. I want DESRONS One and Two to fan out entirely on our southern side. I'm not worried about being hit from the north or even the west right now. Only the south. Have the cruisers fall in between them and us. All scouts on a constant recon basis. I want eyes up all the time."

"Aye aye, Admiral," with that a lieutenant commander gave a quick salute and bolted off to the radio room.

"All right, gentlemen, here we go. We're going to presume Yamamoto thinks we are behind him. Full speed to Pearl."

A lieutenant emerged from below decks with a message that he handed to LeBoutiller.

"Well, Admiral, we'll know sooner rather than later. One of our scouts found Yamamoto's fleet just three hundred miles to the south of us, on a heading toward Hawaii. He's right on our flank. The scout did not think it was detected; said they were flying in very tight cloud cover. Just had one small opening to see the Japanese."

Halsey slapped the chart table. "Recall the other scouts, immediately."

"Sir?" LeBoutiller asked. "Don't you want to know if Yamamoto is turning?"

"Do it!" Halsey barked, and LeBoutiller issued the order. A moment later, Halsey said, "Look, we know where he is. We'll know where he's going by whether we get shelled in the next thirty minutes. But if he sees one of our scouts, which is simply too far to have come from Midway or Hawaii, he'll know we're out here, and not at Point Spades. Now, let's pray our scouts don't get spotted."

The Yamato, 510 miles southeast of Midway
5 Jun 42 0732

"Confirmation, Admiral. Scout Eighteen reported not only a destroyer screen but clearly identified three oilers. It was at the far end of its range and had to turn back. It did not see the carrier or the rest of the ships, but if there are destroyers and oilers, Halsey's main body must be behind them." Sagata paused while Yamamoto digested the report.

Yamamoto lowered his head. *Only a madman strips himself of his oilers and destroyers, especially after losing his only island support. Yet, if I turn now and sail even far enough to bring my scout planes in range to confirm and Halsey is still to my north, he will gain the edge and escape.* "And radio reports?"

"We have been picking up little, but there are occasional messages, as if someone unintentionally broke radio silence. Also, we've heard a lot of signals in the area from submarines and aircraft, but can't determine who they are intended for. It's very puzzling."

More deception? "And the nature of this traffic?" "From what we can translate, Sir, it's almost all providing updates on our location."

Yamamoto sighed deeply. "Very well, Captain Sagata. Signal all ships. Come about. Give them the bearings of the American destroyers. Launch scouts every fifteen minutes until we have confirmation of the exact location of Halsey's carrier and main task force."

Naval Station Pearl Harbor, Headquarters, CINCPAC
5 Jun 42 0847

Nimitz had slept briefly during the night, but was up by 0430, had showered, shaved, and was back at the chart table by 0530. Lamar arrived at 0600, and, thinking he was early, was embarrassed to find the admiral already at work.

"Admiral. I didn't think you'd be at it this early, Sir."

Nimitz gave an obligatory grunt, then turned his attention back to the chart.

"No word from Halsey?"

"Nor would I expect any. He can't communicate with anyone. But we should be hearing soon if Yamamoto is heading north, or south."

"But what if, instead of attacking, Yamamoto turns just long enough to probe the position of the destroyers?

"Then, Art, he'll come about again, and it will be a real race."

USS **Balch,** *345 miles southeast of Midway Island*
5 Jun 42 0851

"Radar contact. We've got another one, Captain." A sailor raised his binoculars and scanned the distant sky where Tiemroth couldn't see the Japanese scout plane with his naked eye. "He's coming straight this way," repeated the sailor.

"That means Yamamoto has turned enough to get his scout aircraft in range." Tiemroth looked at his Officer of the Deck, or "OOD," Lt. Eugene Trulock. "Lieutenant, that's good news and bad news."

"Sir?"

"It means that Halsey should now, or very soon, have the edge in his race to escape Yamamoto's southern pincer."

"And the bad news, Sir?"

"The bad news, Mr. Trulock, is that if he so decides, Yamamoto can have the whole Jap navy on us in a few hours, and we won't have a hope in hell."

"Sir," asked Trulock, "should we put on a show anyway?"

Tiemroth shrugged, "Why not. All right, Lieutenant, let's make some noise. Send to all ships, evasive action." Within minutes, the six destroyers and the three oilers responded, cutting through the water in random zigzags.

"By the way, Captain, since we've been spotted for some time, where exactly are we going?"

"Our orders are, once we are absolutely sure that Yamamoto has considered this to be the main fleet, to head for Point Clubs and return from there to Pearl by any possible route."

"So we aren't to lead them on any further?"

"What's the point, Lieutenant? It will be entirely up to Yamamoto by then, if he wants to eradicate a small force of destroyers and oilers, well, we can't exactly stop him."

Trulock nodded with a glum expression, and returned to his binoculars, watching the Japanese scout head over their position.

The **Yamato**
5 Jun 42 0853

"Scout Number Eighteen has flown more than seventy-five miles beyond the position of the destroyers and the oilers. As you surmised, Admiral, it is a ruse. Do you wish to close with them and destroy them or attempt to catch Halsey?"

Yamamoto stoically stared at the map, performing calculations in his head. If he came about immediately, while he would no longer have the angle on Halsey, he could stay close enough that the slightest problem in Halsey's advance could mark the difference.

"Detach the *Ise*, one cruiser, and two destroyers, and eliminate the ruse fleet. Bring the rest of the task force about, set a course for Pearl Harbor, maximum speed, and plot a course that will allow us to gradually angle on Halsey." Sagata began drafting orders.

As Yamamoto concluded, the phone from the radio room began to ring. A lieutenant answered it, listened, and responded, "*Hai!*" He pulled out a notepad and began writing, nodding, even though the voice on the other end could not see him nod. "Hai! I understand. Yes, I have it."

"Admiral," the lieutenant reported with urgency, "we have just received word from Admiral Kurita. He is in a battle with the American heavy cruisers north of Midway. They have been engaged since early this morning — even with our superiority in night fighting, the Americans stood their ground. It appears the ..." he checked his notes, "*Hyuga* sustained heavy damage, and the *Yamashira* has some light damage. Earlier, he reports, a submarine sank the *Fuso* and struck the *Mutsu*, but *Mutsu* is repaired and making good speed. Kurita wishes to withdraw. He estimates that he has sunk one American cruiser and seriously damaged at least one, possibly two others. The Americans are retreating, but maintaining a blocking position between Kurita and ourselves."

Yamamoto looked at Sagata. *One prong dead in the water, one irreparably delayed on a wild goose chase. That only leaves Nagumo and his carrier force, bringing up the rear. The remaining American cruisers will not place themselves in range of Nagumo's planes.* "Captain Sagata, send this to Admiral Kurita. Tell him to break contact. I am assigning any of his ships capable of making speed to Admiral Nagumo's carrier strike force. If the damaged ships cannot be repaired at Midway, they should put in to the nearest facility that is equipped to deal with their damage. To Nagumo: Proceed with all deliberate speed and rendezvous with my task force, at the same position from which we launched the Pearl Harbor raid. Assume command of Kurita's operational ships. To Admiral Hosogaya: any warships no longer needed for protection at Midway are to be transferred immediately to Admiral Nagumo."

Yamamoto frowned, rubbing his hand. *None of this is going as planned. The invasion was easier than expected, defeating the enemy ships, harder. Halsey has acted completely out of character, running when he should have fought, deceiving when he should have attacked. He split his force and possibly sacrificed his cruisers and destroyers to save the carrier. He has now dictated what I do next.*

A few moments later, Sagata returned to confirm the orders with Yamamoto. After they were sent, he stood near the admiral's bridge chair. "What now, Admiral?"

"In the short run, we will eliminate another half-dozen destroyers and the oilers, and Kurita has removed at least one, and perhaps three American cruisers from the fight. All of that on top of the Hornet, which we sank at the beginning of the battle. And in the exchange, we got Midway. In the long run, however, the Americans continue to exact a cost for every victory. They stall, delay, and escape. I fear we keep winning battles, but are losing control of the war."

"Yet you are still pursuing Halsey?"

"We must. Only now, if fortune does not favor us by slowing him down, we will await Nagumo's carriers and finish the job at Hawaii."

CHAPTER EIGHTEEN

Kaiser Shipyards, Rich-mond, California
5 Jun 42 1003

USS *Enterprise* (Wikipedia)

"Boss, you might want to see this. California Shipbuilding down in Los Angeles just put a Liberty Ship into the water in forty-six days from laying the keel. Forty-six days, Boss." John Eugland waved the sheets that had been sent up the day before from southern California. "I also hear that Cascade Boat Works up in Eugene is hitting about fifty days on theirs."

Kaiser snatched the papers out of Eugland's hand, and studied the data. "Well, no wonder. Those yards are doing a fourth of our volume. Sure, if all you're going to do is make five ships, you ought to make 'em damn fast." He pulled out a cigarette and said, "Johnnie, the men have done a helluva job. Helluva job. They've cut almost a hundred days off the construction time. But we can do a lot better. There's still a lot of wasted effort, wasted time, people milling around waiting for parts ... Here's what I want you to do: take an assistant and randomly investigate three different parts of our construction process — hull, superstructure, interior. Use the old Frederick Taylor time- and-motion stopwatch crap, but obviously, if something jumps out, make a note of that, too. Get back to me in two days. I want to know how we can make one of these babies in under three weeks."

Eugland's jaw dropped.

"Twenty days, Johnnie. All our yards. There are fourteen other shipbuilders making Liberty ships, and right now we're barely ahead of most and trailing a couple. Our Permanente Metals here in Richmond is days ahead of our Vancouver yard. That shouldn't be. At the very least, all yards ought to be on the same pace."

"Boss, I can tell you one thing that might help." Eugland pulled some papers out of the attaché bag he carried and waved them at Kaiser. The boss sighed.

"Your 'just-in-time' idea again?" Eugland bobbed his head enthusiastically. "Oh, hell, all right. I'm willing to try anything." He took the papers.

"I'm telling you, Boss, if we can get some of the junk — parts that are stacked up, and unused machinery — off the work floor and institute this system to bring parts in from our warehouses as we need them, we can shave another ten, maybe fifteen, days off the process."

"But you're assuming that the parts will get here, Johnnie!"

"I am, sir. But if we put one-fourth the effort into streamlining the delivery process that we have the construction process, then the latter will go much faster too."

Kaiser stopped walking, and thumbed through the papers. "You've got a lot of confidence in our trucks and railroads, Johnnie."

Eugland agreed. "They haven't let us down yet, sir. In fact, we haven't begun to push them. I say let's see what they can do."

Kaiser slapped his leg with the papers. "All right, Johnnie. I'll look at this tonight, and if it has an outside chance, we'll institute it this week. Now, you find me some other ways to shave time through these random inspections!"

Eugland hustled off with a broad smile on his face.

USS Enterprise, 250 miles west of Pearl Harbor
5 Jun 42 1126

A sailor handed LeBoutiller a message, as the lieutenant made his way down to the Admiral's cabin. Halsey, who had been on the bridge for nearly 24 hours, finally agreed to get some sleep. LeBoutiller knocked on the door firmly.

Moments later, Halsey opened the door, his dark, sunken eyes looking worse than ever. He jerked his head for LeBoutiller to enter the tiny cabin, as he splashed some water on his face. His paunch, usually well concealed by his uniform, was obvious in his skivvies. Halsey ran his hands over his face, and then put on his khaki uniform.

"Admiral, it appears our ruse worked," LeBoutiller noted confidently.

"Yamamoto pulled up just long enough that he no longer has the angle on us."

"So," Halsey said, still trying to wake up, "what leads you to this conclusion?"

"Sir, DESRON Six sighted several scout planes this morning. They flew well past the destroyers and the oilers. He has to know there's nothing else up there, but the fact that the scouts could get within range means he had to turn north long enough to close the distance and launch."

Halsey let out a long, loud breath. "So they bought it. I'll be damned."

"I made some calculations, Admiral. Even if we assume that Yamamoto turned back southeast immediately after learning he's been tricked, he can't cut us off now. We'll be a good fifty miles ahead of him all the way to Pearl. He doesn't have the fleet carriers. So if he only has a light carrier ..."

" ... he's almost certainly got it stacked with Zeros, and not torpedo planes. Assuming nothing goes wrong, he shouldn't be able to hit us before we reach Hawaii."

LeBoutiller replied, "Yes, Sir. Assuming." "And Kinkaid? What do we know of him?"

"That's the other thing, Sir. He's stayed off the radio because of our situation. Should I go raise him now?" "Yeah, Charlie, we better know what's happening up north. I'll bet he hasn't seen Nagumo, but I'm sure Yamamoto's called in all the dogs for this hunt."

LeBoutiller nodded and walked down the narrow passageway, then down the ladder two decks to the radio room. Inside the cramped space were a half-dozen radio operators, most just listening. LeBoutiller scribbled a message in long hand, and approached the communications watch officer, a chief radioman. "Send this to Admiral Kinkaid." The chief checked the clock, added a date-time-group to the message and passed it along to his crypto operator for encoding. Within minutes the message was in the hands of a circuit operator who sent it on its way. After another few minutes, the reply was received, decoded, and handed to LeBoutiller. He hustled back up the ladder to the navigation bridge, where the admiral had awaited him with the *Enterprise*'s skipper. He found Halsey leaning against the bulkhead, cup of black coffee in hand. Captain Murray was out on the wing of the bridge, scanning with his binoculars.

"Sir, Kinkaid tore 'em up, but he's took it, too." He gave the report to Halsey, who read over it.

"My God. Looks like he took out that whole task force single-handedly. Of course, we all know that ships that appear to be sinking miraculously reappear, but still, that's a helluva scorecard. Looks like he's lost both the *Portland* and the *Pensacola*. Got damage to some others, too. Out of eight cruisers we started this battle with, we're down to five. We've most likely sacrificed DESRON Six and the oilers, and lost the *Hornet*." Halsey slumped back in the chair as Murray came in.

"News from Kinkaid?" He asked, knowing the answer. Halsey nodded and held out the report.

Murry read it slowly, then handed it back. "Seems like we're trading 'em ship for ship, Admiral."

"I'm afraid you're right, George. Kinkaid must have fought a tremendous battle—cruisers against battleships and their escorts. It shouldn't have been close. I don't know how the Japs stumbled into Kinkaid's range."

"Subs, too, sir. Don't forget the submariners." Halsey nodded. "Goddam good job on their part.

As best we can figure, the subs sank *Fuso* and severely damaged another battleship. Perhaps the Japanese got so preoccupied with the subs that they drifted into Kinkaid's range. Either way, it took a stroke of luck just for us to break even, only Yamamoto has plenty more ships in his armada, and we don't. Okay, LeBoutiller, I think we can notify Nimitz of our position—and Yamamoto's. He's going to have some planning to do."

Naval Station Pearl Harbor, Headquarters, CINCPAC
5 Jun 42 1140

"Art, get Admiral Spruance over here, on the double." Nimitz reviewed the dispatch from Halsey, received just minutes earlier.

"Aye aye, Admiral. Trouble?"

"Let's just say I think we're going to have a fight on our hands."

Lamar went to his desk and phoned Spruance's office. The Admiral was at the *Yorktown*'s drydock, supervising repairs, and a messenger was sent out immediately. *Yorktown* had just pulled in the previous night, but already Nimitz had ferried almost 100 repairmen and tradesmen to the carrier and begun work. Once *Yorktown* reached the dry-dock, guided in by the tugboats, 1500 additional workers descended on the vessel like a swarm of bees in order to convert the sick ship into a healthy fighting sea beast. It took a few minutes to locate Spruance. He was already inside the ship, talking to the *Yorktown's* Chief Engineer, when an ensign delivered the message.

"Tell Admiral Nimitz I'll be right there," Spruance said, reading the order. He cast one last glance at the massive carrier in her dry-dock, some 870 feet in length. Built in 1934 at Newport News, and commissioned three years later, the vessel displaced 25,500 tons. Her massive turbines turned four screws that could propel the ship through the water at 33 knots. The crew, whose number varied between 2,700 and 3,400, had been given shore leave while the ship was repaired. All of them were subject to six-hour recall. In the meantime, they were replaced on board by the army of repairmen. Spruance marveled at the ship—he'd heard rumblings of the loss of the *Hornet*, and it troubled him deeply. *With* Lex *and* Hornet *both gone, we're going to need* Yorktown *more than ever. It could still take another ten days to get her seaworthy.*

He wondered what the latest on his friend Halsey was. There had been no news since yesterday, when reports of the *Hornet* came in via the destroyer. *Bill, tell me why you didn't attack while down a carrier,* Spruance thought. It was well known by now that Midway had fallen and that Kinkaid was fighting a running retreat with his cruisers against battleships and had also taken heavy losses. *My God. Nimitz is going to tell me that Halsey's dead, the* Enterprise *sunk, and nothing standing between us and the Jap Navy except the* Yorktown, *which won't even be out of dry-dock for a week.* Saratoga *is making her way west after completing torpedo damage repairs in Bremerton, but it won't get here until it's too late. Yamamoto's not going to give us an opportunity to get off the mat. We're going to be playing defense all the way to San Francisco. God help us.*

Spruance climbed into the waiting Jeep, and his driver took him to CINCPAC headquarters a few minutes away on the other side of the harbor. Walking past the neatly trimmed grass and gently swaying palm trees outside, Spruance made a sharp right, down the corridor, past the map room to Nimitz's office. There he found the admiral and Captain Arthur Lamar waiting for him. *They don't look as grim as I thought they would. Maybe my fears were misplaced. Nimitz gestured to the empty chair.* Spruance sat as Lamar pulled the shades and then sat in a chair to the side.

"Ray," Nimitz began, "it's bad, but it could be a helluva lot worse. You've probably already heard that Midway has fallen and that we've lost the *Hornet.*" Spruance said nothing, but merely nodded in affirmation. "Halsey is running back to Hawaii, fast as he can, and is less than a day out with Yamamoto's fleet hot on his tail. It seems the Japs tried to cut him off in a pincer movement. Tom Kinkaid blunted the northern pincer with his cruisers, but it cost him: we lost the *Pensacola* and the *Portland*, on top of the *Vincennes* lost earlier in the day. Yamamoto came around from the south, and would have enveloped Halsey if Bill hadn't pulled a neat diversion." Nimitz, standing in front of the map, pointed to "Point Spades," where DESRON 6 and the oilers had been sent. "Knowing that Yamamoto was following the destroyer *Balch* and thinking the *Balch* was, in fact, joining up with Halsey's task force, Halsey had the *Balch* rendezvous with DESRON 6 and sent three of his oilers to "Point Spades," behind Yamamoto. The Japs figured Halsey was sneaking past their rear—a belief we encouraged having some 'accidental' transmissions from that area and a lot of intended radio traffic there—and the deception succeeded just long enough to get Yamamoto to slow up. Halsey now has the edge, and should reach Pearl late tonight.

"The good news," Nimitz continued, "is that Halsey has saved the Enterprise, the rest of his vessels, and in the process took out an enemy carrier, two battleships, and several smaller craft. We think even a third battleship is damaged and will be forced to retire. The better news is that he escaped Yamamoto's trap. By God, I wouldn't have believed it—Halsey, thinking defensively and saving the fleet! As for Kinkaid's boys, they are outgunned and will be lucky to get back to Pearl Harbor, but there are some indications that the Japanese have broken off with them. For planning purposes, I'm not expecting to have them. We also expect DESRON 6 and the oilers to be eliminated. It will be sheer luck of any of them escape.

Spruance's jaw dropped. *This was the good news?*

"The bad news is, we think Yamamoto's force that is on Halsey's heels is only comprised of battleships and a small carrier, and Nagumo may be coming in from the north, joining what's left of that battleship fleet with all of his remaining carriers. That could be four or five."

"Coming in, Sir?" Spruance muttered, already thinking. *Coming for us, here?*

"I don't know if Yamamoto would be stupid enough to attack Hawaii itself, especially Oahu," Nimitz said. "All of our air bases are fully repaired from the December seventh attacks. We could put up over a hundred fighters in minutes, Army, Navy, and Marines. Plus the Army has a lot of B-17s and medium bombers ready for any mission. Even the Yorktown air group over at Kaneohe would get into the action."

"Sounds pretty desperate, Chet." Spruance was stunned. Halsey was returning from a major battle with a single carrier and a handful of escorts.

"It might be damned desperate. We'll need every gun, every plane, every ship, Ray. If they come at us here, you and I may be sailing dinghies out."

"I understand, Admiral." Spruance tensed up even more, still waiting for the other shoe to drop.

"Here's what I'm thinking, Ray. Captain Layton tells me Commander Rochefort's people have decrypted enough to indicate that Yamamoto has stripped his invasion fleet nearly bare. He's bringing everything eastward."

"Attempting to cut our lines of communication?"

Nimitz nodded. "When he does that, Ray, we won't have any choice. I'm not a political man, but you know Washington won't tolerate an attack on the west coast. I won't even have to wait for that order."

Spruance understood. "Admiral, what do we know that Yamamoto has . . . for certain, what do we know?"

"I think I can tell you, but it would be better if you heard it from Layton. He should be here any minute. I had Art call him in, and Art said he's bringing Rochefort along. Besides, I think all three of us need to evaluate Rochefort's evidence. I'm told the Commander is quite an advocate, and sometimes, even a CINC can get caught up in his confidence."

No sooner had Nimitz uttered the words than there was a knock at the door. Lamar opened it, and Captain Edwin Layton and

Commander Joseph Rochefort stepped in.

"Admiral Nimitz, Admiral Spruance," Layton said. Nimitz motioned them to sit in the empty leather chairs near Spruance.

"Okay, Captain Layton. You say Commander Rochefort here has a lot of credibility with us because of his call on Midway, this 'AF' business, and all that."

A look of surprise crossed Rochefort's face. He knew, obviously, that the information had been passed up the chain of command, but assumed Layton had claimed credit for himself. "Sir? Captain Layton told you that?"

"He did, Commander. Said you guys came up with the original conclusion that Midway was the target, and that you confirmed that with the water treatment trick?"

Layton dropped his eyes and smiled.

"Well, Sir," began Rochefort, "ah, that's essentially correct. Yes, Admiral."

Nimitz cut to the chase. "What does your merry band of soothsayers over there at HYPO tell us now?" Rochefort went into his predictable, self-effacing, "aw-shucks, we-don't-really-know-all-that-much" mode when Nimitz exploded. "Commander, cut the crap. We don't have time. Now, this morning, you had me believing Yamamoto would not regroup at Midway, but would come at us full speed ahead. Do you mean to say you think he'll dare to attack us in Hawaii?"

Rochefort suddenly became dead sober. "Absolutely not, Admiral. But that would be an opinion. You pay me to provide you with evidence. So here's the evidence: We think, based on radio traffic we've picked up, and the sources of that traffic, that Yamamoto's northern force—we now know it was under Kurita—that his northern force got hurt by Kinkaid's cruisers and the subs. They lost the *Fuso* entirely, and apparently another battleship, the *Mutsu*, was heavily damaged, and we don't think it will be repaired at Midway. The *Yamashira* was fixed up and is sailing out to join Yamamoto's force. Obviously they lost a carrier, some landing vessels, and two destroyers in the battle. On the other hand, we are down a carrier, three cruisers, a whole destroyer squadron—plus the *Hammann*, which had joined it—and three fleet oilers. By my calculations Admiral, that's a helluva bloody nose for us, and Yamamoto knows it. But, again, that's opinion and you're paying me for evidence."

Rochefort pulled out a cigar, but looked at Nimitz first, and lit up after the approval came. "The traffic tells us Yamamoto is still heading east, after briefly taking Halsey's bait and going after the destroyers. Moreover, it appears that he's stripped the landing fleet of everything except the bare minimum. He's got a number of big battleships, including the *Yamato,* which outranges anything we have. And with the reinforcements from his invasion fleet, he'll still have four big carriers and several small ones. We don't know how many, but he had a couple of smaller ones with the landing fleet, maybe one with his own southern pincer. That still won't put him on a par with us in and around Hawaii, with all of our ground-based air cover here. But we can't just ignore that threat, either. He might be counting on that. And, of course, *Saratoga* should get here soon."

Nimitz grunted, "We'll need her."

"Undergoing repairs at Bremerton, right Admiral?" asked Spruance.

"At first, yes," interjected Layton, who realized he had interrupted Spruance, but Nimitz signaled for him to continue. "But then she picked up escorts and planes and left San Diego a few days ago, stuffed to the rivets with aircraft. She'll be a welcome reinforcement."

Nimitz took it all in took a deep breath, then continued, "We can't disregard the threat of him striking here, but he doesn't need to. If I were Yamamoto, I'd just swing in behind us, cut us off from the west coast, and we'll have to go fight him."

Rochefort had already foreseen that possibility and offered an alternative. "Couldn't you just wait him out, Admiral? I mean, he can't possibly supply a fleet that size with Hawaii sitting astride his lines of communication. Why, we could sortie out and annihilate any oilers, and even if a few slipped through, it wouldn't be enough to keep such a massive fleet at sea. He wouldn't last three weeks out there, and on the way back, he's be a sitting duck, unable to burn fuel to maneuver."

"Commander," interrupted Spruance, "you're thinking like a U.S. Navy officer, not like a politician in Washington, or a citizen in California. It would scare the daylights out of the public there, disrupt our war production, God knows what else. If he gets between us and the west coast, we won't have a choice."

Puffing on his cigar, Rochefort glumly nodded. Nimitz added, "There are real, and profound, political implications of an attack on California. Even some important military targets there that we can't completely leave defenseless. What I want from you, Commander, is your best estimate on what Japanese ships are where, and where they are heading."

Rochefort stood up and jerked his head to the chart room. "Is this too classified for out there?" Nimitz shook his head and extended his arm toward the large chart table. Rochefort continued. "Admiral, our traffic analysis and JN-25 decrypts suggest Yamamoto is with his southern fleet here," and he moved a small icon of a Japanese ship into a position about 250 miles southwest of Hawaii. "And the combined *Kurita-Nagumo* carrier task force is coming about here." He moved other icons with several carriers on a northeast line heading diagonally down to Hawaii." They formed two ominous pincers, and no matter the reality of Hawaii's ground-based air, the visual image was disturbing. "However, something is really troubling me."

Layton started to laugh, causing Rochefort to develop a puzzled look on his face. Spruance said, "Captain, what's funny?"

"The Commander," replied Layton. "A Jap fleet outnumbering us at least two-to-one is bearing down on us, and 'something is troubling' you? I should hope to hell so!" The mood in the room lightened, and everyone briefly smiled.

Nimitz asked, "Do you mean, something else is bothering you, Commander? What? I mean, what could be worse than this?"

Somewhat placated by Nimitz's intervention, Rochefort cleared his throat. He took a pencil out and began to slowly rotate it in his fingers, almost absent-mindedly. "We are picking up a lot of signals about what appears to be a rendezvous point, about a hundred and fifty miles out, back toward the north."

"And that bothers you because . . . ." Nimitz didn't follow."

"The Japs have to rendezvous somewhere Admiral, but what I'm thinking is Midway was a different type of operation. It was the first time the Japs didn't use multiple simultaneous fleet movements."

"You mean deception?" Nimitz interjected.

"Not exactly. If you think about it, the early attacks in Malaya and then Pearl Harbor were real attacks—all of them—but pulled off simultaneously or nearly simultaneously. If it was deception, the Japs would have struck somewhere at one time to divert our attention, then somewhere else next. It was a strength for them, which allowed them to pull off several concurrent operations, but a weakness, too, indicating they didn't trust any one thrust to 'win the war.' This operation, on the other hand ... well, I think it was one of a kind, and Yamamoto may think he's played this card and can't repeat it."

"But," Spruance countered, "he did divide his forces after the initial attack and nearly surrounded Halsey. That was typical of their style."

"I agree, Admiral Spruance, but something doesn't seem right. It was almost seat-of-the-pants stuff, an afterthought, not the main plan. Honestly, I wonder if the top brass back in Japan, like this Admiral Fukodome, even approved what Yamamoto did after the initial attack. No, that Midway operation wasn't like him—it's not like his patterns that we've seen before—to use one single main thrust where he has committed all his resources."

Layton nodded at Nimitz, who then echoed Rochefort, thinking out loud. "That whole enveloping plan for Halsey did seem to have an off-the-cuff feel to it, like Yamamoto might have gotten greedy, or modified his original plan based on what happened at Midway. Commander Rochefort, are you saying you think he will return to a more traditional Japanese multiple operations?"

"Admiral, I'm just ..." but a sharp look from Layton told him that Nimitz had tired of the humble intelligence analyst mode and expected an answer. "Yes. I think he'll use that rendezvous to reorganize his fleet, then divide it into separate offensives."

"For what? Hawaii is the prize. The fleet is the prize," Spruance pointed out.

"But," continued Rochefort, "you just said he can't get you here. He'll have to get you to come out. He'll have to guarantee that you'll come out. Think about his forces, and our forces, Admiral: he's got a bunch of battlewagons, which are real good for shelling ports, harbors, and cities— while he thinks we've got no battleships left—and he's got another major component to his fleet, the carriers—and he thinks we've got just one operational. I know what I'd do."

Nimitz saw it clearly. "You're right, Commander. There's only one way he can guarantee he gets us in open water."

It took Spruance a minute longer, then he lowered his eyes and quietly muttered, "Oh, hell."

CHAPTER NINETEEN

Honolulu, Hawaii Territory
7 Jun 42 0927

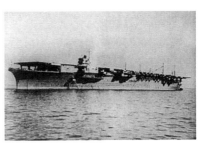

The Zuikaku (Wikipedia)

Earlier, Ensign Gibbons and Miko had gone snorkeling in Kaneohe Bay, so Sam Tomita took his time about getting out of the house today. He didn't have to open the photography store until 10:00, and he could be late, claiming the traditional small business woes of insufficient help. Photography equipment filled the car, and, as always, Sam had gone back to his highly private basement to make certain the radio was off. Just as he was about to lock the trap door, and push the desk back over it, the phone rang. A chill ran down Sam's back. If he answered it, and it was Miko, he'd have to come up with a good excuse why he was home. On the other hand, if he didn't answer it, and it was Miko checking to see if he had left for work yet — and concluded he had — she and her Ensign might return. Paralyzed, Sam sat as the phone rang four times, then abruptly stopped.

He felt perspiration on his forehead, and walked to the kitchen where he grabbed a hand towel and dabbed it off. *Just eight months ago. Has it only been that long?* A Japanese man had come one night when Miko and Elliot were gone. *"How much do you love your sisters?"* That was his question. *Miroki and Hara. How much do you love them, Sam? Enough to risk your own son?* It was a simple and unveiled threat. Information for their lives. Sam had no way of knowing if the man was still on the island, but once, when he gathered the nerve to quit, and was late with a report, a finger showed in his mailbox. Miroki's finger. *It had mama's ring still on it.* Sam hadn't been late again with a report. *And the young men on those ships?* Sam pushed it out of his brain. They weren't his problem: his sisters were his problem. They were helpless. And they weren't the only relatives he still had in Japan. *And Jerry?* Sam had already decided, he wouldn't risk Jerry or Miko — but Jerry's transfer now let him rest easier, and his nights had gotten longer, and his sleep less, until he didn't sleep at all. Now, night after night, he stared out his window at the gentle palms, sometimes interrupted by a burst of rain. Sam left the window open, getting soaked, and didn't care.

Jerry had left his duties at Hickam Field for Wisconsin, to join an all-Japanese regiment. *Hitler is a gaijin bastard anyway. Deserves to be stopped. Jerry can help.* He had convinced himself that the United States would negotiate a peace, especially after Midway. *I had hoped America and Japan could at least be neutrals, perhaps even allies against Hitler.* Now, peace seemed further away than ever. He had been drawn in deeper, and his soul had become blacker, no matter how often he reminded himself of Miroki and Hara.

Sam's greatest talent—aside from being an excellent photographer and a pretty good liar—was in pushing aside the realities of what he was doing. It consisted of one part traditional Japanese patriotism, one part naive wishful thinking about the realities of the war, and one part seared conscience. What he had not buried was the fear of being discovered, and the phone call had thrown him off just enough. Heart still racing, he concluded it was not Miko, and that he could leave for Pearl Harbor and provide his patrons with the reports they needed. In his haste, he pushed his desk over the trap door, but did not notice the exposed corner uncovered by the edge of the bamboo mat which had flipped back.

Less than a half hour after he left, Elliot and Miko pulled into the driveway, Miko having forgotten her face mask, left on the back porch to air out. "Do you want something to drink while we're here," she shouted from the back. Elliott, looking at the family photos in the small living room, yelled back "No." Then he thought of something. "Hey, you wouldn't happen to have a spear gun, would you?"

"I think Father has one." She still used the formal *Father* instead of *Dad*. "Check his closet."

Elliot went into Sam's room, opened the small closet, but didn't see a spear gun. Then he noticed the uncovered edge of the basement door. "Hey, Mik," — his nickname for her came out "meek" — "what about your basement?" She didn't hear. "Mik?" he shouted louder, but Miko had found a spare pair of flippers, and was busy on the back porch smacking them together to knock off the sand. Elliot shrugged and, examining the desk to make sure he wouldn't knock anything off, pushed it aside, and pulled back the mat so he could open the door in the floor. Clambering down the small, rickety stairway, his eyes slowly adjusted to the dim light. He scanned the room looking for the spear gun, and only gradually did it dawn on him what he was actually seeing. A cluttered table, sat in front of a radio set with a few photos of U.S. ships scattered about.

Elliot searched for a light switch, and, finding one, re-focused his attention on the ship photos on what was, obviously, Sam's desk. He recognized the top three photos instantly. *The* Yorktown! There was a date and time handwritten in the upper right: "6-6-42 8:40 AM." *Why is Sam photographing the* Yorktown? *And why is he time-stamping and dating these photos?* Elliot sifted through the pictures underneath those of the *Yorktown* and recognized construction and rehabilitation work on the battleships *Nevada* and *Pennsylvania,* with times and dates in the corner. A chill ran down Elliot's back, then he heard Miko calling up above.

"Down here," he shouted. Momentarily, Miko was sticking her head into the trap-door opening.

"What are you doing down there? I didn't even know this room existed," she laughed. Then she climbed down the ladder. "Wow. I didn't even know this place was here," she said, repeating herself. "This has to be Father's room. I wonder why he didn't tell me about it?"

Elliot shook his head, holding the photos of the *Yorktown.*

Miko shrugged. "What?" She took the photos from his hand, naively shrugged. "So he took photographs of ships. Did you find the spear gun?" she asked, looking around.

"*Miko,*" he said sternly, waving the photos. "Think! Your dad has *times and dates* written on these photos, and they aren't just of 'ships,' they are of specific ships, namely our carrier and the battle-ships that are being repaired after the December Seventh attacks." She still stared blankly at him. "Miko! These are not innocent-look-ing. Any normal person would conclude your dad is spying for someone. This information in the wrong hands could tell our enemy what ships we have available for combat. Don't you get it?"

At first Miko registered anger, then, quickly she began to laugh. "Come on, Elliot. My father, a spy? He's done work for the military in the past."

He pointed to the radio transmitter. "And everyone needs a transmitter in their house, right? Do you know the difference be-tween a transmitter and a radio?" Clearly, it wasn't registering, but she impatiently shook her head.

"You have a radio receiver upstairs. We've listened to music on it. This isn't that type of radio."

Her eyes narrowed. "What are you saying?"

"This is a *transmitter*, as well as a receiver. It's built to send and receive messages, not just pick up music. What do you think is the meaning of all of these pictures sitting right at the spot where someone would broadcast to someone else outside Hawaii?"

Shaking her head angrily, she hissed, "Elliot, you're crazy. You think Father is signaling someone off shore with information about what ships we have here?"

He held up the photos, his finger underscoring the time and date. "Do you have another explanation? Miko, I like your dad. He's been great to me. But this looks suspicious as hell, and as an officer in the U.S. Navy, I'm bound, legally and morally, to report this to Naval Intelligence."

"Report it?" She seemed stunned. "But you don't know that he's actually *done* anything. All we have—all you have—are some pictures with some times and dates on them, and a radio transmitter ..."

"... in a secret basement that you didn't even know existed," he interrupted. "How do you explain that?"

"Okay, that's odd, but maybe Father just has hobbies and needed his privacy."

Elliot began looking around, opening drawers, and pulled out a small black book. Flipping through it, Elliot saw several numbers, each next to a date. "I'm not sure, but these look a lot like transmission frequencies next to the dates." Miko crossed her arms, decidedly not amused. "Today is, what? The seventh?" She nodded unenthusiastically. "Okay, play along with me, and if I'm off, I'll drop it. Let's say he did transmit something to someone. The last date we have here in the book is June first. If this number is actually a radio frequency, and he hasn't sent anything since then, then we should turn on this radio and it should still be set to the June first frequency, 514 kilocycles. He flipped a switch to turn on the radio's power supply, causing the front panel lights to illuminate. A shadowed pointer behind the translucent main tuning dial came into view, casting its gray arrow slightly below the "515" mark on the dial. Elliot looked up at Miko, whose face now registered a frown.

"Elliot, there has to be an explanation for this. It's absurd ..."

"Mik, I'm sure there is, but this is too serious for me to ignore as an officer. I have to let someone know." She glumly nodded and took the photos from his hand.

"We have to put this place back like it was. When he comes back ..." Miko laid the photos on the desk. "What would happen ..." she sighed deeply. "What would happen if these ... if this is what you say it is?"

Embracing her, he pressed her head to his shoulder. "I don't know. It's not good. Maybe . . . maybe there is some explanation, some innocent explanation. That's not up to me. But I don't think he should know that we know. Just in case, I mean, just in case it's nothing."

Suddenly she pushed away from him. "Jerry!" she said. "Jerry is going to be heading for the mainland soon. Wouldn't this endanger him?"

Elliot shrugged. "The pictures seem more about what carriers are in harbor. I'm just thinking out loud, okay, but if he was transmitting information about the *Yorktown,* and if the scuttlebutt I'm hearing is true ..." He abruptly stopped, realizing he had already said too much.

"What scuttlebutt, Elliot. What are you talking about?" she demanded.

He pointed to the ladder. "We need to get out of here." "Elliot!" she pleaded

"Look," he said shaking his head, "maybe it's all rumor, but word is we took a helluva beating out there. May have lost another carrier. Supposedly, the fleet's headed back here. It looks like the Japs, er, Japanese had information, that they knew we wouldn't have all our carriers. Mik, if all this is true—and again, it's just a swabbie rumor—it might look really, really bad for your father."

Tears welled in her eyes as she climbed the ladder, while Elliot repositioned everything as he had found it, then closed the trap door and moved the desk back over it.

"Guess you don't feel like snorkeling, but we can't stay. We have to make it look like we weren't here." He kissed her on the forehead and they slowly walked to Elliot's car.

Once inside, Elliot stared at Miko. "Can you think of any reason he would do such a thing—again, assuming that it's as bad as it looks?"

Miko didn't answer. Instead she lowered her head into her hands and began to sob.

He put his arm around her. "Okay, look, don't tell Jerry. Let me just check this out quietly. There might be something here that

I'm not seeing."

She nodded, still crying, and put her head on his chest.

Aboard the **Yamato**
8 Jun 42 0740

Yamamoto studied the intelligence, complete with the latest reports from midget submarines near Hawaii and the source on the island. Halsey had made it to safety late the previous night, and Admiral Kinkaid had arrived just minutes ago. Kurita's ships had, as ordered, broken off their pursuit for the rendezvous point. More important, the source on the island confirmed that as of two days ago, the *Yorktown* was still in dry-dock, although it was a beehive of activity. *Irrelevant. No amount of work can restore her to fighting status before Operation Tsushima.* Yamamoto silently laughed at the code name he had chosen for this last, master stroke. *Halsey escaped me once through a trick. It won't happen again. There had been no further reports of the American battleships at Pearl Harbor — those we damaged on December 7. Our intelligence is slipping.* Yamamoto reached for an intercom handset and summoned his chief intelligence officer to his quarters. *I must be sure where all the Americans are.*

A knock on his door interrupted Yamamoto's thoughts. "Yes?"

"Captain Sagata, Sir." "Enter, Captain."

Sagata opened the door and stepped in to Yamamoto's quarters, which, by Japanese standards, was spacious. "Sir, Admiral Kurita has now joined us. In addition, six more oilers have been dispatched from Japan for Midway, allowing Admiral Hosogaya to release two more oilers to us. Hosogaya will protest. I'm sure he will claim that his invasion force still needs the protection."

Yamamoto's eyes grew steely and cold. "This is not a request, and Admiral Hosogaya will comply immediately or be replaced."

"*Hai*, Admiral-san." Sagata was chastened by the sharp tone.

With any other officer, Yamamoto would not have spent a second concerned about the man's feelings, but his friendship for the young captain gave him pause, and he added, "Captain, that was not directed at you. I just tire, sometimes, of my admirals thinking they are in charge of strategy. Expect Hosogaya's protest, tell him you will register it, but remind him that we are still in a dangerous situation, and his now-empty landing ships are the least of my concerns." Yamamoto raised an eyebrow and inexplicably added, "Eh?"

Sagata's faith in his mentor was immediately restored, and he responded with an affectionate "Yes, Admiral. As you say."

No sooner had Sagata left than Commander Ashi Naichi, the strike force's top intelligence officer, reported. "Admiral-san. You sent for me?"

Yamamoto gestured for him to enter, then closed the door. "I'm aware you have sources, Commander. Normally, it is not the job of a fleet commander to get bogged down in such details, but we are coming to a critical point in our battle—perhaps in the war, right now. I must be absolutely certain of what I am facing."

Naichi gave a small bow, and responded, "Anything you wish, Admiral Yamamoto."

"Very well. Explain to me the main source from which you have been deriving your intelligence here, which, I must say, so far has been excellent."

"As you wish, Admiral. We of course rely on reports from midget submarines, some of which have penetrated the waters of Pearl Harbor itself. And we rely on radio intercepts, although that has not proven very helpful. My most reliable source is on Oahu, a man whose family is in Japan and whose cooperation has been, shall we say, ensured? He is a photographer, and not only makes notes of what he sees, but takes pictures of the ships in port, so there is no mistaking which vessels are there at a given time."

Yamamoto considered the source. *Reliable? A civilian photographer? Acting out of what motivation?* "What information has he given you in the past? It was accurate?"

"As far as we can determine, sir, yes. It was accurate. He informed us of the exact position of the battleships at Pearl Harbor. He also told us no carriers were in port, but the information came too late for us to incorporate it in our attack."

"I'm impressed. But why does he help us? Is it out of loyalty? Or something else?"

Naichi shook his head. "Admiral, no one has provided me that information. I am a mere commander, apparently not worthy of such high-level clearances. When I have inquired, I am told his assistance is completely reliable and 'guaranteed'—that was the phrase I heard." *At least the man is honest. Others may have blustered and made some excuse.* "Very well. How often do you receive reports from the midget submarine captains?"

"Every two days, Admiral. Their job is quite difficult. They must probe around Pearl Harbor without raising suspicion, which means extremely slow speeds in and around Hawaii. Then they must go to a rendezvous point where they can transmit to yet another source we have on Hawaii, who in turn transmits to us."

Yamamoto's eyebrows raised. "A different source transmits this information than the photographer?"

"Yes, Admiral-san." Naichi knew the danger: double the transmissions, double the likelihood of getting caught. On the other hand, it provided a form of redundancy. But Yamamoto knew that, and there was no need to state the obvious.

"Very well. What do we know?" Then he added, "... with absolute certainty?"

Naichi looked at his notes. "There is one carrier at Pearl Harbor. We do not have confirmation of which aircraft carrier it is, but we believe it to be Halsey's *Enterprise*."

Yamamoto interrupted. "*One*? And the one damaged at Coral Sea? The *Yorktown*? It was in dry-dock two days ago. Where is it?"

"We do not know, but it is no longer at Pearl Harbor, Admiral." Yamamoto nearly exploded, but controlled his temper. Naichi continued. "Of the battleships sunk or damaged on December seven, we have now learned that only the *Arizona* and *Oklahoma* remain at Pearl Harbor. There appears to be no effort to repair the Arizona or re-float her in any way. Perhaps the damage was too great. The *Oklahoma* was capsized, and has been refloated and put into dry-dock."

"And the others? The *Nevada*, the *California*?"

"We simply don't know what happened to them, Admiral. Every evening, Pearl Harbor runs a harbor clearance drill, and the midget subs have to be out of the paths of the destroyers, so they cannot observe. And apparently our photographer cannot raise suspicions too much through regular appearances."

"So they slipped out." It was not a question. Yamamoto's voice was somber. "With their escorts, I presume."

Naichi didn't have to answer. He merely bowed his head in agreement.

"You are saying then, that as the Midway carrier fleet — or what was left of it — returned to Pearl Harbor for refitting and repairs, the battleships that we thought we had eliminated before – all but two of them, at least – have now escaped to open water along with the *Yorktown*?"

"Correct, Admiral. That is an accurate summary of the information I now have."

Naichi is no gutless toady, that's for sure. He states his intelligence reports without concern for how his superiors will react to the news. Yamamoto frowned, and muttered, mostly to himself, "Inconceivable that they could have repaired that carrier. Perhaps the battleships, but not the carrier. Could the carrier in your dispatches be the *Saratoga*?"

Naichi suddenly smiled. "No, Admiral-san. Forgive me – I received this message just before you summoned me, but we have received word that the *Saratoga*, which had been undergoing repairs at Bremerton and was heading back to Hawaii, when submarine ..." he paused and checked some notes he brought, " ... I-168 hit her with at least one torpedo, and badly damaged her. The captain of I-678 reported her heading eastward at greatly reduced speed, but he was unable to get another shot. But he was certain the vessel he hit was the *Saratoga*. Therefore, the carrier that left Pearl Harbor had to be another carrier. Yet how could it be *Yorktown*?"

Yamamoto shook his head. "We shall give that further analysis. But there are two other issues ..." Before Yamamoto could finish, Naichi interrupted.

"... the destroyers and oilers that drew away your strike force, and the cruisers that fought the holding action to the north. Yes, it appears at least four of those destroyers escaped our air attacks, along with two of the oilers. We think they may have headed to Pearl Harbor through some indirect route. But with the oilers, those destroyers could be literally anywhere, and could sail around for weeks. And the remaining American cruisers have not returned to Pearl Harbor yet."

"Have *not* returned? Where did they go?" Yamamoto now rubbed his hand with the missing fingers. *We had them in the perfect trap, but the Americans salvaged enough of their fleet to keep fighting. They know we cannot storm Hawaii, but they also know they cannot let us get between them and California.*

"I have no precise information on the cruisers ..." "... but do you have a guess, Commander?"

Naichi, bowed. "Yes, Admiral. My guess is that they headed for the American west coast, probably California. There is some, incomplete, information that they were on a bearing for San Diego. But, of course, bearings change with the wind."

"Thank you, commander. Keep me posted immediately of any new intelligence." Even before Naichi saluted and disappeared, Sagata had returned from delivering the orders to Hosogaya. Yamamoto gestured Sagata to his side. "I want an officers meeting here, as soon as Nagumo reaches the rendezvous point. We have one chance left to annihilate the Americans." *One chance left to win this war.*

CHAPTER TWENTY

Kaiser Shipyards, Richmond,
California
9 Jun 42 07:45

The USS *Hornet* (Wikipedia)

"You gotta be kiddin' me." Henry Kaiser looked at the telegram, which now was confirmed by a second order from the Navy Department. He bellowed at his secretary already hard at work at her desk outside Kaiser's office. "Eunice! Get Eugland over here, now! And get every yard foreman here for a ten o'clock meeting."

Unfazed, Eunice Wilkens started flipping through her company lists, and called messengers over from the pool. Runners immediately took the handwritten orders to shipyard foremen throughout the Kaiser facility. "Something wrong, Mr. Kaiser?" she calmly asked.

Kaiser looked again at the message, and threw it on his desk. "Not a damn, thing, Eunice. Not a damn thing, except that now they want me to put battleships back together." He had no sooner flopped back in his leather chair, and lit up a cigarette than John Eugland burst in. "What's up, boss? Sounded urgent." Kaiser motioned for him to close the door and handed him the paper containing the message from the Navy Department.

Eugland's eyes opened wide, and he muttered, "King himself." Then he looked up at Kaiser. "I thought we were supposed to be building freighters? Where are we even going to get the parts? And no one here has any up-to- date training on battlewagons."

Kaiser produced the follow-up order from the Navy Department, which Eugland quickly read.

"This must be serious." Kaiser frowned as if to say, *You figured that out on your own?* Then Eugland added, "Well, they've got people on their way here from San Diego, and this says that parts are en route by train. Do we have that many suppliers west of the

Mississippi?"

Flipping down a large map behind his desk, Kaiser said, "Roosevelt's crew got this much right: they spread out production in every state, every city, and every contractor. We can just about assemble most weapons in any one large metropolitan area—New York alone has enough contractors to make tanks or aircraft. You take all the shipbuilders here in California, well, it's possible we have all the parts we'll need."

"But why *us*, Henry? They could have used the repair docks down at San Diego or Long Beach—they're much better equipped for warship work than we are."

Kaiser ripped the cigarette out of his mouth. "Dammit, Johnnie, who do you think I am, the Great Houdini or some mind reader? I'm just following orders here, and you are too! I don't know why they want us to do this, other than we're damn good and setting records with the speed of our work. Next time I sit down with for dinner with Franklin and Eleanor, I'll ask 'em, okay? Meanwhile, we've got a job to do, and from the looks of this, limited time to do it. Our foremen's meeting is at ten o'clock, and I want a plan they can work with, so you need to get busy."

"Yes sir." Eugland hastily departed for his own office, cursing under his breath the circumstances that were now making his shipyard responsible for re-fitting and, when necessary, repairing, a dozen cruisers and battleships in a five-day window.

Naval Station, Pearl Harbor, CINCPAC
9 Jun 42 08:15

Lamar came jogging through the outer office desks, looking positively nimble and holding a fresh radio message. Although he knocked on Nimitz's door, he did not even wait for a response before he burst in. Fortunately, Nimitz was reading the progress reports from Halsey's force, which had pulled in on June 6th. Emergency repairs were nearly complete. The Admiral looked up, surprised at Lamar's unusual breach of protocol.

"Sorry, sir, but I knew you'd want to see this immediately." Out of breath, he handed the radio message to Nimitz, who read it twice, then broke out in a broad smile.

"I'll be damned. I'll be damned. We just might win this yet. All right, Art, first, tell Halsey I want to see him, right away. Then, send this message ..." and handed him a handwritten dispatch:

SECRET
FROM: CINCPAC
TO: CTF 17 AND 18
PROCEED ALL DELIBERATE SPEED TO POINT LUCK

Lamar stopped reading. "Point Luck, sir? I thought ..." Nimitz shrugged. "Spruance wanted a break from the playing card nomenclature, so he gave us the rendezvous point. No one else disagreed. Hell, we can't have any worse luck, can we Captain?"

Lamar shook his head. "Guess not, Admiral." He continued to read the dispatch:

RENDEZVOUS WITH TF 15 ENGAGE THE ENEMY WITH ALL DELIBER-
ATE SPEED WILL PROVIDE INTELLIGENCE AS TO ENEMY LOCATION

"Task Force 18? Is that *Saratoga*?"

Nimitz smiled and nodded. His mood lasted only seconds when an officer knocked on the door and delivered a fresh dispatch to Lamar.

The Captain's face turned ashen.

"Art?" queried Nimitz. "Are you okay? What is it?"

Lamar handed Nimitz the dispatch, which relayed the news that the *Saratoga* had been hit and returned to San Diego. The admiral, never given to hysterics, stared at it for a moment then crumpled it up. "Rewrite the message, Art. Remove Task Force Eighteen from the orders."

"Aye aye, Sir." Lamar started to leave, when he abruptly turned and the cloud on his face lifted some. "Admiral," he said, "they don't know about Task Force Fifteen at all, do they?"

Nimitz winked at him. "Just send the message, Captain."

Naval Station, Pearl Harbor, Office of Naval Investigative Service
9 Jun 42 0845

Just a short walk from CINCPAC, where Lamar was sending his message, Miko Tomita sat on a hard wooden bench in a sterile hallway across from a closed office door, identified only as "NIS/XO." The click of hard military shoes on the linoleum occasionally broke the silence, but otherwise Miko had been alone with her thoughts since Elliot went into the office more than half an hour ago. He thought it best since she was a Nisei, not complicate matters when he presented the photographs and other evidence from Sam's basement to the authorities. She took another sip of the cold coffee that she had nursed since she arrived, when the door suddenly opened and an officer appeared. "Would you step inside?"

Miko obediently entered the office, and was let to a back room where Elliot and two other officers dressed in Navy khakis sat around a long wooden table, the photographs and other materials taken from her home that day spread on the surface. All the men stood as she entered. One officer—she still wasn't very good with ranks —named O'Brien spoke first, coldly. "Miss Tomita, I'm sure you and Ensign Gibbons here have discussed the implications of this information." He pointed to the photos, and to the transmission frequencies. She lowered her head and nodded.

Tears were already forming up. "At the very least, this looks highly suspicious, and at the worst, treasonous. We have already sent a car to pick up your father. At this point, I'm not going to use the word 'arrest,' but that's going to be what happens if we don't get some good answers, fast."

Again, she nodded, and the first tear had already started to inch down her golden cheek.

"I need to be direct here. Ensign Gibbons insists neither you nor your brother had any knowledge of this. But I want you to answer for yourself. Did you have any indication whatsoever of this strange behavior on the part of your father, or did you have any access whatsoever to this information?"

Miko looked up. "Accusing me now?" Her teary eyes flashed with anger. "No. Elliot discovered the secret basement by accident. I lived there for years and didn't know it existed. I never saw any of those photos or materials before that day. And I never once saw my father do anything disloyal."

A second officer, with hard eyes, whose name tag read "Wilson" spoke next. "Do you still have any relatives in Japan?"

"Yes," she offered softly. "My grandmother and two aunts."

"You will give me those names." It wasn't a request. He slid a pad of paper over to her.

"Yes, but I don't know if I'm spelling them right— especially in Japanese letters---and I don't know addresses without looking at father's books."

"That's fine. We're just exploring all angles."

Another officer knocked, then entered and gave a hitchhik-ing gesture with his thumb toward the outer office. "It seems your dad has arrived." The door swung open and Sam Tomita entered, under guard, in handcuffs.

Miko shot out of the chair. "Father!" she sobbed, embracing him. Then she pushed back, anger filling her voice. "Jerry is sched-uled to ship back to the states any day. Did it ever occur to you that your own son might be at risk?"

Sam lowered his eyes. "I'm sorry, my daughter. I'm sorry. I had no choice." One of the officers shoved him into a chair as he continued to mutter, "no choice."

"Mr. Tomita," O'Brien began. "You are in serious trouble. This evidence indicates that you have been spying for the Empire of Japan, feeding the Japanese information on which ships are in harbor, and on their condition." He tapped the photos and papers in his hand against the table, their light flicking becoming the only sound in the room other than Miko's light sobbing.

"I admit, I took the photos," he began. "That's obvious. You have them. Elliot here told me he figured out what frequency my transmitter was set to. I am completely guilty."

Miko raised her head in a look of horror, while Elliot buried his face in his hands.

"What you don't know," Sam continued, "is why. Not that it will exonerate me of my crimes."

"So," instructed Wilson sarcastically, "enlighten us, please."

"Right before Pearl Harbor, I was contacted by an agent of the Imperial Japanese Government. He showed me pictures of my mother and two sisters, still in Japan. The man made it clear that if I did not do exactly as told, they all would die long and painful deaths. All I had to do to save them was call in on the radio once or twice a month as directed, and provide information as to which ships were in the harbor. That's all. I never thought we would be at war, or about who might be hurt—or that any of the ships might be at risk—only of my mother and sisters. It seemed like insignificant information. They told me not to lie or make things up—that they already had midget submarines confirming my reports."

O'Brien and Wilson looked at each other when Sam men-tioned midget submarines, but said nothing.

Sam continued. "I know what I did was wrong. I will take my punishment. If I must die, then let it be so. But I could not sacrifice my mother and sisters. If I am now executed ..." and with the mention of that word, Miko let out a small gasp, "... perhaps the police there will let them go. The honorable thing would have been for me to kill myself when I was first approached, but I was too weak. Now I see I could not win." He turned to Gibbons. "My apologies, Elliot. You are a fine man, a good officer. You did the right thing. I am relieved to be found out. Take care of my daughter." Elliot felt his own eyes mist up. Then, to Miko, he said, "I have brought dishonor on our family. But it is my dishonor. Not yours or Jerry's."

The two officers remained impassive during Tomita's speech, but Gibbons finally spoke. "I knew there had to be a reason, Sam. I don't agree with it. I think what you did was abominable, risking the lives of my fellow sailors. But I do understand it. Maybe under the circumstances . . . . Well, who knows what I would have done."

O'Brien gestured to Wilson, and whispered in his ear. "Perhaps we shouldn't immediately send this guy into the system." Wilson's eyes grew big. "What the hell are you talking about? He's a rat traitor. Should be hanged."

Gesturing to Wilson to calm down, O'Brien whispered, "Will you use your head for something more than hat rack for a minute? Remember last month we got that memo that anything unusual, out of the ordinary, or strange was to be brought to the attention of Captain Layton I think this qualifies as strange, don't you? Certainly out of the ordinary."

Willson rubbed his five-o'clock shadow, already visible at mid-morning, and said, "You got a point there. All right, I'll call Layton's people. But this guy should still see the end of a rope."

Gibbons and Miko were ordered to leave, and told that the Navy had not yet decided what charges to press. Within the hour, Layton showed up, obviously suffering from sleep deprivation.

"All right, boys, whaddya got for me?"

O'Brien and Wilson introduced him to Sam Tomita. Once again, Sam told his story. Layton listened, displaying no emotion, then replied, "You got yourself in one hell of a pickle, there, Mr. Tomita. I don't know how you're gonna get out of this. But you might be able to atone for some of your sins."

O'Brien's eyes narrowed. "What exactly do you have in mind, Captain? He's our prisoner. There are procedures."

Still puffing, Layton nodded aggressively. "Oh, I understand. I understand, Captain. And I think you understand that we are in a helluva situation with the Jap Navy here—no offense, there, Mr. Tomita . . ." and Sam bowed, slightly, ". . . and I think Mr. Tomita here, for all his crimes, just might help us out. Would you be willing to do that, Mr. Tomita . . . Sam . . . if it might, say, affect your sentence?"

Sam expressed little emotion. "I am ashamed of what I have done. Once the Empire learns I am a prisoner, they will kill my mother and sisters, or assume they are of no more use and let them go. Either way, their lives can no longer be used to force me to betray my country." He displayed no insincerity at the term, "my country," meaning America.

"Hang on, here, Mr. Tomita," said Layton, as if the prisoner had an option. "Gentlemen, your phone please?" O'Brien pointed to the phone on his desk. Layton sat down at the desk and dialed a number.

"Art, this is Ed. I'm over at NIS. That's right, the gumshoes. We have something here that you ought to find very interesting. Very, very interesting." Layton paused a moment.

"Okay, thanks Art." He turned to the guards. "Admiral Nimitz's chief of staff is on his way over here. Suffice it to say your prisoner here might give us the break we've been needing for a couple of months." Wilson shot a disgusted look at O'Brien.

"Whatever you need, Captain," replied O'Brien, without enthusiasm. An hour later, Lamar and Nimitz both strode in. When Layton saw Nimitz, he shot Lamar a look, as if to ask, "What's this all about?" Before he could speak, Lamaar whispered, "Ed, he wants to get this, first hand."

O'Brien and Wilson followed the admiral into the room. By this time, Tomita looked ashen. Nimitz glanced at his intelligence officer. "Ed, what do you have for me?" asked Nimitz.

Closing the door to the small room, Layton pointed to Tomita. "Admiral, looks like we have us a repentant spy."

"Didn't think there was such a thing," snorted Nimitz, studying Tomita.

Layton reviewed the story of how Sam Tomita came to be a prisoner, and of his family held hostage in Japan. Nimitz listened dispassionately. When Layton concluded, Nimitz coldly added, "I can sympathize with your concerns over your family, Mr. Tomita, but that hardly excuses the blood that may be on your hands. Many a fine American boy died as a result of your aid to the enemy."

Sam glumly bowed. "I offer no excuses, Admiral. The dishonor is mine. The dishonor to my country, the United States, is also mine."

"So," Nimitz impatiently asked Layton, "why do you think he can help us now?"

Layton turned to Tomita. "Mr. Tomita, the Japanese don't know you've been captured, is that correct?" Sam nodded, still staring at the table.

"And you were not scheduled to file another report until tonight, is that what you told me?"

Again, Tomita nodded, but slowly looked up. "Do you have something I can do to make up for my sins?"

Nimitz scowled at Layton. "Ed, where are you going with this?"

"Admiral, I think Sam should keep his appointment with the Japanese."

"Keep his appointment? I don't ..." Nimitz heard Lamar chuckle rather loudly behind him. Puzzled, he wheeled to stare at his chief of staff with raised eyebrows.

"Sorry, admiral," grinned Lamar. "It's just...Captain Layton's idea. It's a goodie."

USS Yorktown, 200 miles southeast of Hawaii
9 Jun 42 1140

Raymond Spruance peered off the starboard side of the *Yorktown's* flag bridge. Sounds of rivet guns still rang through the piping, while down below showers of sparks still drenched work crews who labored to bring the vessel up to fighting ability. She had left under cover of darkness on the night of June 7, having only half her boilers operating and gaping holes in some of the aft compartments. Tugs had hauled her out, and throughout her slow cruise to Point Luck, destroyers had regularly pulled alongside to take off civilian workers who had completed their jobs. *She's far from one hundred percent, observed Spruance, but she can launch and recover aircraft and maneuver a little.*

Spruance had received his orders from Nimitz on June 6, and while not understanding the urgency, had assembled his staff and planned the operation. Typically, Spruance gave his staff a few general directions, then let them attend to all the details. Besides the *Yorktown*, Spruance's Task Force 17 consisted of cruisers *Astoria* (fully repaired now), DESRON 2 (except for the still unaccounted for *Hammann*, which had joined the decoy force, DESRON 6) and six subs reassigned from the Midway Patrol Group, the *Flying Fish*, *Nautilus*, *Grouper*, *Gato*, *Grenadier*, and *Trout*. In addition, Spruance had been given the oiler *Guadalupe*, which had been ordered into theater once Halsey sent his other three oilers with the decoy fleet. Along with the various destroyer escorts and other auxiliaries, TF 17 numbered 18 surface warships plus the seven subs. And soon it would be double that size, when TF 15 arrived. Of course, until a few hours ago, when he learned about the *Saratoga*, Spruance had hoped he might even get her hundred-plus planes as well. But now all he could count on were a pair of cruisers and three destroyers, as the other vessels accompanied Saratoga back to port.

Ah well, thought Spruance. *Nothing in war goes as expected. And I still have enough to do the job.*

In consultation with Nimitz, Spruance had already thrown out the destroyers in a screen due east of Hawaii, backed up by all the seaplane tenders the Navy could cobble together, accounting for some 25 PBYs that would serve as reconnaissance for the fleet from the west side of Hawaii. *This time, they're carrying bombs. It won't affect their range much, but might contribute to the general confusion if things unfold as we hope.* As the decision at Midway became clear, the Army had reinforced Hawaii with another 28 B-17s and 15 B-26s, and all the practice bombs they could drop. The minute Halsey's fleet began its retreat, Army pilots were training non-stop. *Their performance will be a helluva lot better than it was at Midway, that's for sure. Anyone who expects a repeat of that sorry example of land-based air will be in for a surprise this time around. The AAF got their asses chewed out after that, and they've already improved, changing their bombing levels and adopting other tactics.* Moreover, Spruance knew that the Army had reinforced Hawaii with as many fighter planes as it could find, even if most were P-40s. Between the "Warhawks" and the P-39 "Airacobras," some 50 fighter planes would escort the land-based air into their attack.

Spruance, Halsey, and Nimitz, in the few days they had, worked round the clock to see that the malfunctioning electrical arming switches were ripped out of the SBDs. All bombing would be done by hand ... *the old fashioned way,* thought Spruance. This time, relatively sure of where the enemy would be, TF 17 had 37 Dauntlesses battle ready. *It'll be a tough job coordinating and organizing all those new faces, but we need every bomber we can get.* The Yorktown again had a full complement of Devastator torpedo planes (12 — one simply refused to work, its engine in perpetual "gremlin" mode), and 25 Wildcats to provide fighter escorts.

Nimitz had trusted him with a carrier command, perhaps, given the likely way the battle would unfold, the carrier command — Ray Spruance, a cruiser man. *I know the boys weren't too excited when they heard I was to command. Guess they don't know, or don't care, that I've seen combat.* Spruance thought back to a time in early '42 when his cruiser came across a Japanese fishing trawler — clearly a picket ship and transmitting station from the antennae. Spruance ordered the gun crews to blast it out of the water. He watched through his binoculars and as the ship exploded and the "fishermen" were shot down, one of his officers said, "I pity those devils." Spruance countered, "I do too, but we didn't start this war." Word got around: Spruance was tough, willing to do the dirty work that was necessary.

Now Spruance awaited the arrival of Task Force 15. It better not be late. He pondered the recent debacles at Coral Sea and Midway, how Fletcher, Fitch, and then Halsey had all been out-guessed by the Japanese; how, at each turn, American forces were simply outnumbered and overwhelmed. *Not this time.* He mulled the sudden, unexpected loss of the *Saratoga's* task force. *No matter. With our land-based air, for once the odds are going to be just about even — if everyone comes to the party on time.*

Naval Station Pearl Harbor, Brig Facility #4
10 Jun 42 1335

"Guard, I'm here to see prisoner one six zero one two." The outside gate opened, and Captain Nelson O'Brien presented his credentials to the Marines, who waved him through. In moments, he stood outside the jail cell of Sam Tomita, who lay staring at the ceiling. The cell door swung open with a clang, and O'Brien stepped in, followed by the second clang of the door shutting behind him and the keys turning in the lock.

Sam sat up. "Well, did it work?"

"We obviously won't know for a while. I brought your file. You can read my comments and recommendations to the military tribunal — as a spy, you won't be tried in a normal civilian court."

"I understand," Sam softly responded. "My son? Will this affect him?"

O'Brien took out more papers. "I've looked over his folder. There is nothing there now. If — but only if — your information helps us, there will be nothing added to his file and the Army won't care. If necessary, if your information works, I'm sure Admiral Nimitz will do what he needs to. As for your son, he will only know what you tell him."

Sam chuckled. "It would be hard to keep it a secret, with me here in jail." O'Brien shrugged. *Maybe you shouldn't have spied in the first place*, he thought, but let it pass. "Anything else I can do, I will. It doesn't matter now."

"Certainly the other Japanese spies on the island know of my arrest, and likely think I'll be executed ..." He suddenly stopped. "Wait! You said if I helped I would not be shot ..." "Relax. We gave you our word. You did your part. There will be no execution ..."

"No!" Sam broke in. "No, don't you see? If I were to 'die' — be executed — the other Japanese spies on the island would naturally assume I'm dead, and could not be the source of future information being fed to the Empire. Moreover, they would attempt to take over my job."

O'Brien wasn't following. "But you can't make any more transmissions if you are 'dead.'"

"No, but after this, they won't believe anything I send anyway. Meanwhile, I know what and how they would acquire information. I know the general times, how *they* would get photos. I could help you find them, if there is indeed more than one. And ..."

O'Brien was adjusting to the first set of implications. "And what?"

"It will be a tight timetable, but if word gets back to the Japanese authorities that you executed me, it just might lend even more credibility to the last information I sent."

Rubbing his chin, O'Brien said, "So you want us to 'kill' you?"

"It is proper and honorable punishment for my crimes."

"*Guard!*" O'Brien called, and he heard the sounds of iron

doors being unlocked. Turning to Sam Tomita, he said, "I'll run this by my office, and probably CINCPAC will have to sign off on it. But let's get this straight, Tojo: I had friends on board the *Arizona*. Without your helping the Japs, its possible those men might still be alive. Anything I do for you, I do because it helps us kill more of those bastards, not because I'm impressed with your sudden sense of honor.   It's too bad about your mother and sisters. Its war, and war is hell. If I had your choice, I don't know what I'd choose. But I don't. I have my own job and my own allegiances, and I doubt I would have ratted out my own country. I'll get back to you." O'Brien stepped outside the cell door, and it slammed shut behind him.

Sam, alone in his cell, hung his head.

CHAPTER TWENTY-ONE

*The **Yamato**, 150 miles northeast of Hawaii*
10 Jun 42 1630

Nakalima B5N@ "Kate" (Wikipedia)

Sagata's rap on the door shook Yamamoto out of deep thought.

"Sir, the evening meal awaits in the officer's mess."

Dressed in his dinner whites, Yamamoto rubbed his face. He stood, affixed his cap on his head, and opened the door. "Thank you, Sagata. I trust you convinced the steward to make that plum pudding I've been yearning for."

"I think you'll be quite pleased with the meal, Admiral," Sagata smiled. Yamamoto led down the narrow passageways, through piping and tubing—the entrails of a modern battleship—until he reached the narrow stairs. Even a small Japanese sailor had to take care in negotiating the tiny metal ladder, which, when wet, could be treacherous. The close quarters played havoc with white dinner dress uniforms. Sagata trailed a few steps behind, mentally reviewing any last-minute routine messages that he had been lining up to discuss with the Admiral.

Looking at his watch, Sagata said, "Admiral Nagumo's battleship task force should be about two hundred-fifty miles off the California coast by now, and will be in position tomorrow morning to begin bombarding the northern ports. We have sent scout planes out regularly to the south and west, and still have not located any American ships, but we don't have any recent surveillance in the San Diego-Long Beach area. A submarine is scheduled to arrive there tomorrow."

Too late to alert Nagumo if the heavy ships are not there, thought Yamamoto, but he let it pass.

Sagata continued. "Just in case the Americans try to slip in between us and Nagumo's force, a screen of five submarines has deployed to our south and west. And the last of Admiral Hosogaya's oilers arrived with their escorts last night. We shall have plenty of fuel for this operation."

Yamamoto listened as he walked, occasionally nodding, until

they reached the officer's mess. It was a large room with a beautiful wooden table seating 12, now covered by a fine white linen and displaying a silver place setting at each of the 12 seats. Stewards in blue coats and white gloves stood by to serve the officers the moment they took their chairs. When Yamamoto walked in, the assembled officers all came to attention and saluted. Yamamoto returned their salute and said, "Be seated, please." Never one to waste time when it came to food, he gestured to the stewards to begin their meal service.

Surveying the table, Yamamoto noticed that one chair was empty: that of Commander Naichi, his intelligence officer. Yamamoto glanced at Sagata, who also noticed the absence. Sagata shrugged, his meal already interrupted. Finally he stood and said only, "I'll find out," then departed.

A soft, early banter developed until Commander Ure, chief navigation officer, spoke loudly enough for all to hear.

"Admiral, after we destroy the last American carrier, do we invade Hawaii?" A gentle laugh rippled through the mess, and Yamamoto smiled.

"Would you care to be the first ashore, Commander?" replied the Admiral, to the guffaws of the other officers.

Ure good-naturedly responded to the jibe. "Will the admiral place me in charge of a landing barge?" Everyone laughed harder.

"You are the navigation officer, Commander— could you find your way ashore in one?"

The table was now fully engrossed in the comic exchange, a rarity for Japanese officers' messes, with their incessant politeness and obsessive deference. But with Admiral Yamamoto, it was different. The officers loved him, respected him, and yet felt comfortable around him. He had led them to victory after victory, and to many of them, he represented the new Nippon, a far more human empire than they had experienced as junior officers at the academy or in their training, where beatings were still common.

"Seriously, Admiral," continued Ure. "What happens after we defeat the American fleet?"

Yamamoto's face grew impassive. "That is, Commander, for my superiors to determine. Do you see any troop transports with our Kido Butai?"

Ure would not be dissuaded. "But, Admiral, if it were up to you, what would be our next move?"

The Army; always the Army. They opposed the Midway plan from the beginning, wanting to dig in and fortify their little islands. It wasn't until the Doolittle Raid that the Army agreed to provide invasion troops for Midway. Fools! Don't they realize that if we give the Americans time, they will devise bombs so big that no bunker can survive? They will not hesitate to annihilate an entire island if it saves ten of their soldiers' lives. Don't those bee-heads understand what has happened in Europe? A blind man can see it, even if that maniac Hitler cannot. They are massing thousands of bombers, and will unleash absolute hell on Germany in the next year, all without risking a single ground unit or tank. True, fliers will pay a price, but a small price overall. Germany's cities will be razed. The Americans and British will make it appear like the hordes of the Mongols swept through, leaving nothing standing. German civilians will be lucky to find two sticks to rub together for a fire. And that's what awaits us if the Army has its way, and if the Americans aren't forced to operate out of their own coastal harbors, and induced to sue for peace before things get truly out of hand.

The Admiral was completely lost in thought now, his entire table of officers staring at him. *Braggarts! The Army pulls us into China, then has no way to win, and no way out. Then they drag their feet when it comes to supporting our invasions — the only hope we have of getting Australia and America out of the war.*

"Admiral?"

Yamamoto realized he had drifted off. Clearing his throat and taking a sip of his sake — another rare treat he had permitted tonight — he looked at Ure with a mixture of remorse and impatience. "Have we won this battle already, Commander Ure? Do you know what tomorrow brings? Have you forgotten how fortunate we were at Midway that none of the land-based aircraft scored any hits?"

"But, Admiral, could it not be said that the Americans were all the *more* fortunate? That it was only a stroke of luck that Halsey escaped with his last carrier?"

Ure had struck a nerve with Yamamoto, who still blamed himself for biting on the bait of that infernal task group of oilers and destroyers. He responded with an icy tone. "Yes, Commander, luck and my own error." When Ure began to apologize, Yamamoto raised his hand to signal silence. "I do not take affront to what you said, Commander Ure. If we cannot learn from our mistakes, we shall make worse errors in the future. Sometimes our culture of honor and shame prohibits us from even the most basic self-analysis. The escape of the American ships was my fault alone. Everyone else was in position. I merely want to remind you that we are up against no ordinary enemy, no amateurish Russian navy that will sail into our guns, no British battleships sailing helplessly without air cover into our attacks. No, Ure, we are in a death struggle with an enemy who is every bit as disciplined, cunning, and courageous as we are. Never forget that. Do not think for a moment that this war is over. Even if we were to attain a total victory in the coming days, do you think Admiral Hosogaya's naval infantry—even if it were here with us--- could just walk ashore on Oahu as they did at Midway? And if we did, then what? Does the Empire have enough men and ships to keep a bastion in Hawaii supplied, let alone invade the United States? I don't know the answers to these questions, and, thank the gods, I do not have to have the answers. Others give me orders, and I obey. But remember—all of you, remember ..." Yamamoto said, his voice now commanding the table, "... good fortune in a pair of engagements does not equal vanquishing one's enemy permanently. The tides of war can turn on a few minutes in battle, an entire campaign on the actions of a handful of pilots or ships. And even then, our enemy is relentless, massive. I have never believed complete military victory was possible over the Americans, but rather they had to defeat themselves, through pacifism, laziness, or some other unworthy quality ..." and, realizing he had become inordinately serious, Yamamoto added, "... of which they have a great number." Transfixed by his brutal honesty, the officers now nervously laughed.

"We are in a long war, I fear, gentlemen. We have accomplished remarkable feats. Some would say we have already done the impossible. But in the scope of great conflicts, we have yet done nothing. Our enemy's forces in this theater are temporarily diminished, but at best slightly wounded. In the face of our 'successes,' what has he done? He commits two-thirds of his resources and men to fight Germany. Does that sound like a nation that truly fears the Empire of Japan? Our spies tell us that the Americans have a half-dozen aircraft carriers already operating in the Atlantic convoys, and a dozen new carriers of an advanced class building in their ship ways. I will not tell you how many we have under construction—that information is classified." *I dare not tell them it is only one!* "But it is certainly not a dozen. My point is, gentlemen, that a military victory as they desire in Tokyo may not be possible. We may have to instead inflict such damage on our enemy that he gives us what we want without us having to take it. Does that require us to possess Hawaii? That is not for me to say. I will only say that the sooner we can bring this to a conclusion, the better, for when the Americans defeat Germany — and I have no doubt they will — we do not want to be the 'last man standing' between them and their lazy, peaceful way of life. Once they commit themselves to destroying a foe, they do not relent until they have achieved their purpose. And any of you who have doubts can ask the North American Indian tribes about that."

Several of the officers stared wide-eyed at the Admiral. He had never spoken so long, or so freely, in their entire time on his staff. A few mouths hung open. Sagata, sitting to Yamamoto's right, suppressed a smile, for he had heard it all, many times. *What? Sagata thought. Did they truly believe Japanese forces would land in San Francisco and march ashore in San Diego? Do they have no understanding of the size of the United States, or how unified we have made their people? These are not inept and divided Chinese, or oppressed rejects of the Russian Tsarist army, but the products of a modern industrial nation of immense power.* Despite his own frequent dismissals of Americans as gaijin, deep down Sagata knew better and had never deluded himself into thinking that a traditional invasion and occupation of even part of the United States was even remotely possible. He agreed substantially with Yamamoto. *But for the Admiral to say so, openly, well ... either he is supremely confident in our operation, or he knows something I do not.*

Yamamoto gestured to the officers to eat, and, still digesting what they had heard, they all obediently began with their noodles and crab cakes. No one said a word, although every man at the table itched to ask more questions. While they mulled and ate, Yamamoto remonstrated himself for his honesty in front of the officers. *Ultimately, though, they have the right to know what they are doing, do they not? At any rate, one way or another the die will be cast soon. If the brilliant dons in the Naval General Staff learn of my remarks, and wish to remove me, they will find it difficult to do so if our operations are successful. Admiral Fukodome? He hasn't the spine. On the other hand, if we fail, my honor and reputation will be of little value anyway, so removing me will be viewed as punishment for my military transgressions, not my political views.* He no sooner wrapped his chopsticks around several noodles than a junior officer entered and whispered something in

Sagata's ear, who then stood and whispered the message to Yamamoto.

"Commander Naichi is outside with some updated intelligence that he thinks is urgent."

The Admiral nodded, stood, smiled gently, motioned for everyone else to remain seated, and excused himself. Outside, he found Naichi waiting with some papers in his hands. "We missed your presence at dinner, Commander. Your chair waits for you."

Naichi bowed, and replied "I had pressing matters, Admiral, which I think you will agree took precedence. My source in Hawaii reported in." He handed Yamamoto the transcript of the transmission. "It appears the *Yorktown* has re-entered Pearl Harbor. He reports that apparently it was taken out for a trial run, and limped back in, requiring several tugs just to position her for the dry dock. Further, he reported much activity around the ship—repair crews and the like. I think she is still badly damaged, and the Americans' attempts to repair her have failed."

Holding the transcript, Yamamoto pondered the implications. "So, we know the location of the *Yorktown*, and it is not capable of fighting. That leaves only the *Enterprise*, but your source has no knowledge of her location?"

"Correct, Admiral-san. Nor do we know the location of the battleships and cruisers that sailed several days ago. This source apparently heard some loose talk about San Diego as their destination."

"Did that strike you as odd, Commander? Has it been typical for that source to offer such information before?"

"It did seem unusual, Admiral. However, not long after he delivered the information, I received word from another resource in Hawaii—I try to double check all information—that the source of this information was arrested, and is likely to be executed. It strikes me that in acquiring this information, he may have exposed himself."

"And that makes it all the more credible to you?" asked Yamamoto.

"Yes Sir. That the spy is willing to be executed ... well, few are anxious to die for a lie."

Handing the transcripts back to Naichi, Yamamoto folded his hands behind his back and began to pace slowly up and down the narrow, dark corridor, mulling the implications. "And other, generic radio intercepts? What do they tell you?"

"We can't be certain," answered Naichi, "but it appears there is a sizeable body of ships somewhere to the southwest of Oahu — possibly the battleships."

Sagata looked at Yamamoto, then at Naichi. "Why would the Americans take their battleships out of a more- easily defended harbor, complete with combat air patrol, and send them to open water outside combat air patrol's range? It doesn't make sense."

Naichi shrugged. "I agree, it doesn't make sense, but it didn't make sense that the Americans were completely unprepared for our December seven attack either. I think their phrase is 'caught with their pants down?' You are asking me to assign motivations to our enemy. I only analyze his movements."

"But," Yamamoto responded, "you do have a better feel for these types of intercepts than we do — how they sound, whether their language is appropriate for the size of force they seem to be, and so on. What does your intuition tell you?"

Naichi stared for a moment, uncomfortable that his estimate would provide the basis for Yamamoto's next move. "Admiral, I will offer you only what I know: we cannot account for the battleships, so it could be the battleships producing the signal traffic. But neither can we account for the decoy destroyer squadron that drew us away from Halsey last week. Some ships were destroyed, but the rest escaped, and they might generate sufficient signal traffic to account for this level of activity. Or, for that matter, it could possibly even be the *Yorktown*'s escort force. If, for example, our source is wrong and the damage is easily repaired, the *Yorktown* could be under way in perhaps a day or two. It would not be efficient to bring all her escorts back in if the plan is for her to again rendezvous with them soon."

"Another option," Yamamoto mulled, "is that they were planning to rendezvous the *Yorktown* with the *Saratoga* ..."

"... until the *Saratoga* was damaged and had to return to port in California," Naichi pointed out.

"There is a final possibility," Yamamoto countered: "The battleships are sailing to San Diego at reduced speed."

"In which case it would mean that the Americans are more concerned with defending their west coast than Hawaii, or think they cannot protect their battleships in harbor."

Yamamoto considered his options. "If it is the battleships accounting for the signal traffic, then by the time the Americans figure out what is happening, it will be too late for them to join the fight from that position. If it is the destroyers—the *Yorktown*'s escorts---they cannot affect matters in any way. As for the *Yorktown*, even if she gets underway late tomorrow, it will be too later for her to affect the battle, and we can destroy her at our pleasure."

"There is one element you haven't yet mentioned, Admiral," cautioned Naichi. "What if the battleships have already sailed eastward toward the American coast? Nagumo's strike force would encounter them. I'm sure he could defeat them in open water, however."

Nagumo did well enough against the American cruiser force, although he suffered inordinate losses to the submarines. Still, he has not encountered a force that equaled his in firepower. He thought a moment more, then stated, "Nagumo will be fine against any forces he encounters. Commander Naichi, you have removed the last burden on my mind about this operation, the location of the *Yorktown*. They will not be launching any aircraft from a drydocked ship, and even if naval aicraft launch from land bases on Hawaii, they won't have the range to influence the battle. So we are back to dealing with one carrier, and Halsey. You are dismissed, with my thanks, Commander. Now, will you please have some dinner?"

Naichi bowed, saluted, and then entered the mess. Once the door shut, Yamamoto signaled to Sagata to walk with him down the passageway—not an easy task for two men engaged in a conversation. "We now come back to Halsey. He surprised me last time, choosing flight instead of fight." Yamamoto stopped in a doorway.

Sagata nodded. "Most unusual for the man. Most unusual. Yet he saved his command. Had he stayed, we would have utterly destroyed his fleet."

"So where would he be now, Sagata? If you were Halsey, where would you go?"

Sagata's face screwed up in a puzzled expression. "We don't know what he knows, Admiral. Do you think he is aware of Nagumo's diversionary force? If so, would he pursue it?"

"Or," suggested the Admiral, "would he ignore it and seek out my carrier force?"

"He has one carrier, Admiral. How much can he do? Especially against four fleet carriers and three light carriers capable of putting up a nominal combat air patrol? It seems his only likelihood of success would be to position himself east of us, behind Nagumo, and attack him from the west."

"Perhaps. But Halsey could also stay behind us, with Hawaii's land-based air at his disposal, and attack us from the west."

"That," Sagata concluded, "would give Nagumo free rein to wreak havoc on the American west coast— harbors, shipping, even the cities."

"You have a constant scout patrol up. I want you to increase the number of planes conducting reconnaissance. Use some of the Nakajima attack planes from the carriers if you need to. I want to know where Halsey is."

Sagata turned to execute the order, but Yamamoto uncustomarily grabbed his arm. "Tomorrow, Captain. You may begin the new flights tomorrow. In the meantime, have dinner. It seems we have been trying to eat for the past hour!"

Kaiser Shipyards, Richmond, California
11 Jun 42 1902

"Here comes the *Pennsylvania*, boss." Johnnie Eugland and Henry Kaiser watched tugboats guide the massive battlewagon into her berth against the sunset. Looking down at the report, Eugland added, "There doesn't seem to be much left to do to her—refit some of the 5-inch guns, the number four boiler is still not operating properly, and some of the watertight hatches aren't sealing. But she's essentially battle-ready now. A magnificent sight, that's for sure."

"And to think we almost lost her. Almost lost all of 'em." Kaiser scanned the massive shipyard, his Liberty ships now lining the far side of the harbor in a row of semi- completed vessels. Now he was in the battleship business, and already in berths in some stage of refit were the *Nevada, California, West Virginia,* and *Maryland.* They all were still suffering some damage. Alongside were the newly-arrived *Texas* and *New York.* He took the work list from Eugland and reviewed the remaining tasks. Half the vessels had one or more turrets out; the Nevada had a minor rudder problem, and one malady or another was still afflicting every Pearl Harbor survivor. Still, the fact that they were floating and capable of fighting at all was a marvel.

"Johnnie, you've done some job here. Seems to me these ships are as ready as we can get them without putting them in dry-dock. Oh, there's a few things we need to wrap up on most of them, but I think they could push out of the ways in the next day or so."

"Good to hear it, Mr. Kaiser," came a voice behind them. Kaiser and Eugland turned to see the figure of a vice admiral. "We're going to need them out of here tomorrow."

"And who might you be?" inquired Kaiser. Extending his hand, the officer said "Vice   Admiral Dan Callaghan. I've been detailed here by the Navy Department to get these vessels out to open sea. Of course, the moment they push off, they belong to Admiral Kinkaid, their new task force commander, along with those cruisers he brought with him from Pearl."

"I don't know that all of them will be ready tomorrow, Admiral. We've had two thousand men working on them round the clock since the arrived, and I have to say, even I'm surprised that we've accomplished so much. The Navy Department's been very good at getting us parts. But this was a helluva job, let me tell you. A couple are still only a little better than floating gun barges."

"That might be all we need, Mr. Kaiser," interrupted Callaghan. "And your men have worked wonders. Wonders." Even though the light was almost gone now, he added, "To think that whites and Negroes could work together like this ... Well, let me just say I spent some time in the South, so it's ... it's different. But you did it. Maybe you showed everyone something here. At any rate, you certainly showed the Navy you can build any ship we ask you to build, that's for sure."

"I appreciate it, Admiral, but in all honesty, most of these ships had already been substantially repaired.

Actually, I don't understand why we didn't just leave them at Pearl Harbor and finish the work there."

Callaghan shrugged. "Sometimes it's better if we don't know everything, Mr. Kaiser. Anyway, I've said what I came to say. The Navy wants these ships out to sea tomorrow. I've ordered Tom Kinkaid to assume active command of Task Force Eighteen as of twenty-four hundred hours tonight."

Kaiser and Eugland exchanged skeptical looks, and Kaiser said, "They're your ships, Admiral. At least now we can go back to building Liberty ships."

Callaghan again offered his hand. "Truly, Mr. Kaiser, it's been an honor. Don't think the country doesn't know what you're doing for this war."

Shaking the officer's hand, Kaiser smiled. "Maybe I'll remind FDR when it's over."

Task Force 16, 150 miles northeast of Hawaii
10 Jun 42 1130

A bright moon lit the Pacific, providing Bill Halsey a heaven-ly lamp with which he could survey his armada from the bridge of the *Enterprise*. He still had the cruisers *New Orleans* and *Northamp-ton*, plus the repaired December 7 survivor, *San Francisco*, and five light cruisers who also survived that attack (*Raleigh, Detroit, Phoenix, Honolulu*, and *St. Louis*) but all the other heavy cruisers from the Battle of Midway had been sent east to join Task Force 18. That still left Halsey with the better part of two destroyer squadrons (the old DESRON 1 and the remainder of the Midway refueling unit). De-spite the impressive sight, with ships extending completely into the distant darkness, Halsey knew that alone they were no match for Yamamoto's force of at least four fleet carriers.

He'd received his orders earlier in the day from Nimitz. Ro-chefort's magicians had again figured out where the enemy force was, and PBY patrols had confirmed it. Halsey was up against the main body, almost certainly Yamamoto, which he would engage to-morrow at dawn. Nimitz also informed him of a second strike force, comprised exclusively of battleships and cruisers, plus one light car-rier, sailing for northern California. That would be Kinkaid's objec-tive: he would have all the Pearl Harbor battleships plus whatever could be spared from other operations on the west coast, as well as land-based air and all the cruisers that had been saved from the holding action at Midway. Guns against guns, air against air.

LeBoutiller appeared beside him. "Coffee, Admiral?"

"No thanks, Charlie. Makes me pee too much."

Reaching in his pocket for a cigarette, he found only an emp-ty pack. "I will take a cigarette if you can find one, though." LeB-outiller immediately disappeared, then seconds later held out a new pack. "Courtesy of the OOD."

"Tell him he's promoted," joked Halsey.

"Quite a view, huh Admiral?"

Halsey let out a low laugh. "It'd be a lot better if I saw the sil-houettes of four more flattops out there. Aw, hell. Guess you never go to war with everything you want."

"Admiral Nimitz has a real plan," offered LeBoutiller. "One way or the other, this will be it. Either we get them, or they get us tomorrow."

"Nimitz has done his homework, that's for sure. That ol' Texas boy ain't dumb. Still, I don't like operations that require this much coordination, especially between units that can't even see each other, let alone communicate by radio."

"Kinda forces you to trust Ray Spruance, doesn't it Admiral?"

"Oh, Charlie, I'd trust Ray with my life." Then he laughed, "Hell, I am trusting him with my life. But in combat, it always seems like it's the things you can't plan for that cause your defeat or provide your victory. A faulty catapult keeps a scout plane from finding an enemy force in time. Bombing squadrons go to the wrong coordinates or take off late. Or, like last time, our electrical arming devices cause three or four bombs to drop prematurely. Who knows if one — just one of those — wouldn't have been the bomb that hit the *Akagi*? It's the old poem, 'For want of a nail.' But it's not just that we lack anything. God knows, for being in the war only a few months, I think our people have done an incredible job. It's just the unpredictability of war."

LeBoutiller stood quietly, saying nothing.

"It's like the guys on the ground must feel all the time. Why does the man next to you take a bullet through the brain, but a round glances off your helmet? Why does a guy run through an artillery barrage without a scratch, then get crushed on the netting between a troopship and a landing craft? It's the damndest thing. I've been a sailor all my life and still don't understand it."

"You're not a religious man, are you Admiral?" LeBoutiller knew the answer, but wanted Halsey to state it himself.

Dropping his head, Halsey answered, "No. No, I'm not."

Halsey shrugged. "How can you not believe in God? Yet how can you believe in a God that lets this ..." he swept his arm out to the fleet "occur?"

"You mean war?"

"Hell yes, I mean war. Look, any idiot knows this planet didn't just spring out of nowhere. And these guys who think we came from monkeys?" He uttered a profanity. "I'll show them a monkey! But this Bible God who cares about people? Where was He when the Japs were blowing the hell out of those fine men on December seventh? If there's any sense of justice, where was He when we were getting our asses whipped on June fourth?"

"I understand, Sir," LeBoutiller nodded. "I've struggled with that stuff, too. My dad died of cancer in his early fifties. Never understood it. He wasn't a pious guy. Went to church when he had to. But he was a good man, an honest man. Hard worker, good husband all that stuff."

Halsey paused and looked at his chief of staff. "You seem to have gotten over it. I mean, you're not down very often. Hell, I don't think I've ever seen you with a frown on your face."

LeBoutiller laughed. "Oh, Admiral, I've had my suicidal days. Don't think I haven't. It's just that, well, I don't know. Mom raised us as Southern Baptists. You hear all the fire and brimstone stuff, but it seems as hard as those preachers tried to make God into a giant second-grade teacher, I just always felt close to Jesus. This sounds crazy ...." and LeBoutiller's voice trailed off, but Halsey was intrigued. He'd never carried on a conversation like this with his wife, much less his aide.

"It's okay, Charlie. I'd like to hear this. Hell, can't hurt. We might be dead tomorrow."

"You have a way of putting a real zip of reality on a conversation, that's for sure, Admiral!" laughed LeBoutiller. "Ok, well, see, it all comes down to just one thing: not Genesis and God creating the world in six days, not raining frogs, not parting the Red Sea. It just comes down to one verse in the Bible. One. John 1:1: 'In the beginning was the Word, and the Word was with God, and the Word was God.' Since almost everybody who knows this stuff agrees that 'the Word' there refers to Jesus, that's all I need. If that's true, everything else works out. And if that's not true, then it doesn't matter, because we're just all random, er, atoms, right? What had Einstein said? Atoms. We're just little pieces of stuff, bouncing around for fifty, sixty, or at best, a hundred years then ... poof! We're gone. But if this guy Jesus is real, and if He was with God, well, it all works out." He paused and saw Halsey's beetle-brows furrowed deeply, but the Old Man was listening intently.

"Ah, I'm sorry, Admiral. Really, I didn't mean to preach, least of all to my commander. I'm not a soap-box kind of guy," and he offered Halsey a shy smile.

Halsey stared at him a few moments longer, then said, "Seems to me you've got a career as a preacher when this war is over, Charlie. At any rate, you've given me something to think about. Do you know how often it is I can say that?" Then his face broke out into a grin. "Anyway, neither of us are going to be seeing Jesus tomorrow, because we're going to kick the hell out of the purple-pissing Japs. That's what I think tonight!"

LeBoutiller, exuberant, swept off his cap and slapped it on his thigh. "You're absolutely right, Admiral Halsey. Come this time tomorrow, there's going to be a lot of Japanese wishing they never heard of the United States Pacific Fleet!"

"Now, Charlie," added Halsey, "since it's clear you're a praying man, I am hereby ordering you to pray tonight. Pray that Ray Spruance is like a mind reader tomorrow. Pray that he has 'divine revelation' ..." Halsey's voice contained a hint of sarcasm, "... and that every single attack is perfectly coordinated."

"Aye aye, Admiral," beamed LeBoutiller. "Aye aye"

Naval Station Pearl Harbor, CINCPAC
12 Jun 42 0103

"Admiral, what the heck are you still doing up, sir? It's just past midnight." Art Lamar consulted his watch to make sure. Chester Nimitz was staring at the chart of the Pacific on the large table in the conference room, where tiny models of battleships and flattops awaited movement in the morning.

"Art, couldn't sleep." He gave a snort and added, "I probably should do some drinking, but old fashions just don't seem appropriate, either."

A few yeomen, cleaning personnel, and guards moved about, but the bustle of dozens of officers and enlisted men and more than 20 yeomen were noticeably absent.

"Tomorrow's operation got your stomach in knots, Admiral?" queried Lamar, pulling out a flask of milk. Without even asking, he handed it to Nimitz, who drank it down.

"Admirals aren't supposed to show signs of concern, Art. You know that. We're cool, collected professionals." Nimitz leaned on the map table, staring at the tiny ships.

"But ..." Lamar added.

"But, a whole lot will have to go right for these little Japanese ships to be gone from this map tomorrow. How's your Japanese, Art?" Nimitz looked at Lamar, who shrugged.

"Admiral, there's no one I'd rather share a POW cell with."

"Well, I doubt it will come to that. If everyone does his job, and if Halsey and Spruance get this thing timed up, we may just even the odds a little bit tomorrow."

"Is that what your gut tells you sir? Or your professional experience?"

"Captain, my professional experience tells me Yamamoto has all the advantages except one: he doesn't know where we are, or how many of us there are. And, thanks to Rochefort and that Jap spy ... well, we pretty much know exactly where he is. Even so, professionally speaking, would I play his hand instead of mine? In a second."

Lamar repeated, "Professionally speaking. And what does your gut tell you, Admiral?"

Nimitz began to walk around the table, to the Japanese ships, quietly picking them up, one at a time. Finally he looked up and gave his thin Texas smile. "My gut, Art? My gut tells me that we can't lose with guys like Halsey and Kinkaid and Spruance. Can't lose. They're the best of the best, any one of them can out-think Yamamoto and half his staff along with him. When you couple that with Americans fighting for their home territory? I think this time tomorrow night we're going to wonder how we did it."

That was all Lamar needed to hear. He beamed as he started out when Nimitz called to him. "Art, one more thing."

"Sir?"

"Get the chaplain out of bed and get him over here." "The chaplain sir? I thought ... that is, well, you have never struck me before as the . . . ah, I mean, I never figured you for a 'holy Joe.'"

Nimitz walked over to the captain and laid his hand on his shoulder. "Art, the way I look at it, those Japanese are going to be praying tonight to every god they have. Maybe we better get ours on our side, huh?" He slapped Lamar on the back and jerked his head as if to say, "go on."

Lamar paused a moment, nodded in agreement, and said "God it is, Sir." He took off for the base chaplain's quarters.

CHAPTER TWENTY-TWO

Nagumo's Battleship Strike Force, 40 miles west of San Francisco
12 Jun 42 0520

"You are the lead ship. Swing into line as soon as you come within gunnery range of the port facilities, Captain." Captain Hiroshii Kugo shouted "*Hai!*" and checked his speed, which registered 26 knots. Behind the *Kongo*, which had become Nagumo's flagship, now that Yamamoto had taken the *Yamato* for his own strike force,

B-17 "Flying Fortress (Wikipedia)

came the battleships *Hiei, Haruna, Ise,* and *Hyuga,* then the cruisers *Takeo* and *Maya,* and in the rear, the small carriers *Ryujo* and *Junyo,* along only to provide fighter cover, but with a few torpedo airplanes. Combined, they could only put up 40 Zeroes, 30 of which were circling overhead in combat air patrol, while Nagumo kept 10 in reserve.

Within minutes, the Japanese would be within range of the American coast. Nagumo had received intelligence reports, forwarded from Yamamoto himself that placed the American battleships and cruisers at San Diego. He would have a free run at bombarding the ports, destroying hundreds of freighters under construction, and terrifying American citizens. But something gnawed at Nagumo, a recurring feeling that the intelligence this time wasn't right. He repeatedly sent out scouts, the last ones an hour ago, constantly probing in front of him. Some transmissions were garbled, and apparently two planes were shot down. *Perhaps American air patrols this close to their coast are thicker than normal.* Still, not one scout had reported any American ships yet. *No matter. In fifteen minutes, we will be in a battle line shelling the American ports, and by the time the enemy battleships sail up here from San Diego, I shall be long gone, having done my job of diverting Halsey from the real attack.*

Just as Nagumo thought about the scouts, the intercom from the radio room rang. An ensign picked it up, listened briefly, and said urgently, "One moment. Admiral, you should hear this, sir."

Nagumo took the phone. "Admiral, Scout Number 24 has just reported a battle line, repeat, a battle line of enemy battleships and heavy cruisers dead ahead fifteen miles. You're sailing right into them, sir!"

A look of horror and disbelief crossed Nagumo's face. "Impossible. Why haven't any other scouts reported in with this information? And the destroyer screen, they should be reporting that they have sighted ships as well."

The radio operator briefly spoke to the radioman in Scout 24, then again addressed Nagumo on the intercom. "Admiral, Scout Number 24 says all the other scouts have been ambushed and shot down. He is damaged as it is. He repeats, you're sailing into an ambush!"

Nagumo started to tell Captain Hiroshii to immediately change course when the radio room intercom rang again, and, simultaneously, an ensign came to the bridge door. "Admiral, we are getting flash signals from others ships. The destroyers are under attack. They are signaling 'enemy heavy ships, dead ahead.'" Hiroshii had taken the call from the radio room. More radio messages from the lead destroyers. They were under a hail of shell fire. He didn't wait for orders from Nagumo.

"Full left rudder! All gun crews, prepare to fire." Lacking radar, he didn't really know what to fire at. Behind him, rather than coming into a line, the other Japanese battleships plowed ahead.

Nagumo grabbed the intercom handset to the radio room. "Send immediately from Task Force Commander: 'All ships, hard a port, prepare to fire. Enemy ships coming in range. Repeat, enemy ships coming in range." At the same time, signalmen flashed their lamps at other ships, acting as backup for the often-unreliable ship-to-ship radios. Other ships blinked in reply, their signalmen recording the messages and delivering them to captains. These long messages could be sent by signal lights under normal circumstances, but often only parts of orders were ever received in battle as signalmen squinted through smoke and haze to decipher the blinks.

As Nagumo sent his instructions, he could not hear the thunder of the American battlewagons in the distance. But he could make out the flash in the dawn light. They were opening up on the destroyers. For those in the destroyer screen, however, it was though they had walked into a curtain of death. Incoming 14-inch shells showered the small ships, blasting the first destroyers in the line to bits with hit after hit. PBYs, circling above, provided accurate fire-control information back to the ships. Desperate reports soon came back as panicked destroyer captains broke off and ran for the protection of Nagumo's guns, unaware that the Japanese combat air patrol had never gained control of the skies, and that their every move was relayed to the American gunships.

Nagumo felt the *Kongo* lurch to the left, and wondered why the Americans, if they were in range, had not immediately targeted his heavy ships. A moment later, he found out.

"Enemy aircraft! Torpedo planes! Dive bombers!

Evasive action!" Kongo's five inch guns opened up, soon followed by the small caliber machine guns. Nagumo sought to gain his footing as Hiroshii ordered evasive maneuvers, unaware that in addition to the dive bombers (land-based Dauntlesses) and torpedo planes (Army B-26s), his vessel was also being targeted by high-level B-17s, B-24s, and even all the B-25s that could be rounded up. In all, Nagumo's lead vessels were under attack from more than 120 aircraft, coming in at multiple altitudes and lines of attack, escorted by 60 fighters. They were flying from Hayward, Alameda, San Jose, Santa Rosa, Oakland, and even some of the longer-range bombers from bases as far away as Salinas, Stockton, Sacramento, and Merced. Alerted by Nimitz's intelligence the day before, the Army had begun repositioning every aircraft in California and neighboring states. And Catalinas were passing along position data by the minute.

It's a death trap, thought Nagumo. *The battleships aren't even supposed to be in fighting condition, let alone here!*

Geysers immediately shot up on all sides of the *Kongo*, apparently from the high-level bombers, and a flight of Mauraders leveled off for their torpedo runs. Zeros from the *Ryujo* and *Junyo* started to engage, then, facing two-to-one odds, found themselves overwhelmed by American fighters. Few Zeros scored any hits; many more were shot down by American Army pilots working in teams. Unlike Midway, the American attack squadrons had little to fear from Japanese fighters, and bore in on the battleships.

A chill went up Nagumo's back. *The American heavy ships were holding their fire on us until the air strike was over, so as to not destroy any of their own planes by accident. That means we are in range — we've always been in range.*

Japanese gunners had to divide their fire between the two

types of attackers—they had no chance of hitting the B-17s—reducing their effectiveness. *Kongo*'s starboard anti-aircraft gun turret suddenly exploded in a massive fireball as a bomb from a B-17 actually hit its target.

Smoke poured out, obscuring the approach of the B-26s, six of which released their fish. Reports from crewmen who sighted the torpedoes barely reached the bridge when three explosions rocked the *Kongo*. The massive vessel almost immediately came to a halt and began to list ominously to starboard. Meanwhile, behind Nagumo's flagship, a destroyer captain unexpectedly came hard-a-starboard, causing chaos. Other ships now had to maneuver around him, while still dodging and evading the air attacks from the Dauntlesses. Most ships finally resumed their formation, although a pair of cruisers toward the back of the pack had scraped the paint off each other. Only now were they, and in the process slowed dramatically before reacquiring speed.

Nagumo, trying ignore the damage to the *Kongo,* attempted to pull his battleships into a line. He was receiving sketchy but telling damage reports from the destroyer screen that indicated it was virtually gone. Of the eight destroyers deployed forward, only two were still afloat, and reporting the American capital ships were moving within range of Nagumo's fleet.

Forget forming a line. There is no time. We need to get out of here, now! Smoke filled the pilot house, and Hiroshii struggled to get his bearings after being wounded by shattered glass from the bridge window. Blood streamed in from an ear.

The battleship rocked sideways again, from another bomb hit, and a commander, also bloody, screamed, "Admiral, do you want to transfer your flag? Admiral?"

Transfer? To which ship? He could see out the still-clear port side—a mass of swirling, turning vessels, desperately attempting to evade the bombs. There was no ship close by, nowhere for Nagumo to go. *Any transfer under these conditions would be difficult if not fatal. Still, how else do I manage the battle? The* Hyuga*! Captain Tagawa would be the last in the battle line. He should be the least damaged – the one with the best field of vision.* Nagumo struggled to the bank of radio phones, as Kongo dipped even more to starboard, clearly going down. Hiroshii looked at the admiral, who jerked his head upward. "Abandon ship, Captain." Hiroshii nodded, and gave the order. Then, to no one, Nagumo muttered, "I'm transferring operational command of the fleet to Captain Tagawa of the *Hyuga*." If Hiroshii heard, he did not care, as the wound near his ear seemed suddenly worse.

Claxons blared, and, when combined with the explosions and the sounds of a dying ship, Nagumo could barely hear the radio room. "Radio central control! This is Admiral Nagumo. 'Order to Captain Tagawa on the *Hyuga*. You are to immediately assume command. Repeat: Captain Tagawa of the *Hyuga*. You are now in command of the task force.' Send immediately. Radio central?" He had heard a voice when he first established contact, then nothing. Did the order get out?

Kongo now shifted sharply downward and to the right, causing Nagumo to nearly fall over, clinging only to a bank of instruments. Hiroshii and the helmsmen were helpless, and the captain gestured them to abandon ship. Nagumo shook his head. "You are to leave, Captain. I order it. No officers will die for honor today. NOW GO!" Reluctantly, Hiroshii, now leaning at nearly a 45-degree angle, stood silently for a moment, then gave a curt bow. "*Hai!*" Nagumo followed him off the bridge, and only when he cleared an abandoned 20-millimeter anti-aircraft gun did he see the full devastation of the *Kongo*. Fires burned from bow to stern and men were jumping into the water or throwing life rafts overboard all along the side of the ship. As *Kongo* shifted again, Nagumo lost his balance and slipped through a railing, grabbing the cable. Hiroshii was pitched over the side, and he screamed as he hit the water. When *Kongo* reached a 60-degree list, Nagumo let go and fell straight down nearly 25 feet, into the water. The impact took his breath away, but he managed to pop up near a life raft where several sailors pulled him in.

U.S. Task Force 18, 15 miles off the California Coast
11 Jun 42 0615

Admiral Tom Kinkaid watched through his binoculars as his battle line eviscerated the enemy squadrons. Many of his vessels exacting a terrible revenge for Pearl Harbor. An ensign handed him a report from the Army Air Force squadrons. The *Kongo*, one of Japan's finest battleships, was gone, sunk entirely by air attack, and the Army boys were still at it.

Kinkaid couldn't wait any longer. "All battleships, open fire, repeat, open fire on enemy battleships." New targeting coordinates were signaled to the heavy ships, and after a few minutes of re-calibration, the massive guns opened up. Each salvo shook the ship like a colossus smacking it with an open hand. Inside the close confines of the turrets, double ear protection was required, including earplugs and special noise-abatement headgear. Between the narrow confines of the gun turret and the unprecedented noise, it took a special type of sailor to work the big guns, and the turret personnel knew it. Automatic loading machinery brought the next monster shell up and rammed the 14-inch armor-piercing shell, followed by several round powder charges into the breach. The second the loader withdrew, a crewman slammed the breach shut and locked it, then covered his ears and opened his mouth. The fire control officer triggered the burst. Even the *Kongo's* eight inches of side armor were no match for the heavy shells, and the more lightly armored cruisers and destroyers had even less chance.

"Looks like Admiral Nimitz was right, Tom," said Rear Admiral Dan Callaghan, who had requested permission to join Kinkaid's force as an observer. "They walked right into it."

Kinkaid lowered his glasses and his eyes revealed a grim, sad visage. "It's a slaughter. Ships without proper air cover? If they'd deployed in battle line, and if we'd had no air, well ... it might have been a fight. But they don't stand a chance."

Callaghan looked at him with a puzzled expression. "Are you feeling sorry for the Japs, Admiral?"

"A lot of brave fighting men are being sacrificed, and I bet half of 'em don't even know why. We have to do our job, but this borders on murder." He raised his glasses to see a trio of shells land nearly simultaneously on the cruiser *Takeo*, lifting her out of the water and breaking her in half at the same time. Kinkaid lowered his head.

Callaghan looked on, mystified. "I don't see that it's much different than what they did to us at Pearl Harbor. We were sitting ducks, and that didn't stop them."

Kinkaid slowly looked up. "No, and I guess that's what bothers me. We're better than them, dammit. We occasionally question bad policy, or bad orders. Sometimes, like Billy Mitchell, it costs us our commissions or our rank. But we're free to speak out. I don't know about you, but for me, that's one reason we have to win the damn war. And God help 'em, that's why I'm going to put every last damned one of those bastards at the bottom of the Pacific. But don't think for a minute I enjoy this."

A chastened Callaghan said no more, and merely returned to watching the battle through his glasses. He noticed American heavy cruisers were sailing forward, not pulling broadsides to fire. "What are you doing with the cruisers, Admiral?"

"I figured the Japs would run after we creased them the first time, and I don't want them escaping. I've asked the Army for a second bombing wave laid down fifteen miles west of the Japs' last location. While the battleships keep up their fire, I'm leapfrogging my cruisers up so that the Japs will still be in range even when they run."

"Aren't you afraid of your battleships hitting your cruisers?"

"Normally, absolutely. But today, well, it's a clear day, and we have solid scout plane spotting. They are getting the coordinates down to us like an announcer at a baseball game ticks off the plays. Sure, there's a risk, but the payoff here — wiping out an entire strike force — is too great to ignore. So I think we can keep the pressure on. Like I said, none of 'em get away today."

Kaiser Shipyards
11 Jun 42 0713

Henry Kaiser heard the battlewagons booming in the distance and scrambled for his telephone. A dazed and sleepy Johnnie Eugland, who had gone 48 hours straight before tumbling into bed the night before, slurred his words. "Yes? Oh, sorry boss. Yeah, boss. What? Gunfire?"

Eugland turned away from the receiver for a moment and heard the distant booming. "Yeah, boss, I hear it too." He rubbed his eyes and stared at the coffee pot, which he would soon need. "A plane? Okay, boss."

Eugland knew the coffee would have to wait. He called the airfield where Kaiser had his own modified C-47 for trips to the east coast and for transporting Navy Department officials to his various plants. Within minutes, crews were scrambling to get it fueled and ready. Kaiser and Eugland arrived by 7:30, and the C-47 was lumbering down the runway by 7:38. Kaiser was determined to see this battle for himself — one in which he had a direct stake.

It didn't take long for the C-47 to come within range of Kinkaid's battleship line, but notifying the American anti-aircraft gunners that he was a friendly posed more of a challenge. Two 5-inch puffs of flak exploded near Kaiser's aircraft before Kinkaid himself, with a few choice curses, approved Kaiser watching the battle—he had better things to do than worry about a civilian and Kaiser did have some right to be there.

By that time, Kaiser had inserted himself into the co-pilot's seat, and Eugland stared through the cabin door over the pilot's shoulder. The scene in the distance was, to say the least, breathtaking. They could see, almost below them, Kinkaid's battleships blasting away, but another rank of ships was sailing straight for the Japanese. Neither Kaiser nor his pilot knew those were the cruisers, nor did they have any idea what the Admiral was up to. Then, a few miles ahead of the advancing line of American vessels, they saw a dozen burning hulks of Japanese ships, which, by their size, were obviously destroyers. In the far distance, they could see Nagumo's heavy ships, now also under attack from the aircraft, and some of them in obvious distress.

"My God," Eugland muttered. "My God, Henry, we got 'em. We got the whole Jap fleet." Struggling to keep his legs in the choppy air, Eugland sat down and pulled out a note pad, sketching the positions of the vessels below. "The Battle of San Francisco ... and we won it. We won it, Henry," he yelled from inside the cabin. Kaiser leaned into the window to take in the panorama.

"This is for Pearl Harbor, you bastards," he said, although no one else heard him over the din of the C-47's engines. "This is for Pearl."

The **Yamato,** *northeast of Hawaii*
11 Jun 42 0703

An endless stream of reports had been brought to Admiral Yamamoto on the bridge, all of them staggeringly bad. *The Americans had been waiting for Nagumo. How did they know?* Although he should have been furious, he accepted the news with impassivity. But he did call Naichi for an explanation. The Commander arrived moments later, clearly distressed and, no doubt, concerned for his own life, which would have been forfeit in some commands.

"How?" asked Yamamoto. There was no anger in his voice.

Naichi had heard the reports. "Our source on Hawaii, the one from whom we got the report yesterday."

The Admiral shook his head. "That only explains some of it. They could scramble their air cover as they did with such intelligence. But the battleships? How did they know? And how did they repair them so quickly?"

Quickly surveying the battle reports that flooded in from Nagumo, whose strike force was now in danger of being eradicated, Naichi replied, "Admiral, to your first question, my answer is, Nimitz guessed."

Yamamoto turned and squinted. "He got lucky?" His voice contained a faint scent of sarcasm.

"Admiral, Midway was the only operation in our recent history where we did not use multiple forces. By now, our methods are known: we strike at multiple points, forcing our enemy to choose which to defend, sometimes concealing our true intention. Only at Midway did you change that doctrine, and with great results. If you're asking my opinion, I think the Americans calculated we would return to our old strategy. That accounted for the large number of battleships off San Francisco. How they were made ready, I am very sorry indeed. I have no answer."

I do, Commander. The Americans, when aroused, are superhuman at building. As a young man I read stories of Andrew Carnegie, whose steel companies out produced entire nations, or John Rockefeller, whose oil empire defeated the mighty Russian companies. Their Civil War histories are replete with innovators and builders who accomplished amazing feats, mostly supplied by the private sector. Already, our spies tell us their freighter yards were turning out a ship every ten days. Ten days!! We struggle to turn out an airplane in that amount of time. No matter. We could not have foreseen that the battleships would be sent back to the American west coast.

"So, Naichi, what do you know for sure—that does not come from your now-discredited source?"

Gesturing to Yamamoto to move to the map room, Naichi continued. "Radio traffic, scout planes, and submarine reports all indicate that Halsey's carrier force is here," pointing to a spot northwest of Hawaii. "That was confirmed by sources other than the impeached spy. I think it is reliable. Admiral Yamamoto, the dishonor for Admiral Nagumo's ambush is mine. I expect to be summarily judged for it. But I would risk any credibility I have left that Halsey's carrier is just to our west, and likely within range of Pearl Harbor's land-based air cover."

Yamamoto thought for a moment. "I agree. Naichi, the spy business is difficult. One never knows when one is being fed small successes as a set-up for a big failure, or whether sources—who themselves always are at root dishonorable people—can ever be trusted. After all, to be a successful spy, one must lie from the beginning, itself a dishonorable act."

He certainly has the correct perspective on the espionage-intelligence business, thought Naichi, but decided it was best to let the Admiral continue.

"Here is the central question: if we were misled once about the location of the battleships—and we can still win a great victory by destroying the last American carrier, which would greatly offset Nagumo's ill-fated attack— what else have we been misled about? Is there one carrier, or two? We don't know where the *Yorktown* is, now, do we? Your spy's earlier report that it was at Pearl Harbor cannot be trusted."

Naichi agreed. Yamamoto looked at him for an opinion. "Obviously, Admiral, it is essential that we find out not only where Halsey is, but how many carriers he has."

"I agree, Commander. Your mission now is to re- examine every intercept or radio transmission that we have taken since yesterday and see if you can identify the *Yorktown* on the basis of that evidence. And if you do so, tell me where she is. Dismissed."

"*Hai!*" Naichi saluted and turned to leave when Yamamoto added, "And Commander Naichi ..." The intelligence officer spun around.

"I do not view you as dishonorable. Events in war occur that we cannot control, and cannot plan for. You are the finest intelligence officer I've ever known, and I will not have you beating yourself over a doctored report from a twice-dishonored spy. Do you understand?"

Bewildered, Naichi paused, then replied, "Yes, Admiral. Thank you, Admiral." He bowed deeply, then turned and went to work.

Naval Station Pearl Harbor, Headquarters CINCPAC
11 Jun 42 1052

The commode flushed, and Nimitz tucked in his shirt, buckled his pants, and stepped outside the stall to wash his hands.

Straightening his tie, he suddenly remembered, *Three months ago I ordered that ties were no longer required at sea or at HQ except in dress uniforms.* He carefully un-knotted it and slipped it off, sticking it in his pocket. *There. Now it looks like I'm ready to do some work.* His guts rumbled again, and he passed a small bubble of gas. *Nothing brings out the stomach acids like a big fight.* Nimitz sighed, and opened the door, running smack into Art Lamar.

"Good God, son, you almost knocked me into the toilet. What's the rush?"

"Kinkaid's latest, sir." Lamar held several transcripts of radio transmissions. They had been flooding in all morning. "Looks like the Battle of San Francisco is going to go down as a helluva victory."

Nimitz scoured the reports, but Lamar summarized for him. "As of an hour ago, the *Kongo* was sunk by Army aircraft. Apparently all the Japanese air cover had been destroyed, because B-26s were coming in damn close and put two torpedoes into one of the Jap small carriers. Admiral, it appears that a couple of bomb-armed PBYs even dropped ordnance on the other carrier, which was last seen smoking and listing. All but three of the Japanese destroyers were sunk in the opening minutes, and Kinkaid's cruisers moved forward while the battleships were still firing overhead and tore the heck out of the Jap cruiser force. All the while, the land-based air made more attacks. Bottom line, Admiral, the battleships *Hiei*, and *Kongo* were sunk—and that's confirmed, Sir, and *Haruna* and *Ise* were badly damaged and retreating. Kinkaid says they were barely making fifteen knots, and would be destroyed within the hour. The last battleship in Nagumo's line, the *Hyuga*, and two cruisers, *Takeo* and *Maya*, along with a couple of escorts, tried to make a run for it, and Kinkaid reports they are under air attack now. Since they have to maneuver for evasive action, Kinkaid has his battleships double-timing to re-acquire range, but, as you know Sir, it's doubtful he can catch them."

"No matter," countered Nimitz. "The air will finish them off." The admiral had allowed Lamar to nudge him back into the head where he could lay the reports out flat. The enormity of it suddenly hit him, and Nimitz slowly sat down on a toilet. "My God, Art. Kinkaid has wiped out a whole Jap fleet. And we haven't even gotten to the main event yet." *My God. Perhaps the tide has indeed turned. It's now all up to Halsey and Spruance.*

"Admiral," noted Lamar, "are you confident Halsey knows what to do?"

"You mean, attack, Art?" Nimitz laughed.

"Well," countered Lamar, "it does run against all logic—to attack four carriers with one?"

Nimitz grew grim. "Bill Halsey knows his mission, and understands his part in this plan. No one can do this better, or be more convincing in this role."

"Okay on that, Admiral. And I don't doubt him, but it's strange, almost funny: the guy has a reputation for being aggressive and impetuous, yet he saves the fleet by retreating. Then, when on the surface logic says he should retreat and play it safe, we need him to attack."

"It's a brilliant plan, don't you think, Art?" smiled Nimitz, folding up all the reports in a single stack.

"They'll say you were a genius when this is over."

"Or they'll send me to the brig if I lose our last assets in the Pacific. So far, however, it does look like our prisoner Tomita did his part. I don't excuse one thing he's done, but we gave our word, and it was his idea to 'execute' him. No telling how much that reinforced the deception. Art, in the morning I want you to draft a strong, confidential recommendation to the military tribunal. Mr. Tomita should be acknowledged in his contribution to our victory, if we pull it off."

"Five years to ten, with time off for good behavior? He will be out in three or four years."

Nimitz shrugged. "He'll have to live with the deaths of two thousand American sailors, soldiers, and civilians on his conscience for the rest of his life. Plus he endangered his own son. With his family in Japanese hands, it's somewhat understandable, but I'll not forgive him. However, he's atoned some. Perhaps if he saved us tens of thousands of lives, it's a wash. Meanwhile, we'll know soon enough if Yamamoto has forgotten about the Yorktown. Now, Art, I want to be sure: is all ground-based Army Air on full alert?"

"Absolutely, Admiral. I just checked with General Emmons. Pilots are in their cockpits and are ready to take off on short notice. We can put more than one hundred and fifty planes in the air on a few minutes' warning. Radars are up and fully manned."

"And the PBYs?"

"Per your orders, sir, we still have flights of twelve at a time going out in a forty-five-degree arc between Halsey and Yamamo-to."

"So we're sure where Yamamoto is—that he will be within range of the Army's bombers?"

"Yes sir. He's trying to stay at the far end of our range, but it's obvious he really wants the *Enterprise*, so he keeps inching back westward toward us. He's sailing a big 'figure eight,' but each new loop move brings him a little closer to our bomber range."

"And the bombers are standing by as well?"

"As part of the hundred and fifty Army planes, yes sir." La-mar checked his notes, but had the material memorized by now.

"Ok. Let's get out of the head or they'll think we're strange. What do Layton and Rochefort say?"

"Sir, Captain Layton said that Rochefort has full confidence in the message that we had Tomita send. He's sure Yamamoto thinks he's facing one carrier, to the northwest, and that it's all lining up."

Leaving the head, Nimitz headed back to his office, then add-ed, "Captain Layton and Commander Rochefort can afford to think it's all lining up. I'm the one whose butt is on the line for all of this."

CHAPTER TWENTY-THREE

*The **Yamato**, northeast of Hawaii*
11 Jun 42 1130

"That's a second confir-
mation, Admiral. Halsey is almost due west of us, 75 miles.
He has one carrier." Sagata read
the report from scout number
thirteen, repeating the report of
a scout that had spotted the fleet
an hour earlier. Yamamoto had

F4F3 Wildcat (Wikipedia)

not launched any planes, wanting to make certain the Enterprise
was alone.

At least the admiral has calmed down, observed Sagata. *I've never seen him so angry, so animated, as he was earlier, when the reports of
Nagumo's battleship fiasco came in.* Yamamoto had lectured his aide
about the utter vulnerability of battleships lacking air cover, and
again brought up his opposition years before to the construction of
the behemoth battleships *Musashi* and *Yamato*. Sagata recalled that
many in the Imperial Japanese Navy thought Yamamoto had coined
the saying, "There are three great follies in the world: the Great Wall
of China, the Pyramids, and the *Yamato*," but had never confirmed
it. The admiral's rant today seemed to offer proof, but he had re-
gained his composure.

Now calm and focused, Yamamoto pretended the loss of the
battleships was irrelevant. "This is it, Sagata. Nagumo's battle was
a sideshow, and ultimately of no consequence   when   we   turn
the   carriers on those battleships." But first, we will eliminate the
last American carrier in the Pacific."

"And the *Yorktown*? You trust the intelligence that she is back
in port?"

"Not entirely, Sagata, but our scouts have swept the area
around the *Enterprise,* and one thing is certain: the *Yorktown* is nowhere near her. If *Yorktown* should appear later — likely in much de-
bilitated condition — we will finish her as well."

"Commander Naichi is comfortable with this assessment?"

Yamamoto scowled at Sagata. "You forget yourself, Captain! I am not interested in Naichi's 'comfort' with my decisions. He has not exactly proven infallible."

"My apologies, Admiral. Your orders?"

"All aircraft aboard the *Kaga*, *Hiryu*, and *Hosho* will attack Halsey's force immediately. *Akagi* will provide air cover for the fleet in case of American land-based air attacks, although we are at the far extent of their bombers. Attack, Captain. Signal the carriers, attack!"

Task Force 17 and Task Force 15, 150 miles south of Yamamoto's fleet
11 Jun 42 1147

"Any word yet, Admiral?" Commander Oscar "Pete" Pederson, the *Yorktown*'s air group commander, in whom Ray Spruance had placed all air operations in his carrier force, entered the bridge after spending time with the aviators on the deck. It was Pederson who had conceived of the "running rendezvous" that had given the Americans an edge in air operations.

Spruance, who had come up from the flag bridge at Captain Buckmaster's invitation, merely shook his head and nursed his coffee. Buckmaster reviewed charts from his captain's chair.

"Well," continued Pederson, "the boys are ready to launch. We can push 'em off in a few minutes." There was no response from Spruance, who was unusually quiet, even for him.

Damn, Pederson thought. *He's nervous. Didn't give the most rousing or inspirational speech this morning.* "The successful conclusion of this operation will be of great value to our country." *Not exactly, "Don't give up the ship!" He's been in that chair ever since. Hasn't even peed yet.*

Buckmaster merely said, "Just stand by, Commander."

"Aye aye, Captain," and Pederson assumed a position out of the way of the bridge crew.

He knew that an hour ago, *Yorktown* had turned north. What he did not know was that it was sailing directly at Yamamoto's fleet at full speed, which the ship's damage had reduced to just 24 knots.

If Yamamoto didn't attack Halsey soon, Spruance would

have to turn the task force around, and possibly lose the element of surprise.

"Holy Jesus, Billy, they're launching!" Carl Elliot's Catalina had dipped out of the clouds, and saw the armada of Japanese planes in the distance. "I'm getting back up, now. Send to headquarters. *Make sure you give him the coordinates! Do you read me?*" Radioman Billy Mason immediately began transmitting.

"Red Raven, Red Raven, over. This is Blue Whale. Blue Whale. We have three ..." and suddenly Elliot dropped out of the clouds again for another peek, "... make that *four* enemy flattops." He paused as Elliot commenced a big turn.

"Tell them one's a light carrier, not a fleet carrier. Got that?" Elliot yelled.

"Copy that, Skip. Red Raven, we have four enemy carriers, one of them is a Charlie Victor Love, Repeat. One is a light carrier. My posit zero eight five degrees true at six four zero miles, enemy course two four zero, speed two five. They are launching. Repeat, they are launching." Suddenly the PBY lurched upward as Elliot spotted Zeros closing in.

The lieutenant merely smiled as the Catalina disappeared again in the clouds. *They ain't gettin' me. It's amazing. The sky over that Jap fleet is pure blue, but to the west here, we've got a perfect cloud cover. I can duck in and out of this all day and they'd never find me.* "Did you get 'em sent, Billy?"

"We got it, Skip. I repeated everything twice. There won't be any screw-ups on this."

Elliot smiled broadly and waggled his wings to no one in particular.

"Repeat!" LeBoutiller shouted to the radio room, holding up a note pad, copying as he went. "Roger, got it," he said and hung up the phone. Bill Halsey, smoking his fourth cigarette of the day, swiveled in his chair toward his aide.

"Well?" he asked.

LeBoutiller slapped the papers against his hand. "We got 'em, Admiral. We got 'em. They're launching on you right now. We should pick them up on radar in twenty minutes or less."

Seldom in naval history has a commander, upon learning that he was about to be under attack from an air armada from four different carriers, been so relieved. He already had a combat air cover up of a dozen Wildcats, with the rest standing by. Now Halsey sprang into action, stamping out his cigarette on the arm of the chair and punching the NAVBRG button on the intercom.

"George, launch your strike. Go get 'em. Our guys are working out the coordinates now, and we'll have them to you before your last plane clears the deck." On the *Enterprise*'s deck, engines were already warmed up. The pilots, waiting their call, leaped in the cockpits and strapped in. Ordnance men in their red jerseys hustled to the sides, while blue-jerseyed plane pushers got the aircraft ready, then finally the yellow-jacketed chief launch officer waved the first Wildcat off the deck with a checkered flag. In tight precision, 16 other Wildcats followed, and in what seemed record time—less than 12 minutes—all the fighters were off.

As the last one lifted off, the squadron leader, Lt. James Gray, cupped his hand to his ear to receive the coordinates: "bearing one six five degrees true, range one, one, zero miles, speed two five knots." All pilots heard the transmission on their fighter director frequency. *We'll get the jump on 'em, that's for sure, but from what they said in the briefing, we'll be outnumbered. And we're cutting it close. Their flight time to us barely gives us time to get our remaining fighters airborne.*

Once the last Wildcat had cleared the deck of the "Big E," Halsey had ordered Task Force 16 to come about hard and make full speed bearing northwest. He looked at his watch.

"Charlie, let's hope the Army's on time." Then he noticed Leboutiller's uniform. His khakis were already soaked under the armpits and across his back. Halsey chuckled, "You nervous, Charlie?"

LeBoutiller wiped his brow with his sleeve, staining it, too, and blurted, "Nervous as hell, Admiral."

"We'll be fine. Nimitz and Emmons got the info before we did."

"Like you said, Admiral, let' just hope the Army's on time."

U.S. Army Air Base, Hickam Field, Hawaii Territory
11 Jun 42 1208

Gentle breezes rustled the nearby sugar cane fields, providing a stark contrast to the beehive of activity a few hundred yards away at Hickam Field, where 28 B-17s and 17 B-26s revved their engines. The first B-17's were already lumbered down the runway, having been given the "go" sign just moments before after receiving Nimitz's orders that had been relayed through General Emmons. Their fighter escorts were already airborne. Unlike carrier operations, Army B-17s could line up and take off in rapid succession, and within 15 minutes both bomber units were on their way to Yamamoto's last reported position.

Task Force 15 and 17
11 Jun 42 1225

Ray Spruance calmly watched his Wildcats, Dauntlesses, and Devastators lift off the deck of the *Yorktown*, while in the distance, the USS *Wasp* (CV-7) mimicked *Yorktown*'s operations. *Wasp* had been commissioned the April before Pearl Harbor and had been performing anti-submarine duty in the Caribbean and Atlantic until the news of the *Lexington*'s sinking reached Washington. King began to make adjustments, and by late May *Wasp* and her escorts had already sailed for the Pacific. Now, she added her 80 aircraft to those of the *Yorktown*, en route to attack Yamamoto's carriers from the south.

Pederson had been busy overseeing the launch, but as the last Wildcats and Devastators lifted off, he flashed Captain Elliott Buckmaster the thumbs-up sign. Buckmaster picked up the intercom to Spruance on the flag bridge below.   "Admiral, our planes are off."

"Thank you, Captain," and turned to a nearby staff officer. "Signal *Wasp*: 'Launch your strike." Then, checking to see if anyone was watching, Raymond Spruance gave a stifled "ya-hoo."

An explosion rocked the big carrier, starting a fire on the hangar deck. Before the ship even stopped shuddering, the automatic fire suppression CO_2 had come on, and damage control crews followed up with hoses, screaming to communicate above the din of anti-aircraft blackening the sky.

A single reserve Dauntless was on fire, and without a second thought the damage control parties pushed it out the open hangar bay into the Pacific. The Japanese had no such advantage on their carriers due to their enclosed hangars.

Halsey's flag bridge had already seen the windows shot out and a bomb go off, drilling a large, smoking hole into the side of the island. The black cloud that billowed out obscured his view from the bridge. LeBoutiller frantically relayed messages from damage control, engine room, and the gunnery units, competing with the cacophony of real-time radio transmissions of the dogfights above that filled the bridge.

One deck above, on the navigation bridge, Captain George Murray paced from port to starboard, visually assessing damage, all the while maneuvering the big vessel.

"OOD! Damage report!" Murray bellowed.

"Two fires, sir. Hangar deck forward, not bad. They've got it contained. Aft, we've got the number two elevator working, but there's a real danger of the fire spreading to the fuel and ready ordnance. The guys have apparently sealed it off for now and are pushing some ammo over the side." American carriers had unarmored decks, unlike the Brits. The bad news was that bombs could penetrate the wooden flight deck easily and detonate on the hangar deck below, but the good news was that the American flattops carried a lot more aircraft, and had much larger hangars than even the Japanese. Also, as the *Yorktown* demonstrated, a wooden deck could be repaired more easily. It was a tradeoff: power projection for armor.

Murray slammed his fist down on the metal table. "Damn! How are the fighters doing?"

"We're counting fifteen kills already, but we've got eight down of our own. AA has taken out probably another six of the enemy."

That probably means they've got thirty-five to forty attack planes left. Of those, how many already released? How many do we still have to evade? Murray picked up the intercom to Halsey. "Admiral, we've knocked out twenty. They probably have thirty or forty left."

Halsey looked at his watch. "Ten minutes until Yamamoto gets a taste of his own medicine, George." Under his breath he uttered a prayer. "Hold 'em, boys. Hold 'em."

The radio chatter seemed to increase even more. *"Lou, he's on me. Lou, help!" "God Almighty, I tore him apart." "My eyes! I can't see. Oh, my God!"* On and on. Murray picked up the transmissions, but Halsey had the volume down on the flag bridge. It was impossible for a task force commander to make sense out of all that anyway. All he knew was that the Japanese torpedo planes seemed to be vanishing in bright bursts as the escorts of the Big E riddled them, but the Vals were tough, and increasingly the remaining Wildcats shifted their attention to the dive bombers.

"Another wave, coming in one o'clock, Admiral," announced LeBoutiller. He could barely see through the smoke from the explosion below, and the bridge itself was becoming warmer.

Obviously the fire below isn't completely under control.

Suddenly the Enterprise shuddered, then there was a second's worth of delay, then a massive explosion shook the ship. LeBoutiller and Halsey looked mutely at each other.

Torpedo, Halsey thought. He didn't interrupt Murray with a query about damage control. One deck above, Murray had received a rapid report from aft damage control, which reported flooding in numerous compartments. The boiler room reported half the boilers out, and the *Enterprise* slowed dramatically, making herself a limping, fat target. *We won't make ten more minutes of this.*

Nearby the destroyer *Morris* burst apart in a titanic explosion, having intercepted a torpedo on course for the *Enterprise*. To the port, a Zero, smoking and the pilot clearly dying, angled his aircraft for the Big E's deck, but overshot, plunging into the water just feet ahead of the bow. *Ten minutes? We might not make two minutes.*

Murray grabbed the intercom handset and punched the ENG button. "Engine room, this is the captain. I want a no-crap assessment. Can you keep this ship moving?" He listened to the response, then stabbed the FLAG BRG button on the intercom. "Admiral, we can get eight knots and if we get the fires under control, maybe fifteen soon. We just can't take any more hits; and I'm out of people. Damage control personnel are completely assigned, and with their own dead and wounded, well ... They're gonna need help." Directing the *Enterprise*'s operations in battle was the captain's my job, but fighting the broader battle was the Admiral's. Murray deferred to Halsey, as the *Enterprise*'s next move was now a part of grand strategy.

Halsey took his cap off and ran his hands over his hair—a clear sign of agitation, or thinking, or both. "Captain, here's what I'd do. We have plenty of escorts who can put up AA for us, but we—this ship!—is the only one the Japs want. So long as she stays afloat, they'll have to keep attacking, and every minute their planes are here ..."

"Understood, Admiral." Murray jumped back on the intercom to damage control, who passed the word down to the gun crews. Every other AA gun was to be abandoned and its crews to report to damage control. Perplexed, the obedient gunners jogged to the closest fire or damage control unit, reported in, and doubled the size of the forces battling the fires and the leaks. An eternity of minutes went by as the guns hammered away, Wildcats chased Vals and Kates into the ocean, and the Big E's captain maneuvered his sick carrier as best he could. The sky over *Enterprise* was black with dots of anti-aircraft fire, and geysers sprang up on all sides of the ship, like choreographed fountains.

The OOD responded to a ringing intercom phone. "Captain, it's the boiler room. They've got us eight knots. Say it's looking better. Sir, ah...he says 'watch those torpedoes.'"

Murray gave a snort. "Tell that arrogant SOB to get me some more speed and I'll worry about the goddamn torpedoes!" No sooner had he disconnected from the boiler room line than Halsey was on the intercom from the flag bridge.

"Whaddya got left, George?" Coming out as one word.

"You mean our CAP, Admiral?"

Halsey replied, "That's right, our CAP. How many are still flying?"

"I figure there's no more than a half-dozen, Admiral. The Japs sent plenty of Zeros with their strike."

"Let's hope they sent 'em all, George."

Over the **Yamato**
11 Jun 42 0107

Warning claxons sent gunners scurrying to their positions. Yamamoto, eyes trained toward the distant battle to the northwest, which he could not see, calmly asked, "Halsey's planes?"

Sagata, on the phone to the radio room, instructed, "Repeat that. Confirm." A look of concern crossed Yamamoto's face. Land-based bombers out of Hawaii, sir.

Looks like high-level bombers, certainly B-17s, and their Army torpedo bombers."

Yamamoto frowned. He had turned away from Hawaii immediately after launching, but knew he still was within range of the enemy's land-based planes. "I had hoped they would be inefficient and slow to launch. No matter. We have more than enough Zeros left from the *Akagi* in combat air patrol." Already, above, faint silhouettes of fighters attacking the B-17s could be identified. The first geysers began to spray upwards, surprisingly close. *The Americans have improved their land-based air bombardment since the fiasco of Midway. Already, a destroyer, the* Arashi, *is ablaze. But the Americans aren't after destroyers, and as long as the carriers are safe.* Still, it troubled him that the geysers were walking their way steadily closer to the *Hiryu* in the distance, when a bright flash and smoke appeared on her deck.

"Admiral," Sagata shouted. "They hit *Hiryu*!" *Enough!* Yamamoto screamed in his head. "Sagata, signal Admiral Aoki. Launch all of Akagi's fighters. Signal all carriers, any fighter reserve, deploy it now!"

"Yes, Admiral." Sagata grabbed the phone to the radio room. Both Kaga and Hiryu had sent 13 of their 18 fighters with the strike forces. They now launched their last five each, Hiryu doing so with great difficulty due to the gaping hole in the left side of her flight deck. Hosho had no fighters, only eight Vals. Fleet protection was largely the responsibility of the 24 Zeroes from the Akagi, which had all been retained for that purpose. Now that the initial combat air patrol from the Akagi was attacking the B-17s and B-26s. Fleet protection largely rested on the 10 remaining Zeros from the other carriers.

It is more than enough to counter anything coming from Enterprise *and these land-based bombers. A massive geyser shot up all the way to the Yamato's bridge. At least, I'm counting on it.*

Sagata shot a concerned glance at Yamamoto, who gave him an noncommittal shrug.

Bombing Squadron 3, Yorktown, above the **Kaga**
11 Jun 42 0112

Lt. Commander Maxwell "Max" Leslie marveled at the scene in front of him. Above, B-17s had dropped their bombloads, and were now battling swarms of Zeros. The many defensive guns of the big planes were interfering with their attacks. Below, B-26s were completing their torpedo runs, generally ineffective, but forcing the carriers into wild turning maneuvers. Together, they had set fire to at least one carrier, damaged several smaller vessels, and had the battleship — apparently, the *Nagato* — dead in the water. Most of the combat air patrol was gone, absorbed by the Army attacks.

Leslie looked out his cockpit to see the 17 other Dauntlesses from VB-3. Scanning the horizon below and left, he could barely make out Lt. Commander Lance Massey's Devastators coming in for their run. Directly behind Leslie, having rendezvoused almost immediately after takeoff, were the 18 TBDs of the *Wasp*, and behind Massey. Slightly above, in visual range, were 50 Wildcats from the two American carriers. *Wasp* had armed her scouting squadron of 38 SBDs and was already launching them in a follow-up raid. What he didn't know was that, having located Yamamoto's fleet, Admiral Nimitz had approved a dozen PBYs armed with bombs to also attack. In all, 112 different attack aircraft, escorted by 50 Navy fighters were descending on Yamamoto's fleet, which had just survived the first wave of land-based air attacks.

Leslie immediately identified the most southerly ship, the *Kaga*, right in front of him. "All right, gents. Let's take out this fat baby right here."

His pilots didn't respond as they peeled into their dives. *No gung-ho, chatty crap today*, thought Leslie. *All business. Good. Today is all about business.* By Leslie's estimates, only a couple of Zeros were in position to intercept, the rest having been drawn to the attackers from the west.

Kaga's anti-aircraft guns opened up, as did those of her escorts, and three of Leslie's squadron members were hit, but he knew — and those on the *Kaga* knew — it wouldn't be enough.

Line her up. Line her up. Adjust for the wind. Hell, there isn't much wind today. Concentrate, Max. He heard the chatter of his twin .30s behind him, and blocked it out. The fat red rising sun seemed to grow to the size of a football field, and he released his bomb. He didn't even have to confirm. *"That's one for the Hornet!"* Leslie shouted. "I got the bastard! That's a hit." Seconds after he announced it, a massive fireball shot off *Kaga*'s deck, instantaneous with a double hit by the lead Devastators. Gutteral screams of victory went up as two more SBDs plunged at the *Kaga*. Massey called off the rest: "Go after the next one. This one's finished." *Rest in peace, guys. You have been avenged.*

Seeing VB-3's success, the squadrons from the *Wasp* next lined up the *Hosho*, whose slightly slower speed and minimal anti-aircraft guns made it even more vulnerable. Mitchell Merritt, claimed the first hit, putting a bomb squarely on the bridge. Black clouds puffed out, obscuring the target for the rest of the Wasp's bombers, but once they determined wind direction, they merely aimed for the smoke column and adjusted to the port side. Five more explosions turned the baby flattop into a gigantic fireworks display. *Wasp*'s squadrons were congratulating themselves when Leslie broke in.

"Shuddup out there. We've still got *Akagi*, and have to finish *Hiryu!*" The latter appeared to again be under way again with its fires under control.

"Aye aye, Commander," came the response. Six more Dauntlesses from the *Wasp* broke into their attack dives on the *Akagi*. At sea level, the entire *Wasp* TBD squadron, plus three from the *Yorktown* that had not yet released their fish, began their torpedo runs.

The **Yamato**
11 Jun 42 0120

"Where are all these aircraft coming from?" Yamamoto shouted at Sagata. "They are all from the south. Halsey is under attack right now to the northwest. *Where are they coming from?*" Sagata stared glassy-eyed. *Hosho* was sinking; *Kaga* was on fire and listing badly, explosions still going off. *Akagi* was now under attack from no fewer than three squadrons of aircraft. The Americans were buzzing like bees. They were everywhere.

"Admiral, a destroyer picked up the pilot from a downed

American torpedo plane. They interrogated him— he's from the *Wasp!*"

"Impossible," Yamamoto countered. "*Wasp* was last reported in the Caribbean! What of the other aircraft? They can't all be from one carrier."

"No sir. They are from the *Yorktown*. We also learned that from the *Wasp* pilot."

Yamamoto staggered slightly, and felt himself lean against the bulkhead. *Impossible. No, it's not impossible. The Americans have set a perfect trap, perfectly coordinated with land-based air. I set a trap for them, and they escaped, then lured me into one of their own design.*

"Sir, look—it's the strike force that was attacking Halsey." In the distance, Sagata could see the returning Vals and Kates—less than half those that went off earlier that morning. But right now, only one thing mattered.

"How many fighters are with them?" Yamamoto glumly asked.

Sagata counted as they came in range. "Five, sir." He lowered his glasses.

"Then it is over, and the end has come even sooner than I imagined."

CHAPTER TWENTY-FOUR

The *Kaga* (Wikipedia)

The **Yorktown**
11 Jun 42 0134

After hearing from some of the officers aboard *Yorktown* about the despair coming over the radios on June 4, Spruance was energized listening to the real-time reports over Yamamoto's fleet that crackled over the radios. "Hoooo-wweeee. Lookit her burn." "Mike, I shot down another Zero. See it?" "Dammit! I'm all out of bombs, every one of 'em's a sittin' duck." In between, the pilots laced their descriptions with profanities. They had lost all radio discipline in their exuberance. Spruance, straightened up, crossed his arms, and sent for his flag communications officer, Lieutenant Melvin Andrews.

Andrews arrived from flag radio, soaked with sweat and panting from being summoned by the admiral. Was he in for some sort of reproach? He came to attention.

Spruance, steely-eyed, said, "Lieutenant, do you have a transcript of what just took place?"

A puzzled look came over Andrews' face, but he replied, "Yes Sir."

"A detailed transcript? Verbatim?"

Andrews, now completely confused, reaffirmed he did. "Sir, I had two of my best guys copying. They got every word, sir."

"Very well, Lieutenant. I want a clean transcript typed up. I want to send it to Admiral Nimitz so that he will know what our boys think of the Japs." Andrews slumped a bit, then Spruance added, "And Lieutenant?"

"Sir?"

"Make sure I get a copy for my files. Our pilots seemed to be enjoying themselves."

"Permission to enter the bridge, Captain?" Admiral Halsey stood in the doorway. Looking up from his charts, Captain Murray beamed, "Permission granted, Admiral." The two shook hands.

"By God," said Halsey, "you kept her afloat, George. I don't believe it, but we're going to get this carrier home in one piece." Halsey slapped Murray on the back and the captain hung his head in utter exhaustion and relief. "You did a great job, George. Your crew was superb. No one could have pulled this off like these men."

LeBoutiller, who had accompanied the admiral, was still scanning the horizon for other Japanese aircraft. But he concluded the attacks were over. Below, the fires that had plagued *Enterprise* all day were under control, and the Big E was now plowing through the waves at a solid 12 knots. The engine room intercom rang, and Murray picked it up. "Tell your guys, good job," he said, then replaced the intercom handset.

"Admiral, the damage control guys say they'll have the number four boiler on line in a few minutes. We should be able to get fifteen to eighteen knots, and they'll have the number two boiler back at full capacity in another hour."

Halsey took his cap off once again and ran his hands through his hair. "I'm putting you in for a commendation, George. Well done." Then Halsey slapped LeBoutiller on the back as well. "And you, too, Charlie. You were terrific today. You still keeping that diary?"

LeBoutiller nodded. "I marked today as the day the war would be decided, one way or another. Guess I can finish it tonight. And Admiral ...?" Halsey cocked his head. "I'm going to describe Nimitz's plan. Never saw anything like it. But it wouldn't have worked without your guts." LeBoutiller swore he saw Admiral Halsey blush, for just a moment. That night, LeBoutiller would outline the details of the Battle of Halsey's Bluff, writing a memoir that would become a classic in military literature.

Then the admiral changed the subject. "And what about Spruance? My God, the man came through. Hell, even the Army did a good job today. I'd say that calls for a cigarette!"

Gesturing to the captain's chair, Halsey looked at Murray, who said, "Absolutely, Admiral. Be my guest." Halsey slumped into the chair and inhaled, more deeply than he ever had in his life.

The Yamato
11 June 42 1400

"I see them. In the distance. It's at least two more squadrons." Sagata lowered his glasses, aware that the incoming aircraft would finish what remained of the proud Japanese fleet that only weeks earlier had dominated the Pacific. In the far distance, *Hosho* was barely visible above the waves, and would sink within the hour. *Kaga* and *Akagi* were pouring smoke, both dead in the water. What this wave of attackers did not finish, the American submarines would. The only unscathed ships were the battleship *Nagato*, cruisers *Tone* and *Chikuma*, and a dozen of the destroyers, plus, of course, the *Yamato*—all sitting ducks, now, with no air cover whatsoever.

Admiral Yamamoto had directed them to run for the open ocean, but Halsey blocked his path to the west. And most remarkably Halsey still had aircraft. Any minute, the bombers from Hawaii would return, refitted and rearmed. And already another wave of dive bombers and torpedo planes bore down on the capital ships, whose anti-aircraft blotted black marks on the perfect azure sky. They will get through, Yamamoto realized. Ship-based anti-aircraft fire is woefully ineffective. The only real defense is the fighter plane. And we have none.

Moments earlier, he had broken radio silence to Nagumo, but had reached the captain of the *Hyuga*. It was being assaulted by the American battleships, which, along with their ground-based air, had shredded Nagumo's remaining force. *Hyuga* alone remained, and Nagumo himself had been killed. Support ships, seaplane tenders, ammunition and supply ships all were now coming under attack from B-17s and B-26s, plus submarines, which had accounted for a dozen kills this day.

All that remains of the 100 ships I came to Midway with is this handful of battleships and cruisers, and Hosogaya's tiny invasion support fleet. The Americans will sweep that from the Pacific in minutes, especially if he is not warned.

"Captain Sagata, I would like you to personally contact Admiral Hosogaya at Midway. Order him to evacuate as rapidly as possible. Tell him the Americans can be there in three days, and there is nothing—repeat, nothing - that can stop them. If he wants to save any of his men and ships, he will leave by midnight tonight. Is that clear?"

Sagata, the reality of the disaster now registered on his face, responded "Hai!" and left for the communications room. By the time he returned, the Yamato was under attack and had already sustained a hit.

"Sir, given the situation, perhaps you should transfer to the destroyer *Sendai*. If we immediately order the destroyer screen to scatter, some of them can escape. The Americans can't pursue in all directions at once."

Yamamto was numb. It was as if Sagata had not spoken.

"Operation Tsushima. That's what we called this, right? In commemoration of our grand victory in 1905 when we utterly destroyed the Russian navy, marking the end of the war." Yamato shuddered with another direct hit as her captain struggled helplessly to evade the attackers. In the distance, another destroyer went up, sending plumes of fire and smoke and charred metal in all directions, like a fireworks display. "Who would have thought that it would be the end of our navy, the destruction of the flower of Japan's fleet, which this 'Tsushima' would commemorate?"

"Admiral ..."

"And it's my fault. In my obsession to remove the American carriers as a threat, I exposed myself, walking into a trap a junior officer would have avoided."

"Sir, everyone agreed with your analysis. Nagumo, Naichi. Myself—for what it's worth. No one could have ever dreamed the Americans could restore and repair the Pearl Harbor fleet, or make the *Yorktown* operational, or bring another carrier into the Pacific, all so quickly. You were right, Admiral. You were right! This was not a war we could ever win. Perhaps it will convince them to ask for terms, before it's too late." Yamato absorbed another hit, and creaked menacingly. "We need to abandon ship, Admiral. You should transfer to a destroyer. There is still an opportunity ..." Yamamoto waved off his explanations and nodded. Having insisted that so many other captains not go down with their ships, he could hardly do so himself.

Arrangements were made, and the *Sendai* pulled nearby. Yamamoto climbed into a small boat, saluted the *Yamato's* captain, Keisuke Yamanami and left. His final words were, "Captain Yamanami, when appropriate, you are to also abandon ship. There is nothing to gain today by a grand and glorious death." Yamanami saluted, and the *Yamato* lurched with yet another impact.

The remaining ships, including most of the destroyers, were now under attack. *Nagato* belched smoke from several successive explosions, then seemed to raise out of the water and break in half. By the time Yamamoto and Sagata reached the *Sendai*, American land-based torpedo planes were chasing down the surviving destroyers. Everywhere, the remnants of the massive armada were in flames, most of them still absorbing hits from the B-17s circling above, the never-ending waves of dive bombers raining down on them, and the B-26s, which presented with stationary targets, promptly peppered them with torpedoes. Unable to fight off subs, panic now swept the vessels as reports of torpedoes coming from every direction spread through ships. Once reliable sailors abandoned their positions, jumped into the Pacific, or committed suicide, convinced the Americans would torture them. With the arrival of American submarines, it became a turkey shoot.

CHAPTER TWENTY-FIVE

B-25 (Wikipedia)

"It appears to be over, Admiral. An utter bloodbath. Theirs." Art Lamar handed Nimitz the initial battle reports from Halsey and Spruance. The Admiral scanned them and passed them along to Layton. "A few of their destroyers are running, and our PBYs say the Midway force is already evacuating, so I doubt we can catch them, but all of Nagumo's heavies and all the carriers are at the bottom of the ocean." Lamar suddenly slumped against the doorway, and tears came to his eyes. "Admiral, we did it. In one day, we made up for Pearl Harbor and Midway and all the rest."

Layton, reading the reports, merely marveled and shook his head. "Absolute helluva job, Admiral. You, Halsey, Spruance ... helluva job." He straightened out his wrinkled shirt and extended his hand. My congratulations on winning the battle, Admiral."

"Ed," Nimitz said, shaking his hand, "without you and Rochefort's outfit, no one could have accomplished any of this. I'm putting you in for a commendation, and the HYPO group for a unit commendation." Looking at Lamar, Nimitz added, "Art, start the paperwork, and I'm putting Halsey in for a Distinguished Service Medal."

"Sir, have you heard? Have you heard what the men are calling the battle?"

"What, the carrier battle?"

"Yes, Sir... They're calling it the Battle of Halsey's Bluff."

"What, like a hill? Halsey's bluff? But it's the wrong use of the word."

Lamar shook his head. "Won't matter, Admiral. You know how these things go. 'Bull Run,' not Manassas. 'Bunker Hill,' not 'Breed's Hill.' Once a name is fixed on a thing, it kind of becomes final."

Nimitz thought for a moment. "'Halsey's Bluff.' Well, it's

damned appropriate, that's for sure."

Lamar lingered in the doorway. "Something else, Art?" asked Nimitz.

"Sir, we got an incredible performance out of Mr. Kaiser and his shipyard there in California. It's not my place, Sir, but ..."

"Relax, Art. I've already looked into the highest civilian award I can recommend for the yard, and Mr. Kaiser."

Lamar saluted and chirped, "Thank you, sir. Thank you, Admiral." Then, afraid to shout a "yippee," he looked at the outer room and said loudly, "God Bless America!" Nimitz laughed.

Layton shook his head. "Is that boy all right, Admiral? Never mind. Oh, I thought you might like to see this verdict by the base military court." He pulled out a thin envelope from his attaché bag and handed it to Nimitz.

"Our spy?" Nimitz grunted, and Layton gently bobbed his head. The Admiral skimmed the verdict: "... guilty of treason ... Sam Tomita was sentenced to execution by firing squad ..." Nimitz closed the folder and gave it back to Layton. "I assume this sentence has already been carried out?"

"Seems this man was so vile, we needed to deal with him as soon as possible." Layton slithered the folder back in his bag.

"And am I to assume that word of this execution made it to the proper Japanese, ah, 'authorities' on the island, as identified by the defendant?"

Layton closed his bag. "I think we may assume, Admiral, that as far as both the Empire of Japan and the United States of America are concerned, Samuel Tomita died by firing squad yesterday." Nimitz sighed, and stared at his desk. "Oh, don't worry, Admiral, he'll be out in a few years, if someone in prison doesn't find out about his spying activities and kill him."

"Then what?" Nimitz found the whole situation depressing.

"Then he leaves the federal prison at Leavenworth   a free man, and if he's smart, he changes his name. "The FBI has agreed to cooperate with us on this, and they will give him a new identification if he serves his term."

"Pretty strange, huh, Ed?" "What, Admiral?"

"We'll be awarding medals to the men who fought this battle. Even a civilian. But without Tomita, we couldn't have pulled it off."

"True enough, Admiral. But without Tomita, we might not

have had December seventh in the first place."

"I suppose you're right, Ed. I just find it perplexing and deeply interesting how the fortunes of nations — heck, the whole world — can turn on the actions or motivations of one man, and that same man can display the basest, most despicable traits we have, then turn around and do something good, noble, worthwhile."

Layton let it sink in and softly replied, "You've just described the whole human   race, Admiral." Then he thought for a moment and added, "Everyone except that Hitler fella. I can't find one good thing about that nut."

He smiled and turned to leave, when Nimitz added, "Keep me up to speed on the boy. Tomita's son. I'd like to know if he makes a good soldier after all this."

"I'm already ahead of you, Admiral. I've got my own spy in the unit — by the way, it's going to be called the 442nd Regimental Combat Team. All Japs. Er, all Nisei."

Nimitz thought for a moment and said, "No, Captain. All American. See you later, and thanks, not just from me, but from the nation. And tell Rochefort I'll buy him a new pipe."

"He'll appreciate that, Sir." Layton paused, then nodded and disappeared.

"Now," said Nimitz to himself, "there's only one loose end to be tied up."

Epilogue

*Over the **Sendai**, 230 miles northwest of Hawaii*
12 Jun 42 0630

The PBY's droning engines had almost put Lieutenant Junior Grade David Jones to sleep, not once, but several times. Lt. "Red" Lattin, the Patrol Plane Commander, was scanning below for the handful of refugees which had escaped what had already been termed the Battle of Halsey's Bluff, a strange name for a fight at sea, but appropriate for those who knew the details. Technically, the Navy would likely label it the Battle of Hawaii or

Isoroku Yamamoto (Wikipedia)

some other plain-as-mud name. For the sailors and officers, it was already ensconced in the history books.

Lattin ordered Jones, who suffered incessant jokes about his name, "Davy," to swing the big Catalina to the south.

"Sir? Our grid is here."

Lattin usually played it by the numbers, a trait that irritated the spontaneous and free-wheeling Davy Jones. But now, he moved the aircraft out of its designated patrol lane.

"Dunno," replied Lattin. "Just got a hunch. Keep yer eyes peeled, will ya?" He pointed with his forefinger down at the Pacific, and Lattin grudgingly complied.

"You get hunches, Sir?" Jones replied with a grin.

Moments later, Lattin punched his finger at the cockpit window. "Hey, Ensign. I think I see something down there."

Jones swung down lower, as the shape of a destroyer of the Imperial Japanese Navy came into view. "That's one of 'em, all right. Radio the other PBY in this sector, but we're goin' in now." The Catalinas had been armed with 500-lb bombs, at the expense of their range, to allow them to attack any of the fleeing destroyers. It was thought that with the minimal AA fire a destroyer could put up, a flying boat might have a chance to score a hit, and two or three might actually sink a destroyer.

"Bullfrog Two is on his way, and he called Bullfrog Three and Bullfrog Four. Between us, we ought to be able to get him."

Within minutes, the PBY pulled in a flat trajectory 700 feet above the destroyer, which was now turning in evasive maneuvers.

"Lieutenant," Jones noted, "Bullfrog three doesn't have a bomb—it's got a torpedo!" Jones had heard that the Navy had been outfitting a few PBYs with torpedoes, but was still unsure how they performed.

"Fine. I'll hold off my attack until he gets here," and Lattin pushed the PBY out of small-caliber AA fire. With only one 5-inch gun, the destroyer was helpless to shoot it down at the higher altitude. It was stuck. It couldn't shake the faster airplane, and couldn't fight. Soon, other PBYs, circling like sharks, arrived on the scene. After brief discussion, they coordinated an attack in which three came in overhead with their bombs, while the fourth came in amidships with its torpedo. Only one bomb hit, but the torpedo landed square, ripping a giant hole in the small vessel, and within minutes, fires raced throughout the *Sendai*. Few of the destroyer's sailors escaped, soon to become captives of the Catalinas who picked them up, one of them the chief of staff for Admiral Yamamoto, a captain named Sagata. In his personal effects, they found a series of sketches he had done—maps of the admiral's brilliant envelopment plan at Midway that came within a whisker of succeeding.

As for Admiral Yamamoto, he had been on the bridge when the lone bomb went off, killing him. In the end, he had gone down with his ship after all, and with him the last faint reminder of the glory of the Imperial Japanese Navy.

President Franklin D Roosevelt
(Wikipedia)

Acknowledgments

Thanks to several individuals associated with the "Battle of Midway Roundtable," and who offered excellent details on the operations and technology of World War II fleets. Among those who provided information or comments were R. W. Russell, Otis Kight, Frank DeLorenzo, and Sam Laser. My cousin, Colonel Michael Jackson, USMC (ret.), also helped with naval and Marine procedures. Barney Geary provided wonderful artwork.

About the Author

Larry Schweikart is an Arizona native who attended Chandler High School and Arizona State University graduate who played in various rock bands, opening for such acts as 'Steppenwolf' and 'Mother's Finest'. Returning to academics in the 1970s, he decided he wanted to be a history professor, and earned his MA from ASU, then went on to the University of California, Santa Barbara for his Ph.D. In the process, he taught at Brophy College Preparatory in Phoenix, Eloy Public Schools, and the University of Wisconsin, Richland Center. In 1985, he was hired at the University of Dayton, where he has taught ever since.

He began his publishing career while still in the Master's program at Arizona State, with *A History of Banking in Arizona*. Along with several books on banking, he co- authored the 1984 history of the Trident submarine program, Trident with D. Douglas Dalgelish of ASU. By the mid-1990s, he had begun to write on issues of banking and finance, as well as national defense. In 2004, he and Michael Allen of the University of Washington, Tacoma published their best-selling survey of American history, *A Patriot's History of the United States*. Now in its 5th printing, this work has become a standard in the field for classical, conservative history. In 2006, he wrote *America's Victories: Why the U.S. Wins Wars*, which came to the attention of President George W. Bush. Schweikart was invited along with five other military historians to attend a private session in the Oval Office with the President to discuss history, politics, and the military. His most recent non-fiction book, *48 Liberal Lies About American History* is already in its 6th printing has been through several printings and has made him a fixture on Fox News, where he comments weekly on textbook errors and biases.

Schweikart has been interviewed by Rush Limbaugh for the Limbaugh Letter, has been on over 200 radio shows, and has appeared on C-SPAN's BOOK TV as well as Al-Jazeera Television, the i700 Club, and Hannity & Colmes. He is a ghost writer for prominent American celebrities, and is working on a book with Mark Stein about the 60's super-group 'Vanilla Fudge' about rock and roll.

After 9/11, Schweikart thought a motion picture with the scope of James Cameron's 'Titanic' needed to be produced that would capture the events of the day. In the process of attempting to write a screenplay for such a movie, he discovered he needed the story to be developed first, and that led him to write his first novel, *September Day* (2006), which was published by Lightning Source. Halsey's Bluff is his second novel.

Look for more books from Winged Hussar Publishing, LLC – E-books, paperbacks and Limited Edition hardcovers. The best in history, science fiction and fantasy at:

https://wingedhussarpublishing.com

or follow us on Facebook at:

Winged Hussar Publishing LLC

Or on twitter at:

WingHusPubLLC

For information and upcoming publications

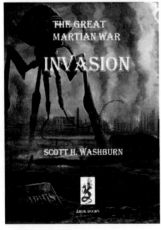